BLINDED

The Dragon's Game
BOOK VI

H. N. Henry

Presse Dragon Libre

Free Dragon's Press

Trois-Rivières, QC, Canada

FREE DRAGON'S PRESS
Huard, Norman Henry
220 B Farmer
Trois-Rivières, Québec, Canada, G9A 3E6
www.hnhenry.com

Publisher's Note: This is a work of fiction. Names, characters, places, and incidents are a product of the author's imagination, except for his use of the Cree language in Roman orthography to number and title chapters and as one of the languages spoken by certain characters; and also for his use of certain Tai Chi exercise names. Locales and public names are sometimes used for atmospheric purposes. Any resemblance to actual people, living or dead, or to businesses, companies, events, institutions, or locales is completely coincidental.

Book Layout © 2014 BookDesignTemplates.com

BLINDED The Dragon's Game BOOK VI by H. N. Henry—1st edition.
Print-On-Demand 2022-12-12

ISBN: 978-1-998882-00-7

Dedication

To my editor, Staecy-Lee,
and
to my proofreader, Randi.
They were like angels watching over my words.

"Stay, you imperfect speakers, tell me more:"
Macbeth to the witches
—WILLIAM SHAKESPEARE

Chapters

— † —

FROM BANISHED

THE DRAGON'S GAME

BOOK I

Legend tells us dragons fly so high they can see the future.

Reason tells us that to know the future is a curse.

Our hearts tell us the seeds of hope are sown in the reality of the present.

— † —

FROM BRANDED

THE DRAGON'S GAME

BOOK II

Reality tells us that to lose hope is to welcome death.

— † —

FROM BETRAYED

THE DRAGON'S GAME

BOOK III

Hope tells us light lives even in the darkest places.

— † —

FROM BRED

THE DRAGON'S GAME

BOOK IV

Darkness tells us it will change us if we venture there.

— † —

FROM BLAMED

THE DRAGON'S GAME

BOOK V

Light tells us darkness wraps the gift of fate in the fear of the unknown.

At Maze Point
Miniwatimik

— † —

*The curse of fear tells us we are blind
to what we think we see.*

— † —

Nagora sat up in bed, covered in sweat. The dream woke her. At least it wasn't the recurring nightmare of when she had branded her twin sister, Sagora. Each time, in that tormented dream, she hoped for a different outcome. This one was different, though. It too involved twins. They are dark as shadows, but not shadows. Dark as night and as mysterious. Black as coal and in that blackness, their beauty glows. Together they beckon to me, each with a hand outstretched, their fingers curling like ebbing waves on a mist-shrouded beach in moonlight.

Mother Danuka, are you trying to tell me something, like in the days in the cave when I was your Dragon Talker apprentice? I will ask you when I see you again, for in these Dark Twins I sense hope and foreboding.

BOOM! "Dannor!" Nagora fell back onto her pillow, her right hand landing on Lars's hip. He half grunted and half laughed as he turned to raise his upper body onto his elbows and look at her with sleepy eyes. "Don't blame me for the rude wake-up call. You're the one who taught him to use that sling."

"Guilty as charged. I was awake before his stone hit the door."

"The branding nightmare again?" asked Lars.

"No, not this time. Something I've never dreamt. It could be a premonition. If it sticks with me, I'll tell you more. I think Dannor's stone hitting the lodge door might have knocked the dream out of me."

Lars swung his legs out of bed and stood to dress.

Nagora admired his strong back. Her eyes traveled down to the scars on his left buttock where an arrow had, in his words, "pinned my ass to my saddle." If my trusty horse, Storm, had not fallen, I might have witnessed your valiant fight for me.

"I'll start the fire and put water on to boil," said Lars as he left their room.

"I'll be down soon." Just about everything she admired in her man, she now admires in her son. Not only had he grown to resemble Lars in physique, but in his mannerisms too. There's no doubt my son is a man now. He's grown so much in these past three years. As tall as his da, and almost as strong.

Nagora recalled the day Dannor had found the war stones and the two slings.

†

That day, Dannor had come into the lodge after finishing his chores in the stable. He was juggling three of the war stones. "Mum, what are these? I found two buckets of them in the saddle room." He set the stones on the table and pulled two rope slings from his scrip. "And I found these too."

"Ah! Your da hung them there. We didn't know when you'd get around to finding them." Nagora picked up one of the knobby stones with its symmetrical, circular grooves. "This is a war stone, made by the Stone Standers. You've heard of them, haven't you?"

"Aye, two came to work on the inner circles of the maze. I was a young lad then."

"Aye, you were. Those were Grim's lads who came to raise the enormous lintel pieces and sit them atop the pillars of the inner circles."

"Why would they bring war stones?"

"Your da and I can only guess, since the Stone Standers didn't allow us to watch them work. Possibly to protect the secrets of their trade. Your da thinks they used the war stones to help pivot the huge lintel stones and act as measured counter weights to help raise the stones that high. We know they had lots of solid pieces of lumber, their hammers, chisels, pry bars, and these stones to help them do their work. Grim's lads left those for you as a gift. They hoped you would become skilled enough to join the Stone Standers' ranks as a slinger. Though, to become one, you'd need to carve your own war stones."

Dannor looked at the stone in the sling. "I can't even imagine how I would try to carve one of these out of stone so hard."

His mother smiled. "You would need a Stone Stander to teach you that skill." Nagora picked up one sling by its knitted, net-like pocket of hemp. Then she waved the war stone and set it in place before holding it suspended with the braided ropes. "This is a sling. It's used to hurl one of these at a target such as an enemy, an animal you hunt, or a contest object in a game."

She pointed to the bumps and grooves on the surface of the stone. "Imagine hitting an enemy on the head with one of these. I don't care what sort of helm they'd be wearing; I can guarantee it would knock them out, if not kill them outright. These symmetrical furrows help the stone find its ideal resting spot in the pocket. They make loading the sling easy and, above all, quick."

Dannor picked up the other sling and a stone. He spread the braided ropes with his fingers and, like his mother had said, the stone found its place in the pocket when he let go of it. "How accurate are these?"

"In skilled hands—deadly accurate. It takes practice, but once you get the knack, you can hit whatever you want, even a target in flight."

Dannor held up the loaded sling. "Mum, do you know how to use one of these?"

"Aye, I do. It was the first weapon I ever learned to use."

A big smile filled his face. "Will you teach me?"

"If you want to learn," she pointed at him, "promise not to complain about losing war stones and not being able to hit your targets like you want. It takes time, lots of practice, but once you get it, you won't lose it. Trust me."

Dannor nodded. "I promise, Mum."

✝

Now with over two years of practice, Dannor has become an accomplished slinger and a chaser of war stones. He's been teaching his sister, Sarah. That's all I need now: two stones hitting the lodge door to wake us up. For the past six months, Dannor had taken to hurling a war stone from the stable, four hundred paces away. When it hits our timber door, we know they're almost finished tending the horses and cleaning the stable stalls. Soon they'll come for breakfast. His accuracy has improved. His stones are hitting the middle of the door more often than not. If he keeps it up, we'll end up with a hole in need of a window to fix it.

Nagora got out of bed, dressed, and made her way to the kitchen. "Do I have time for my exercises?" she asked Lars as she hugged his back.

He was preparing a batch of skillet bread. "Sure, you'll probably make it back before they do."

"Good." Nagora reached for her set of blades on the hook near the door, adjusted the three holsters of the throwing knives on each shoulder strap, and checked the latch that secured her big skystone blade in its leather sheath. She slipped her blades onto her shoulders and opened the door a crack, checking in case Dannor had just slung another stone at the door. Some days he did. Coast is clear. No sign of him near the stable in the valley below.

Nagora hurried out, closed the door, and rounded their lodge to make her way up to the spot where she did her daily ritual exercises, pausing only a moment to look over at the maze and the growing village on its inland side.

Her hand, as it always did when she looked over at the maze, reached for her thigh. Her fingers felt the scars beneath her leather legging. They were from the cuts she had made as a reminder not to fail in her duty again. They also told another story of her unique relationship with her dragon and how the maze came to be. *Will I ever see that golden-handled dragon dagger again?* That thought sent a shiver down her back. *Why do I wonder about that now?*

Before going to the stables, Dannor and Sarah did their morning exercises like Nagora. Their footprints were still visible in the dew on the grassy parts of the path leading up past the big stone bluff perched above the sea. That they exercised together made her smile. Her uncle, Dangor, had taught her the moves many years ago: Ward off, rollback, press, push, pull, elbow strike, shoulder strike, advance, retreat, look left, gaze right, and center balance. Since then, Nagora has repeated them a hundred times each morning with a different weapon in hand, no matter the weather, one day deliberately slow, the next blindingly fast. Nagora had waited until her children asked her to teach them. Just like her uncle had waited for her to ask.

She had also taught her sister, Sagora.

Does Sagora still do the exercises? Can I blame her if she doesn't? Not a day goes by without a thought of her. If only they hadn't forced me to brand her. Then again, perhaps she's lucky I was the one. I best not dwell on Sagora any more than I have to.

Nagora gazed out to sea, breathed in the salty breeze, and spread her legs to balance her stance before pulling her sky-stone blade from its sheath. When she held it before her face, she stared at the two Tiwaz symbols—the one engraved on the blade and the reflection of the scar branded on her forehead. They meant for a higher cause. Focus. Nagora did the exercises in rapid succession, letting the morning dream that woke her play out again and again in the back of her mind. Flashes of images of the Dark Twins appeared.

They each held a spear in their right hand. The arms of their beckoning left hands bore symbols on the skin at their wrists and upper arms.

When they spoke, it was not in unison, but one after the other. Nagora could not hear the words their lips spoke, but she was certain of what they said. One said, "Come, sisters," and the other said, "Join us."

A gold ring hung from their left ears.

Their hair was pulled back tight on their heads, gathered at the back somehow so that the rest of their hair spread across and down their shoulders.

When Nagora completed her exercises, she reached over her head to slide her blade back into its sheath and flip the latch over the crossguard. Standing with hands on her hips, she looked out to sea. Danuka, I will ask you about the Dark Twins. I am certain you are the one who sent me this dream. Why do they call to me? It must be important. Do you know?

On her return to the lodge, Nagora bent over to pick up the war stone that lay on the ground at the side of the doorstep. They must be back. The smell of baked skillet bread filled her nose as she opened the door.

...

Sarah was chopping chives on the board next to a basket of eggs. A pail of fresh goat's milk rested on the floor near her feet.

Dannor was cracking eggs, emptying them into a big bowl.

Lars held a plate of skillet bread in one hand and a plate with smoked venison and a chunk of goat cheese on the other.

"We beat you back," said Dannor, glancing over his shoulder at his mother.

Sarah turned to face Nagora. "We had help from Jari and Jenni. They were early on the job today. They say they have a big day planned. The frost heaved up lots of stones in the garden plots. Jenni wonders if it'll ever end. In her words, 'Every spring, there seems to be more and more stones growing.'"

Lars laughed. "Comes with the territory. Eventually there'll be enough for stone fences to replace the stick fences."

Sarah emptied the chives into the bowl of eggs. "If only all crops needed as little tending as our chives growing right next to our doorstep and always first to harvest." She took a cup and bent to the pail to fill it with milk. She nudged Dannor. "Too much, or not enough?"

"Pour away. That should do," said Dannor, as he reached for the whisk made of bark-stripped maple twigs bound with a halved willow sapling branch.

As he whisked the egg mixture, Nagora stepped next to him and waved the war stone before his face. "Soon, young man, there'll be a hole in my door."

Dannor smiled at her. "You've always wanted a window there. I'm just trying to help."

Nagora poked him on the shoulder with the stone. She turned to Sarah. "When you gain distance with your sling, I don't want you joining your brother in destroying my door." She kissed Sarah's cheek.

"How about me?" asked Dannor. He bent and offered his cheek.

Nagora kissed it and then smacked his behind. "Back to work, cook! I'm starved."

Dannor whisked faster. "Aye, Mum! Won't be long."

Lars laughed and said, "My lady, weren't you the one who wished to sleep a wee bit longer in the morning, but no later than sunrise? Dannor offered to wake you. Doing it his way with a stone saves him many footsteps when he's not finished his chores."

Nagora, feigning anger, took several long strides toward Lars with the war stone in her raised hand. "I've a good mind to boil this and feed it to you!"

Lars grinned. "I thought stone soup was an evening meal."

Nagora pretended to bite his arm and then pulled him to her for a kiss. "You promised me a window." She waved the stone at him.

They all laughed. It was an ongoing joke with them ever since Nagora had expressed the wish for a window in the door, and Lars promised he would make one. Being an ever busy man, he kept putting it off.

After their meal, Nagora asked, "What have you got planned for today?"

Lars leaned back in his chair. "Weapons practice in the morning at the training grounds with those who've signed up to be future dragon riders. Today we'll focus on how to shoot a bow from horseback. If they can't master that, they won't make it as dragon riders. Dannor will help me. I have issued all the trainees bows, arrows, and wooden practice blades, except for the throwing knives. They're the real things.

"In the afternoon, rider training on the wooden dragons. We've just completed six of them. They've got saddles, bits and bridles, and reins. The trainees have temporary goads. Dannor will teach them how to approach and saddle a dragon, and how to use a goad to control it in flight. If only it was as easy as with a Dragon Talker." Lars looked to Nagora, Sarah, and Dannor. "Isn't that right?"

Nagora nodded and took a breath. "How many girls in the group?"

"There are five young women, as I prefer to call them. If you ask me, out of the thirty people who signed up, they show the most promise. They learn fast and focus well on task details. I wish I had more like them and more young men with attitudes like theirs. Perhaps when they ride their first dragon and hold a real skystone blade, their attitudes will change. When the men realize they'll get to keep the blade if they earn it, maybe then they'll focus."

"Sounds like most young trainees. It takes a while for them to see the value of the skills they're learning. I think they'll surprise you as soon as it gets real," said Nagora. "Aren't you meeting with someone this afternoon?"

Lars placed a hand on the table, fingers spread. "Aye, with our dragon estate managers. We'll look at the inventory numbers for our farm areas: poultry, sheep, and goatherds. We'll ask how to increase production to continue adding variety to the dragons' diet of fish. And we'll examine whether to continue with sealing on the cove ice in winter since the dragons hunt seals further out on the ice floes. If we can convince the dragons to bring some of their catch in, we could recuperate those hides and then butcher and smoke the meat so the dragons would have it in the coldest days of winter when they don't venture out. Or for variety in the summer. If that works out, our smokehouse will run near full capacity."

"The dragons like smoked sheep and goat meat. I think they'll like smoked seal. Now they'll be going into their fourth year. They eat anything Danuka eats," said Nagora.

Lars touched Nagora's arm. "If the meeting ends early enough, I'll ride to Skull Bay to meet with Gabe and his assistant for an update on how the building of the trade route is going. I should be back by tomorrow evening."

"That's good to know," said Nagora.

She understood why her door window had to wait. They had built a community on the lands surrounding the maze to care for the needs of the dragons and the dragon rider trainees. So much of that work needed their attention. They had to oversee the management of all the various farming operations to feed the people and the livestock of the community, and to provide additional food for the dragons. Plus, they had to keep abreast of the building progress of the overland trade route between the Land of Skulls and the Land of the Danu because, when ready, dragon riders would patrol it as well as the coastlines.

Besides training the new dragon rider recruits, Nagora and Lars also oversaw those who worked to attract skilled craftspeople and workers to Maze Point. They needed such artisans to work in all the trades that supported the community and its people. If Nagora named just about any trade, from butcher to baker to candlestick maker, she knew it was in need of an apprentice or a person possessing those skills.

Over the past three years, the growth of Maze Point had been nothing short of miraculous. It was mostly thanks to the Little People who worked unseen at night, helping build so many of the stone buildings and lodges needed for the village families to thrive and work in their occupations. Nagora could never thank them enough for all their help in building the stone maze. That took fifteen years, with mostly only Lars and her working on it. If the Little People hadn't helped them at the time, they would still be sorting and stacking rocks to build it.

Nevertheless, there it was, massive and so mysterious. Not only for the dragons it now held in the caves beneath it, but because it was impenetrable. Only the Dragon Talkers had the gift to find their way to its center and, of course, the dragons that flew there.

It was no surprise that during every summer season, the maze attracted an ever-increasing number of visitors to see the fifteen dragons. To see them fly above it and perch on one of the lintels of the two raised inner rings was a spectacle.

Most visitors came to hike the surrounding hills and admire the maze's beauty from different perspectives. They tried to let their eyes find a way to the middle from one of its four entrances. That was part of the mystery. As soon as one keen observer exclaimed they had found the way to the center, and then tried to show a bystander, the path would lead them out by a different maze entrance without ever taking them near its center.

Nagora had put a stop to the more adventurous visitors who came with great lengths of stout twine. They unraveled the cord as they attempted to navigate to the unknown center of the maze. Rescuing intrepid explorers lost in tangled webs of their own weaving became a chore that wasted much of the Dragon Talkers' precious time.

Since then, the Dragon Talkers had marked off a single path leading from the entrance nearest to the village, into the maze, and out by what they called the sunset entrance. While exiting there, visitors had a limited view out to sea. The guides guaranteed them they would spot a dragon in flight and perhaps even a whale and if lucky, early in the season, an iceberg.

Over the past two years, dealing with visitors to the maze had become a thriving business for the community: catering to their needs for lodging, sharing dragon lore and sightings, and selling souvenirs such as replica dragon eggs.

"Sarah, what are your plans?" asked Nagora.

"Since the young dragons will shed their skins again soon, Danuka has been flying nets filled with food into the cave. I'll finish sorting the stashes of smoked-meat pieces and fish the hungry dragons will need to replenish their strength. Then I'll check the condition of the shedding chambers along the main tunnel. I want to make sure the water basins are clean and free of debris that might block the flow of the underground stream. We don't want the water to stagnate in the pools. Last, I'll check that the pillars are clean and ready to help the dragons rub out of their old skins.

"As usual, if I can nab one or two of the young female dragons, I'll continue to instruct them in the ways of people," said Sarah.

"Remember the dragon promise they'll make after this shedding?" asked Nagora.

"Yes, Mum. I just want to prepare them to make it easier for them to accept the riders. Danuka told me her dragons will make their promise together as a group. She said their collective experience with riders and other people will influence how they understand their oath to not harm people. And something else too that has to do with dragon history," Sarah's brow furrowed as she paused, "or group memory that Danuka hasn't been able to make clear to me yet.

"I understand and accept that, as a Dragon Talker, I must obey and serve the dragons. I can ask them and inform them, but never try to force them to do something contrary to their oath. All I can do is care for them, love them, and protect them. It's my destiny."

Sarah pulled the dragon-tear amulet from her shirt and held it out. "You gave this to me at great cost, just as your mother gave it to you, and your father gave it to her. I don't know what it will cost me. Perhaps the dragons do. Like you, Mum, I'll deal with it when that day comes."

Nagora swallowed the lump in her throat, and her eyes teared at the memories of all she had suffered in service to her dragon, especially the cost of abandoning Sarah only days after her birth and only finding her again years later. I have a feeling it's not over. There's more to come.

Sarah reached across the table and took hold of her mother's hand.

Dannor and Lars each reached a hand to her shoulder. "We're all in this together with you, Mum. Look at what we've built. Aye, at significant cost. Given the chance to start all over again, I for one would not have it any other way," said Dannor.

"Nor I," said Lars, as he pulled her close to him. "We have a busy day ahead of us. What'll you be doing?"

Nagora looked up into Lars's eyes. "I have something to talk about with Danuka, but before I do, I will meet with Jari and Jenni about our meals at home over the coming busy days." She looked from Lars to Sarah, and then to Dannor. "Are any of you planning on eating evening meals in the village? Or will you be able to make it home for that meal? Like last year at this time of the year, we seem to be missing more meals at home or having meals later to the point we should be in bed by then." Nagora held up her hand. "I know, I know. Things come up, and it's convenient to stay and take care of business rather than ride here and back. I just want to avoid wasting the good food that Jenni and Jari cook for us."

"Mum's right," said Dannor. "This time of the year is busy, not only for us, but for Jari and Jenni too. They've got the animals, the barn, the stable, and the gardens to tend. If we free them from the evening meal, they'll have more time. And when we show up, we can make our own meal from our supplies. Jenni could leave us with a fresh loaf of bread each day. That wouldn't go to waste."

"I'll go along with that," said Sarah.

"Me too," said Lars, as he winked at Nagora. "You?"

Nagora rolled her eyes and knocked his shoulder with the side of her head. "You men go easy on the ale when you eat at the inn."

"Men?" Dannor raised his voice in surprise. "Sarah sips her share of ale too! No dregs left in her mug. I can bear witness to that!"

Sarah stood and leaned across the table, pretending to take a swipe at Dannor. "That's because you finish mine instead of ordering another for yourself, ale-thirsty thief!"

Dannor pushed back his chair. "Mum! Sippy Sarah wants to hit me! Help!"

Lars chuckled and stood. "I think I'll go saddle up before a brawl erupts. Come on, Dannor."

Nagora had just finished speaking with Jari and Jenni next to one of the garden plots. They had been pulling stones from the ground and loading them into a wagon when Jenni pointed. It was Danuka in the sky, flying from the maze. Iridescent shades of red, blue, and green light fractured and ricocheted from the fine mesh scales of her skin as she slowed the flap of her huge wings. The dragon glided above them and arced upward along the slope to land on the bluff above Nagora's lodge. It wasn't the first time Danuka alighted there to converse with Nagora. *You've read my thoughts, Mother. Okâwîmâw, I'm on my way.* She turned to Jenni and Jari. "Thank you, both. I'll let you know if we make changes."

Nagora's thoughts were not only on her dream as she walked up the slope; they were on another moment over twenty years ago when she realized the amulet she wore then controlled her destiny.

†

Nagora looked at her amulet. *I've worn you since birth. In these past two years, you've revealed so much to me. I understand now, but at times I was sure my mind was playing tricks on me.*

A voice spoke words that set me on this path. Words, though strange, that I understood as if they had always been part of me. That voice called me *Ka Peyakot Mahihkan*, Lone Wolf, the name Godomor used when he spoke to me in private in the tongue of *The People*. He had confirmed it's the same tongue the dragons speak. Now I know I speak their tongue. What other powers will you reveal?

✝

Danuka, it was you all along who controlled my destiny through the amulet Sarah now wears. I freed you to become your Dragon Talker apprentice, your protector, and the guardian of your precious eggs.

When I was your apprentice, you often sent me messages as unsettling dreams. That was when you had to touch your snout to my forehead to speak to me, though sometimes you still do. On the day you deemed my apprenticeship over, you and I talked to each other only with our thoughts, without touching. That day, I became a true Dragon Talker. Is there a reason for the dream of the Dark Twins? I guess I'm about to find out.

Danuka's wing talons rested on the ground before her. She had wrapped her long green tail around her twice. Its red-finned, bulbous tip lay near her hind leg. The dragon's red eyes followed Nagora as she approached and sat cross-legged on the ground.

Nagora spoke first in her mind. *Okâwîmâw, kîya kanesotipeyihtamihk asici niya opawamow kaskitewiyâs nîsotewak?* Mother, you shared with me a dream of dark spirit twins?

Danuka answered. *Ehâ, namoya mwasi opawamow. Nîso onâpehkâsowiyinîs asici powâkan. Ehkapachik.* Yes, not dream spirits. Two young warriors with spiritual powers. They come from a lake to this shore.

Mother, in my dream when they call to me, I do not hear their voices, but I can read their lips. I am sure one says: Come, sisters. The other says: Join us. Are they calling Sagora and me?

Each day I get messages from your father, Yogari. Each day the messages get stronger because the Dark Twins are coming. They bring something of great importance to me and my young. They will give us much knowledge, so much more than my mother dragon gave me when I was young. Danuka paused.

This surprised Nagora. My father, Yogari, sends you these messages? The last news she had of him was that he had sailed to Kemet, known as the Black Lands, with her mother and his crew. They were on a quest to return the stolen dragon gold and to bring Raganora to justice.

Is my father still in the Black Lands?

Yes, he is in the Black Lands.

So the Dark Twins come from a lake in the Black Lands to bring something important to you. Mother, what did you get when you were younger?

The power to see into the future as it will affect me, but not the power to trust what I see.

Mother, that means you know what the future will be?

No, because at the moment I see it, to me it is a prediction, a guess, or a feeling. Only after it happens do I realize I glimpsed into my future. And since there is always the unknown, the unknowable, I fear sharing those glimpses with you, as acting on them might harm you.

Danuka's words prompted Nagora to speak aloud to her dragon what she felt.

"Mother, I have always felt that somehow you controlled my destiny; that you put me on the path I have taken in life to serve you without question, to help you, and to protect you. Could it be that you have been sharing the glimpses into your future with me so that I can help you?"

Perhaps that has been so. I cannot answer with certainty until I fully have that power, learn how to use it, and trust it. Lone Wolf, I will share with you what I feel. I am eager for the Dark Twins to arrive because I fear for my young and that once again I will be in danger.

"Mother, what is this danger you speak of?"

The danger brought by those who promise unprovable rewards to believers.

Danuka raised her upper body from the ground and spread her wings.

Beware of them, *Ka Peyakot Mahihkan*. They are near.

She flapped her wings and lifted off the ground.

As Nagora watched the dragon fly out to sea, she wondered about Danuka's last words. Who could they be? What promises could they make that would be of danger to Danuka and cause her to fear for her young?

Nagora stood.

Sometimes she speaks in riddles, as if she does not have all the words to explain what she means. Who do I watch out for? How will I know what they are promising is a danger?

...

That night when the others were fast asleep, Nagora was still awake, sitting before the fireplace and watching the last of the embers die out. She was trying to fathom the unknown and guess why Danuka hadn't answered whether the Dark Twins were calling to her and Sagora. I guess the answer to my question was obvious. What other sisters would they call to?

Why join them? Danuka says they are warriors with spiritual powers. What does that mean? Powers to do what?

The last red ember faded into darkness. Nagora stood and found her way up the stairs to her empty bed. Sleep, bring me rest tonight.

Instead, sleep took her back to the nightmare. The branding was just two days after she had helped Danuka hatch her dragon eggs in the center rings of the maze. Lars and Dannor were still in the Land of the Danu.

✝

Gabe and Sagora had traveled to Maze Point to bring Nagora to Skull Bay for the branding. She had no choice because soon Prince Gabe and Sagora would embark on a journey to the Land of the Danu to bring back their sons. It would be a journey of mourning and diplomacy.

Mourning because seven-year-old Raean's twin brother, Baerik, would return under escort in a coffin.

Diplomacy because Prince Gabe and Sagora, with the new brand on her forehead, would reassure King Raynhard and his people that the warriors of the Land of Skulls no longer threatened to invade.

Nagora stood on the third topmost step of the wide stairway leading up to the Grand Hall of King Godomor the

Terrible. Sagora knelt before her on the hall landing. Sister, I knelt before you on the same spot seventeen years ago when you branded me. Now it's my turn to brand you.

Godomor stood to the left of Sagora. He was wearing his leather crown with the gold chain loops, symbolizing the domains of his kingdom, and a black raven wing that spread over his head.

His son, Gabyndor, Sagora's husband, stood to the right of her. To the right of Gabe and behind him, a blacksmith stood by a burning metal brazier, pumping its bellows to heat the brands that rested on the hot coals.

Behind Nagora, the people of Skull Bay stood in the street below to witness the branding. As was custom in the Land of Skulls and to appease the signers, who still held to their rigorous hand signals to protect themselves from twins who they believed to be evil, Sagora's new brand would again mark her as different from her twin, Nagora. The signers would, once more, be able to see them as distinct sisters.

Gabe raised his hand, signaling the smith to bring the brand. He took it and handed it to Nagora.

"No!" Nagora screamed in the Skullian language on seeing the brand. It was the Gebo symbol. One could interpret it to mean a gift for a curse. That would have been fine if it were to hide the Tiwaz symbol Sagora had branded to her own forehead to make her appear identical to Nagora, but the size of this red-hot iron horrified Nagora. "No!" She held Gabe's eyes with hers. "This isn't just a branding, Gabe! This is disfigurement! It's meant so no other will look upon her with love. How can you ask me to do this?"

Nagora turned her gaze to Godomor, continuing to speak in Skullian. "Is your son ordering this to earn the title of 'Gabyndor the Terrible'? Has he thought this through? He'll be the one to behold that scarred face every day. As will their son, Raean. And you too, King Godomor, will live with the consequences of such a disfigurement.

"A brand this size will scar Sagora so she can no longer smile on any of you ever again. Sagora is a healer. Your people trusted her when she worked with my mother. Those she healed called her Sagnuska. Her smile will no longer comfort those she could heal should your people ever forgive her and put their trust in her again. There is no love in such disfigurement—only hate. Hate you will grow to regret."

Nagora looked to Gabe again. "How will you explain to Raean your reasons for doing this? Will such destruction of his mother's face foster his love for you? What about his love for his mother, who raised him all these years away from you?"

Nagora pointed at Gabe. "When Raean arrives, ask him what King Raynhard told him about his mother's role in those unbelievable events. Yes, that wedding invitation was a painful affront to you, Gabe." She swept her arm back to show the people behind her. "And to all people in the Land of Skulls. However, Sagora and Raynhard were under the spell of a powerful witch who is no more. Forgive Sagora!"

Nagora looked at her sister. Sagora stared back at her with lifeless eyes, resigned to the fate that awaited her.

Nagora looked to Godomor. His face was unreadable. She looked to Gabe. His jaw was set and determined. The big Gebo brand had lost its red glow. "Gabe, I'm the one who risked all to travel to the Land of the Danu. There I risked my life to learn the true reasons behind that heartbreaking insult to you and set things right. If your reason to brand Sagora in this way is a punishment, then I should not be the one to deliver it. However, if it's to distinguish between the two of us, then let it be a smaller symbol such as Othala to cover the Tiwaz symbol we both share. That I will do as Sagora did to me on this spot."

"Why Othala?" asked Godomor.

Nagora turned to this man she loved like a father. "I returned to the Land of Skulls as a returning twin, banished from this land. I returned for a higher cause. That is why I chose the Tiwaz. Sagora has returned here, to Skull Bay. Our mother raised her here. This is her homeland. She has come home to find herself and the man she loves. Othala would be fitting."

Godomor looked down at Sagora, who stared back at him with tears on her cheeks. Then he looked to Gabe, whose expression had not changed.

Nagora followed Godomor's gaze and spoke. "Gabe, if you let me brand her with Othala over the Tiwaz, I promise you will never see me within a hundred paces of Sagora ever again here in Skull Bay." She set the Gebo brand on the step a stride away from where she stood.

Then Nagora performed the signing ritual of those who still feared twins in Skull Bay. In rapid sequence, she covered her eyes, ears, and mouth; pulled her fists to her chest; brought the backs of her hands to her forehead; pushed her hands in front of her toward Sagora; and then struck out twice with her fists crossed. All the while she chanted the ritual formula in Skullian to ward off the evil twin. Nagora did it a second time. "Consider Sagora banished from my life. That way both of us pay double the price as look-a-likes."

Gabe looked to Sagora and then to his father. He turned to walk to the brazier.

Sagora spoke in Danuian to Nagora in a whisper. "You played to the audience so my man would save face. I hope they heed you and you don't regret it. I love you, little sister."

Gabe returned with the glowing red Othala brand and handed it to Nagora.

She turned to her kneeling sister. "Ready, Sagora?"

"Do it."

Nagora did not hesitate. She aimed for the Tiwaz and touched the Othala brand to her sister's forehead, pulling it away as soon as the skin sizzled.

Sagora stood as Godomor placed a hand on her shoulder and proclaimed, "Our daughter has returned!"

✝

Nagora sat up in bed. She had just relived branding Sagora, and no, the condition of banishment had not changed. Do I regret making that call? Am I destined to never reunite with all the members of my family? How many times have the four of us been together? Only once. That was on the day of Uncle Dangor's funeral in Windhaven. That day I mourned the man who raised me all those years in place of my parents. All that time, he kept their and my sister's existence from me. A secret to protect me.

Sagora, what I did was to protect you, but in doing so, I've taken you out of my life. Yes, I regret it because it has kept me from getting to know you better. That day I couldn't disfigure you. I love you, my big sister. Now I learn about you from Sarah when she tells me of her visits to you. She presses Gabe with my requests to find a way to lift this ban I've imposed on us.

Nagora lay back down. That night she missed having her man to nestle against for comfort. She had discussed possibilities of resolving the ban with him many times. He always offered hope with the suggestion that Sagora could visit since Nagora's own words of self-imposed banishment specified Skull Bay, thus limiting the area of the ban. Yet would Gabe allow it? What would the signers say? They're so stuck in their belief that twins are evil, even if branded. Nagora was sure that, in his heart, Gabe wanted them to reunite, but he would have to convince the signers the banishment had gone on long enough.

Her mother's words to explain the meaning of the signers' ritual signing came back to her.

†

"It is their way. Banished from the eyes—not to be seen; banished from the ears—not to be heard nor heard spoken of; banished from the lips—not to be spoken of; banished from the hands—not to be touched; and the most difficult, banished from the mind—to be forgotten."

†

Sagora, I may not see you, but I see you in myself when I look in a mirror. I may not hear you, but I remember your laughter and I speak of you often. And though I cannot touch you, I have not forgotten you—banished you—from my mind.

Lars thinks there might be a way soon. Since we will train the dragons and dragon riders as scouts to patrol borders, and as fighters capable of defending themselves and mounting attacks on land positions and on enemy boats at sea, this would be the opportunity for Gabe, as Prince of the Land of Skulls, to become the commander of such a dragon force. His prestige and respect as a leader would only grow. Gabe has battle experience. We could train him to become a dragon rid-er. He could set up his headquarters here in Maze Point and best of all, Sagora would be here too and could work as a healer. And their son Raean, when old enough, would make his dream to ride a dragon come true, as he had expressed to Dannor in the castle yard in Windhaven upon seeing Danuka land there with Sagora and Sarah.

Lars, perhaps you'll return with good news, or at least hopeful news, like Sarah does when she returns from visits with Sagora. Even if I gave birth to Sarah, Sagora is more of a mother to her than I've ever been. Nagora pulled her man's cold pillow to her and fell asleep.

Of Dragons and Riders
Paskwaskisiw ekwa Otêhtapiw

Nagora's sleep was light, allowing her to hear Lars's late return. She speculated that one or both of his meetings had been short. I won't ask now. You must be tired. He crawled into bed next to her and kissed her sleepy eyelids. They both fell sound asleep.

In the morning, after the booming sound of Dannor's sling-launched war stone woke them, Nagora informed Lars of the details of her dream of the Dark Twins. Then she told him what she had learned from Danuka about them. "Should I tell Sarah and Dannor?" she asked.

"They need to know, but I'd wait for more information. I'm sure Danuka will inform you as soon as she learns more. Besides, they'd just have questions about who and what to watch out for. You don't have those answers, at least not yet."

"You're right. Let's go get breakfast ready."

During their morning meal, Sarah was eager to fill them in on her work in the cave beneath the maze. "I can't get over all the help I get from the Little People to prepare the sheddings. Again they cleared all the pools of debris. They had piled it in one spot on each pool shore. All I had to do was shovel it into a wheelbarrow. That made for simple trips back and forth to the mouth of the cave to dump the loads over the cliff into the sea." Sarah made a heaving motion with both hands, showing how she worked the handles on the barrow.

She continued. "It's obvious the dragons are getting used to fishing at sea and then coming back into the cave, nice and clean. That helps. Now they're not bringing in as much dirt. In the past two years, when they played so much on land, dirt got lodged in their scales, claws, and talons.

"Oh! Mum! Danuka came to me while I was down there. She told me that she too will shed this time with her dragons. The young shed every four months in their first year, then every six months in the past two years. She said after this shedding, some dragons would be ready to mate for the first time. And after the shedding in the fourth year, all of them will be ready to mate."

Sarah held out her hands. "Think about it! We will be busy at the maze with all those dragon hatchlings!"

Before Nagora could speak, Dannor did from near the washbasin where he stood. "It doesn't mean the dragons will lay hatchling eggs right away. You know they have pouches inside them to store the semen and can decide when to fertilize their eggs with it."

Sarah nodded. "I know that, Dannor, but imagine if they did! It could happen. I mean, look! The maze is the ideal place for them to do it. Mum and Lars built it for that purpose. The hatchlings would be safe in the maze. The dragons won't have to wait until the last moment to lay eggs, like Danuka had to. Why wouldn't they?"

Lars had been listening. He looked at Nagora. "To Sarah's point, you have been planning for that contingency with Danuka and the Little People, haven't you? I recall you told me that Danuka would ask the dragons to not lay all their hatchling eggs at the same time so as not to overwhelm us and the Little People."

"I did," said Nagora. "We and the Little People are at the service of the dragons. Danuka knows we want what's best for them. Like sheep herders who manage their flocks, the dragons want us to help them manage and care for their young in a way that's comfortable for all involved, and to increase the chances of survival of all the hatchlings.

"Remember, Danuka herself delayed inseminating her eggs almost until the last moment. That was close to her fifteenth year of captivity in the cave with my da. She has assured me she'll instruct her females on when they should inseminate their eggs based on their order of successful mating to ensure safe, manageable conditions for their hatchlings to survive. They'll be easy to spot. They'll be the ones laying feeder eggs for their hatchlings. Danuka says we should be able to handle hatchlings from three of the females at a time. Once their young start flying and hunting on their own at sea and on land, another three dragons will lay eggs. Not in winter, though."

Lars held up a hand and brushed over its outstretched fingers three times. "I'm speculating like I think Sarah is. We're dealing with fifteen dragons, one male and fourteen females. If Danuka and all the females were to mate, and each lay fifteen hatchling eggs, that would mean two hundred and twenty-five hatchlings. Can you imagine dealing with that many?"

Sarah was nodding her head. "To care for that many at a time would increase the risk of losing young ones. I feel better knowing Danuka wants what's best for future hatchlings. Still, I can't wait to see the eggs they'll lay.

"I remember Grandda showing me Danuka's red-, blue-, and gold-veined hatchling eggs before she hid them in the cave again. They were the same size as the red- and blue-veined feeder eggs, but so much more beautiful.

"And I can't wait to see the baby dragons attack and eat the feeder eggs. Mum, the way you described how full their bellies became, causing them to curl up and sleep next to feeder eggs, I can't wait to see that! Oh! Something else Danuka said! Since she'll be shedding too, we must add some meat to what we've set aside."

"Did Danuka tell you anything else?" asked Nagora.

Sarah stopped short of biting into the piece of cheese she held. "Aye! Mum, she said after the shedding, I must measure the dragons for their first saddles, and the saddles are to have pouches to carry things. The young dragons will fly only with saddles for a time before taking on riders. And we three Dragon Talkers," she pointed to Dannor, Nagora, and back to herself, "will be the first ones to ride her dragons. And before any rider attempts to ride one of her dragons, they must ride her first. They have to prove they can use a goad to control her."

"Did she say anything about her own saddle?" asked Nagora.

"I asked, and she said with the added holes in the saddle straps and her bridle, it should still fit fine. Danuka also said she has begun training the dragons to land and then line up and sit near the saddle room, along the maze wall and face out to sea. That way, they'll behave when being saddled."

"Thanks for reporting this, Sarah," said Nagora.

She turned to her son. "Dannor, how's the bow practice with the riders going?"

"It's a slow start. First, we've got the riders training the horses to get them used to the thrum of the bowstring. They're learning to trust that they can hold on to their mounts with their knees while their hands are busy with the bow. We'll build on the riders gaining confidence first before adding arrows and shooting positions. Accuracy will come later."

"Good." Nagora remembered learning from Paruline and Geirador. It's amazing what you can do when you trust yourself and your mount.

"And Mum, you promised that you'd demonstrate with Storm," said Dannor.

Nagora sighed. "I did. I'm working on it with Storm. It's been such a long time since I've shot an arrow from horseback."

Lars winked at Nagora and said, "I look forward to seeing that."

Nagora returned his wink with a grin. "I'm not all talk and no action. You'll see soon enough."

Lars held up his hands. "I believe you."

Nagora placed her hands with spread fingers on the table.

"Remember, in our plans we want every rider to take training or apprenticeship in at least three other occupations that interest them. We want them to be active members of our community when not riding dragons in the long months of winter. As riders, they'll have the privilege to drop whatever they're doing when called to duty in emergency situations. Replacing a pregnant rider who is giving birth would be such a situation.

"Our dragons have so much to teach us. We're only beginning to learn. I hope we and the dragons will benefit." However, Danuka's words, "I feel fear for my young," gave her cause to worry. The unknown.

A half-dozen dragon rider trainees were picking themselves up from the ground in the central training ring. Nagora stood at its center, leaning on her staff as she scanned the faces of the two dozen other trainees standing around the perimeter. She looked back to the six who had volunteered to attack her. They'll have bruises for a few days and dislike me for a few days more until they realize they have skills to learn.

Once the last one had picked up his staff and taken his place in the circle with the others, Nagora spoke. "That was lesson number one. Never underestimate a skilled opponent. Six of you tried and did not take me out. You failed because your lack of skills failed you. Learn the skills I'll teach you, and you'll stand a better chance of beating me the next time. Your chances will only increase if you practice and the staffs become a part of you, an extension of you."

Nagora looked around at them once more, gauging reactions. They're still green and don't know what they're capable of. "Each of you is holding a staff. In eight days from now, I want you to return with a piece of wood the same thickness as your staff, but only half its length. It will be a most important piece of wood for a dragon rider. I'll teach you how to make it into the goad you'll use to control a dragon in flight." Now their eyes light up. They have a goal to work for, with a promise of adventure few will ever experience. "Dismissed."

Dannor approached his mother as the trainees left the ring for their midday meal. "Some of them will be sore in their saddles today. Are you still going to demonstrate with your bow this afternoon?"

"Aye. I'm looking forward to it, as is Storm. I think he's due for some excitement beyond the occasional calls to service a mare, or me taking him on brief rides." Nagora relished those rides just to get away and be alone for a while. Secluded spots on the coastal shore with a view to sea and salty grass for Storm to graze were her preferred destinations. *I need more of those moments with my Storm.*

Dannor touched her sleeve. "Mum, can I say something personal?"

"Aye, Dannor." Nagora came out of her momentary reverie to look into her son's eyes.

He averted his gaze as he took a breath before looking at her again. "This is not a criticism. It's an observation and I just want to understand."

Nagora tilted her head and gave a slight nod. "Go ahead, son."

"You don't smile when you teach them." He pointed to the last of the trainees as they rounded the corner of the equipment lodge. It not only housed their training weapons, but a hall where they received instructions before practice sessions.

Nagora couldn't help but smile. "Well, this is serious business. I want them to become the best dragon riders they can be. I expect them to understand the responsibilities that come with that role. It's not a game. They'll get a smile from me when they earn it.

"Uncle Dangor trained me that way. He was hard on me. He was patient with me. Sometimes I wanted to give up. I felt I'd never be good enough for him. Sometimes I swore I would never talk to him ever again. And then there were the times when he smiled at me because I had earned his approval. Those were the times when I realized I had mastered the skills he had been teaching me."

Nagora paused and placed a hand on her son's shoulder, looking up into his eyes. "And with all those lessons learned, sometimes I did the most foolish things. Things Uncle scolded me for. I'm not perfect. I haven't always made the best decisions. At least I've learned from those mistakes.

"That's all I can expect from the dragon riders. If they show they have the skills, I can only hope they'll make the best decisions in most situations. And when they make a wrong decision, I can only hope they learn from it and don't get killed because of it. This is serious business."

Dannor smiled. "I think I understand, Mum. Let's go find Da. That rescheduled meeting with the dragon estate managers should be over by now. I'm hungry."

"Me too. Your da's lucky. When the managers heard he was going to Skull Bay, they put off the meeting until this morning. Still, he came back late. We'll find out what he learned from Gabe this evening." She placed an arm at Dannor's back as they walked to the stables to get their mounts.

Maze Point was in a continual state of construction. On some days when Nagora rode into the village, she had the impression there were more stone structures surrounded in scaffolding than there were of finished stone buildings. Today was such a day.

The village sat on a hillside of stony land. Across the valley from it rose the outer circular wall of the maze. From the hamlet, a well-worn path led down the valley, over the stone bridge straddling the stream, and up to the inland entrance of the maze.

From there, as far as one could see to the left and to the right, the path followed the outer maze wall that stretched and curved around the prominent point of land. Standing at any intersection of the small town, one only saw the tops of the inner walls of the labyrinth.

To view the inner perching rings of the maze, one had to climb or ride the winding trail on the hill high above the village to the best lookout point at the top. Every time Nagora rode up there with Lars, the immensity of what they had built with the Little People struck her as beyond belief. Eighteen years ago, it was a massive mound of scattered stones. *What tricks had my mind played on me to convince me that rebuilding the ancient maze was doable?*

As she and Dannor rode toward the inn, Nagora mused about the tricks being played on the minds of the people living and working in Maze Point. They too were getting help from the Little People to build their hamlet. In the night, tiny pinpricks of light came in the thousands to work their magic. Each villager knew the Little People came and worked for them, though not one of them claimed to have seen one.

This place did not spring up like many she had visited in her travels. People here did not build their homes around their places of work. The Little People, caretakers of the dragons and harvesters of the gold from dragon hatchling eggs, played a role in laying out the plans of this village. They situated workplaces, such as smithies and tanneries, which produce smoke or use foul-smelling by-products, on the far outskirts of the village where the prevailing winds blow away from them. And here, like in Windhaven in the Land of the Danu, sewers brought waste out to the sea.

Nagora felt at home in the village. No signers here, only smiling faces. An inn attendant took their horses.

"Da's here. I see his mount over there."

Inside, they made their way through the busy noonday tables to the staircase that led to the second floor. Lars was sitting at their usual corner table. His great sword in its scabbard stood propped up in the corner. The room had window views to the market square on one side and to the maze on the other. "It's quieter up here," said Nagora as she bent to kiss her man's cheek, keeping him from standing.

Lars smiled up at her. "You're the busy one today. Staff combat training this morning. Horseback archery this afternoon. You could, while you're at it, take them on a night patrol to Skull Bay. There'll be a half moon in the sky tonight."

Nagora dug her fingers into his broad shoulders, squeezing with all her might. "And you'd not catch a wink of sleep without me at your side. I know you well, Lars Marraden."

He squirmed as he reached for her hands. "And so you do." He pulled her hands forward and across from his shoulders, so her arms wrapped around his neck and her cheek was next to his. "I'm so hungry I could take a bite out of you."

Nagora wrestled free of his grasp. "In that case, I'll sit because I'm hungry too. And if I'm not mistaken, the cook has made spring lamb stew."

Lars watched her sit in her chair. "Your nose tells no lies. Somehow, Clarence knows when you're coming. He always makes a pot of your favorite stew."

Nagora gave Lars a knowing smile. She had the best view out both windows. That he and Dannor always left that chair to her made her happy. Not to mention her man had told Clarence she was coming for a meal.

An inn maid came to their table carrying three mugs of ale. As she set them down, Nagora said, "Thanks, but none for me today. I'll have the forest tea instead."

"With mint leaves?" asked the maid.

"Aye, please, that will taste good after the spring lamb stew," said Nagora.

Lars reached for Nagora's mug and looked up at the girl. "Leave it. I'll share it with my son. I'll have the stew." He looked at his son. "You, Dannor?"

"Aye, stew for me too."

The girl smiled at Dannor. "I'll be back with a bowl of bread and a plate of cheese."

While Lars and Dannor sipped at their ale, Nagora looked out the open window over the market square. She saw beyond the curve of the maze's outer wall. Her land wasn't in sight.

"Mum, I've been wondering about using stones with the dragons as an attack weapon." Dannor's words brought Nagora's gaze back to the table and to her son's face.

He had piqued her interest, and Lars's. In unison they said, "Tell me more."

"Aye, okay, here's what I've been thinking: Would it be possible to use stones dropped from special pouches tied to the dragon saddles? I was thinking of big stones."

Lars frowned. "I like your idea. Are you thinking of stones like the ones on the stone beach? They're all well rounded and come in many sizes."

Dannor was nodding. "Aye, like those. What do you think, Mum? Is that something worth testing?"

"Definitely, Dannor. I like your idea. Plan the pouches for different sizes of stones, and we'll try them once we've trained the dragons and the riders. There's an endless supply of stones on that beach."

"And Mum, we should ask Danuka about that too. Are there limits to the loads she or any dragon can carry? For how long and for what distance?"

"Excellent points," said Lars.

"I agree," said Nagora.

The maid brought the bread and cheese. "I'll be right back with the stew."

Nagora pointed at the plate and smiled. "Look! Honeycomb! I'll have that with the cheese after the stew." She reached over to squeeze Lars's hand. Their larder's supply of honeycomb had run out a month earlier.

Dannor had more questions to ask. "Should the dragon riders have a uniform or a set of clothing to wear? I'm asking based on my experience when flying Danuka at night. It can get cold, even at her normal speed of flight.

"Another thing I've been wondering about, do we Dragon Talkers just tell Danuka with our thoughts about where we want her to go? We don't have to worry about seeing where she takes us when flying fast. We just close our eyes and hold on for the ride.

"Dragon riders won't be able to do that, since they must guide the dragons with their goads." Dannor's hands were in motion, as if helping him to express his thoughts. "They would need to see at those speeds when the wind blows and it rains, and when in battle and focusing on enemy movements. This will sound silly, but the dragon riders would need a mask. And so would we. One with a window that would allow us to see in those conditions." He looked from his mother to his father. "Would that be possible?"

Lars and Dannor looked to Nagora. She bit on her lower lip in thought. "Dannor, those are excellent ideas! Worth serious consideration. A uniform that would make the riders comfortable in all conditions would be an asset to help them carry out their duties."

Now she was pointing at her son. "That idea of a mask to allow them to see in the conditions you mentioned makes so much sense. I know who can make such masks for us to test." A smile crossed her face as she looked from Dannor to Lars.

"Not Geirador? I've never seen nor heard of him working with glass," said Lars.

Nagora shook her head no.

"Well, who?" asked Dannor.

His mother winked at him as she pushed her chair back and stood. "The Little People."

"But … "

Nagora cut Dannor short with a wave of her finger. "Trust me." Neither Lars nor Dannor, nor even Sarah, had ever seen, let alone spoken, to one of the Little People. And Nagora had shared none of the conversations she'd had with her family, nor with anyone else except for Geirador and Godomor. And she had something else to ask the Little People. That, she kept to herself.

Nagora rode Storm to the maze as soon as she had finished her archery demonstration and answered all the questions of the impressed trainees. She left her mount at the entrance closest to her lodge.

While walking to the center of the maze, Nagora planned the questions she would ask the Little People, provided Sarah was not in the caves. Chances were she wouldn't be there, as by this time of day she was usually back at their lodge.

Nagora stepped into the middle area of the maze and walked past the tall lintel support pillars of the two inner rings to the center well hole that led to the caves below. Years ago, Lars had built a stout wooden tripod above the well hole, its three legs resting against the raised rim of the well. A pulley hung from the apex of the tripod. He had attached other pulleys to the tripod legs, ready for use when needed to raise or lower heavier loads. Now the apex pulley rope hung unfastened to the cleat on the rim of the well. That means Sarah is still down there.

Most of the time, they anchored one end of the rope to the metal grate at the bottom of the well. It allowed one to slide down the rope rather than take the narrow steps that spiraled down the well's inner wall.

Nagora imagined Sarah rigging the rope with several pulleys to lower the extra sacks of smoked meats for the dragons to feed on after their shedding.

That's most likely something you won't have to do once the dragons are mature and trained to carry supplies. Riders will fly dragons into the cave entrance on the sea cliff face and unload whatever the dragons need. Will you still be here to see that, Sarah?

Stepping closer to the well, Nagora detected movement in the rope as it ran through the pulley at the apex of the tripod. She stopped and waited. Sarah's climbing the steps and holding onto the rope with one hand. I don't want to give her a fright.

Sarah's head appeared above the rim, and then she climbed over it. She spotted Nagora. "Mum! What are you doing here? Weren't you supposed to be shooting arrows from horseback this afternoon?"

"That's done. I thought I'd come by to see if you were still here."

Sarah finished tying the rope to the cleat and then raised her arms. "Aye, I am. How did your show of skills go?"

"I think they liked it. They had many questions." Nagora waved a hand in dismissal. "It all comes down to the riders trusting their mounts and relaxing so they can focus on their aim."

Sarah laughed. "You make it sound easy. It'll take them a while to gain the confidence you have. It took me a good amount of time to feel confident. How about the staff combat training? I think I still have a few bruises from when you trained me."

Nagora smiled. "You're right, there a few bruised bodies and a few with bruised self-esteem. They'll survive, just like you did." Nagora put an arm around Sarah's shoulders. "How was your day?"

"I finished adding to their food stashes. I laid out all the pieces of meat in neat piles. After lunch, I spent the rest of the afternoon at the mouth of the cave. I had the company of a few young dragons.

"They had questions about the food we eat. Again, I had to explain the hard work involved in growing crops in gardens and fields. A few of them are still raiding crops that haven't ripened yet. I reminded them they have to respect those parcels of land because a good part of what grows there will go to them, but only after harvest."

Nagora smiled at Sarah. "I'm glad you brought that up with them. Will you do the same with others?"

"I plan to after the shedding. Only two or three are still doing this. I think the others will press them to stop going for easy pickings."

"Are you coming back here tomorrow?"

"I wasn't planning to. Why?"

"Just wondering. There's something I want to talk to you about. I know how attached you've become to the young dragons. And I'm impressed with how you've taken to your role as Dragon Talker. And how you've adapted to living here with us.

"Sarah, what I'd like to know is how you feel about returning to Windhaven with some dragons. That day will come, perhaps sooner than you think."

Sarah stepped away from her mother's arm to look at her, face-to-face. "Mum, there's something magical about this place. I feel I belong here. Nevertheless, I also have a duty to my father, King Raynhard, and to his people—the people of the Land of the Danu. It is the Land of the Dragon and you, as Edana, promised the dragons would return. I want to make good on your promise."

Nagora took Sarah in her arms. "If you do, Sarah, you'll make me proud. You'll make your father proud. And you'll make the people of the Land of the Danu happy."

Sarah stepped back from Nagora's embrace and took hold of her hands. "But I plan to come back and visit—often!"

"Good! That's what I like to hear! Listen, Sarah, Storm is saddled and waiting at the entrance. I bet he was expecting more of a workout today. Why don't you go take him for a ride? It'll do you good. You've been down in the caves these past few days. I haven't been down there in a while. I'd like to look around and admire the work you've done. The walk back to the lodge will do me good."

Sarah swung Nagora around with her in a merry dance. "Mum! I love to ride Storm! I'm taking your offer. Kimmo won't see me ride off on Storm. He won't be jealous."

Nagora squeezed Sarah's hands. "Oh! Lars and Dannor say they'll be home for supper. You missed the spring lamb stew we had at lunch." Nagora patted her tummy. "It was so delicious! Could you surprise us with something from the larder?"

Sarah laughed. "I'll see what I can dig up. But I warn you, supper might be late. I'll let Storm take me wherever he wants!"

"Enjoy the ride!" Nagora watched Sarah skip away toward the exit gate that would take her to Storm. Now to see if the Little People are there.

Nagora let go of the rope as soon as her feet touched the metal grate. She took a candle lantern from its hook and lit its wick. From there, Nagora walked ahead toward the forge the Little People operated when young dragons hatched from their eggs. She came to the wall with the picture of the dragon painted on it, holding the lantern high to illuminate it. She couldn't suppress the memory of the first time she had seen it eighteen years earlier, nor the feelings it had given her.

✝

They stopped in front of the drawing. Lars moved his taper across it.

"Wow! Lars! The colors and details of the scales! So realistic! Almost like Danuka is before us. The drawings in the other section are all done in black and shades of gray. This one glows in iridescent tones of red and blue, like the colors on Danuka whenever the day's rising or setting sun shines on her!"

The single eye looked deep inside of Nagora, as only Danuka could. It makes me feel weak and vulnerable, just like when Danuka looks at me, like she can see inside me and read my every thought. Though I have no proof of that, other than the decision I made after the first time Danuka looked at me that way. I surrendered to her. I accepted she had powers beyond anything I could ever imagine possessing. When I did, I realized I was on my way to becoming a Dragon Talker.

✝

Nagora sighed, lowered her lantern, and turned left to walk the twenty-five paces to the forge room. The cave passage opened onto a vaulted, rectangular chamber. In the dim light of the lantern, she saw the terraced levels on the wall opposite the entrance. The many miniature staircases that climbed from one terrace to the next were just visible. Tiny forge equipment such as anvils, pulleys, chains, and other tools covered each level. Nagora would need the light from a taper to see to the top level projection where the twelve little bellows and their hooded furnaces stood.

However, that wasn't what she had come for. *Mê-mêkwêsiw,* are you here? Will the Little People signal their presence? Do I have to open the concealed door like the last time they led me here in the middle of the night?

Nagora turned right to face the patchwork of shelf spaces that ran from the floor up to the edge of the ceiling. The entire unit of shelves was a concealed door. All the staggered shelf spaces had vertical ladders of different lengths leading up to them from the bottom of the unit. There were no such ladders the last time I was here. The handle to open the door is right in the middle, at the back of the only empty shelf without a ladder leading up to it. Do I open it?

"*Namoya kâtac,*" spoke a distant voice from somewhere among the shelf holes.

"Unnecessary?" asked Nagora to confirm what she had just heard. To the right at the periphery of her vision, she caught the flicker of a tiny light. She moved toward it, but now the pinprick of light flickered to her left. Nagora stopped where she was and faced the shelves square on.

"*Miyoteh ka wisamiht awîyak. Peyakwanohk kâyâhk,*" said the voice, not as distant this time.

"Thank you for welcoming me. I will stay in one place as you ask," said Nagora as she lowered the lantern to her side. "I seek your help."

"About masks for the dragon riders?" asked the voice.

They already know? They must have been listening at the inn. I'm not surprised. They built this place so long ago and helped me rebuild it, and now they're helping build the village. Why wouldn't they have an interest in anything of concern to the dragons they too serve?

"Yes, is it possible to make such masks? And I have other questions."

"It is possible. In seven days we will have completed one we think would be best for the riders. We will make it for you. If you approve of it or make suggestions to improve it, we can prepare to make others like it."

Nagora bowed her head. "Thank you." She planned her question, wondering if the *Mêmêkwêsiw* too could read her mind like Danuka. "From the shed skin of Danuka, you made a skin of armor that can make me invisible when I wear it. It fits only me. My question is this: Would it be possible to make such invisibility skins of armor for other dragon riders?"

The answer did not come right away. As she waited, she was aware of the palpable tension in the air. *Should I even have asked?*

When the voice spoke, Nagora swore it came from behind her. "Possible, yes."

Then the voice continued from in front of and above her. "But no. We will not make such armor for the riders. Think well on all the wrong ways they could use it. On the harm they could do with it. On the power such armor gives the wearers. And think well on whom the blame would fall." The voice stopped.

Then it continued. "We cannot trust how the riders would use the armor. They are not Dragon Talkers like you. You used the armor for a just cause, and no one was the wiser. To this day it remains a secret you share with us, Geirador, and Godomor. You understand its power and respect how to use it."

Again, Nagora bowed her head. "You are right. I gave no thought to how the riders might use the armor for wrong. I feel foolish for asking."

The voice came from her right side. "Do not feel foolish. We know you think to benefit the dragons, just as we do. We can offer you this." There was a long pause. "A single suit of dragonskin armor made to measure for a single rider. It will have only a onetime use. The rider wearing it will be able to will it invisible only once."

Another voice spoke from her left. "And the wearer of that skin will have to return it to you within three days of use."

The voice from the right said, "If you do not return it to us within three days, the one who wore it will die."

Nagora's stomach tightened. That offer portends an extreme situation and places a heavy burden on my shoulders. Why would I want to take on such a responsibility? Do they see something in the future like Danuka has been showing me in my dreams? "Do you know anything about the Dark Twins?"

This time the tension in the air raised the hairs at the back of Nagora's neck and down her arms. The flame of the candle in her lantern flickered and jumped. She listened for a voice, but heard only a low buzzing noise that rose to a loud hum, then stopped, leaving her frozen on the spot where she stood.

"Run to the cliff entrance. We will meet you there," ordered the voice.

Nagora turned on her heel to run out of the forge chamber, past the wall painting of the dragon, across the metal grate of the well, and into the broadening tunnel. She did not slow down to admire the images of the dragons on the walls, but ran with determination.

When light from the entrance appeared in the distance, Nagora picked up the pace and ran faster, wondering about the urgency in the last word the voice spoke.

As she reached the entrance, Nagora slowed to a halt. Standing two strides from the cliff edge, she caught her breath and looked out to sea. Now what? She wondered.

"Face me and look beyond me."

The voice caused her to obey. Nagora looked from the cave floor up along one top side of the wall, along the ceiling, and down the other side. She saw no one standing before her, not even like the tiny one she had seen years ago. Looking back into the tunnel, as far as the light from the entrance allowed her to see, she saw no one.

Then it came, spreading in her direction all along the cave floor and up the side walls, an intricate net of hair-thin, glowing green filaments. In an instant, the net had spread under her feet. Nagora turned to face seaward. Her eyes followed the net as it fanned out past the mouth of the cave. It reached out into the air, where it spread out wider and curved down into the waves of the sea.

Then it became invisible for ten heartbeats before reappearing for the briefest moment, only to disappear again. When the voice spoke again, it seemed as if it came from someone standing at her side. "We have cast our net of the finest thread spun from the scales of shed dragonskin. We, like Danuka, are looking for answers."

Nagora waited, sensing the Little People would continue to speak.

"Danuka flies high seaward each day, spreading her wings wide to catch any morsel of information. Our net spreads further out to sea to catch what may come our way by water. Information comes in small pieces, but not enough to put together to make sense."

Nagora felt her jaw drop as she tried to understand. "How does this net work?"

"You remember how you called us to help you in the secret mountain cave, and then here to this cave we had abandoned ages ago?"

"Aye, like Geirador had instructed me. Each time, I tied the dragon coin to the crossguard of my skystone blade, then positioning it so the flow of water made the coin dance and ring out its calling song on the blade."

"On those occasions, our net caught the distinctive signal of the calling song made by the coin on your blade. This time, we have expanded our net to search for signals that do not have distinctive call notes. The notes are out there and mixed with many others not related to the information we seek."

Nagora tried to understand how the Little People did this. Catching signals with a net made of spun dragon scales made sense to her, though how they spun the scales was beyond her comprehension, as was how the signals traveled in water and how the Little People deciphered them. Was her father signaling with the Little People too?

"Is my father sending messages to you like he is to Danuka?"

"Indirectly, through the Dark Twins who travel over the water to come here."

Better the Little People than me to understand the mystery of how they catch those messages.

"What do you know so far?" asked Nagora.

"Like you, we know the Dark Twin warriors are coming, and what they bring is of unimaginable value to the dragons. We cannot tell you more, except you are right. They are calling to you and Sagora to join them."

"Will you be able to share more information once you decipher it?"

"Danuka will. We share what we learn with her."

"What do you know of the danger Danuka fears?"

After a lengthy pause, the voice spoke. "Alas, it too approaches. Beware the teller of stories who promises unprovable rewards. Your eyes may not recognize the teller."

Again, the unknown. Will it never leave me alone? Sometimes I worry it will be the death of me.

"Dragon Talker, we will call on you in seven days. Do not come to us."

Nagora stood at the mouth of the cave, looking and listening intently. Nothing. I'm alone. Time to head back. Before she could reach for her scrip to take out flint and a pinch of milkweed fire starter to relight the lantern, the flame sputtered to life on the tip of the candle, and the lantern door closed. "Thank you, *Mêmêkwêsiw.*"

After the evening meal with her family, Nagora sat back in her chair at the table, smiling at Dannor. He was standing with one knee on the seat of his pulled-back chair. He used gestures as best he could to describe for Sarah the horseback archery demonstration their mother had given.

"Sarah! You should have seen their faces after they watched Mum hang off to the side of her saddle. She had pulled two arrows from her quiver. She held one with her teeth and nocked the other." He made the motion while leaning over to one side, pulling back an imaginary bow string. "Mum let loose at the hanging dummy target. Right in the chest! Didn't she, Da?"

Lars nodded and smiled.

Dannor stood straight. "Then as she rode by, she had already nocked the next arrow." Again he acted out the motion while leaning over again and, this time, twisting his upper body away from his attentive audience. "Mum twisted to take aim as she was riding away from the dummy! She released the second arrow! Her arrow struck the dummy square in its back, right between the shoulder blades!"

Dannor straightened up and moved to the front of his chair, preparing to sit, but he stopped as he pointed to his chest with one hand and his back with the other. "Mum struck the dummy with two arrows! One to the middle of its chest, the other to the middle of its back! The trainees couldn't believe it." He held his pointing fingers to his thumbs before his eyes as he sat in his chair. "Their eyes were round as saucers and their mouths hung open as they looked around at each other to confirm what they had just seen Mum do."

Nagora waved her hand. "I expect them to hit their targets. I just wanted to show them what's possible once they gain self-confidence and trust their mounts."

Lars stood, pushing back his chair and pointing to Nagora. "I've seen you train Dannor and Sarah, but I've never seen you shoot from Storm like that until today. To think, all those years ago, I could have avoided taking an arrow here if Storm hadn't stumbled and thrown you!" he exclaimed as he twisted his hip toward Nagora and slapped at his left buttock. "I could have used an archer like you back then!"

As Lars sat, Nagora shook her head. "Well, if I had been there to help you, I wouldn't have those two scars to admire today, would I?" She reached to his hip with a pinching motion of her hand.

"Oh! Mum! I bet I'll get a dozen retellings of your demonstration when I go to help tomorrow. I wish I had been there to see it," said Sarah, tilting her head and smiling in admiration at her mother.

Nagora shrugged her shoulders. "I wasn't sure I'd be able to do that trick. However, three days of practicing with Storm brought it back. I'm lucky to still be so limber." With those words, she twisted in her chair and jabbed a punch at Lars's shoulder with her hand farthest from him.

Lars leaned away from Nagora's playful attack and looked to Sarah and Dannor. "I don't want you two to say a word about your mum beating me."

With that, Nagora was out of her chair and pummeling Lars's shoulder with both fists. She paused for a moment and looked at her offspring. "Sometimes you have to let the one you love," she pulled up a fist and drove it to his shoulder, "know," she struck again, "how much you love them!"

Then she turned her back to Lars and let herself fall onto his lap.

His powerful arms encircled Nagora in a gentle embrace from which she spoke. "You can tell people how much I love my man." She leaned back to look at Lars's face, and then back to Sarah and Dannor. "Beatings and all!"

Laughter erupted around the table as Lars tickled Nagora, who squirmed and begged for mercy.

...

With the table cleared and the spoons, bowls, and mugs washed and put away on their shelves, the four sat down to business.

Lars started by reporting on his previous day's meeting with Gabe and one of his assistants. It was about the growing inland trade route between the Land of Skulls and the Land of the Danu. He spread his hands on the table. "Labrys filled us in on the state of the work being done on the forest and mountain trails bordering our two kingdoms."

Labrys? Nagora wondered if he was the same one who had thrown the axe to stick its blade into the top center beam of the sawyer's frame structure? That axe was part of the trap she had set to capture Vorpinger, a sworn enemy of her mother and a vassal who threatened King Godomor's rule. Another situation where the unknown caught me off guard. The memory of the entire ordeal brought a shiver to the back of her neck.

She reached for Lars's hand. "Labrys? Is he who I think he is?"

Lars smiled at her. "Aye, that he is. The man who swore he'd protect you on the battlefield if you were in danger and within range of his axe throw."

Nagora nodded and pursed her lips in a smile.

Dannor spoke. "Sarah, that's the story Da told me when he took me to the victory bridge named after Mum."

Sarah nodded. "I remember. You told me when we crossed it. Mum was your age back then when she came up with that plan the axe thrower helped with."

Nagora waved her hand. "Let's listen to what your da found out from Labrys."

Lars winked at Dannor as he leaned his elbows on the table. "First, work on the trails on both sides of the border is coming along. They're being made more wagon friendly for smaller merchants wanting to travel inland to trade with Godomor's people. On the steep mountain trails in the Land of the Danu, builders are working on wagon-to-mule transfer stations. Merchants will move goods to the pack mules to take them over the steep parts. Once at the transfer station on the other side, they will move their goods from the mules back into wagons.

"Second, these stations will also have inns where travelers can buy meals and spend the night and get feed and water for their animals.

"Third, with the wider trails and the rough spots cleared, Labrys is running trials with loaded wagons to calculate where along the route they should set up other traveler stations."

Lars rested four fingers on the tabletop. "This brought about a discussion about having dragon riders patrol the forest and mountain trade route to discourage attacks from bandits. For now, they encourage merchants to travel in caravans and hire trained fighters to escort them."

Dannor held out a hand. "That means we must examine how to use our dragons and their riders. We must set priorities. If we don't, people will call upon us for protection for many reasons." He held up his other hand and waved both in front of him. "I'm not saying to not patrol the trade route. It should be a priority."

Lars nodded. "You are right, Dannor. I've already assured Labrys we will schedule dragon patrols of the route, and I informed him we will decide how many dragons will patrol, how often, and at what times of day. I told him we would work out a staggered, ever-changing schedule to reduce the predictability of when a patrol will fly by."

Sarah spoke. "And we don't know how long such a patrol flight will take. We must take that into consideration too." She leaned onto the table with an outstretched hand. "Also what the riders will look for, since bandits can hide under the cover of forest trees. Maybe we can train them to watch for signs of ambush?"

Now Sarah's two hands were in motion as she talked. "And we don't want our dragons vulnerable to attack from an unseen archer. We must work out a patrol procedure. To my mind, that means the riders, as part of their training, must do a thorough study of the land, on foot, before even flying by with their dragons. That way, they'll have a better understanding of potential danger areas along the route and how to approach them."

Invisibility armor could be part of the solution, but the Little People are right. Nagora put the thought out of her mind and spoke. "Excellent points, Dannor and Sarah. Lars, thanks for reporting this to us. I think we have a better grasp of what we have to plan for."

Lars said, "I have a few more things to mention. Remember last fall when Gabe and I went to Geirador's in Cairnmase for a meeting with Raynhard to discuss these trade route details?"

"Aye," said Nagora.

"At that meeting, Gabe had brought up building a bridge across the Blood River and setting up an inn with a records station on the site of Sagora's half-way lodge. Well, they've since razed the lodge, prepared the land, and begun building the inn and the station. And soon Godomor should approve the plans for the bridge."

Nagora turned to her daughter. "Sarah, are you writing up notes of our talks?"

"Like I do every time we get together to share information. Lars, can you describe what goes on at the records station for me?"

"Sure. It'll be a place to record how many merchants cross into the Land of Skulls and the number and kinds of goods they bring to trade. Godomor and Raynhard will have people working there to gather that information. It'll help merchants decide what to make for trade, and it'll help ensure that what's traded is fair for sellers of both lands. It's similar to what's being done at the harbor in Skull Bay and other port towns."

Sarah nodded. "Thank you. Now I understand."

Nagora touched Sarah's hand. "Good. I've spoken to the Little People about the masks for the riders."

Sarah's face turned into a frown. "Masks? For the riders? Mum?"

"True! You weren't at our noonday meal at the inn. Dannor brought up having a mask with a window on it so riders can see when the dragons fly fast."

Dannor interrupted. "And I brought up uniforms for the riders. To keep them warm and comfortable when flying. What did they say, Mum?"

"In seven days, I should have a mask to show you. We'll be able to approve it as-is or make suggestions to improve it."

"Great! I can't wait to see it!" Dannor smiled.

"Aye, I want to see it too," said Sarah. She pointed at her brother. "Consider that information noted."

Lars cleared his throat. "Do you want to hear about my rant at the community council meeting this morning?"

Nagora looked at him with a questioning frown on her face.

"Do I have to write notes about that?" asked Sarah.

Lars smiled at her. "No, no. These council affairs don't concern us directly." He leaned back in his chair, arms bent at his sides and hands spread open as he talked. "They were discussing a plan to outlaw beggars who've been showing up here in the summer with the visitors."

By the look on Lars's face, Nagora judged he had taken a unique position on the matter.

"I told the council that outlawing beggars would not solve the issue, but only create more problems. I proposed we integrate any who come into our community so they don't leave and spread word this is a grand place to come to beg."

Lars made a fist. "Instead, since everyone here earns their keep, we should offer beggars that opportunity no matter their infirmity. Be they one-armed, one-legged, one-eyed, or even blind, there's a job they can do. Be it as a bellows operator, a seed sorter, or a fletcher, we could teach them a trade that interests them. They'd get food, clothing, shelter, and pay if they do well."

"And if they don't want to work?" asked Dannor.

Lars leaned forward with an elbow on the table, looking Dannor in the eye. "Food for the dragons."

Silence filled the room.

Lars leaned back in his chair. "I'm kidding! I'd never do that. Your mum, on the other hand … "

Nagora nudged his arm. "Dannor has a point. What if?"

"They'll not be welcome here and will have to leave to go beg elsewhere. I'm betting most would take us up on an offer to learn a trade. I think it's worth a try."

Nagora reached for his hand. "Do you truly think it'll solve the problem? I think it just might attract more beggars. What did council say?"

Lars shrugged. "As long as they're begging for work, I have no problem with that. Council is taking my suggestion into consideration and will bring it up for a decision at the next meeting."

"Lars, I think they'll come around to see your reasoning," said Sarah. "Perhaps it's the drunk beggars that cause the council to worry. Rare are the drunk ones who want to find purpose in their lives again. Nevertheless, there's always hope. There is no simple solution."

"Da, did council discuss anything else?" asked Dannor.

Lars nodded and turned to Nagora to get her complete attention. "The last thing they discussed was planning and developing products to sell to the summer visitors. One council member suggested we could make rides on dragons available to visitors."

Nagora's jaw dropped. She closed her eyes and shook her head. When she opened them, she said, "I don't even want to think about that right now. Strangers on our dragons? No! I'll not say more about it today. If I even consider it, I'd have to think long and hard on it."

Nagora leaned to the table, holding its edge with one hand, while her other formed a fist she shook. "And the decision, if it ever comes to that, will not be mine to make!" She pointed in the maze's direction. "The dragons will decide!" She sat back with arms crossed before her.

"Mum?" Sarah leaned forward, her voice hesitant. "I want to talk to Danuka about something."

"What?" said Nagora, regretting she had coated her word with her anger. "I'm sorry, Sarah. Tell me."

Sarah sat straight and smiled. "I will ask her about building a maze in the Land of the Danu. She might know of one from the past. Or maybe the Little People do. Were there mazes? And how about the Stone Standers? They might have information about mazes in their history."

Into Nagora's mind slipped the memory of the Stone Stander, Grim, leading her to meet with the Council of Elders in their unique council chamber.

✝

Nagora entered the chamber ahead of Grim. No one else had arrived yet in this amazing room. Could she ever in her life have imagined such a place? No. It was longer than it was wide. Its two long walls curved inward and met at a point at one end. The door she had come through was at its other pointed end. Almost like the shape of a ship.

To her left, a full stride from the wall, stood a single long bench and table carved out of the stone, stretching in a curve almost all the way to the other end. Both were well worn. Wow! How long has this place existed?

All along the center of the chamber's ceiling, oil lamps hung from hooks. They lit up detailed relief carvings on both chamber walls. They must be of the works of the Stone Standers. For there it was, on the wall opposite the table, a carving of the Twin Rivers dragons drawn with all the details the original statue must've had. Proud Stone Stander art, defaced and destroyed on the orders of vengeful Queen Raganora. How could she be so stupid?

...

Nagora stopped before one of the relief carvings. Beautiful pillars stood in a ring, with images of dragons carved upon them and on the stone lintels spanning the tops of the pillars.

Grim placed a hand on her shoulder. "Ever see something like this?"

"In a field on my way to Gallanford. I saw rough pillars standing; some lay on the ground, and only a few had the top slabs on them. I couldn't see any dragon images."

Grim sighed. "Defaced. Destroyed. Nothing on the inner ring of pillars either, right?"

"Nothing. Just rough, chipped surfaces. What were they?"

"Dragon rings. Dragons from all parts of the land would fly to meet at the rings. They brought their eggs, placed them in the middle ring, and perched on the outer ring to watch their babies hatch."

He pointed to the carving they were looking at. "It was one of the biggest of the dragon rings. There were many others in the land. Most were smaller, though, but well-loved by the dragons. Those times are no more."

His words sounded heavy with loss. They even seemed to press down on his shoulders. Then he straightened up, took a deep breath, and looked at her. "But today you are here, Edana. You bring us hope."

Now the weight of his words was on her. What have I done? How can I ever bring back such greatness?

Grim touched Nagora's arm. "I'll be gone for a few moments. I want to check on Council. They should be here by now. Can I leave you here?"

She was still admiring the distinct reliefs. "Sure, Grim. Take your time."

...

She stood before a most intricate relief. It was a maze. Could she find the way through it before Grim returned? She picked one opening on the outer edge and let her eyes walk into the maze. When she blinked and lost her place, she returned to the starting point she had chosen and focused on the path.

"Does your leg hurt?" This time, Grim's words pulled Nagora from the maze.

I was almost there. "No, my leg doesn't hurt. Why?"

"You were rubbing your thigh as I came in."

"Was I? I didn't realize it. I was trying to find the way to the center of the maze."

"Few can." Grim pointed. "Look. Council arrives. Stay with me until they're seated."

†

Nagora's hand rested on her right thigh as she looked over at her daughter. She's waiting for me to answer. "Sarah, ask Danuka. I'll ask the Little People, and if your father in Windhaven can't put you in touch with the Stone Standers, I will. If there were mazes there, the Stone Standers most likely have a record of any remnants of mazes in the Land of the Danu. I know there were many dragon rings, like those at the center of our maze, and I know where the ruins of the biggest one are near the town of Gallanford. Have you ever seen that place, Sarah?"

Sarah looked to Dannor, and then to Lars. She wasn't smiling as she blinked back a tear. "Only once on the trip here when we escorted the wagon that carried Baerik's body." She turned to Dannor. "Remember when you pointed to the ruins in the field as we rode by?"

Dannor nodded.

Sarah pursed her lips before speaking again. "I want the dragons I take back to the Land of the Danu to have a safe place to lay their eggs. It will have to be as safe as our maze. If not, I'll have them come lay their eggs here, or at least bring them here to hatch."

"Sarah, we will help you do what is best for those dragons," said Nagora, looking from her daughter to Lars.

He was nodding. "Sarah, the maze will always be their home and they, like you, will always be welcome to return."

"Don't worry. We'll help you, and the dragons too," said Dannor as he reached over to hug her.

Ghost
Cîpay

Three days later, Sarah returned from the maze after her morning visit to check if the dragons showed signs their shedding was at hand. Nagora met her in the stable where they would saddle up for the ride to the training grounds to help Dannor.

Nagora had just finished brushing her horse. She was about to pick up Storm's saddle when Sarah spoke.

"Mum, yesterday when I rode past the maze entrance opposite the village, a big fat man dressed in rags was sitting on the ground next to the entrance. He didn't beg for anything, but he asked me if I liked oak trees. I found his question strange. I didn't stop to answer. I ignored him."

Nagora left the saddle on its rack. Instead, she leaned an elbow on it and listened to her daughter.

Sarah frowned and scratched her cheek. "Today, when I came out of the entrance we use to go into the maze, he was sitting there, his back to the stone wall. Again he asked me if I liked oak trees. This time I told him, 'Not any more than other trees.'"

Nagora listened, her eyes on Sarah's face.

Sarah held up her hand as if something dangled from it. "Then he held up a silver medallion he wore on a chain around his neck. It was shaped like an oak leaf. He said, 'Trust in the secret to a future life of riches. Join the Community of the Leaf and plant acorns to make your life prosper.' I said, 'No thanks. I'd rather put trust in my own skills to make my life a prosperous one.'"

Nagora smiled.

Sarah continued. "Then he held out a handful of acorns and said, 'Lassie, you're on the road to a life of poverty with thinking like that. Put your trust in the Leaf and you'll be on the road to riches.' Mum, I was in no mood to argue with someone dressed like a beggar making such promises, so I wished him well and came here. I don't need to plant trees."

Nagora grabbed her saddle and turned to Sarah. "Well, let's saddle up. You go on to the training grounds. I'll ride by the maze entrance. If he's still there, I'll have a few words with him and then send him on his way. Then I'll meet you at the grounds."

"I'll tell Lars and Dannor you might be late," said Sarah.

Nagora stopped Storm about twenty paces from the maze entrance. Staying in her saddle, she examined the bearded man sitting with his back against the maze wall. He wore layers of what Nagora guessed to be hemp sackcloth. It was hand stitched together to make a hooded garment with ample sleeves and a ground-length hem that covered one of the man's sandaled feet. The rope of a bulging hemp sack crossed his chest from his right shoulder to his left hip. Beneath it, the leather strap of a covered basket of woven bulrushes crossed from his left shoulder to his right hip.

I see no weapons other than his staff. Though it looks more like a walking stick. She reached to the middle of her back and tapped the sheath of her skystone blade. I don't expect to get you wet with blood today.

She dismounted. "Wait here, Storm."

When he saw Nagora approach, the man moved the hemp sack and rolled the weight of his rotund body onto his hip before struggling to stand with the help of his walking stick.

The closer she got, the less Nagora liked the way the man looked at her. The gaze of his eyes was bold, and it did not hide the lecherous desire of his thoughts. I've seen these eyes before. Why do I feel they haunt me once again?

The man bowed, holding out the silver medallion that rested on his chest. "May the promise of the Leaf be with you this day and guide you to better and richer days ahead."

Nagora stopped several paces away. He needs a bath and a change of clean rags. "I have no need of promises or guidance to richer days, let alone from a leaf. You'd best keep the peace in this land and be on your way."

"Aye, but if you'd only put your trust in the Leaf and join its Community," he said, his other hand reaching into his hemp sack and pull out a handful of acorns, "these that you plant today will reward you with gold in the tomorrows to come."

"What if I already have all the gold I'll ever need? Why would I want to plant acorns?"

The man let the acorns fall back into his sack and then reached out to touch the maze wall. "No one, no king, no queen, in any kingdom anywhere, has ever had enough gold. Besides, you have plenty of space to hide more gold in here, don't you?"

Nagora waved a hand at the maze. "You're the first person to ask me about any gold I might hide in here. Is your information based on fact or on rumor? Or are you using your empty promise, hoping I'll give you a coin to put in your empty purse so I won't have to listen to more of your idle chatter?"

The man removed his hand from the wall and placed it on his chest above the oak-leaf medallion. "I'm not the beggar I appear to be. I'm a rich man in waiting." He chuckled. "The acorns I've planted are growing, and in time I'll reap the rewards they'll turn over to me. I know more about you than you can imagine. I know you control that which will increase the yield of the many thousands of oaks the Community of the Leaf has planted over the years. You can reap untold benefits from the Leafers if you join them."

Nagora grinned. "Now you want to line my purse with coins, gold ones even, which will fall into it only in the distant future? I'm guessing you think shipbuilding in the years ahead will require such a volume of oak trees to provide stout ribs for bigger and better ships, that you'll reap the benefits from harvesting them? I doubt that in our two lifetimes combined, those trees will reach the size for a shipbuilder's needs.

"And I'm guessing that you will tell me that dragon manure will increase the yield of oak trees? Make them grow bigger, faster? The dragons don't shit in the maze! And you don't know a thing about me other than what you've heard from others."

"Aye, oaks for ships' ribs are only a small part of it. I'd like to tell you more, but I won't because you won't believe me. Join the Community of the Leaf. The Head Leafers, more proper-looking folk than I, will tell you why you should join and convince you. However, I can show how, thanks to you, I found my way to become a Leafer. Perhaps then you'll consider joining them." The man held out a hand.

Nagora waved her hand. "Don't bother. I don't know you, and I don't know any Leafers. You've shown up here at the wrong time of year when few visitors come to solve the mystery of the maze. You have no one to beg coins from. If you had a pitiful enough story, I might have parted with one and sent you on your way, like I'm trying to do now in all kindness."

The man leaned in her direction, staring at her. "You don't recognize me, do you, dragon lassie?"

Those last two words froze Nagora in place. A long-ago rage built inside her as the words brought back the memory of the cruel jailor in the dungeon sea cave. He was the only person to have ever called her by that name. Is it possible? Could it be he survived?

"You're asking yourself if it's possible he survived. The one you judged and took upon yourself to punish and leave to die a terrible death. Aye, him. Dragon lassie, what you did not know at the time is you gave me the sign that led me to the Leafers!"

Once again at the back of her mind, Nagora opened that drawer of puzzle pieces. She raced to put them together to see if what she was hearing from this man was possible. "If you are Worsham, Prince Acindor's jailor in the dungeon at Yhorgal Cliffs … " Nagora's insides quaked, and the muscles in her body tensed. She fought to control her rage. " … and you know I was the Dragon-Warrior Princess who returned to serve justice upon you for all the young women you and your prince raped and tortured!" Nagora shook her fist. "If you are him, I failed in my sworn duty to those women on that day!"

Nagora reached over her shoulder and pulled her skystone blade from its sheath. "But today, Worsham, believe me! You and I will bear witness to my just actions! For I will—not—fail this time! Turn that way and start walking! Follow the maze wall until we reach the cliffs! There your days will end, and I will fulfill my promise!"

Worsham let his walking stick fall and held out both hands, palms facing Nagora. With his right hand, he pointed to his left palm. "See the scars in my hand? Those are the scars from the wounds you made when you pinned it to the tabletop with the knife. Those scars and the other lines I was born with complete the shape of an oak leaf in my hand. Do you see it?"

Nagora saw the oak leaf, and she remembered. The pointed knife tip had struck bone the first time she plunged it into his hand. The second time, though, she pinned his hand to the table with it. His only chance to free himself was to cut off his own balls with that dull-bladed table knife. Somehow, he must have. And now she wanted confirmation of how he had, and who had helped him.

Worsham held the medallion next to his scarred palm. "See? Just like the medallion."

Nagora pointed her blade at him. "I should have killed you on your own torture table! You would not be here today! Tell me! Who helped you, Worsham?"

Worsham stepped back and kept his hands held out in front of him. "My friend, Chive the Idiot. He pulled the knife from my hand and folded my fingers around its handle."

Raynhard! Once my king, The Watcher, and Chive the Idiot, scrounger of herbs and mushrooms for the witch, Hag—all the same person! Raynhard, were you under Hag's spell all along when you freed this piece of shit? "What did Chive say to you, Worsham?"

"Of the many words he uttered in his strange stutter, I only understood four of them when he pointed to me and then away."

Nagora flicked her blade closer to Worsham. "What were those four words?"

"Windhaven, Raganora, Acindor, boat."

"Did you think he was telling you to go join Raganora and Acindor on a boat in Windhaven?"

"Aye. He pointed to my hand, then to his own, and then to his heart before repeating the four words."

Nagora frowned. "And that led you to the Leafers you now serve?"

Worsham shook his head and his hands. "No. No. Not right away." He pointed below the rope that ran around his thick waist. "I was on the floating tabletop in the sea cave. The tide was rising. I had to," his face grimaced as he made multiple slicing motions at his crotch, "and rip my cock free from under the iron dog you used to pin me to the table. All I wanted was revenge. To find you and torture you like no person alive has ever been tormented."

"How did you survive your wounds?"

"Hag sewed me up. I was with her in the wagon to Windhaven. There, she left me in the care of one who would put me on a boat with Raganora and Acindor should the battle not turn in the queen's favor."

Those last words brought questions to Nagora's mind. Did Raynhard have knowledge of Raganora's plan? Why would she flee with her son? While captive in the dungeon, Nagora had overheard Acindor discuss with Worsham his strained relationship with his mother, the queen.

And later, at the fortress on the Isle of Smoke, Nagora had spied on a conversation Raganora had with the captain of the fortress force, Grallimdor. The choice words the queen had about her son, when reacting to the news of his capture by Edana, came back to Nagora.

✝

"What woman in her right mind would want to mate with him? I'm his mother and I can't even love him as a son. She can have him for all I care. Let's face it. He hasn't the brains to rule a chicken coop! How could she even think or believe he could rule a kingdom?"

✝

Fleeing with her son wasn't adding up. Unless Raynhard had, through Hag, informed Raganora of the plan to raid the Isle of Smoke Fortress, and Raganora was speaking for the benefit of any spies who might be listening. Was that treason, or was he under Hag's spell?

And wasn't Sagora supposed to have beheaded Acindor and brought his head to Raynhard? Raynhard told me so. I accepted that as truth. Why hadn't I ever asked Sagora if she had done so? Come to think of it, is that something she would have done of her own choosing? Perhaps if ordered to and with the knowledge of his crimes. I didn't give her all the details of what Acindor had done. Who in her contingent would have given such an order? Only Raynhard. From the way he told it, it didn't seem like he had ordered it. Perhaps Acindor is still alive? That could only be if Raynhard freed him.

"That means you sailed away with Raganora, Acindor, and Hag?"

"No."

"Did you see them sail away?"

"No, the last time I saw Acindor was the day Edana err, you captured him. The last time I saw Hag was when she left me in Windhaven. I had last seen Raganora a year before in Windhaven when she sent me with Acindor and Hag to the fortress at Yhorgal Cliffs."

"Where did Hag leave you in Windhaven?"

"At a small inn near the harbor. It was one of many on a narrow street known as Lonesome Lane."

"Someone there was to put you on the boat that sailed without you. What happened?"

Worsham pointed to his crotch. "Infection down there. It gave me terrible pain and a fever like I've never had. Two women in the inn took care of me. I was so delirious, I didn't know who I was or where I was. I didn't remember that I was to leave on a boat. It was only weeks later when the fever broke and I regained some strength that I remembered. So much time had passed that I figured they must've left without me."

"Did you try to find out if they had sailed?"

"No." Worsham looked to the ground.

"Why not?"

He held up his scarred left hand. "One woman who took care of me at the inn made her living there reading palms, telling patrons events from their past and predicting their futures." He pointed to his hand. "She read this, told me it was a sign and that if I wanted work and to become rich, she would connect me with someone who'd make that happen, but that I'd have to forgive and forget about getting revenge for this." Again, he pointed to his crotch.

"And you believed her?"

"She told me so many things from my past that were true that to this day, I don't doubt her predictions about my future."

You poor fool. You must have talked so much in your delirium. She just had to recall some of what you blabbered.

"Then she connected you with someone from the Community of the Leaf. A Head Leafer?" Nagora asked.

"The Head Leafer."

"Does this person have a name?"

"I don't know it because it was never told to me. I've only met the Head Leafer in the appearance of a different woman many times."

"How do you know it's the same person?"

"Whoever it is knows too much about me for two people to keep all the details straight in their heads. That person just might be a master of disguises."

"Do you mean disguised as different women?"

"Aye, that's what I mean. Each time it was someone different in appearance, but the same in her choice of words and her knowledge of me."

"What do you do for the Leafers?"

"Plant acorns and spread the word about the Community of the Leaf, like I've done to you today." Worsham held up the medallion with one hand and patted the hemp sack with the other.

"You said I control that which will increase the yield of the many thousands of oaks the Community of the Leaf has planted over the years. What do you mean?"

Worsham spread his arms wide. "Like I said, you won't believe me if I tell you."

Nagora jabbed her blade in his direction. "You said you know. Now you say you won't tell me. Well, that's fine with me. You've told me a fine tale, which I don't believe a word of. Your usefulness in life has ended. Did your palm reader predict my blade would remove the remains of what hangs between your legs and that I'd make you stuff it in your mouth before offing your head?"

Worsham backed up a pace. "Dragon lassie, you're about to make a grave mistake. Don't do that!"

"Not a grave mistake, Worsham. I'll be fulfilling a long-ago promise to serve justice. Executing you will make me proud today! Now turn around and keep moving!"

Worsham took another step back. "I have forgiven you for what you did to me. I no longer carry the desire for revenge in my heart. Believe me, please! I'm just a messenger."

Nagora took another step toward Worsham. "But I haven't forgiven you. While you're at it, you can forgive me for what I am about to do—keep a promise! I always keep my promises, eventually!"

Worsham backed up two paces and, as he did, he reached into his robes. "Perhaps this will change your mind, dragon lassie." In his hand he held the golden-handled dagger Raynhard had given her those many years ago as a symbol of her duty to him, her king.

The sight of the dagger flooded Nagora's heart with mixed emotions and the taste of bile. The scars on her right thigh now burned as if she had just pulled the dagger's tip across her skin and sworn her oath once more—I will not fail in my duty to my king.

To seek sunlight outside of the cave, where she had con-fined herself as apprentice Dragon Talker, Nagora left Danuka's eggs unguarded. While she was gone, Pug, who was a sworn bully to Nagora and controlled by the ancient witch, Hag, stole two of the dragon eggs for the sorceress.

Nagora eventually captured Pug to use him in her plan to protect Danuka and attempt to kill Hag. The witch had taken on the body of a dark-haired beauty, Aliza, to seduce King Raynhard.

In the secret cave, the Little People created a likeness of Danuka with her shed dragonskin and placed Pug's wounded body inside it. This allowed Nagora to stage her illusion of killing Danuka with the king's dagger, as witnessed by Raynhard and Aliza. In the appearance of stabbing the dragon, Nagora actually stabbed Pug, killing him and spilling his blood onto her hand and arm as the dragon likeness fell over.

However, another witch, Heqet, also present and invisible to Nagora, cursed Aliza as she reached for what she thought was the last dragon egg. That curse turned Aliza into the child witch, Alizarine, whom Nagora could not kill by herself.

Alizarine lived in an ageless body with Nagora's family for fifteen years, carrying the dragon egg everywhere she went. After being crowned queen and then crowning her own daughter, Sarah, as princess, together they carried out Heqet's curse by plunging the dagger into Alizarine's ancient heart to kill her and end the curse.

It was the last time she had held the golden-handled dagger. It was her last duty to her king, the father of her daughter.

Worsham extended his hand which held the dagger. "The king calls his queen to duty. Take it. He can tell you how you can increase the yield of the oaks."

Yes, he made me his queen for one night only, consummated without a crown. My daughter, Sarah, was the issue. And yes, unwittingly, he crowned me queen; not to be his, but only so I could carry out the conditions of the witch's curse to save him and his kingdom. My days of duty to him are done.

"You have the wrong person, Worsham. The queen is no more. Gone, as is the witch, Hag; the queen killed her on her wedding night in the castle maps room. Her daughter, Princess Sarah, was witness to that event and a participant in the execution."

Worsham spread his arms wide. "The king does not doubt the Dragon-Warrior Queen has the power to disappear—She did so after executing the witch!" He stepped forward, pressing the dagger toward Nagora.

"I have no duty to this king."

"The king's belief in the promise of the Leaf says otherwise. That is why he calls you to become a Leafer, so you can carry out the greatest duty of your destiny."

The tip of Nagora's blade stopped Worsham from coming any closer. "The promise of the Leaf? What do you mean by that?"

Worsham pointed at her. "You control the source that would increase of the yield of the oaks. Only you can make it happen."

"Horseshit! I should have run you through without saying a word to you. Why would I want to believe in your unprovable promise? For gold?" Nagora spat on the ground.

Worsham was quick to clench the fingers of his hand into a fist. "Aye! For gold, and for the duty your king calls you to perform!"

"And what duty would that be?"

"To obey your king and carry out the ultimate duty destined to you by the dagger."

"Enough! You've gone from horseshit to bullshit. Speak. What do you mean by ultimate duty destined to me by the dagger?"

Worsham reached out a hand and touched the stone wall of the maze. "You built this maze. You serve the dragons. You protect them. You do so for the one reason you don't yet understand—your ultimate duty! Perform it, and you'll reap the rewards for the service you render to your king and to the Community of the Leaf."

"That—is not—an answer to my question!"

He leaned in Nagora's direction, pointing at her. "You are blind to the curse of this dagger. You will only see the destiny it holds when you truly see as only the blind can see, not before."

"Do you know the dagger's curse?"

"I don't. The dagger knows!"

"I'm not blind! The dagger is not destined to me!"

"That's right, dragon lassie. Even when your king tells you your ultimate duty, you still will not see it."

Nagora took a step back. "No! Your riddle makes no sense whatsoever! Raynhard will command me to do something that I will not understand?"

"No, you will understand your duty. Your king awaits your arrival."

"Well, he will wait a long time because I don't believe any of this!"

Worsham held his hand up, palm facing Nagora. "The king said you would say that, but that you will realize you must go to him."

Those are strange words from the one who has always been blind to the dangers that assail him. This is so wrong. Why am I not surprised?

Nagora stepped toward Worsham with her blade pointed at his chest.

Worsham reached into his robes again. This time he pulled out a pair of leather slippers. "You know these are yours. I know they're yours because I took them from your feet." He grinned. "You remember that, don't you?"

The memory made Nagora's skin crawl. It was her first encounter with the cruel, lewd jailor.

"Somehow they came into your king's possession. He wants you to wear them when you meet with him in Windhaven to inaugurate the Assembly Hall of the Leaf, once known to you as the Center for the Dragon Arts. Prophetic are the stained glass windows there, as you will see when you carry out your ultimate duty."

"Worsham, you know what that duty is, and you know I control what will increase the yield of the oaks. If you value your life, tell me. If you don't, I will end your life now!"

Worsham nodded. "I'll tell you." He wrapped the leather lanyards of the slippers around the sheath of the golden-handled dagger and placed the bundle in Nagora's hand. "Your king told me he saw you kill a dragon once before with this dagger. He says he knows you can do it again, and again, and again.

"King Raynhard, like his father before him, is a Leafer. The roots of the oak trees, planted by the Leafers, attract dragon-gold nuggets from the ground. If the Leafers spill dragon blood on the ground around those oak trees, the yield of gold nuggets will increase a hundredfold. Your true Dragon Talker destiny, dragon lassie, is to become the dispenser of dragon blood to the Community of the Leaf."

Nagora remembered the warning of the Little People: "Beware the teller of stories who promises unprovable rewards. Your eyes may not recognize the teller." This is the danger Danuka fears! And with reason. I have to sort this out.

"Worsham, I was about to commit, as you say, a grave mistake by killing you to keep my promise. Instead, today, I will spare your life so you may bring my message to the king. Though, I feel I will once again regret this decision. Tell Raynhard he does not know me, but in not knowing me, he knows me only too well."

Nagora put away her blade and pulled the golden-handled dagger from its sheath. "And tell him when I come to Windhaven, I'll be armed for my duty, a queen's duty."

Worsham bowed with a smile on his face. When he stood straight, he held up a hand. "There will not be enough scales to weigh the rewards of gold you will reap."

Nagora watched Worsham step over to where his walking stick lay, bend to pick it up, and leave without another word.

Over my dead body! Not one of my dragons will die at my hand.

As soon as Worsham was out of sight, Nagora sheathed the dagger and entered the maze, making her way to its center. She sat on the stone slab on the ground, her back to the stone rim of the well. She laid the bundle on the ground between her spread legs and stared at it.

I have so many questions! Worsham, from what I understand, doesn't know Raynhard was Chive. If he did, he would have guessed that was how my slippers came into Raynhard's possession.

Would Hag, if she had control of Chive, have also known he was Raynhard? Would she have shared that knowledge with Acindor? Or with Raganora? Or would she have kept it to herself to manipulate them for her own ends?

Hag's goal was to kill all the dragons in the Land of the Danu to earn the reward of eternal life promised her in the body of beautiful Alizarine. What benefit would the witch have gained by sharing that information?

Ultimately, Hag wanted to control Raynhard. If others knew of his dual identity, they might have interfered with her plan. By keeping the identity of Chive to herself, what she might have learned from him about the secret plans of The Cause to free Danuka and win back the throne for the rightful sovereign, Raynhard, would surely have benefitted her.

Raynhard knew all aspects of the planned uprising to free Danuka and overthrow Raganora. Was he a willing traitor to The Cause, or was he under Hag's spell without knowing it?

Whose control is he under now? The Community of the Leaf? Who among them? The Head Leafer?

Or is Raynhard in control of them and somehow using them for his benefit? What benefit? Whose benefit? To what end?

Nagora reached for the bundle and unwound the lanyards, separating her slippers from the sheathed dagger. She pulled the dagger from its sheath and let the blade rest in the palms of her hands. Examining the golden handle was like seeing it again for the first time.

A dragon's spread wings, body, and tail curled around the hilt. The dragon's neck and head completed the handle's pommel, with the dragon's open mouth holding a crown. Its studied workmanship was so fine the handle was comfortable to hold. The dragon's tail formed the crossguard, which looped out on each side of the blade's edges and ended with the tip of the tail pointing down on one side of the blade.

Of all Raynhard had spoken to her on that day when he had offered her the dagger, these words and the determination with which he declared them rushed back into her mind.

†

"We are the People of the Danu. This is the Land of the Danu. We will give it back its greatness once we free the dragon."

†

Raynhard, this doesn't seem to be the underlying message you had your messenger bring me. If you and the members of the Community of the Leaf believe in the promise Worsham told, then I only see greed as the reason you call me to duty. I don't see how greed can bring greatness to the Land of the Danu.

Why send my slippers? To wear at the inauguration of the Assembly Hall of the Leaf, as Worsham said? To confirm Worsham's identity? Or as a warning—to watch my step and be careful? Wait! I was younger when I wore those slippers. I didn't know who Raynhard was then. I knew only of The Watcher before my time in the dungeon. Only after my escape did I learn of Raynhard, and that he could take on those two other identities. Is he telling me I won't know him? That he's taken on a new identity? Why not just send me a coded message?

She turned the dagger over in her hands. He wanted the dagger delivered to me in person. Why? Nagora took a deep breath as she tried to figure Raynhard's actions. He told Worsham he had seen me kill a dragon with it once. Raynhard knows that's not true. I revealed the illusion the Little People had helped create. Is he truly expecting me to kill the dragons with it?

Worsham says the dagger is cursed. Did Raynhard tell him that too? Cursed? A chill took hold of Nagora's body as she recalled the voice of Heqet in the secret mountain cave pronouncing her curse on Alizarine.

†

Aliza raised her hands and looked upward as she yelled out, "Heqet! Oh! Heqet! Come witness me end the curse you put upon me. Witness my destruction of the last egg of the last dragon in the Land of the Danu. Witness too the dead dragon. And then grant me the eternal youth promised me! Heqet! I call upon you to come witness what I am about to do."

"Alizarine." The ancient voice echoed loud off the cave walls.

Nagora twisted to find the speaker. Where is it coming from?

"Alizarine, I have come to witness what you do not see. I have come to grant your due, eternal youth for as long as you find beauty in that which you wish to destroy. Mark, Alizarine, this will hold true until the day a queen and her daughter join their hands on their king's golden-handled dagger to pierce your heart. Only on that day, Alizarine, will you truly see what you now do not."

✝

In the moments that followed, Aliza turned into the child witch, Alizarine, infatuated with what she thought was the last dragon egg. In a way, it was, since it contained the last male hatchling of the fourteen hatchling eggs Danuka had laid. That's one definite curse connected to the dagger. Sarah and I ended it by killing Alizarine.

However, something else bothered Nagora in those moments in the cave after Heqet pronounced her curse. Because of the curse, I couldn't kill the child witch right there, even if I wanted to. It wasn't because Raynhard had regained consciousness and yelled to her not to. It was something else later on. What am I not remembering?

Was there another curse on the dagger? The cuts I made on my thigh with it? Could it be I was cursed to make those cuts? Perhaps, because like killing Alizarine, the cuts benefitted the dragons. So maybe not a curse; rather, the cuts were part of my destiny as a Dragon Talker.

What else happened to me when it was in my possession? Raynhard gave it to me, but I left it in his secret cave while I went to free Danuka and Da. Then when I came back and was apprentice Dragon Talker to Danuka in the cave … Oh! My! Could that be it? Or was it just Danuka's smell? Her essence controlled me while I was her apprentice. Two moments from Raynhard's two visits to her in the early days of her time in the cave flashed into her mind.

✝

Mother, why do you do this to me?

She won't answer me. However, in her mind, Danuka's answer was clear, as if spoken out loud. "He is our king. We will not deny our king." I can't believe I'm hearing this.

Raynhard climbed back in through the crack. Without a word, he stood behind Nagora, put his arms around her, and brought his cheek next to hers. "Where are you looking?"

"The Woman Waiting."

He repeated her words in a whisper and his lips brushed her ear as he spoke them. The spasm pressed her into him as her back arched. She waited no longer. She grabbed his wrists, pulled one hand to her breasts, and pushed the other between her legs. Her mouth found his and bit at his lip as her body abandoned itself to him. She did not deny her king.

✝

I conceived Sarah. That made her the king's daughter. When I became his queen, we were able to carry out Heqet's curse on Alizarine. Was that another curse connected to this dagger? Am I making connections where in fact there are none, but only coincidence?

Then Worsham's earlier words came back to her: "You are blind to the curse of this dagger. You will only see the destiny it holds when you truly see as only the blind can see, not before."

After their evening meal, Nagora took Lars for a walk up to her practice spot on the cliff, past the big stone bluff next to which they had built their lodge. Dannor and Sarah stayed behind to complete the evening chores.

Nagora informed Lars of her encounter with Worsham and her own thoughts and questions on the matter. "Has Raynhard gone mad? Or is there something behind this I'm not seeing? It makes little sense. Not after all we've planned for at Maze Point, and with Raynhard's agreement and his encouragement of Sarah to return to the Land of the Danu with dragons. I just can't believe it!"

Lars took Nagora's hands. "What if there is something behind it and Raynhard needs your help again, but fears you'll not heed his call? This could be his way of getting you to go to him without revealing his true motives."

Nagora let go of his hands, raising hers. "Then why? What are his motives? He knows I'll not kill the dragons! Never for his professed belief in a Leafer promise!"

Nagora pounded one fist into her other palm. "Why haven't I heard about the Leafers before this? How many times did he tell me as a young boy he saw the dragons bring gifts of knowledge of the fire arts to the Land of the Danu? Gifts that benefitted blacksmiths, stained glass window makers, and even beekeepers. And how many times did he tell me he shared his father's dream that dragons and people would live forever in harmony in the Land of the Danu? Something's not right. If that's the case, why didn't he send a coded message?"

Lars waited for Nagora to calm down. He looked her in the eye. "Maybe the message is in the dagger—the curse it holds. It must involve you. Otherwise, why send the dagger? I think he wants you to uncover its curse, if in fact there is one. Are you going to go to him?"

Nagora threw up her arms. "No! Not at this critical time! Danuka and her dragons will come out of their shedding. We'll train her young to accept riders. I need to speak to her to find out what she knows about this."

She hung her head and bit on her lower lip before looking at Lars again. "Perhaps there's a connection to my dream about the Dark Twins. I feel Danuka is trying to communicate with me through dreams like when I was her apprentice. Perhaps it's easier for her."

Lars took a deep breath. "You should tell Dannor and Sarah about this."

She took hold of his arm. "I will, right after I talk to Danuka, but I won't mention anything about the curse. I need to know more about it before I do."

After the Shedding
Miyaskam Pinawêwin

A week later, on the night before the dragons would leave their cave after their shedding. Nagora wondered if she would fall asleep that night. She did, and she had another dream of the Dark Twins. Again, she awoke in a sweat from it, recalling its details.

The Dark Twins appeared in more vivid detail. They were tall, slender, dark-skinned young women with hair and eyes of black, dressed in black, sleeveless leather tunics reaching to their knees, with side seams split just below their hips. A line of round, knotted-leather buttons fastened the tunics from their necks to their waists.

They wore black leather boots, lace-wrapped up to their knees.

In their right hands, the women held tall spears with long, slender blades. A variety of painted white symbols circled their left wrists and upper arms.

A golden arrow circled three times against itself to form a band that gathered their hair at the back of their heads.

The lips of one twin moved, and then the other's, as if they spoke to Nagora together as one in words she could not hear. The Dark Twins pointed at Nagora and then appeared to show others, as if three people were standing at her side. They pointed to themselves and motioned with their hands, bringing together those they had designated.

Nagora swallowed as she leaned back on her hands, searching the darkness of the room as if to find an answer to her question. Who are the other three? What will we and the Dark Twins do?

Nagora lay back, leaving the blanket off as she watched the Dark Twins turn to walk away and recede into the distance. Her eyelids grew heavy as deep sleep overtook her.

Nagora awoke in the twilight of morning to Sarah tapping on her shoulder. She was out of breath as she put a finger to her mother's lips. She made an urgent gesture with her other hand for Nagora to get up and follow her.

When they were downstairs in the kitchen, Sarah spoke in a hushed voice. "Mum! The dragons are out and flying!" Sarah paused. She was still catching her breath, most likely from running to their lodge from the maze. "But when I called to them, none of them came to me."

Now Sarah spread her arms wide with obvious excitement on her face. "And Mum! They've grown so much!"

Nagora reached for her daughter's hands. "Give them the day to set their new skins and enjoy their extra strength. Tomorrow, they'll be proud to come to you and show you their fresh coats of scales."

Nagora examined Sarah's face. "Did you get any sleep?"

She shook her head. "No, I spent the night in the maze, gazing at the stars from the top of a lintel on the outer ring. Soon as the morning star appeared, I climbed down and ran out of the maze to the sea cliff above the cave entrance."

"You were eager to see the dragons. You saw them take flight as shadows in the early morning light?"

Sarah nodded.

Nagora hugged her. "Tomorrow you'll see them in their magnificent colors. Why don't you eat and go to bed? Food and sleep will do you good."

Sarah stepped back from Nagora. "I'll try. I just can't get over how much they've grown."

"Well, most of them are young adults now and will soon be ready to mate."

"I know, Mum! I can't wait to see the first hatchlings!"

"That will be a good while yet. Be patient."

"Are you going back to bed?"

"No, I'm off to do my exercises." Nagora walked over to the rack near the door, put on her sheepskin vest, and then donned her holster of blades. "Maybe as the sun rises, I'll glimpse the dragons while I'm out there."

Sarah stood at the counter near the water cistern, setting a mug beneath the spigot. "I'll make the morning griddle bread. It'll help calm me before I try to sleep."

"Good. If Lars comes down before you go up, let him know so he can keep quiet. Though Dannor's war stone striking the door will wake you."

Sarah touched the side of her head and rolled her eyes.

...

While making her way up the trail to her spot on the cliff, Nagora planned what she would do after her exercises. The mask the Little People worked on should be ready. They asked me not to go to them, but I want to check the situation in the cave. Have the dragons eaten all the food stockpiled for them? Have the Little People taken the shed skins? Maybe they will contact me when I'm down there not looking for them. I'll eat before going.

At sea, the edge of the sun's red disk had climbed into the orange sky as Nagora took her stance at her spot on the cliff. With a throwing knife in each hand, she began her ritual exercises. Today, she did them slow and let her mind work on her dream of the Dark Twins. Perhaps the hidden meaning of the dream will show itself.

When Nagora finished slipping the small blades into their holsters, Danuka rose from below the cliff in a slow glide. She was an imposing silhouette against the red ball of the sun behind her. With a single beat of her wings, she floated over the top of the cliff to land several paces from Nagora. There she set her wing talons on the ground before her as her tail wrapped around her twice in her usual sitting position.

Her fresh dragon's skin was a milky translucent color, with only hints of the coming red and blue along the edges of her wings and snout. Green showed on her lower neck and belly.

When Danuka's red eyes looked into Nagora's, she knew she was ready to speak to her dragon mind-to-mind.

Okâwîmâw, you have grown in your new skin. I was not expecting to see you so soon.

Ka Peyakot Mahihkan, so have my daughters and son.

Mother, you make me proud when you call me Lone Wolf, the name you gave me those many years ago.

Ka Peyakot Mahihkan no longer feels like a lone wolf. Now she has her children at her side.

And you, *Okâwîmâw*, have yours.

Danuka's long neck curved seaward. Nagora looked in the direction her dragon pointed. In the distant sky, dragons spiraled higher and higher.

My young are happy with their new strength.

The dragon brought her head back to peer into her Dragon Talker's eyes.

They are not aware danger is near. They do not have that power yet. I have some of it. Enough to warn of what can harm me and mine. That power, I cannot give to them on my own.

Mother, the Dark Twins came to me in a dream again. You projected the dream to me. What more do you know?

Yogari sends the Dark Twins to me. They are as you saw them in your dream.

In my dream they pointed to others. Who were they pointing to?

To you, Lone Wolf, and to those with blood ties to you.

To me, Dannor, Sarah, and ... and Sagora?

I am certain.

Why, Mother?

I know not yet. I will try to learn more on the first high flight with my dragons.

Your first high flight with your dragons? What do you mean?

A flight higher than any rider can survive. At that height and in formation with mine, I am sure I will capture the messages about the Dark Twins that Yogari relays to me. As you know, the *Mêmêkwêsiw* are also trying to gather information.

When will you and your dragons take that flight?

We must first practice flying in formation. It will not be easy. The flight will last from sunrise to sunset.

Mother, I met the one who I believe is, or at least represents, the danger that you fear is coming.

They who promise unprovable rewards. They who wear symbols of the promise around their necks. Those who plant the seed of greed to control the lives of those who believe the promise.

Mother, how can that be?

Greed can blind people to such a promise, preventing them from seeking the truth because they believe in others who have joined that group without seeking proof the promised reward exists. They do not see it is greed that gives their belief a semblance of meaning and guidance to their lives.

Danuka's tail unwrapped itself from around her as she pushed with her wing talons to shift her weight onto powerful hind legs. Then, as she spread her wings, she had a last message for Nagora.

Ka Peyakot Mahihkan, see Godomor to further discuss those who promise unprovable rewards to believers. As soon as I learn more of the Dark Twins, I will share it with you.

I will do as you say, *Okâwîmâw*.

As she watched Danuka fly toward the young dragons, Nagora questioned herself. If Raynhard is a Leafer, as was his father before him, has he sought proof of the promised reward? If so, and the Head Leafer convinced him, will he be able to convince me? However, if he sought proof and found it to be lacking, then what? Call me to this supposed duty to help the Community of the Leaf? Why call me in this way? To warn me? I am warned by its urgency. Why? I wish I knew. The sooner I find out more, the better.

What gives my life meaning? I once swore duty to a king for a higher cause. Also, I wear the scar of the Tiwaz brand on my forehead because I fought for The Cause—to free Danuka and give Raynhard back his crown and throne.

If anyone or anything has ruled my life, it has been my dragon, and for her benefit. When my mother placed the dragon-tear amulet around my neck at birth, it destined me to become Danuka's Dragon Talker.

Did I do that for a promised reward I have no proof of? If protecting my dragon and the future of her kind is the reward, so be it; but I'm not done with that task. I will continue to serve and protect her, to make this a better place for the dragons to live, because I believe the dragons can help people in ways we have yet to even imagine. I don't do it for an unprovable reward, but because I have taken on this responsibility. It is my goal—a right and just goal.

Now Worsham, a Leafer who believes he will be a rich man, tells me my ultimate duty is to be the dispenser of dragon blood for the benefit of the Community of the Leaf. They expect me to kill Danuka and her dragons? That is senseless!

It's the exact opposite of everything I've fought for all these years. How can the Leafers believe such a thing? Who started this? Who is this Head Leafer, anyway? I have to find out more.

...

Nagora found Lars alone in the kitchen, sitting at the table, finishing a bowl of forest tea. With a hushed voice, she asked, "Has Sarah gone to bed?"

He nodded with a smile on his face. "She's excited about the dragons and can't wait to see their new colors. Sarah's that way each time they shed."

"Where's Dannor?"

"Helping Jari with the fence. He did Sarah's chores for her. He'll be hungry when he comes back. I expect he'll be here soon. I came down just before Sarah went to bed. Later when Dannor came down, I told him to hold off with the war-stone wake-up."

Nagora bent closer to Lars, taking hold of his forearm. "I've something to tell you and something to ask you, but first, food for my belly."

He put his arm around her. "Sit. I'll bring you tea and a plate of bread and cheese, and a surprise Sarah found in the larder."

What can that be?

On his third trip back to the table, he sat, hiding the surprise at his side with one hand. "To you, the pleasure of opening it." He placed the wax-sealed earthen jar on the table.

"Umma's pickled herring!" Nagora clasped a hand over her mouth to keep more words from coming out as loud. "I thought we had gone through all of it before the end of winter. This is a treasure!"

Between bites, Nagora told Lars about her recent dream of the Dark Twins and her talk with Danuka. "She wants me to go to Godomor to discuss the Leafers and the threat they pose to her and the young dragons. Can you send a rider to Godomor to arrange for me to meet with him?"

"Aye, I'll dispatch two riders soon as I arrive at the training compound. They should return before nightfall with an answer from Godomor."

"Thanks." Lars had set a rule for riders traveling outside Maze Point. They must always be at least in pairs. The rule had two purposes: First, as a learning experience for the ones accompanying the messenger. Second, to have witnesses to the message and to any harassment the riders might suffer from signers. Two or more riders were a deterrent to threats from the close-minded ones who still held to their beliefs that twins are evil, and who wanted to expand their superstition to those associating with twins.

The door opened and Dannor came in. "I'm starving!" Both Nagora and Lars made a sign for him to lower his voice.

"Sarah's asleep," said Nagora.

Dannor nodded and smiled. "I smell pickled herring. Can it be?" He approached the table. His nose seemed to lead him there.

Lars pointed to the open jar. "Sarah found it in the larder."

He reached for his son's arm. "Is the fence repaired?"

Dannor's eyes were still on the jar as he spoke. "All done. And a good thing too. There were sizeable holes in the fence. Frost heaved some posts right out of the ground." Now he held the jar to his nose and licked his lips. "Someday we'll dig deeper holes and plant longer posts."

Lars pointed to a chair. "Sit and enjoy. I'll bring the tea. Next time I see Geirador, I'll ask him for plans to make post-hole augers. I've seen his. Our smiths could make them. They will dig well where the ground isn't thick with stones. We could set posts deep enough so frost won't affect them."

Nagora stood and rubbed Dannor's shoulder. "I have business to attend to at the maze. I'll meet you at the compound when I'm done."

Dannor waved his hand. His mouth was too full to speak.

In the cave beneath the maze, the shedding pools appeared to be clean, even if the water was not as clear as it was before the shedding. Nagora found no dragonskins at the pools. The Little People must have harvested them for their own use. They value the dragonskins.

The dragons had eaten almost all the stockpiled food. I guess we can leave what's left for a few more days. If they don't eat it by then, we can store it for the coming winter.

At the cave entrance Nagora stared out to sea, wondering what information the invisible net she stood on would find. Will it catch more fish than information? The Little People probably designed it so fish can swim right through it.

Nagora looked to the sky. Not a dragon in sight. The high flight, so high no rider could survive it. I didn't ask why. Because of how cold it gets? Or because of lack of air to breathe? I've seen dragons dive into the sea and stay below well beyond three full counts. A day's work is twenty-four counts. I know of no person who can do that.

When Nagora stood on the metal grate just above the surface of the water of the well, a voice spoke to her. "Go to the wagon room."

She hadn't been to that high-vaulted, rectangular chamber in a long time. It was where the Little People stored what she called the "stone boats." She had given them that name because of their rectangular shape, with rounded corners and edges on their bottoms.

Nagora recalled riding to the maze on Danuka just in time to help with the hatchling eggs. The Little People had illuminated the outer and inner hatching circles where the dragon had, days before, brought the feeder and hatchling eggs.

The Little People had placed the hatchling eggs on the stone boats that rested on stone slabs spread around the inner circle near the support pillars.

Danuka had instructed Nagora on how to find which eggs were ready to hatch by their temperature. She had to take a feeder egg, walk around the hatchling eggs to find the warmest one, and hold the feeder egg above it, almost touching it, until it grew hotter and hotter. The gold veins of the egg glistened as they melted, turning into liquid gold that flowed into the depression of the stone boat, allowing the young dragon to break through the shell. When one did, Nagora led the hatchling to the feeder eggs at the outer ring to attack its first meal.

The Little People lifted the stone slabs to slide the boats down tunnel chutes in the ground connected to the well. When a boat landed in a net at the bottom of the well, the Little People loaded it into a wagon to haul it to the forge room, where they minted the gold into coins.

Nagora took a candle lantern, lit it at the oil lamp, and then made her way to the wagon room. It was twenty paces to the right of the painted image of Danuka on the wall.

In that room on one wall, granite boats lined the shelves. Two paces from the shelves, the Little People had parked two dozen wagons on the floor in neat rows. A folded leather harness lay in each of those wagon beds.

The memory of the child witch flashed into Nagora's mind. Alizarine was sitting in one wagon with her hands on her precious dragon egg, which rested on the stone boat between her spread legs. The image vanished. Good riddance.

One wagon stood by itself, away from the others. Something other than a harness lay in its bed.

"First, the mask we made for you. Examine it. Tell us what you think," said the voice. It appeared to come from the shelves, though Nagora couldn't be sure.

She stepped to the small wagon and placed her lantern on the wagon bed next to the mask to get a better view of it. Nagora didn't know what to make of it. It wasn't what she expected. It was a soft leather helm with two eye windows and a protruding nosepiece, below which hung a flap.

Nagora bent to get a closer look at the symmetrical eye windows. Each was made of two pieces of clear glass fastened at an angle, stained-glass-window style, but with finer soldered joints. The bigger front pieces would allow the wearer to see forward, and the smaller pieces would allow them to see to the sides.

"Try it on."

"I will!" Nagora picked it up, turning it over in her hands to figure out how to put it on. *It's like an unattached hood with a full face cover. I'll fit it over my head.*

Once she had pulled it on, the fleece of the sheepskin lining wrapped her head in warmth. The eye windows had slipped up to her forehead. Nagora reached up and took hold of the windows, letting her fingers feel around the perimeter of the affixed padding strip on each one.

Then she moved her fingertips to the outer sides of glass and found the two-finger-wide straps that held the windows to her forehead. Her touch told her the straps were made of several layers of the fine mesh of shed dragonskin; so it didn't surprise her when they stretched as she pulled the windows forward to move them down over the eyeholes in the mask. Once satisfied with their placement, she found they held snug in place. Her vision to the sides was clear when moving her eyes in those directions.

Her fingertips followed the straps to the back of her head, where a leather buckle covered what she realized was the single strap attached to the windows. It kept the strap in place on the leather helm.

The fleece-lined nosepiece formed a comfortable bridge between the eye windows and spread out across each of her cheeks. From there, it covered the sides of her face, her chin, and neck.

The holes in the nosepiece below her nostrils allowed Nagora to breathe in. When she breathed out from her mouth, the leather flap hanging from the nosepiece swung outward.

Nagora ran her fingers up to the top of her head, down the back to just below her shoulders, to the edge of the sheepskin hood. From there, her fingers ran along the edge to meet at the front below her neck at the top of her chest.

Nagora searched for a person to speak to, but no one was there, so she looked toward the shelves. A tiny point of light flickered. "*Mêmêkwêsiw*, this … this helm or window mask is beyond what I could have imagined it to be. You have put so much thought into it! On night flights and in chilly weather, it will be warm and comfortable. The dragonskin strap you fashioned holds the windows snug against the sheepskin underneath. The window glass is free of impurities."

Nagora held out her hands. "*Kinanâskomitin*, I am grateful to you."

"We accept your thanks, Dragon Talker. Show the … " The voice paused. "We prefer to call it an eye mask. Show it to the other Dragon Talkers. Have them try it on. If you or they have suggestions to improve it, tell us."

Nagora pulled the eye mask from her head. "I will."

"On the windows, inside and out, is something you cannot see. When dragons shed their skin, they also shed the fine skin of their eyes. You would not recognize it if you found one. We have sealed the glass with this strong clear skin. That way, if the windows break, the broken pieces will stay together and not be a danger to the eyes of the one wearing an eye mask."

What Nagora was learning amazed her. Will Sarah and Dannor believe me when I tell them? It only makes sense the *Mêmêkwêsiw* added this protective feature to the mask.

"Again, Little People, you impress me with your detailed craftwork. Thank you. I am grateful to you."

To her left, a tiny light flickered on the corner of the wagon.

The voice spoke again. "Go to that shelf. We have also made these for the riders."

Nagora set the eye mask back in the wagon and reached for what turned out to be a pair of gloves that rested atop of the stone boat on the nearby shelf. She examined them before trying one on. She spotted a rectangular piece of metal on the back-hand part of each glove. Its surface was polished to make it into a compact mirror. A sewn strip of leather, over-laid around the mirror's perimeter, held it to the back of the glove.

What she noticed next was the outer palm side of the gloves. Here too, her fingertips told her she was touching dragonskin. It overlaid the leather of the glove from the heel of the palm to the tip of each finger and thumb, making her recall the first time she had tried on the dragonskin armor the Little People had made for her.

†

It clung to every bump, curve, and indentation of Nagora's skin, but not in a manner that was restrictive; rather, becoming part of her, another layer, transparent, seamless, and comfort-able. Looking at her hands, the fine mesh of dragon scales was impossible to detect in the light of the lanterns.

†

Not only could she breathe and drink through her armor, it allowed her to pick up tiny objects with ease and not lose hold of them. Nagora was sure her grasp would be firm and not slip, no matter what she gripped with the gloves.

She liked the long, wide cuffs of the gloves. They would fit over a rider's coat sleeves to keep the warmth of the gar-ment from escaping.

Nagora picked one up and slipped it onto her right hand. The fleece lining covered the cuffs on the inside. In the glove section, the lining covered the back of the hand and fingers. For the riders, these gloves will make for a slip-free, confident grip on the reins and goads when controlling their dragons.

Nagora looked at the mirror on the back of the glove, puz-zling over its use.

Just as she was about to ask, the voice spoke. "So riders can look behind them when flying in formation with other riders. Seeing where others are will help them better guide the flight movements of the dragons. Not being Dragon Talkers like you, they have to control their dragons with a goad. To maneuver, they must know where they are in relation to other dragons."

"You are right. I have never flown in formation with other dragons, only alone with Danuka. I am pleased you added the mirrors. The gloves will be a helpful addition to the garb of our riders in more ways than one. I will show them to the others and tell you if they have suggestions. *Kinanâskomitin*, I am grateful to you."

Nagora removed the glove to place it with the other, slipping them into her scrip along with the eye mask. Should I ask if they have learned anything new about the Dark Twins?

The light of her candle flickered, almost dying out, and then it burned brighter for a moment. I guess not. Time to go. I'll show these tonight after our meal. Should I tell them of my latest dream and my discussion with Danuka? Or wait until after I've spoken to Godomor? I'll wait.

"Well, you've tried on the eye mask and gloves. By the looks on your faces, you're as impressed as I was this morning," said Nagora as she sat back in her chair, holding Lars's hand.

Dannor's antics amused his father; wearing the eye mask and gloves, the lad turned his chair around to sit facing its back, pretending to be riding a dragon and holding its imaginary reins. He leaned left and then right to imitate flying maneuvers while glancing from one glove mirror to the other.

"Do you have any suggestions or changes you'd like to make?" asked Nagora.

Sarah stood and reached to pull the eye mask from Dannor's head. "Listen up, rider! Mum's talking to you, too!"

Dannor was smiling as he held out his gloved hands, turning one, then the other, to look at the mirror and palm sides. "Mum, these are amazing! They've really considered the riders' needs." He held his hands out to Sarah.

She pulled the gloves from them. "I think their work shows how much they value our dragons. If you think about it, their dragons too. They helped rebuild this ancient maze. They were most likely the ones who had built it in the first place so long ago. We do not know when that was."

Sarah folded the gloves and placed them at the center of the table next to the eye mask. "And now they're helping us with these. I think they're perfect. I don't have any suggestions or changes I'd like them to make." She looked at Dannor as she sat.

He held out his hands. "I wonder about the rest of the garments the riders will wear: the coats, leggings, and boots. What color should they be to make them uniform? Do we stick with natural leather, like the color of Danuka's saddle? Or do we make everything black?"

Nagora leaned toward the table. "What you're saying is we should choose a color. My choice is to go with the natural color of leather as it ages well as we oil it to care for it. Like the sheaths of our blades. To me, black requires more care. Scuffs and scratches are quick to show up and stick out."

Sarah nodded. "I'm with Mum's choice."

Dannor was biting on his lower lip. "Seen that way, I'd go with Mum's choice too. I was thinking of Godomor's and Gabe's men on horse patrol. Their leather armor is black."

Lars spoke. "And they wear black paint on their eyelids and grimace at their enemies. It's for a purpose—to frighten the foe. To make them think twice before engaging in a fight with warriors reputed to drink enemy blood from the skulls of those they kill in battle. I see no need to fashion rider uniforms on the Land of Skull warriors. Our riders will create their own reputation as dragon riders. What person has not dreamed to fly like a bird? Our riders will make that dream come true."

"Aye, Da. I'm with Mum's choice too. Natural leather it is." Dannor held up a finger. "We should think about where to place the coat pockets."

"And for ease of sitting in the saddle, I suggest the coats have open seams at the sides from the knees up to the hips and a split front and back to at least crotch level," said Sarah.

Nagora sat up and pointed at her daughter. "That, Sarah, is an excellent suggestion! And I would add front buttons from the neck down to the waist, no lower."

"How about knife sheaths on the outside of the boots? Knife handles mustn't stick out over the tops of the boots. I suggest the boots be knee high," said Dannor.

"I like that," said Nagora, pointing to her son.

"Don't worry, Mum. I'll note these suggestions," said Sarah.

A loud knock at the door brought Dannor to his feet. He walked over and opened it. A rider stood in the doorway. Another stood nearby, holding their mounts. Dannor showed the young man in.

As soon as he saw Lars, he pulled a sealed, folded vellum page from his scrip and handed it to Dannor. "Message reply from Prince Gabyndor. For your mother."

"Thank you!" said Nagora.

He smiled at her, bowed, and said, "Good evening to you," before turning to leave.

Nagora looked to Lars. "From Gabe?"

"The riders I sent delivered your request to Gabe. He handles Godomor's personal missives. His scribe handles only the king's business documents," said Lars.

Nagora reached a finger under a corner of the folded vellum page, ran it over to the seal, and popped it open. She recognized Gabe's writing done with a fine brush. Nagora read it once to herself and then read it out loud for the others.

✝

✝

Nagora,

In three days, my father will receive you at his lodge.
Sagora will be with Umma for the day, ensuring you two will not meet.
Someone you will be glad to see will be in Skull Bay on that day.
Come with an escort of two.

Gabyndor, for Godomor

✝

✝

Nagora looked at Lars. "That's curt and to the point. At least I know that Sagora and I won't cross paths. An escort of two? Is that necessary?"

Lars folded his hands in his lap. "Gabe likes my policy when sending escorted riders. It helps keep the signers quiet. He's adopting it too. It gives him peace of mind. And I'll have peace of mind knowing you're with an escort."

I can take care of myself, but then Lars has a point about keeping the signers quiet. The rule should apply to me. If I were alone, they'd jump at the slightest glance I'd give them as a provocation to make their beliefs heard.

Lars touched Nagora's hand. "When I sent the riders to Godomor, I sent a request of my own. He'll tell you if he agrees with it or not. Don't be surprised."

"Will you tell what it is?"

Lars smiled and shook his head, no. "You'll find out. I'm sure Godomor will make it pleasant news."

I don't know what to expect. What's he up to?

"Mum, you must plan a new training session with the riders. You wanted them to bring a stick on that day. Remember? And could I go as one escort? I could go visit Sagora while you meet with Godomor," said Sarah, looking from her mother to Lars.

"Thanks for reminding me, Sarah." Nagora looked to Lars. "We'll respect your rule. Choose two riders, a man and woman, to escort us. Have them meet us at our stable at sunrise. I want to make the most of that day."

Lars took her hand. "Consider it done."

A Talk With King Godomor
Pîkiskwewin Asici Okimawiw Godomor

The next morning on their way to Skull Bay, Nagora, Sarah, and their two escorts rode in single file. Armand, a young man a few years older than Dannor, took the rear. Henna, a young woman with tight, curly, fire-red hair, took the lead. The color of her hair reminded Nagora of her friend, Moreena.

When they neared the gates of Skull Bay, Henna fell in behind Nagora and Sarah as ordered before they left. Nagora wanted a good view of the town as they rode in.

Nagora spotted archers at the top of the wall, waving their bows. She could hear their chant. "Edana! Edana!" They were probably with me on the campaign to free Danuka.

Ahead, in the stone wall, the skull-covered timber doors of the gate opened.

The four rode past garden plots where families were preparing the soil for planting. Several members looked up, waved, and called to others as they pointed to Nagora. They smiled and called out in their language: "Nagnuska tykommi iyammani."

The first time she had heard the chant was when she returned to Skull Bay with Lars and the child witch, Alizarine, who had adopted Nagora as her mother. Lars had translated for her, "It means 'Nagora, bringer of medicine and truth.' They're acknowledging what you did."

Again, today, it warmed her heart that they recalled she had helped save the life of their king and exposed the plot to kill him all those years ago. Only two of the townsfolk in a far garden stopped working to sign.

On reaching Godomor's stone lodge, Nagora dismounted while the escorts rode on with Sarah to Umma's infirmary.

Nagora approached the guard who had knocked on the door to announce her arrival. When he opened the door, King Godomor was standing with open arms. He looked strong as ever since recovering from the poison that had almost killed him years ago. Now his trim beard was white, with a few strands of black hair on each side of his chin.

"*Mitânisimâw! Miyoteh ka wisamiht awîyak.*"

Nagora stepped inside to Godomor's warm embrace. That he still called her "Daughter" made her eyes water for to her, he truly was like a father in more ways than one.

"*Ohtawimaw kitatamihin anohc,*" said Nagora when he held her by her shoulders to look into her face.

"I make you smile today, *Ka Peyakot Mahihkan*, with tears in your eyes."

"Father, Lone Wolf always has happy tears when you call her 'Daughter.'" She blinked, and her insides shook with admiration and affection.

Godomor took her hand. "Come. We will sit by my fire. You need to talk with me." He led her to the fireplace and showed her to the guest chair.

Nagora sat and waited while Godomor looked into the fire. She would let him speak first. It was the way. No need to rush. He would answer all her questions.

Godomor looked from his fire to Nagora. "Daughter, you come with questions today. Ask them. I will try to answer."

"Father, Danuka instructed *Ka Peyakot Mahihkan* to come to you to discuss those who tell of promises of unprovable rewards. She fears them and so do I, with good reason. Can I start by telling you my dreams and then my encounter with one of those tellers?"

Godomor's smile left his face. Nagora guessed he might already know what she wanted to discuss.

"Tell me of your dreams first."

Nagora recounted her dreams of the Dark Twins and her discussions of them with Danuka.

Godomor had been sitting back in his chair, listening to her. One forearm lay across his belly, holding the other at its elbow as two fingers and a thumb held his bearded chin. When Nagora finished, he sat forward, leaned his elbows on the armrests and crossed his fingers without taking his gaze from her face.

"Know this, Lone Wolf: The Dark Twins are your *pawâkan*."

"Dream spirits?"

"Yes, of you and Sagora. You are in them, and they are in you. They need you, and you need them to help Danuka. When you and they unite, powerful magic for the dragons will be born. What you find disturbing now, afterward you will understand. That understanding will give you the peace you need to find the path to reason and overcome evil."

Nagora wanted to speak, but Godomor held up a hand.

"You do not wear the name Lone Wolf without reason. In your life, your duty has isolated you from your loved ones and made you lonely. You have even doubted yourself. Yet you have always carried out your duty to Danuka with great care and intention. You have always sought the truth and spoken the truth. Because of that, unknown friends come to seek you." He pointed to Nagora. "Like you sought me many years ago."

Godomor crossed the fingers of his hands and sat back in his chair.

He speaks the truth. We are more than friends. With him I can speak of what is important to me. He has always helped me find direction. With him, I never feel alone.

"Father, once more you show me who I am in a way I do not see myself. From the time I have known you, you have always shown me the path I am on. That path has been one of discovery of who I am, and of finding strength to carry out tasks I thought as beyond me. You give me the confidence to continue on my journey."

Godomor smiled at Nagora. He was a wise father to her.

Godomor stood and picked up several pieces of wood to place on the ember-laden grate of his fireplace.

He sat, watching the flames grow and attack from beneath the logs, before turning his gaze to Nagora again. "An enemy armed only with words and unfounded promises has recently breached the walls of Skull Bay."

Godomor glanced at the fire. "This Community of the Leaf wants my people to plant acorns. I refuse to let my people plant such trees within the walls of Skull Bay." He placed a hand on his knee. "Now Daughter, tell me what you have learned of them."

Nagora told of her encounter with Worsham, explaining who he was and the message he brought from King Raynhard, and where the Leafers planned to inaugurate their hall in the Land of the Danu. She ended her telling with a question. "Father, how can the Leafers attract so many followers in our lands?"

Godomor took a breath. "As you know, I descend from *The First People of The Land*. We were one with *The Land*. We were part of it, and it was part of us. The trees, the grasses, the rocks and stones, the rivers, lakes, and streams. As were all living things.

"A common spirit bound us. We lived in harmony. There was a balance. If we respected the balance, *The Land* always provided for us. We believed we were connected to *The Land*. The responsibility we took in maintaining the balance gave our lives meaning.

"When the Outlanders came, they destroyed the balance. They came with greed in their hearts, fought us for our land, and took all that was best from it. They brought disease. Most of us died.

"Still, to this day, I try to live with the beliefs of my ancestors. If people form their own ideas, they learn from what they observe. They judge those things as true or not." Godomor waved a hand in dismissal. "They don't believe senseless stories." He held up a finger. "When they take responsibility for their actions, their lives have meaning and value. That meaning gives them self-respect and respect for others. It allows them to take a stand on what they trust makes sense."

Now Godomor wagged that finger. "On the other hand, I have learned that if people do not forge their own beliefs, but allow others to shape them with unprovable promises," he jabbed at his other palm, "such people are open to deception. They will place the responsibility for their personal actions in those promises, more so if greed leads them to that belief." He held his hands open. "And so, greed blinds them as it overtakes their lives."

"Like the Leafers," said Nagora.

Godomor nodded. "One can never know what stories a person believes. It is their right. I as king cannot dictate what they believe."

He held up a finger. "All it takes is one from the Community of the Leaf to come in peace inside our walls and speak his words. He tells the story of the promise of riches that await those who plant acorns. That story comes with no proof. Those who join the Community of the Leaf buy that promise. It costs nothing, only the work to plant acorns and tend the oaks that grow."

Godomor spread his hands. "Before we know it, the Leafers will grow in number and clamor for their right to plant their acorns wherever they want."

Then he raised his hand above his head and looked upward. "In the forest where oaks grow, many acorns fall from the trees. Forest animals harvest them, hide them, bury them in the ground, eat some, and forget where they hid the others. Time and *The Land* decides which are most suitable to become oaks, and even then the survival of the seedlings is a struggle."

Godomor lowered his hands and looked at Nagora. "The Leafers plant acorns and tend them for the promise of the dragon gold their roots will attract. Ha!"

Nagora was nodding. "They believe that, and now Worsham tells me they want dragon blood to spill on the ground around the oaks to increase the yield of gold. How can they believe that?"

Godomor shook his head. "You already know greed has blinded them. You already sense what they will clamor for next—the blood of dragons. Imagine as more and more Leafers join to demand that blood. That is your coming battle, Lone Wolf. Who will you trust to help you fight it?"

The words of Uncle Dangor came back to her: "Trust no one but yourself." How many times had she struggled with whom she could trust? Here it was, coming back to test her again. Can I trust what I believe in my heart? That Raynhard is calling me to help him, not to kill the dragons, but to save them? There just might be sense in that.

Nagora looked at Godomor's face. "How many in Skull Bay have joined the Community of the Leaf?"

Godomor raised an eyebrow. "A handful have formed a first Leafer cell with the acorns given them by the same Leafer who visited you. Come the end of summer, they will spend time and energy to find more acorns in the forest and to find spaces to plant them according to the rules of the Leafers."

"So that's why I've only heard of them from Worsham."

"And because they are cowardly signers. Once the numbers of Leafers grow, then they will openly call for the blood of your dragons for their trees. Does that surprise you?"

"No, Father. Today two signers, working a garden plot, showed me they didn't want me here."

Nagora shifted her weight in her chair from one armrest to the other. "What of the vassals in your domains? Have any of them become Leafers?"

"I have asked my counselors to report on the visits Worsham, or any of the converted Leafers from Skull Bay, make to their domains."

Godomor continued. "Finding groups of twelve, or 'cells' as the Leafers call them, will be the hard part for the five new Leafers here. They have to be like-minded and willing to put in the work. Those who form cells early will seek to form as many new cells as possible. Their goal will be to get a share of the future harvest of gold nuggets from those new cells.

"My guess is that the original Leafers formed long ago in the Land of the Danu, but in a more discrete and calculated way as they grew in numbers in the towns across the land. Now that a Leafer recruits so openly here in the Land of Skulls tells me that a more sinister plan is in the works. It will unfold before the Leafers even begin their first harvest of gold."

"That is what I have to find out."

Godomor turned his gaze to the fire. "Yes, Lone Wolf. Listen to your heart. Follow it. You will find answers."

Nagora had one more question to ask, hoping that Godomor might have an answer to guide her. "*Ohtawimaw,* earlier when I spoke of the man Worsham and the message he gave me from King Raynhard, I told you he gave me the golden-handled dragon dagger."

Godomor nodded and pointed to her thigh. "The one you used to make the cuts that were the key in making the map to the maze?"

"Yes, Father. Worsham said that I am blind to the curse of that dagger. That I will only see the destiny it holds when I truly see as only the blind can see, not before. Is the dagger cursed?"

Godomor sat back in his chair and turned his gaze to the fire.

Nagora waited.

After taking a deep breath, Godomor looked at Nagora. "If I showed you the dagger for the first time and told you the blade was sharp, would you believe me or want to see proof?"

"I would want to see proof." Nagora realized the terrible dilemma before her as soon as she had spoken the words. It sent a chill through her entire body. Will I ever have to make that choice—choose to become blind to see the curse?

Godomor reached out and took hold of her hands. "If ever you must make that choice, come to me before you do."

Did she feel the slightest bit of hope in his words, or was it the strength his hands delivered to hers?

Godomor stood and helped Nagora stand. "A dear friend of mine and yours is here today. His business here is done. Because he brings urgent news for you from the Land of the Danu and news from those close to your heart, he will ride with you to Maze Point."

"Father, that has to be Geirador!" I can't wait to see him and learn what news he brings. If it's urgent, what could it be about? And about whom? She was going to speak her questions, but Godomor raised a hand.

"At the request of your Lars, Trowan will ride with you today to Maze Point to speed up the archery training of your riders. She will stay until no longer needed."

Now Nagora's mouth hung open. That's a surprise! Lars couldn't have asked for a better person to help with the training. Trowan had proven her worth on the campaign to free Danuka and Yogari.

"Father, thank you! Trowan has so much experience and skill. Our riders will benefit from her teachings."

Nagora hesitated before asking her next question, as she knew Sarah would have news for her, but she wanted Godomor's opinion. She wondered if he was expecting it. "*Ohtawimaw*, can you give me news of Sagora, Gabe, and Raean?"

He pursed his lips before answering. "Sagora no longer smiles. Many here shun your twin. She spends most of her days with Umma, assisting her with the sick or injured who need day and night care at the infirmary. Though, if they voice their distrust in her, she does not argue. Sagora lets her healing actions speak. Over time, she will win their trust again. Your mother left many writings of her healings here. Sagora studies them. She finds comfort in those notes from the time when she was happy here."

Godomor took a noticeable breath. "Sagora wears her blades wherever she goes. Signers have thrown threats and insults her way from the shadows. If she could identify them, Gabe would intervene. I fear her smile will return only when she finds a greater purpose to her life and moves toward it."

Godomor raised a hand to shoulder height. "Raean grows taller. He is nine, soon to be ten. He spends more time with Gabe. Often the boy goes with him when Gabe oversees the roadwork and building of travel stations, and even into the Land of the Danu where we have work teams. Gabe has had the half-way lodge razed. We are building an inn on the site. It will house our workers until they complete the bridge over the Blood River. Raean gives his father a reason to live."

Godomor shrugged. "Gabe has not yet come to a true understanding of what Sagora lived through in Windhaven. To find forgiveness requires a journey to the heart. Few are prepared to go there. We cannot push them. They must first set one foot and then another on that path and be prepared to suffer in the dark. In the dark, they can find light."

I have been on that journey to forgive myself. I know who I am, the pain I suffered, the terrible harm I can do, and the good I can do. When I can, I do good.

Godomor placed a hand on her shoulder. "Geirador is ready to travel with you. An early start on your return to Maze Point is in order. The sooner you learn the news he brings, the sooner you can plan for what is coming."

He knows what Geirador will tell us.

"*Ohtawimaw, kinanâskomitin.* You have helped me."

"*Mitânisimâw*, I thank you for your visit. You are always welcome to sit with me at my fire. If I can be of help to you, ask. I will make it happen." He took Nagora in his arms, and she held him close, taking solace in his repeated offer to help and the perspective she had gained from their talk.

Godomor opened the door and pointed. "Our friend, Geirador!"

Geirador was standing next to his mount, reins in hand. He waved to Nagora to come to him.

She waved and returned his smile as she ran to embrace him, reveling in the strength of his arms as he lifted her off her feet and hugged her to his barrel of a chest.

He put her down. "Have you lost weight? Is Lars not feeding you, lass?"

Nagora jabbed him in the belly, smiling up at him. "From the looks of it, what some lose, you gain. I weigh the same. You've grown stronger. That's from being back at your forge, and it has brought back your appetite."

Geirador laughed and patted his belly. "Aye! It has! And it makes me a cheerful man."

"How was your trip here?"

"Slow, but safe. I had two mules and travelled in a caravan. In the future, the trip will be faster once work crews complete all the work on the roads and stations."

Trowan approached on horseback. Like Geirador, her horse carried loaded saddlebags and a bedroll wrapped in a rain cape tied behind her saddle. Her bow stuck out over her shoulder from the quiver on her back. Nagora enjoyed seeing this proud, battle-ready warrior again. Each time she accompanied Godomor on his visits to Maze Point, it was like their first meeting when they campaigned together with Godomor's Hundred Best.

As always, Trowan waved with the dragon-chord salute: two middle fingers folded into her palm, the other two and thumb splayed outward, and extending her hand from her heart until her arm was straight and high, pointing in Nagora's direction.

Nagora replied in kind. It brought back the memories of that day when her unwitting salute and words to the crowd became the new rallying cry of The Cause, renewing the people's hope that their dragons would return.

Now here I am, about to fight for my dragon and her young again. How?

Nagora returned her attention to Trowan as she dismounted and walked over to greet her. "What a surprise, my friend! You do us a great honor in accepting our request." Warrior-style, they grasped one another's forearm with one hand and pulled their bodies closer to slap each other on the back.

"I am honored you asked me," Trowan said, pointing and waving to Godomor who was standing by the door of his lodge, "and my king granted me leave from his personal guards with permission to serve you."

Henna and Armand arrived with Sarah. Nagora pointed to them. "Trowan, you know my daughter, Sarah. Henna and Armand are our escorts today and two of the contingent you'll be training."

Armand came alongside Nagora, leading Storm. He held out the reins for Nagora. "Henna and I can't wait to tell the others this legendary archer will train us."

"You have heard of her?" asked Nagora.

"Aye, by reputation."

Trowan smiled at them. "Best you judge me on my actions than my reputation."

Sarah dismounted and ran to hug Trowan. "This is good news! We're so lucky to have you come to help us."

Nagora heard Godomor call out to Sarah. "*Piwi Mahihkan,* come give me a hug!"

Sarah waved to Geirador. "You'll be next." Then she dashed over to Godomor to embrace him.

Trowan walked over to Geirador to greet him. "Good to see you again." She reached behind her head to tap the handle of the skystone blade she wore beneath her quiver. "Best set of blades I have ever had. I am proud to wear them still, as are those who guard our king."

Geirador smiled. "You earned them. They're a small thanks for what you've done."

He looked at the others. "Soon as I get a hug from Sarah, we'll be on our way."

Sarah skipped to Geirador, leaning into him for a hug. "So good to see you! I can't wait to hear the news you bring."

The six mounted, waved to Godomor, and rode single file, following Henna out of Skull Bay.

Letters
Omasinahikaniw

When the group stopped to eat their trail rations at noonday, Geirador reached into one of his saddlebags and pulled out three missives. He motioned to Nagora to step away from the others. Out of earshot, he handed Nagora two letters, one from Paruline, and one from the sisters, Moreena and Erin. "Should be good reading, with good news," he said, as he tapped a third letter against his chest. "Raynhard asked me to give you this one when in Maze Point." Geirador kept it in his hand. "I don't want to forget. It's not for you, Nagora, but for Sagora, and for her eyes only, from Raynhard. He wants you to deliver it to your sister in person and says to tell you it's not a love letter, that it has no offenses to anyone in the Land of Skulls. He told me to ask you if you can deliver it as instructed. Can you?"

How will I even try to do that? My oath makes it impossible. "There's ... well ... you must have heard. I banished myself from seeing her in Skull Bay." She looked to the others, then back to Geirador. "I can't promise I'll do it, only that I'll try."

Geirador nodded. "Raynhard said you would say that." He handed her the sealed missive. "For Sagora's eyes only."

Nagora took it. "Aye, for my sister's eyes only. Is there a letter from Raynhard for me?"

Geirador shook his head. "No, he spoke the information I'm to share with you; though he said he would also send you a messenger," he said as he looked her in the eyes, squinting with what she guessed was concern, "to give more weight to his message. Did that messenger get here before me?"

She placed the letters in her scrip. "Aye, and you won't believe who the messenger was when I tell you tonight. Let's eat so we can be on our way."

Do I open Sagora's letter? Is that what you want me to do, Raynhard, even though Geirador says it is not for my eyes? It appears so, but I won't. It would, though, be my chance to get back at Sagora for all my letters she intercepted, opened, and burned. However, she wasn't herself then. Was she, or wasn't she, under the witch's spell?

What information can it contain? Will Sagora share it with me? I'll ask her to when I deliver it to her.

The six rode over the last grassy hill well before sunset. From there, Nagora's lodge and the maze came into view, with Maze Point further in the distance where the outer wall of the maze curved away, receding in size.

Henna and Armand stopped alongside Sarah. Geirador and Trowan pulled up next to Nagora. They were staring at the display of the dragons flying in the sky.

Sarah turned to Nagora. "Mum, that's new. I've never seen them fly like that before. Do you know why?"

Geirador spoke before Nagora answered. "They're flying in formation. They must have a reason."

"Aye, they do. I'll tell you why later," said Nagora, as she focused on Danuka and her young. Three dragons flanked their mother on each side. Another six flew in an evenly spaced row beneath them. The two youngest dragons flew in a third row by themselves, one at each extremity.

The formation flew as one giant dragon, turning over on itself before leaning left to bank downward in a slow glide over the maze. Then the formation rose straight, the dragons pumping their wings in unison. They banked right, continuing to gain speed as their flight path curved above the village, and then they leveled out to fly in Nagora's direction.

"My stars! I never dreamt of seeing such a sight!" It was Trowan.

Before any of the others could speak, the formation flew over their heads, only a stone's throw above them. By the time the riders controlled their horses, the formation was flying out to sea. Past the cliffs, the dragons rose as one, flying higher and higher until they were almost out of sight. At that moment, the formation broke and the dragons each took a different flight path. In a slow glide, they spiraled downward.

"Wow!" said Sarah. "They're amazing!"

As Nagora's eyes followed their descent, she couldn't help wondering when Danuka would take her young on the high flight. Soon, I hope.

Henna and Armand shouted out in unison. "We riders be! We riders be! We riders be!" Henna turned her mount to ride to Nagora. "To think someday soon I'll fly with them like that! I can't believe my luck! It will be a true honor!"

Henna's excitement made Nagora smile. "I hope the other trainees have seen this. And I hope their reaction has been like yours. When I give the signal, lead us to the training compound. We have to find Dannor and Lars."

Nagora turned to Trowan. "Knowing Lars, he has planned for you to lodge in comfort during your stay. We'll get you set up first thing. Dannor will be happy to see you. He still retells the stories you told him when he was a young lad just learning to pull a bowstring. And your hunting tips when you were here with Godomor's escort on his last visit! Lars is jealous because Dannor won't share any of them."

"I have no worries about where I will lodge. I have fond memories of Dannor as a young lad, and it has been a pleasure to watch him grow. Now I look forward to working with the man he has become," said Trowan, smiling at Nagora.

Facing Geirador, Nagora asked, "And you, Geirador? I'm sure you've brought something in your saddlebags for our smiths and for Lars."

"Aye, I have the recipes I promised to bring my lads when I was here last fall. I can leave those with them now or when I visit their forges tomorrow, when riders from Skull Bay will bring my pack mules. They carry chunks of skystone to make the alloy for the skystone blades, and walrus hides for the handles of those blades," said Geirador.

Nagora remembered how happy Lars had been when Geirador came to Maze Point with two of his apprentices to set up the forges. He was even happier when, on Geirador's recommendation, the smiths stayed on to work the forges and train their own apprentices. One of Geirador's maxims was:

"Teach something you've learned. It'll reinforce your understanding."

Nagora waved to Henna, and the others fell in behind her.

That evening, Nagora, Sarah, Dannor, and Lars gathered at the table in their lodge with Geirador and Trowan. Nagora decided now was the time to inform her son and daughter of her dreams of the Dark Twins. She would share the details of her encounter with Worsham, but omit the part of the dagger's curse. She would tell of the reason for Danuka's formation flights with her dragons, and her talk with Godomor, again omitting the dagger's curse. Without knowing what news Gcirador had to share, she felt it might be related to her information. Afterward, they would have time to speculate on their plans.

While they ate, Nagora spoke. Dannor and Sarah listened with keen interest, as did Geirador and Trowan.

Later, after their meal, Lars set mugs on the table. He had filled them with ale from a cask he had brought back from the inn at Maze Point.

"You have our attention, Geirador," said Lars, as he sat and glanced around the table.

Geirador took a sip from his mug and wiped the back of his hand across his mouth. "I'll tell you how I learned of the Leafers from King Raynhard. Not a month ago, I was on a business trip to Windhaven and to visit Pare and Harri."

The mention of her dear friends' names made Nagora eager to read their letters.

"While there, Bardas came to make a delivery to Harri's store. He had brought Moreena, Erin, and Erin's baby boy, Rogan, with him to visit Pare.

"One piece of business I had was to meet with Raynhard to carry the approval of the construction plans for the bridge over the Blood River back to Gabe and King Godomor. I've done that. He also wanted me to do a quick survey of the work being done on the trade route, reporting to him the next time we meet.

"And then he wanted me to share everything I knew about gold with him: where it's found; how it's mined; how it's worked to create coins, rings, bracelets, chains, and even crowns."

Geirador looked around the table. "He wanted all the factual knowledge I have, what I knew about dragon gold, and any information about gold that might have come from stories, legends, or rumors. And what credence I had in those. He wanted every detail. I told him everything, even about the whispered stories of the existence of the Community of the Leaf and their belief in the promise of future gold. That's when he spoke of the Leafers, his relationship with them, and his worries."

Geirador looked at Nagora. "Raynhard, like Worsham told you, admitted that he was a Leafer, like his father before him, and explained how that came to be."

"Please tell us what the king explained," said Nagora.

"I'll tell you as best I can because he mentioned you and your parents. He said that, when he was a young boy, about three years before Yogari and Tagnya landed on the beach in Windhaven, his da, King Bernhard, took him on horseback to the hill overlooking Windhaven and its castle.

"There, they walked until they came to a place in the forest with stone circles about the diameter of a man's outstretched arms, and waist high to a man. He said he could see over the stacked stones. An oak tree was growing inside each of the circles they stopped by. His da said the stone circles protected the young oaks. They continued walking until we came to a much larger stone circle that, to Raynhard, appeared to be surrounded by the smaller circles they had passed. Within the big stone circle, thirteen bigger oaks also stood in a circle.

"His father said that he and the members of his personal guard, thirteen in all, had planted the trees four years before Raynhard was born, and that every year after, for twelve years, he and each of his guards had planted acorns and built a stone circle around each new tree that grew. That made for 156 small stone circles around the big one. When Raynhard asked why they had planted acorns that way, his father told him that in good time he would learn why. In the meantime, all he had to know was that the oaks would be worth their weight in gold someday."

Lars stood and showed he would refill his mug. "Anyone else?"

They shook their heads no, except for Geirador, who took a big swig and said, "Later. Thanks, Lars," before continuing.

"Raynhard said that today, the thirteen oaks in the big circle are forty-eight years old. The youngest oaks in the smaller circles are thirty-six years old. Until recently, those trees had been out of his mind until Ardal," he pointed to Nagora, "the one you knew as the Captain of the Guard, spoke to him about the oaks. He's now captain of Raynhard's personal guard. Being the youngest of King Bernhard's personal guard back then, Ardal is the only survivor of that group of thirteen who had planted the acorns."

"Wouldn't other oaks have sprouted from acorns over the years?" asked Nagora.

Geirador smiled. "Surely, but as oaks, these are young. The oldest will reach peak acorn production five or ten years from now. Still, they've been producing acorns for almost twenty years. Deer, squirrels and rabbits feed on them and on the tender seedling twigs in spring. The Leafers would have culled any other variety of trees sprouting during those first twelve years. Though, according to Ardal, since then, they haven't tended the oaks."

He glanced around the table before continuing. "From Ardal, Raynhard learned about the one who calls herself the Gold Planter. She told a beguiling story of the power of oak trees, which had led King Bernhard, with much skepticism, to plant acorns. He half-heartedly hoped the roots of his future oaks would pull nuggets of dragon gold from the earth. However, he had done so knowing that someday, builders would use the wood of the oaks to build the strong keels and framing ribs of sailing ships.

"Ardal too had put the trees out of his mind until late last fall, when the Gold Planter approached him. She wanted to speak to Raynhard about King Bernhard's oaks and how to increase their future yield of gold. Raynhard said he figured he had nothing to lose by hearing the Gold Planter out. She insisted they meet late at night at the Center for the Dragon Arts.

"Ardal went with Raynhard. The Gold Planter told them she was travelling the land to speak to the Head Leafers of all the original, secret cells, inviting them to King Bernhard's circle of thirteen oaks where she will show proof of how to increase by a hundredfold the yield of dragon gold each oak will attract to its roots."

Nagora touched Geirador's arm. "That means she hasn't proven it yet. Do you know when she will?"

He nodded. "Not exactly when, but on a night of the full moon. Most likely soon."

Dannor spoke. "The moon phases spread over about thirty days, with three of them being full moons. If I had a ship's logbook, I could find where we are in the cycle and predict in how many days from now we'll have those full moons." He looked to Lars.

"True. I think Jari keeps track of the moon phases. He could tell you when they are coming." Lars stood, offering to pick up Geirador's and Dannor's mugs. "Nagora?"

She took a big swig and held out her mug to Lars. "Top it off, please."

"Trowan? Sarah?" They shook their heads no.

Nagora looked at Geirador. "Did Raynhard say the Gold Planter told him that dragon blood would increase the yield of gold nuggets?"

He shook his head. "No, only that she'd prove how to increase the yield."

"Why then would Worsham, if he is indeed Raynhard's messenger to me, tell me dragon blood spilled on the ground around the oaks will increase the yield? Was he lying? Or did the Gold Planter tell other Leafers? Is it meant to be a rumor that will spread fast? That's what King Godomor thinks."

Nagora wondered, how can King Raynhard not know about the dragon blood, and then she asked, "Did Raynhard tell Worsham when the Leafers can harvest the gold?"

Lars placed the filled mugs in front of those who had taken his offer.

Geirador nodded his thanks to Lars and answered Nagora's question. "Since meeting with Raynhard, everywhere I go now I hear of people joining the Community of the Leaf and working to form cells. Raynhard said he was told his trees would yield gold nuggets when they reach fifty years of age, but that if he could wait another five years, the yield would increase a hundredfold."

"But why are all these new Leafers joining if they have to wait fifty years?" asked Nagora.

"Maybe their Head Leafers promised them a shorter yield time because they'll start using dragon blood earlier," said Sarah.

"I have heard that said in Skull Bay," said Trowan. "Twenty years to harvest nuggets."

"Have you planted any acorns?" asked Lars.

Trowan rolled her eyes and shook her head. "I live one day at a time. What tomorrow brings, we do not know. Maybe dragons do, but not us."

Geirador looked around the table. "I will say aloud what most of you are thinking. If more and more people buy into what the Leafers are promising, it's only a matter of time before they show up here demanding the blood of your dragons, Nagora. Now the question is: How do we stop what's coming your way? There's something about this that points to a bigger scheme. That makes me ask: Who truly benefits? Who is the Gold Planter?"

"And why did she insist on meeting Raynhard at night in the Center for the Dragon Arts?" asked Nagora. "And why will she give proof in the forest on the night of a full moon?

To me, that's sinister. There must be a benefit to her, but what?"

"And your gut tells you to find out more about her," said Lars.

She nodded. "If new Leafer cells have spread so fast, I can only imagine how fast the Leafers will demand dragon blood for their oaks if the Gold Planter proves the hundredfold increased yield of gold nuggets. The call and cry for dragon blood will be loud." Her own words almost made her stomach turn.

Lars reached for her hand. "I sense your urgency to act on this, but first take time to think about how you'll act. Know that we're here to help you, and that we'll be thinking of ways to do just that."

Nagora squeezed his hand and glanced around the table. "I know you will. I appreciate your concern, and your support."

Dannor leaned closer to the table. "Geirador, since speaking to the king, have you noticed anything else in the places you've traveled to for business?"

"I noticed another thing before, but only after learning more about the Leafers from Raynhard. Then what I had seen fell into place and made more sense."

"What was that?" asked Sarah.

"Leafers seek fellow Leafers in the towns where they live. If they are in business, they do business with fellow Leafers. Rub my back and I'll rub yours."

He pointed to Sarah and Dannor. "Not a Leafer? Too bad, you'll get ignored. They won't tell you outright to your face, but they'll only deal with you if they can't get what they need from one of their own. Members of a same cell stick together and help each other out."

Dannor was nodding. "To join the Leafers is a business decision. All it costs is joining. Then your business benefits from you belonging and planting acorns."

Geirador leaned back in his chair and spread his hands before him. "There you go."

Dannor was shaking his head. "But that sounds stupid, doesn't it?"

Geirador pointed at Dannor. "Not if you're a member of the gang that believes what you've just bought into. Especially when they welcome you and you reap the benefits of belonging."

"Are you worried about your business?" asked Lars.

"No. No others make goods that compare to the quality we make. Eventually, someone will prove the promise the Leafers make untrue. The false promise will be exposed, but will it stop those who joined long ago to cease believing? Will they be ready to admit the Head Leafer has been playing them for fools? As for planting oak trees, I'm not foolish enough to join based on a promise I have no proof of. Though some do, to benefit their business in the present. This could play to our advantage. They might take the loss and abandon the Leafers."

Dannor said, "This whole thing of wanting the dragons killed for their blood makes little sense. Let's face it, the supply of blood would run out. Then what?"

Sarah said, "Perhaps the Leafers won't kill all the dragons. They could keep some to reproduce to have a continual supply of blood. Or not kill any, but bleed them to get what they need."

Nagora shook her head. "I can't see the dragons accepting that. How would Leafers force dragons?"

"Have the people of the Land of the Danu forgotten what dragons did for their kingdom? How they've benefitted from the secrets of the fire arts of the dragons?" asked Dannor. He pointed to Geirador. "You're the best proof of how the smiths in the Land of the Danu have benefitted, as have the smiths in the Land of Skulls, thanks to you."

Dannor continued. "In the years when crops failed in parts of the land, the dragons distributed grains from the secret mountain granaries to help people survive over the winter. Have people forgotten that? When they have nothing left to eat, gold won't keep them alive. Stone Standers have rebuilt the dragon statues and artwork that Queen Raganora, during her reign, had forced people to deface and destroy just to avoid starvation. Now those works of art are back and they remind people that the dragons will return to fly across the Land of the Danu."

Geirador held up a hand. "Not all the people are Leafers. More people count the days until the dragons return than Leafers plant acorns."

Sarah leaned toward the table, holding its edge with one hand. "But if my father has sided with the Leafers, won't more of his people join the Community of the Leaf?"

Geirador looked from Sarah to Nagora. "That's a good question, Sarah. The answer will lie in the Gold Planter's proof of increased yield of gold from the king's oaks. If her proof is solid, then it's possible more of the people will join the Leafers. Do your son and daughter know who The Watcher is?"

Nagora and her children nodded. "One of Raynhard's secret identities," said Nagora.

Geirador smiled at Sarah. "I met with The Watcher in Cairnmase just before leaving on my trip here."

That's when Raynhard must've given you the letter for Sagora. Why not one to me? Why not have Geirador give it to Sagora? Maybe Raynhard wants me to open it. What's his actual reason for sending Worsham to me?

Geirador looked around the table. His eyes stopped on Nagora. "I can count on you to keep this to yourselves. Raynhard is doing his best to expose the Leafers. He's doing it for the future of the dragons because he sees the rising threat the Leafers pose."

Nagora couldn't help but speak her thought. "So the king must know about the dragon blood supposedly increasing the yield!"

Geirador nodded and continued. "Days before we met, Raynhard learned of an added threat headed for our shores. The Leafers have enlisted a giant dragon slayer to come slaughter our dragons, because they fear fighting Edana who protects them. The king wants to protect the dragons."

"Then what's his plan?" asked Lars, before Nagora could speak that question.

Geirador took a breath. "Raynhard has the eyes of The Guard in the major cells belonging to the Community of the Leaf, learning whatever they can. As for more details about how he will make his move, he's only told me his plan is developing as he gains more information, but that he has a backup he's keeping to himself."

Are Sagora and I part of it? Probably. What about the Dark Twins? Will they become involved too? Does Raynhard know about them? I can't see how he would. He will when Geirador reports to him in person. Am I going to be the key to his plan?

I should go to Raynhard, fly to Windhaven or nearby on Danuka as soon as I can. Is he being watched by members of the Leafers? He could be. Why else would he go to Geirador as The Watcher? Or was it to gather information anonymously? So many questions I want answers to.

Dannor set his mug on the table. "Do you know anything about their dragon slayer?"

Geirador shook his head. "Only what Raynhard told me."

Dannor looked from Geirador to his mother. "Even if he's a giant, I doubt he travels alone. I bet he has an armed force with him. If he does, they might even have ballistae to hunt dragons with, like when the Raganora's mercenaries captured Danuka."

Nagora nodded. "Aye, and if he's a dragon slayer, he enjoys the kill. Those sorts perform for an audience."

Dannor asked Geirador, "Have you any idea how big this giant is?"

Geirador pursed his lips and shook his head. "I do not know how big the bugger could be. His size could just be a legend." Smiling, he looked to Lars, and then back to Dannor. "When I first heard of your da, I imagined him much bigger. Mind you, among men, Lars is a big man. You're well on your way to be in his company."

Dannor looked to his father. "Da, when you sailed with the Moroes Island whalers, you put in to foreign ports. I docked at only one that summer I sailed on the whaler. I never heard talk of dragons in that port, nor even among our crew. Did you, in your years of sailing with them?"

Lars sat up straight. "Not once. Are you guessing this dragon slayer giant is a made-up story?" He laughed before continuing. "And that the Leafers are betting your mum will kill her dragons instead of letting their giant do it?" He put up his hands. "Dannor, I don't want to make fun of your question. I'm just speaking aloud my crazy thought."

Nagora leaned forward in her chair. "There might be validity to your crazy thought, and to Dannor wondering if it's a made-up story. Were you wondering that, Dannor?"

He nodded yes and shrugged his shoulders.

Nagora pointed to herself. "I never considered that as a possibility. What if it were so? Why would they think I would kill my dragons? To become a Leafer and their dispenser of dragon blood for a cut of dragon gold? How could they even think I'd do that? What would make them think of that? They'd truly have to believe in the power of their promise to put their coins on such a bet."

"We must wait and see when the giant arrives. I want to see how big he is, and I want to see his weapons," said Dannor.

Sarah leaned close to her brother. "And I want to see the horse he rides. It too must be a giant horse. Once I saw a horse on the deck of a boat docked in Windhaven. People in the crowd said it was at least twenty hands. You should have seen the feast of vegetables and apples it was eating."

"If he exists, I need to know when he arrives," said Nagora. Her mind sifted through ways she might put an end to the giant's threat. A surprise attack. If I get that opportunity, I'll take it.

Lars leaned his elbows on the table and looked around at each of them. "Even with what little information we have so far, we must protect our dragons at all costs. Right now, the best defense we have is the maze. We need to think offense so we can fight on our terms, but we need more information." He pointed to Nagora. "You and I should travel separately to Windhaven and gather information that will help us. On our own, we'd attract less attention and cover more ground."

Geirador squeezed Lars's shoulder. "Well spoken, my friend. Just the same, don't lose sight of using that maze as an attack weapon. Keep all your options open. If I learn something that can be of help to you, I'll get it to you." He pointed to Nagora. "You haven't forgotten our code?"

"Oh! No." She recalled how he had taught her and his daughter, Paruline, to use it; and how she had used it in missives from Danuka's cave to contact him for help.

"Good." Geirador held up his mug. "One more of these and I'll be ready for bed."

"Dannor will set a cot near the fireplace, and we'll wake you for an early meal to start your day," said Nagora.

"Trowan, I can share my bed with you," said Sarah.

"Thank you, but I have a quiet room waiting for me at the inn."

"Be careful riding there," said Lars. "I can go with you."

She stood. "The moon is in its last quarter. Enough light for me to find my way."

The next morning, before the others had finished eating, Nagora informed them she would stay behind to read the letters Geirador had delivered. She promised to include their greetings in her replies and have them ready for Geirador to deliver on his return. She also promised to share her letters with them upon their return from Maze Point.

First she read the one from the sisters, Moreena and Erin.

☦

☦

In my 37th year from Dromester

Our dear friend, Nagora,

We hope our missive finds you and your family well. My happy little Rogan just turned two and is walking with confidence. Rogan is our dearest desire come true. Joni and I are so lucky the stars have favored us with a child at my age. He loves to listen to me play your flute. It has a calming effect on him. It helps me put him to sleep at night. "Flute" is the third word he spoke after "Mum" and "Da."

Moreena knits clothes for him. She stitches a tiny bell to each piece. That way, she can follow him when we bring him to work at Da's smithy.

Da has a morning routine with Rogan. It has become a ritual for a happy start to the day. First, they put on leather aprons. Then they go to the bellows to pump it to start the fire. Next, they choose a nail blank to throw on the coals. Pump the bellows to heat the blank red. Pull the blank from the fire. Drop it into the anvil nail hole. Hammer the blank. Knock out the nail. Cool it in the bucket for Rogan to place in an open nail barrel.

Joni and Jani helped Da make changes inside the shop to improve our cutlery production. On the outside, they added a section in back where we produce copper pots and pans. The demand for our products at Harri's Windhaven store has been steady. Our regular work, along with making cutlery and producing pots and pans, makes our days full. We will have to hire help.

Moreena has had a copy of her harp made, though not of gold, but of wood like mine. Since the Leafers will take over the Center for the Dragon Arts as their hall, it has filled Moreena with worry. She does not want to relive past events. To have peace of mind and for the safety of our family in these changing times, she accepted payment from the king for her golden harp.

Da will melt its gold and cast it into a giant oak leaf. It will sit atop the spire the Leafers will build above what is becoming the Assembly Hall of the Community of the Leaf.

We deliver our goods to Harri when he and Pare are at their shop, like they are today. Pare has fallen in love with Rogan. Whenever he's near her, she becomes his playmate. She always has a new toy for him.

Send news when you can. We are always happy to read it.

Your friends,
Erin & Moreena
✝
✝

Nagora looked up from the vellum page. That can't be! Not Moreena's magnificent golden harp. Her mum sacrificed her life to save that harp from confiscation. Moreena, you sacrificed your eyes! This must be like losing a child. Your mother's harp was most precious to you. It was like a part of her giving you strength and courage for so many years. Did you do that out of fear of the Leafers' desire for dragon gold? And the king paid you for your harp? Geirador didn't bring this up. He must've known you'd have Erin write about it.

And Nagora's eyes teared at the images of young Rogan her friend had described in the letter.

Erin had given the boy his name.

Nagora recalled Erin's words from an earlier letter announcing the little redhead's birth.

✝

I have taken one of each letter of your name to name my son, Rogan. I do so to honor you. If you hadn't risked your own life to save mine, I would not be here today to hold my baby boy. Joni thinks Rogan is a most appropriate name for our son.

✝

In her mind, Nagora planned her reply to the letter. The hard part would be how to express her dismay about Moreena's harp. The simple part would be to express how happy she was for the joy Rogan brought to their family, and to Paruline.

What will I say about the Leafers? We are planning to deal with what these changing times have brought to our lands. Do not lose hope. The dragons will return.

Nagora set Erin's letter aside and slid the blade of one of her throwing knives beneath the seal of Paruline's missive.

✝

✝

In my 44th year in Windhaven

My dear little sister, Nagora,

How I miss calling you by that name. You were an enormous part of my life for at least seventeen years. Whenever I travel with Harri to Cairnmase, the memories of our times together come flooding back. They were such carefree times of learning and training and just riding our horses for the pleasure of being together with them.

These days, I ride with Harri wherever he goes on business. It's a splendid opportunity to visit places in the Land of the Danu I have never been. I am keeping a map of the places we visit. I log how many times we have gone and the interesting things we see.

Harri has encouraged my drawing talent. He wants me to come up with unique designs for door hinges and cutlery handles for the shops that sell his wares in the communities we visit. The designs have to represent those places in special ways. It's a challenge that adds extra excitement to our travels.

One thing we have noticed is the recent increase in the number of Leafers in town and in market squares, offering information about the future benefits of joining the Community of the Leaf. Harri says they are skillful with their words to convince the curious to buy into their unproven promise of gold. He says he has toyed with one day joining them to get an insider's view of how they think and operate. Though, he worries about pressure being put on him and his business by members of a Leafer cell if he joins one. He doesn't see a worthwhile benefit in joining.

I agree with Harri and have encouraged him to resist any pressure to join the Leafers.

I'm Harri's escort, armed with my skystone blade and bow and arrows, when we take certain routes to make deliveries. Outlaws haven't bothered us yet. We try to join a group of other merchants who've hired armed escorts to travel those roads.

Harri and I look forward to taking the trade route to the Land of Skulls. Da is keeping us posted on the condition of the trail and wagon transfer stations. Who knows, we might show up for a surprise visit to Maze Point sooner than you think. I miss seeing Danuka fly. I'll never forget my flight on her to go help you deliver Sarah. She must be a beautiful young woman by now, and Dannor a handsome young man, as tall as Lars.

We've given up on having a child of our own. It's just as well. At my age, carrying a child can be difficult, and it comes with greater risks for the child and the mother. Instead, we take pleasure in our curly nephew, Rogan. We give him as much attention as we can when we or his family visit. Today, he is helping me bake bread. I love spoiling him with toys I find on my trips.

Your big sister, Pare

†

†

Again Nagora wiped at the tears in her eyes. Paruline's single reference to flying to the mountain cave on Danuka's back to help her give birth to Sarah brought those memories back like a fresh wound. For only four days she had held and nursed her *Piwi Mahihkan*, Little Wolf, as she called baby Sarah.

Then Paruline left with Sarah. It was the price Nagora paid Danuka for the single, precious dragon egg she would use in her attempt to defeat the witch, Alizarine. Fifteen years later, she reunited with her daughter to fulfill one witch's curse upon another.

Pare, I'm happy you've found joy in your young nephew. I hope he gives you as much pleasure as when Uncle Dangor brought me to your mother. The stories Geirador told of how you helped your mum care for me made you my big sister.

Be careful on the road, Pare. I know you have the skills to fight and defend Harri. I wouldn't want either of you to get hurt. Someday soon dragons will patrol trade routes and help keep you safe.

I hope to see your designs you draw. Your hands can work magic with whatever they touch. I will write these thoughts to you, and more.

Nagora folded Paruline's letter. Before going for her writing box, she picked up the letter that was for Sagora's eyes only. She turned it over in her hands, closed her eyes, and ran her fingertips over its surface, trying to divine the words on the other side of the vellum.

For your eyes only, my sister. I'll get it to you. And you'll surely tell me what those words are.

...

Nagora had written and sealed the missives for the sisters, Moreena and Erin, and for Paruline. In the light of the candle lantern, she reread the one she had written to Raynhard before sealing it.

✝

✝

In my 37ᵗʰ year in Maze Point, the day before the messenger departs

To The Watcher,

I promise I will make the delivery as instructed.

You have a plan. I need to know it so I can help. Can we meet in the place where your father left his sheepskin vest?

A friend can bring me there at midday, on the day of the next waning moon.

If you cannot be there, I will try to meet with you the next day at a mutual friend's stable near you.

Edana

✝

✝

If Geirador can deliver this on time, I might learn what I need to do. Though that could change. Again the unknown.

Nagora folded the vellum page. Instead of using the stick of green sealing wax from her writing box, she dipped the tip of the blade of her throwing knife into the pot of honey.

Next, she held the tip to the flame of the candle in the lantern, allowing the honey to bubble and drip next to the candle wick.

Then she pulled the candle from the lantern and let the sticky, melted wax drip on the letter where the vellum overlapped.

Before it could congeal, she pricked her little finger with the tip of the blade of her throwing knife. She squeezed a drop of blood onto the honeyed-wax mixture where it had spread as a cloud. Before it set, Nagora pressed her seal to it. My blood, not that of the dragons!

Eighteen years earlier, Nagora had carved her personal seal onto the handle of that knife. She had chosen Tiwaz and Dagaz inside a circle. Dagaz resembled a dragon's wings in its shape, and one of its many meanings was "disappearance." A dragon in flight can will itself invisible for a short time.

On her way to the stable, Nagora stopped to see Jari at the gardens. He and Jenni were still busy clearing stones at the lowest level plot, each working their way from opposite ends toward the middle. Nagora waved to Jenni, who had spotted her arrival and was calling to Jari. They leaned their rakes against their wagons and walked to Nagora.

"How goes the stone harvest, Jari?"

He and Jenni laughed. "We should finish here by day's end. Then we'll start spreading manure. Once we rake it in and pull a few more stones, we'll mound the rows to ready them for the seeds. We planted celery seeds in the lowest plot two weeks ago. Sprouts should come up any day now."

"Would you like me to find you help from the village?" asked Nagora.

Jari glanced at Jenni, who was shaking her head no. "Nah, we'll manage. The worst is over. We'll set the rows to our liking. Planting seed will be a pleasure."

"You're sure? It's not a problem."

Jenni smiled. "We're sure. Dannor lent us a big hand with the fences. If he hadn't, we wouldn't be this far advanced. We're good."

"I'm glad to hear that. I wanted to tell you Geirador will come by to visit your box hives to see how your bees wintered. He's curious if they fared better than the bees in the skeps."

Jari had a grin on his face. "Aye, it'll be a pleasure to show him. We're pleased with how our bees wintered so we'll be building more boxes. They're easier to build than weaving straw to make the skeps, and easier to shelter and cover for winter."

"A big time saver!" said Jenni. "Geirador was right about the bees building their combs onto the branch frames we placed inside the boxes. We'll be on the lookout for swarms to put in the extra boxes we'll make."

"When will he come by?" asked Jari.

"Before sunset, for sure. He'll be busy with the village smiths most of the day. I'm on my way there now. As always, you two impress me with your work. May the rest of your day be good."

"To you, too," they said. They waved and returned to their work.

Nagora walked along the growing stone fences on her way to the stable, noting the places where posts and rails had been repaired. Maybe there'll be a bigger honeycomb harvest this coming fall. Dare I look that far ahead with what I fear is coming? She took a deep breath. Take it one day at a time.

A shadow moved on the ground ahead of her. Nagora looked up. The dragons were flying in formation again. Danuka is preparing her young for the high flight. What will she learn from it? Information that will help us prepare for the unknown?

Nagora made it to the inn for the noonday meal. She brought a dragon rider's goad with her. It was the one she had carved the past winter during the three stormy days when they were snowed in. She fashioned it from her recollection of a conversation she had had with her father in the secret mountain cave where she guarded Danuka's eggs. That was over eighteen years ago.

Nagora brought the goad with her to their table on the second floor. Lars, Geirador, Sarah, and Dannor sat in animated discussion. She stepped between the chairs of the two biggest men at the table and reached for Lars's mug, taking a sip before setting it back down. "Now, who do I bonk first?"

Sarah giggled. "You wouldn't dare, Mum!"

Geirador yanked the goad from her hand and held it out of her reach. "Sarah, please! Never dare your mum. She'll always take you up on it." Geirador laughed. "Right, Lars?"

Lars was laughing. "You've been on the receiving end too? The bruises I could show you!"

Nagora jabbed each of their shoulders before moving to her chair. "Sarah, someday you'll have a man of your own. Before you marry him, let him see you have a dragon goad, and let him know it has other uses if he doesn't treat you right." She smiled at Sarah. "I'm kidding!"

Dannor leaned back in his chair, rubbing his chin. "I don't know about that, Sarah. I could … "

Before he could finish, Nagora reached out to Geirador. "Give me that goad! Sarah, I'll show you how a good mum uses it on her son."

Now all of them were laughing.

Geirador held the goad up by the carved ball at its thicker end. "So this is a dragon rider's goad. I remember Yogari describing one to me, saying each rider had to make his own. Is that right?"

"Aye," said Nagora. "It makes for more personal and more precise contact with the dragon as they ride. It's designed to touch the dragon's wings or neck during flight. Riders can also touch the dragons, when not in flight, on their wings, underbellies, and tails."

Geirador pointed to the smaller ball at the thinner end of the goad. "Why is one end thin and the other thicker?"

Nagora pointed at Geirador. "Excellent question," and then pointing to her son, "Do you want to answer it, Dannor?"

Dannor pointed to the goad and then his right wrist. "The wrist strap and goad loop that slides from one end to the other are missing. Those balls keep the loop from slipping off either end when a rider lets go of the goad that's still attached to the wrist.

"The thick, or heavier, end makes the goad slip down on the loop so it hangs within reach of the dragon's wing. A rider will touch the wing more often to control the direction and speed of flight. The heavier end ensures the dragon feels the intended command a rider gives. A rider presses against the dragon's neck with the ball on the thinner end less often to get it to look in a specific direction without changing flight direction or speed."

Geirador nodded and handed the goad back to Nagora. "Makes sense to me. You'll show the trainees how to make one of these today?"

Nagora shook her head. "No, but I'll show them this one so they can gauge the weight and shape of it. They can only guide and control a dragon with a goad they themselves make. They have no choice if they want to become dragon riders. And they'll be less likely to lose their own goads, knowing the work that goes into them."

Sarah pointed to the goad. "They can use any tools they want to make one, as long as they make it themselves."

Geirador said, "If I were to make one, I'd carve a tapered stick to shape, rub it with coarse, damp sand to smooth it, let it dry, and then rub it with finer and finer sand. To make it ready for an oil finish, I'd give it a last sanding with a piece of oiled leather dragged through the finest sand and shaken to keep only the finest particles.

"I'd use a damp linen cloth to remove any wood dust or sand particles. Then I'd let the stick dry before wiping on, then off a coat of flaxseed oil. I'd let the goad dry and then repeat with as many coats as needed until I get the finish I want."

Sarah nodded. "That's how Mum did it."

Geirador smiled and looked to Nagora with one eyebrow raised. "You'll tell them that part, right?"

She laughed. "Of course. It's the part they'll ask the most questions about, as they won't have had your experience making things."

Geirador nudged Lars. "And you made those wooden dragon horses Dannor showed me this morning?"

Lars grinned. "Aye, to practice control and guide gestures with the goads. Also, that heavier end helps hold the goad out of the way of their bowstring when they draw it. Something they'll practice when they finish their goads.

"And they can use their goads as a weapon of last resort if it ever comes to that."

The inn maid came to the table with a mug of ale for Nagora. She looked around the table. "Cook says he made this season's last pot of fresh lamb stew. No more until next year. Do I have any takers?"

Geirador pointed to the tabletop with both hands. "Bring the pot! Set it right here! I've heard how good this stew is." He laughed, as did the others.

Nagora touched the girl's arm. "I think I can speak for the others. We're takers."

Early the next morning, the two riders who had brought Geirador's pack mules to the smiths in Maze Point showed up at the stable to ride back to Skull Bay with him. Geirador gifted the mules to the smiths to rent out to those not needing such animals year round.

Lars had gone ahead to the stable with Dannor and Sarah to groom and saddle Geirador's mount.

On their walk to the stable, Nagora handed Geirador the three missives she had written.

When he saw the one with "The Watcher," written on it, he stopped walking and turned to Nagora. "I'll be traveling light and fast on my return. No mules. Raynhard should get this in ten days. I'm guessing you considered the possibility he might not get it for whatever reason."

"Aye, I did."

"Good." Geirador pointed back up the hill above Nagora's lodge. "What a sight!"

Danuka and her young were flying in formation again. This time they were circling in a wide arc, climbing higher and higher.

Geirador patted her shoulder. "Prepare with care, Nagora. Put everything Danuka learns on her high flight together with whatever you learn about this supposed giant coming to slay your dragons. Think well on all this information. Knowledge is power. Like a story, a plan built with knowledge can be powerful. We see the power of the promise the Leafers make."

"I will. Thanks for your advice and for all you're doing for our community and our riders." She put an arm at his back. "Hug Pare for me when you see her. And Moreena and Erin."

"I will."

At the main stable door, Jari and Jenni greeted Geirador. "We want to thank you again before you leave."

Jenni looked up at Geirador with a shy smile. "We'll follow your suggestions. Thank you for your help."

Geirador smiled at them and spread his hands. "Even without my suggestions, if you keep on working with your bees like you've been doing, all should go well. I'm glad the boxes are working to your liking. I've yet to convince Godomor to try them. When I tell him what you two have accomplished, it might tempt him to come visit you."

Jenni grabbed Jari's arm. Nagora could see the prospect of the king visiting them to see their bees thrilled the young woman.

Geirador shook their hands.

Sarah and Dannor came out of the stable, leading their guest's mount. Lars followed. "Ready for your inspection," said Dannor.

Geirador walked around Caim, giving a quick check of the bridle and girth straps before pulling on one of the saddlebags and the wrapped bedroll fastened behind the saddle. "Good work." He patted Caim's rump. "They spoiled you, old boy, didn't they?"

Lars had been watching. "For an old boy, Caim looks good. Still strong and eager."

"Aye, that he is. He loves traveling. If I fell asleep in the saddle, he'd take me home. We'll be together for a few more years yet."

After shaking Lars's and Dannor's hands and hugging Sarah and Nagora, Geirador climbed into his saddle. He adjusted the quiver and the attached bow on his back. He waved to the two riders from Skull Bay. "Lead the way."

As Nagora watched them ride down the valley and up the next hill, she wondered about Geirador's age and other events that connected her to him. *He's younger than Da. Early sixties, for sure. He has been like a father to me. His Sarah nursed me after losing their baby boy at birth. Uncle Dangor always said I was her consolation.*

When I was four, she died of a fever and Pare, at eleven, became the woman of the house, caring for me whenever Uncle came to visit. That was often. Geirador was the warrior turned medic. Uncle was the warrior scout. Both had served in the good king's force, fighting invading Outlanders. The arrow Uncle took in his calf brought them together on a battlefield.

Now here I am, a lone wolf warrior, carrying on their legacy and preparing to fight an Outlander who threatens my dragons, our dragons.

That night, Nagora awoke from another dream of the Dark Twins, but this one was different. They're here in my room. No! This is a dream. They can't be here. Or can they?

At that moment, a light in the window caught her eye. She tiptoed to the window. Outside, many tiny lights on the ground formed in the shape of an arrow. The Little People! They're pointing to the maze.

Nagora took her clothes and made her way downstairs, where she lit a lantern. She dressed, put on her blades, took her bowl from the shelf, and placed a knife in it, handle first. It was her signal she had gone to the maze.

Poison
Piscipowin

Danuka and her young dragons, except for the lone male, sat perched on the lintels of the outer ring in the center of the maze. The male lay on the stones near the well. Nagora stopped to gaze at the dragons that looked down at her. Then she ran to the prone dragon's head with her lantern. His eyes were closed. She could hear him breathe. She knelt to touch his head. Fever!

Nagora looked to Danuka and spoke to her mind-to-mind.

Okâwîmâw! How long has he been lying here?

Since sunset. I thought with some sleep he would be better, but when the fever came, I knew I had to ask for your help.

What has made him sick? Is he hurt?

He said he ate something he found here in the maze, hazelnuts.

Hazelnuts? Dragons love those nuts. They have eaten them in the past and not become ill. They aren't ripe yet on the trees.

Mother, is your son in danger?

The fever is helping him. If it leaves him and he cannot stand and fly, he will die.

Nagora swallowed. The future of your kind depends on his survival. Tell me what to do.

Bring a healer.

Yes, Mother! Umma!

Umma and your sister.

Nagora's mind raced. Mother, can you fly me to Skull Bay? We could bring them back here before sunrise.

Danuka pushed off from the outer ring and glided to the inner ring. Then she reached down with the talon of her wing to lift Nagora up onto the lintel.

Nagora stepped onto Danuka's extended wing. *Okâwîmâw*, take me to my lodge. I will wake Dannor and Sarah. They will bring blankets to cover your son to help keep his fever. Then bring me to the stable to get your saddle and a rope. Then we will fly to Skull Bay.

She climbed onto the dragon's back. Mother, I am holding onto your scales. Go when you are ready. Danuka pushed off the lintel with her powerful hind legs. She glided upward with spread wings, high enough to pump her wings and fly from the maze.

"Wake up! Help! Wake up! Danuka needs your help!" Nagora yelled at the top of her lungs to wake the sleepers. At the same time, she grabbed the eye mask and gloves.

Lars was first down the stairs, followed by Dannor and Sarah. "What's wrong?"

"The male dragon is sick with a fever in the center of the maze. Something he ate. Bring all our blankets and rugs to cover him. Danuka says he has to keep his fever until he can stand and fly on his own. If he can't and his fever goes, he'll die."

Sarah and Dannor turned to climb back up the stairs.

"I'm flying with Danuka to Skull Bay to bring back Umma and Sagora."

Lars rushed to the closet next to the stairs, pulled out a coat, and threw it to Nagora. "Put it on! Go!" Before she could put the coat on, he had returned to the closet and pulled out four candle lanterns.

Near the stable, as soon as Nagora finished adjusting the eye mask to her face and the gloves onto her hands, she took hold of the reins and hugged Danuka's broad neck. "Fly, Mother, as fast as you can! Take me to King Godomor's lodge."

It was the fastest she had ever flown on Danuka. She barely had time to think of what to say to Godomor, let alone worry about the commotion her late night arrival on Danuka would cause the guards on duty at the wall. Instead, she focused on what to tell Umma and Sagora, if they allowed her to speak.

To Nagora's surprise, Danuka flew over the section of wall near the cliff below which Godomor's Grand Hall sat. From there, the dragon slowed to a glide that took her to the assembly space in front of Godomor's lodge. The two standing guard at the king's door drew their swords.

Nagora removed the eye mask and slipped out of the saddle. She hopped off Danuka's outstretched wing. "I am

Nagora! There is a life and death emergency at Maze Point. I must speak to Godomor. Now!"

A guard knocked on the lodge door before going inside. Moments later, Godomor emerged bare-chested with his great sword in hand.

Nagora spoke to him in Skullian, so the guards understood. She described the situation and Danuka's request to come for Umma and Sagora, and that the women should wear coats for the flight to Maze Point. "King Godomor, please, we have no time to waste!"

He raised his hand and ordered a guard to fetch Gabe and Sagora. He ordered the other to run and inform Umma of what Nagora had described, and then bring her back with her medical scrip.

"I will stay with you, Nagora. The alarm will summon my guards. They'll be here soon." Just as Godomor finished his words, twelve guards arrived from three directions with arrows nocked on drawn bowstrings. The sound of running feet followed them. Another twelve, armed with spears, took up positions surrounding the archers.

Godomor raised his hand and ordered them to stand down. He described what was happening. Except for two of his personal guards, he ordered the others back to their posts.

Gabe and Sagora showed up first. Raean was with them.

Gabe was about to speak, but Godomor held up his hand. "We have a mother dragon in our presence because her only son is ill and in danger of dying. She requested Nagora come for Umma and Sagora to help. I will not deny the dragon the help of our healers." He pointed to his guards. "They are witness to my words this night. For this emergency, I see fit to lift the ban Nagora imposed on herself when she put the brand to her sister's forehead. I will hear no arguments against my words at this time. Understood?"

Gabe and the guards nodded.

Sagora pointed to Umma, who arrived with the guard.

Umma signaled her to join her and motioned to the guard to give the medical scrip he carried to Sagora. Together, they confirmed the condition of the sick dragon, as Nagora had earlier reported to Godomor.

Umma then led Sagora over to Nagora. "We are as ready as we can be." She tapped the cover of the big, rectangular leather-covered box that hung from the strap slung over her shoulder. "We tie these scrips to the backs of our horses' saddles. Can we ride on the dragon, carrying them like this?"

"Aye." Umma's get-to-work approach impressed Nagora. However, Sagora didn't seem to believe what was happening to her. She wore an uneasy smile and kept glancing over at her son. Does she think she's living a dream?

Nagora waved to Raean, signaling him to come quick. "Give your mum a hug. I'm not sure how soon I can bring her back to you."

He reached for his mother. "Mum, if anyone can heal a dragon, it's you and Umma. I'm proud of you. You're a warrior healer! Go heal the sick dragon!" He ran back to Gabe.

"Umma, you will sit between Sagora and me. Follow me. Do what I do to climb onto the saddle. I tied an extra rope to it for you to hold. Sagora, you have done this before. Umma, tell me when you are ready."

...

The return ride to the maze was not as fast, but it still chilled the riders.

Lars, Dannor, and Sarah greeted the healers as soon as Danuka lowered them from the inner ring lintel where she had landed. "We covered him with blankets. He hasn't moved. He feels hot to the touch," said Sarah.

Dannor pointed. "We've hung lanterns around the inner ring and placed three on the well rim. If you need more, tell us."

The two healers approached the sick dragon. Sagora placed a hand on Umma's back. "Don't worry. He won't hurt us. Think of him as an enormous horse."

Umma handed the lantern to Sagora and knelt near the dragon's head. In the lantern light, she lifted an eyelid with both hands. "That's a huge eye. Still unconscious," said Umma.

As she looked at the others, Sagora placed her wrist on the dragon's head. "He's burning with fever. You said he was fine until he ate hazelnuts, and that usually they aren't a problem with the dragons. He found the hazelnuts here, in the maze?"

Dannor pointed. "Over there, next to the wall near the exit gate."

"Have you found out who put them there?" asked Nagora.

Sarah shook her head. "We asked the other dragons if they had other details. They shared only that he was the first to land here after their high flight practice. When the next dragon landed, she said her brother told her what he had found, a mashed pile of hazelnuts, as much as we can hold in our two hands."

Sagora stood and put her hands on her hips. "Umma, if he were a horse, I would say he had acorn poisoning. Wouldn't you?"

Umma nodded. "We have tended horses for acorn poisoning before. He is becoming dehydrated. That can lead to constipation. We have to treat him and watch for any stools he passes. When he does, we will examine them to see what shells he swallowed. Perhaps not only hazelnuts."

An excellent reason for Godomor to not want oak trees planted within the walls of Skull Bay, thought Nagora.

Sagora reached for Umma's arm. "We have what we need to treat him in our scrips, but not in enough quantity for his size." Sagora looked around at the worried faces. "Here's what we need. Speak up if you can get it. Hear me out until I finish before running off to get it. We need charcoal ground into a fine powder, as much as fits into a beer mug."

"I can make that from the charred pieces of wood from our fireplace," said Dannor.

"Good," said Umma. "With as little ash as possible. We want ground black charcoal. Can you bring kindling wood and a pot to heat our ingredients on a small fire?"

"I have what you need, a small ceramic stove! I will bring it with the kindling," said Dannor.

"We need a pot of liquid honey," said Sagora.

"Liquid, not crystallized," said Umma.

"We're out of honey, but Jari and Jenni must have some. I'll ask them," said Sarah.

"Good," said Umma. "We need a beer mug full of dry dulse, chopped into fine pieces."

Sarah said, "I can get that too from our larder, but I must chop it up. If I don't have enough, I'll go to the beach above the high-water mark to pick more."

Sagora continued. "We need a pail of clear seawater and a big funnel with a tapered tube on it. The end should be no bigger than your thumb. And we need a bucket of fresh water."

"I'll get the seawater and the funnel," said Lars. "We can get fresh water from the stream in the cave that runs from the well. There are buckets down there."

"We need a tube longer than the neck of the dragon to fit it down his throat to his stomach."

"Where are we going to find that?" asked Dannor.

"Out there," Nagora pointed seaward, "is a seaweed known as bullwhip kelp. It has long, leather-like tubes with roots on their bulbous ends that anchor them to stones underwater, and long flat wavy ribbon tips that lie on the water at low tide. Sometimes they get washed up on beaches."

Nagora told Danuka in her mind what the healers needed.

I will send one of my daughters for the kelp. We often eat its ribbons.

Thank you, Mother.

A young female dragon pushed off from the outer ring and flew seaward.

Nagora pointed at the flying dragon. "She will bring back the kelp."

"Good," said Umma as she smiled at Sagora. "Are we missing something?"

"Aye! A bridle, a bit, and three stout hardwood branches tied together to keep the dragon's jaws open so he won't cut through the tube once we feed it into him. Oh! A length of rope to wrap several times around the upper and lower jaws to keep them in position on the branches. We'll have to remove them if he starts to he comes to." Sagora held up her hand. "And we need tarps to cover the dragon if it rains, since Danuka says we have to maintain his fever until he can stand and fly on his own."

"Will Danuka's bridle and bit do?" asked Nagora. "I can take them off her now."

"Aye," said Umma and Sagora in unison.

"I will bring the tarps, ropes, and branches," said Lars.

Danuka was already lifting Nagora up onto the lintel.

Sagora looked around at the others. "That's it. Bring your items here as soon as you can."

Having also removed Danuka's saddle, Nagora brought the bit and bridle to the healers. "We should put these on him now. He has never worn them before. It will be easier while he is still unconscious. If you two can hold his jaw open, I can slip the bit in. Then I'll put the bridle on and adjust its fit."

The healers didn't hesitate.

Nagora made quick work of the task. When she finished, she reached out to touch the rim of the well. "I am going down to fill a few buckets with fresh water. I'll jiggle the rope on the tripod to signal you to haul up a bucket. Will three be enough?"

"Aye, for now," said Sagora. "The sooner we get him hydrated, the better. Then our mix of charcoal, honey, and dulse with seawater should slow the effect of the poison in his stomach and bowels."

"The ... " Umma hesitated, "high flight dehydrated him?"

"I will explain later," said Nagora.

"That means if whatever he ate was poisonous, it reacted faster," said Umma.

Nagora nodded and stepped up onto the rim of the well. "I won't be long."

As Nagora filled the buckets from the shallow underground stream with the big ladle Lars had made for that purpose, her mind struggled with the notion that somehow someone had come into the maze intending to poison one of Danuka's dragons, or even the mother dragon herself.

A mashed pile of hazelnuts? As much as we can hold in two hands? Left next to the wall near the exit gate? Those who can find their way in wouldn't do that. Could it have been a stray animal found its way in and regurgitated what it had eaten, and then found its way out? Would Danuka and her daughters have searched the maze for that possibility? Most likely. Worsham! Danuka said she feared for her young from those who make unprovable promises!

How did Worsham make his way to the center of the maze? Impossible! He's not a Dragon Talker. Could he have followed Sarah or Dannor? Without being noticed? I doubt it. He had acorns in his hemp sack. What did he have in that basket of woven bulrushes? Hazelnuts? Or something else? How will I find out? Would the Little People know? They led me here tonight.

"Dragon Talker," the voice came from behind her, "we share your concerns. We have searched the maze for clues. No footsteps other than those we recognize have walked the maze path to its center. But there is the trace of an animal having been here, a frog."

"A frog?" Nagora hung the ladle's handle from the lip of the bucket. "I have never seen a frog in the maze. *Mê-mêkwêsiw*, have you?"

"Not since the child witch, Alizarine, was here with you."

Alizarine? A frog? A connection Nagora's mind wanted to make wasn't happening. "Tell me more about that frog."

"Alizarine kept it in her basket with the egg. She played with it whenever she was alone in the maze. You were nearby, busy rebuilding the walls of the maze."

"All that time and I never saw that frog? Not even in her basket?"

"We thought it was her pet."

Then the distant memory flashed like a bright spark in her mind.

†

Nagora reached down to Aliza and touched her shoulder. Aliza looked up at her. "I think your beautiful egg deserves a good basket so you can carry it wherever you go. What do you think?"

Young Aliza nodded.

"I know where we can find one for you, not far from here. Do you want to come and get it with me?"

Aliza nodded and stood up with her arms around her dragon egg. "Let's go get the basket."

As Nagora looked up, a frog croaked, hopped into the lake, and disappeared. Strange, I've never seen a frog in here before.

†

Aye, strange. That was just after Heqet spoke her curse on Alizarine. Could Worsham have carried that same frog in his basket of bulrushes? And could that same frog be the witch,

Heqet? How could a frog carry that much paste? I've seen frogs with stomachs distended with the field mice they've eaten. Could she have made several trips in and out? Who knows what power Heqet has as a frog?

"Thank you, *Mêmêkwêsiw*. You have given me an excellent reason to suspect who that frog might be. It could be the witch, Heqet. If Alizarine had it in her basket all that time, Heqet could have learned, like Alizarine, how to navigate the maze."

"Dragon Talker, from now on we will guard the maze and keep a lookout for the frog witch. And we will help in any way we can to heal the sick dragon."

"Can you help the dragon keep his fever?"

"That we can do. Warn the healers and the others we will come. Tell the healers to work as if we are not there. We will not be in their way."

"I will. Thank you. I am grateful. Danuka will be too."

When Nagora stepped down from the rim of the well, Umma and Sagora were sorting through the pile of wet seaweed tubes the dragon had brought back. They set aside six of the longest ones. Sagora cut the bulbous end off one of them. "This will be perfect. I can't believe how tough and thick the wall of the tube is." She took several steps to reach the long, wavy ribbon that grew on the tube and cut it off.

Sarah was the first to return with her ingredients, followed not long afterward by Dannor and Lars.

Once they had laid out their items, Nagora called for everyone's attention. "We will have help from the Little People. They asked me to warn you they will come. Don't be frightened. They'll appear as thousands upon thousands of tiny pin-pricks of light. They will help the dragon keep his fever. Healers, not to worry, they won't be in your way. Treat the dragon as if they aren't there."

From the looks on their faces, Nagora guessed the Little People were arriving. She looked over her shoulder. A continual moving stream of light poured up out of the well and flowed over the blankets and rugs that covered the dragon's body and onto his uncovered parts, covering it completely in three distinct pulsing layers of light.

"We have no time to waste," said Sagora. "Dannor, set up your stove and start the kindling fire.

"Sarah, I want that pot half full of seawater. When it boils, add half the dulse and half the charcoal. Once you mix it well and it boils again, remove the pot from the fire and add half the pot of honey and stir well.

"Lars, bring a bucket of well water and the funnel. You and Sarah will hold his jaw open while we slide a tube down his throat. Then once we put the branches in place, let his jaw close on them and tie his mouth shut. That done, we'll hold the funnel and you'll pour water into it.

"Nagora, you figure out how you will suspend those tarps over us and the dragon."

As Nagora judged the size of the tarps and the length of rope she had to work with, she worried about the sick dragon. How long had he been sick? Since sunset. Counting time over the years had become an effortless habit in the daytime with the sun. At night, it was a guessing game. Since a day's work was twenty-four counts, and a day was three times that, she guessed he had eaten the paste at least twenty-four counts ago.

For how many of those has he had a fever? How long will it be before he shows signs of getting better? I best let the healers be the judges of that. When Dannor finishes, I'll get him to help me string the tarps from the lintels.

Once the tarps were in place, Nagora turned her attention to Danuka, speaking to her mind-to-mind.

Okâwîmâw, Geirador brought news two days ago that will not please you. The Leafers have sent for a giant dragon slayer to kill the dragons because they are afraid to fight me.

I am right to fear them. The giant who comes and the poisoning of my son increase my fear. If my son dies, it will be the end of our kind. Without him, we dragons cannot fly high enough to capture the messages Yogari sends about the Dark Twins. Also, I fear that without my son, they cannot give us the knowledge they bring.

Mother, you have glimpsed the future. It must look terrible to you. You will not know for sure until it comes to pass. One thing I have learned over the years as your Dragon Talker is to never lose hope. Your son needs you to stay in the present to give him strength so the healers can give him the care he needs. Speak to his mind. Tell him what we are doing for him.

Ka Peyakot Mahihkan, your words are true. I will heed them. The *Mêmêkwêsiw* told me you think a witch, Heqet, is the one who poisoned my son.

That is true, Mother. I promise you I will find her and destroy her. I did so with Alizarine. Heqet will be next. It is my duty to protect you and your dragons.

The *Mêmêkwêsiw* have assured me they will guard the maze and the caves. And they work with the healers to save my son. My daughters and I see how much our Dragon Talkers and Lars and the healers care for my son. Thank you, Lone Wolf. Try to rest.

I will, *Okâwîmâw*. You and your dragons should too.

All Nagora could do now was hope that Raynhard might lead her to Heqet. She'll pay for this! Except that she's a witch. Is she cursed like Alizarine was, but to live in a frog's body? If so, the only croak I ever heard from her was in Raynhard's secret cave. How did she find her way into Alizarine's basket, never to be seen by me nor Lars nor Dannor? Dare I try to fathom a witch's powers? And what of the golden-handled dagger in my possession once again? Worsham says it's cursed, and that I can't see how. Who cursed that dagger, and what is the curse? Will I ever discover it? Do I want to know it? Maybe I won't have a choice.

By the time the sun rose, the healers, with Lars's help, had given the dragon his first treatment, along with three buckets of well water.

Now all they could do was wait and watch for changes.

Umma was napping while Sagora, with Nagora at her side, checked on the dragon's fever and watched his eyes for signs of his coming to. "We might not see change before sunset. If he passes stools before then, it'll be a good sign. His fever is holding, thanks to the Little People. How they do it is a mystery to me." The three layers pulsed over the dragon's body, alternating like the rolling waves on the sea. Sagora took hold of her sister's hand. "Like you, they understand what's at stake. We cannot do much more, Nagora."

Lars had gone down to the well to fetch more water. Now he was on his way to warn Trowan she would take charge of the rider trainees until he and the Dragon Talkers finished helping with the emergency in the maze.

Dannor and Sarah were at the lodge preparing food to bring to the maze.

Danuka and three of her daughters perched on the outer ring lintels, keeping watch, while the others slept in the caves below the maze.

"Big sister, I will sleep. Wake me if you need my help," said Nagora as she stood. "I'll be on the other side of the well."

"Sleep well, my little sister. Thank you for bringing me here. I needed this change, though it's not something I'd wish on any dragon."

"I believe you. Danuka did well in asking for you and Umma."

The downpour, along with the commotion on the other side of the well, woke Nagora. Sagora was yelling orders. "Protect his head! That's it, Lars! Don't let go of the bridle! Dannor help your da! Be careful, everyone!"

Nagora saw the dragon trying to push up with the talons of his spread wings as she ran to the other side of the rim. Lars and Dannor were fighting to keep his head off the ground. As the dragon arched his neck back, they held the enormous head between them thanks to the bridle. They fought to keep their balance as the dragon tried to sway its head from side to side and lift it.

Nagora ran to the dragon's head, grabbing hold of the edge of the nostrils on its snout.

"Hang on, Mum! He wants to lift his head!" shouted Sarah.

Nagora spread her legs and bent her knees, ready to join Lars and Dannor in their dance to keep the dragon from hurting his head.

"You're making the difference! Don't let go!" said Lars.

The dragon freed his hind legs from under his belly and steadied himself in a squatting position.

Sagora crouched to peer under the wing. "He will pass a stool! Watch out! He'll pee, too!" Sure enough, the dragon did as she had announced. "Look at the dark color of his urine! We'll give him more water for sure. Here comes the stool!"

On unsteady hind legs, the dragon moved away from where he had defecated. His wings trembled as he pivoted on their talons. "Be careful! He's going to lie down again. That's it! Follow where he wants to lay his head."

The Little People too adjusted to the dragon's movements, keeping the blankets in place while their layers maintained their undulating pulse.

Nagora, Dannor, and Lars relaxed their grip, eased the dragon's head to the ground, and stepped out of Umma's way. She lifted an eyelid and then placed her wrist on the dragon's head. "Still unconscious, and his fever is holding. Let's make sure the tarps keep the rain off him. It's time to give him his second treatment."

Sagora waved to Sarah and Dannor. "You two, like the last time! Fire in the stove. Boil the seawater. Mix the ingredients."

"Nagora and I will adjust the tarps," said Lars.

Sagora and Umma ran to the stool.

"You must be hungry," said Lars.

"Aye, I am. How long did I sleep?"

"It's mid-afternoon. You needed to rest. Let's get these tarps set, and then I'll take you over to our food tent."

Nagora looked around to the lean-tos and tents set up beneath the lintels of the outer ring. "You people were busy while I slept."

Lars grinned. "Sheltered, we'll be more comfortable with this rain. We have food, a place for those needing sleep, and a latrine."

She hugged him. "Thanks. Let's do this."

Sagora called out to them. "Soon as you're finished with that tarp, come see."

Danuka and her three daughters looked on, stretching their long necks down from where they perched on the inner ring lintels. "There you have it," said Umma. "Sagora was right. Acorn poisoning." With the tip of a knife, she pointed to the two piles they had separated from the stool. "Hazelnut shells here, acorn shells here. No sign that the dragon chewed on them like horses do, but someone mashed them together with something, perhaps a mix of flour, water, and honey. I'd say someone formed the acorn mash into a ball and then patted the hazelnut mash around it to make a bigger ball. Enough for a dragon to scoop up with its tongue and swallow in one gulp."

Sarah leaned over Umma's shoulder. "The mixture is ready."

"Good," said Umma. "No time to waste. Let's go make this dragon feel better. He's young and strong. His body is fighting the poison. Our treatment is purging the poison. The

Little People are controlling his fever. By this evening, we might have a hungry young dragon on our hands."

Sagora put an arm around Nagora's waist. "When Umma speaks that way, she's sure the sick one she's treating will take a turn for the better."

Nagora spoke her sister's words in her mind for Danuka's benefit.

I hear my son in the distance in my mind. I will keep speaking to him.

Another good sign, Mother. I am glad to hear it.

After the healers had poured the second treatment through the tube and into the dragon's stomach, Nagora approached her sister. "I'm going to my lodge to get something for you. I won't be gone long."

"What is it?"

"It's for your eyes only." Nagora headed toward the exit gate, leaving her sister with a frown on her face.

The rain stopped when Nagora returned to the maze. She approached her sister. "When you can spare a count of your time, I'd like to talk to you." Umma motioned for Sagora to go now.

Nagora led her sister to the far side of the outer ring, away from the tents and activities of the others. She reached into her scrip. "When Geirador came, he gave me this missive to give to you in person. It's from Raynhard. Sagora, I will ask you only once. Can you, if possible, tell me what's in the letter?"

Sagora didn't reply. She took the folded vellum page and slipped her fingers under the edge of the page to break the seal. She read it once, frowned, and handed it to Nagora.

✝

✝

In my 44th year at Windhaven Castle, Land of the Danu

Dear Sagora,

I need your honest opinion based on what you have heard of and know of Nagora's loyalty to the dragons she protects in the maze. Have you ever heard of or seen any signs of negligence on her part toward the dragons? Have you ever heard of or heard her express resentment or animosity toward the dragons? Have you ever heard her discuss or express an interest in poison? Have you ever heard her say that she will not allow Sarah to bring dragons back to the Land of the Danu?

I ask you these questions as I have it on good authority from one you may have heard of as the Gold Planter that your twin has been secretly planning a terrible deed of revenge on the dragons. I have witnessed events and was present when Nagora threatened Danuka in her secret mountain cave. So I am weighing the information I have, hoping to prevent her from carrying out her plan.

Please send your reply with Godomor's courier as soon as you can.

King Raynhard

✝

✝

My poor king, once again you are being manipulated. Is this Gold Planter in fact the witch Heqet? I have no proof. The concerns you express in this missive contradict the message Worsham delivered with the dagger. This missive must pre-date your instructions to him. Nagora folded the letter and held it out to Sagora. "What'll you answer?"

Sagora shook her head. "You keep it. My answer will be one word—never."

"You won't be telling the truth. I discussed the healer's secret with you. It is a poison." Nagora pointed to the sick dragon. "Someone poisoned Danuka's son. Here in this ancient maze I rebuilt. I'm one of the few that can find their way in and out. Wouldn't that make me a suspect? My first victim. The one who'll allow Danuka's kind to survive into the future if he survives the poisoning. That would be the ultimate revenge, wouldn't it? Imagine the pain and heartbreak his death would cause Danuka and her daughters."

Sagora stared at her sister. "You might think I don't know you well enough, but believe me when I tell you I know how devoted you are to the dragons here, because Sarah and Godomor told me. You wouldn't dare harm them. You had so many opportunities in the past to do it. I'm sure the thought never crossed your mind. You've always fought for truth and justice, and to protect the dragons. Look at the life it has brought you. I don't think you would want to live it any other way." She took Nagora in her arms and held her close. "Little sister, I've wanted to do this for so long. I think of you every day! I miss you. I want to get to know you more. Today is a start, a new beginning for us."

"I hope it is! I want you in my life. We are sisters."

Nagora stepped back, but kept hold of Sagora's hands. "I have to ask you a question that might seem silly to you, but your answer might be helpful to me."

"Ask me."

"From the time you brought Alizarine to Windhaven on Danuka until Sarah and I killed her, did you ever see her with a frog, or see a frog in her room or anywhere within the castle?"

Sagora let go of her sister's hands and held her own together under her chin as she closed her eyes. When she opened them, she said, "Once I could have sworn I heard a frog croak in Alizarine's room, just as I entered it. She was kneeling on the floor next to her basket. She was covering the dragon egg with that red silk cloth. Then she pushed the basket closer to the wall. It made a scraping sound on the stone floor. I thought to myself the basket had made the sound I heard as a croak.

"And once in the courtyard, there was a frog that Alizarine, Raean, and Baerik were trying to catch when I went to call them in for supper. I didn't see where the frog had gone. Alizarine always had her basket with her. Wherever she wandered, the egg followed. Does that help?"

Maybe Heqet rode in the basket. Could she have been teaching Alizarine to relearn how to use her powers?

"Aye, it does in a way. It gives me another perspective on what I learned from the Little People when I was fetching water. I better get you back to Umma. I'll give you a quick explanation on the way."

The sky had cleared. A cool wind was blowing over the maze and in another two counts, the sun would set. Sagora waved to Nagora to join them. "He's coming to. We're going to pull out the tube. Can you take off the bridle and bit as soon as we have it out?"

"Aye, I'm ready."

Umma pulled the tube from the dragon's mouth, and Sagora walked away with it until the end of it dragged on the ground.

Nagora unfastened the buckles to remove the bridle.

Lars approached. "I'll hold his jaw open while you take out the bit and branches."

Umma touched Nagora's arm. "Do you think you could sit with your legs stretched out so we can rest his head on them?"

"Of course."

While Lars helped the healers lift his head so Nagora could slide her legs under it, the Little People flowed off the dragon, bringing the blankets and rugs with them and leaving them at Dannor's feet. He called to his sister. "Come, Sarah, let's get the tarps out of the way."

Once the dragon's chin rested on Nagora's thighs, Umma said, "Good. Stroke his head and talk to him, like you do to Danuka. Keep your eyes on his."

Son of Danuka, you are strong. Your body has battled a poison. The healers gave you medicine to help make you better. Your mother and sisters are waiting to see you stand and spread your wings. They want to fly with you again. They have been waiting for you to go fish with them so you and they can build extra strength. Awake, Son of Danuka.

While Nagora spoke, the Little People split into groups that climbed the stone pillars of the inner ring, illuminating the dragon.

His eyelids fluttered and lifted to reveal red eyes as they stared into Nagora's.

I see you, Son of Danuka. You were in the deepest of sleeps. Now you are waking up and feeling weak from the battle your body fought, but not as weak as before. Now your hunger will give you strength to stand and spread your wings.

He shook his head and blinked his eyes before lifting his head from Nagora's legs to look around at Danuka and his sisters perched around the outer ring. His wing talons came forward, stopping an armspan from Nagora. He arched his neck back and raised his head and chest. His hind legs spread out and lifted his body. He pushed up with his talons to spread his wings wide and flap them. With a push of his hind legs, he glided up to the top of the inner ring lintel.

The other dragons flapped their wings in unison with his, and when he pushed off skyward, they followed.

Sagora hugged Umma. "That's a first for us. We healed a dragon!"

Umma nodded and wiped tears from her eyes as Dannor and Sarah hugged the healers.

Nagora and Lars wrapped their arms around them. "You two are amazing!" said Lars.

"We did it with your help," said Sagora, as she hugged her sister and Lars.

"I wish I had more than words to tell you how grateful I am," said Nagora. She turned to the Little People, who still kept the center of the maze illuminated. "*Mêmêkwêsiw*, you worked without stopping. We owe you a great debt. Thank you for your help."

The pillars pulsed with waves of light.

Dannor stepped away from the group and motioned with his hand. "We should take advantage of their light to break camp."

"Excellent idea, Son. Then we can enjoy a meal at home. I'm offering to cook."

"I'll help you, Lars," said Sarah.

"And I'll make the beds for our guests," said Dannor.

Nagora was the first to awake before sunrise the next morning. She dressed and made her way downstairs as quietly as she could, being careful not to wake Dannor, who slept on the cot next to the fireplace. He had given up his bed to the healers. Nagora donned her blades and slipped out the door to climb to her exercise spot at the top of the cliff.

The sun hadn't yet reached the edge of the horizon. The wind had died overnight, leaving a cool breeze in its wake that settled the waves into long, gentle rollers that crashed and tumbled onto the shore below.

Nagora drew her skystone blade from its sheath and began a hundred slow repetitions of her ritual exercises, allowing whatever thoughts or worries she had flow through her mind without interrupting her focus on the movements.

With the sun well above the horizon, Nagora returned her blade to its sheath on her back as she gazed out to sea. Each time her dragon surprised her, as she did again this day. Danuka's silent silhouette glided up from below the cliff on wings spread wide, to land before Nagora. She greeted the dragon mind to mind.

Good day, *Okâwîmâw*. Is all well with your son?

Ka Peyakot Mahihkan, today my son has the appetite of two dragons. He says he has never felt better. He wants me to reward the healers. I will do that before we bring them back to Skull Bay this morning. And he wants us to resume our practice for the high flight. He and I and all his sisters must learn more about the Dark Twins so we can prepare. I will decide if we practice or not when I return from Skull Bay. You have time to eat with the healers. I will return when you call me.

Thank you, Mother. Your saddle is at our lodge. Come for us there.

The dragon flew off in the maze's direction.

Nagora had not told Umma and Sagora that Danuka's son had asked her to reward them, only that she would take them back to Skull Bay after their morning meal. She wanted to live the moment with them.

Lars had left for the Maze Point training grounds. Sarah and Dannor were still busy with the extra chores at the stable, caused by their previous day's absence, even if Jari and Jenni had taken care of the minimum for them.

Nagora called to Danuka in her mind. As they stepped out of the lodge, Nagora carried the saddle, Sagora the bridle, and Umma the bit. She set the saddle on the grass and pointed to it. "Set those on it for now."

When the dragon landed, she extended the talon of her left wing to Umma. It held a small, cinched leather pouch. Nagora said, "Go ahead. Take it. It's for you. Danuka's son wants her to reward you for your work."

Umma placed a hand on her chest. "I didn't do it for a reward!" She took the pouch and pulled on its gathered edge to open it. "Oh! My! This medallion is beautiful!" She looked up at the dragon. "Thank you, Danuka." She lifted the gold chain over her head and placed it around her neck before holding up the gold medallion to show the others. Tubular silver wrapped its circular edge. On one side was a dragon, like on the gold-dragon coins. On the other side was the Ehwaz rune symbol.

Danuka spoke its intended meaning to Nagora's mind.

Then Nagora spoke the words to the healer. "Ehwaz, because your harmonious teamwork with Sagora created a bond of trust with her son. Danuka thanks you, Umma."

Umma had tears in her eyes as she looked to Sagora and then back to the dragon. "It's perfect."

The dragon's other wing talon also held a pouch. She offered it to Sagora, who took it and opened it. Her mouth hung open as she shook her head. "No! I can't accept this! I don't deserve it, and even if I did, I'm not ready to take on the responsibility it comes with." It was a dragon-tear amulet tightly wrapped in cat sinew, hanging from a leather lace, just like the one Nagora had worn from birth until she put it around baby Sarah's neck.

The dragon spoke in Nagora's mind.

"Danuka says you have earned it, that you should wear it while you think about whether you want to become a Dragon Talker. At your age, the choice is yours to make. If you choose to serve the dragons, she will reward you with the amulet, with the powers of a Dragon Talker, and the gift to speak to her in the Language of the Dragons. And she reminds you, you descend from a direct line of Dragon Talkers from our father, Yogari. That means if you choose to be part of that line, your son, Raean, can join as well if he earns an amulet like Dannor did."

Sagora looked from her sister to the amulet. For a long moment, she turned the black stone over in her hand.

Nagora wondered if she saw the red crystal inside it. There's a pink filament inside that crystal that appears to move when you hold the amulet up to the sunlight. Will she discover it like I did?

Sagora placed the amulet's leather lace around her neck. "Thank you, Danuka. I'll wear it and think about your offer. To be honest, I'm uncertain if I'll be able to decide. I need time to think." She reached for the bridle on the saddle. "My son must be eager for my return. Shall we get ready?"

After Umma placed the bit in the dragon's mouth, Sagora fit and readjusted the bridle to it, while Nagora strapped the saddle in place.

Once they were all on, Nagora conveyed the dragon's message. "Danuka says to enjoy the view. She won't fly as fast this time." We're ready, Mother.

The dragon flew to Skull Bay along the coastline, varying the height at which she traveled to give her riders a unique view. She flew low past Skull Rock at the mouth of the bay and let herself glide to a stop near Godomor's lodge.

The twins helped Umma out of the saddle and onto Danuka's wing. Nagora guessed the healer's smile told her king that their mission was a success.

Gabe and Raean showed up as Sagora and Umma were relaying the details to Godomor. The prince waited for the king to acknowledge them. Godomor sent a guard to the spot where he wanted them to wait. Once they were in place, he sent Sagora to join them.

Nagora could make out what Raean said: "Mum! How did it go?"

Sagora hugged her son and Gabe. "We healed our first dragon. He suffered from acorn poisoning. It was more work than caring for a sick horse. I'll tell you all about it later."

"I knew it! I knew it! Mum! You and Umma are true warrior healers!"

Nagora waved Raean over to her and Godomor, and spoke to the boy in Skullian. "Raean, Danuka says if you ask the king's permission, she'll allow your mum to take you for a brief ride on her. Your mum won't have to use a goad to guide her. You won't be away for more than a count because we have to fly back to Maze Point."

"May I, Grandda?" asked Raean.

The king tussled the hair on the boy's head. "Don't miss this opportunity."

Raean ran back to his mother to explain the dragon's offer.

Sagora looked to Gabe.

He gave them a gentle shove in the dragon's direction.

Sagora led her son by the hand onto Danuka's wing and helped the boy into the saddle. She got on behind him and took hold of the reins.

As soon as the dragon took flight, Raean yelled, "Woo hoo!"

They flew out over the waters of the bay and turned right past Skull Rock, then out of sight.

Nagora conveyed the dragon's thanks to Godomor.

Umma showed him her reward, explaining the intended meaning of the Ehwaz symbol on the back of the medallion.

Godomor hugged her to him. "You make me and our people proud. I too offer you my thanks for the service you rendered."

"Please excuse me. I will go speak to the prince to reassure him Raean will come to no harm," said Umma.

"*Ohtawimaw*, Lone Wolf learned who poisoned the son of Danuka. I am sure it is the witch, Heqet."

"*Mitânisimâw*, tell me how you learned this."

In the time it took for Raean's ride, Nagora explained how she had come to her conclusion, as well as the contents of King Raynhard's letter to Sagora.

"Daughter, he is mistaken and is being misled."

"I realize that, Father. I will set him straight and sort this out when I meet with him."

Raean's walk was unsteady, but his smile split his face in two as he stepped from Danuka's wing and headed for his father.

Gabe was all smiles as he held his wife and son close.

"I must go now." Nagora gave a quick hug to Godomor, waving to her sister and Umma before climbing into the saddle. Let the news spread in Skull Bay. Let my sister regain her status as a trusted healer. Ready, Mother, let's go home.

High Flight
Ispimihk Pimihawin

It was a second night of restless sleep for Nagora. Dreams were not the cause: Worry about the high flight her dragons would take was. She drifted in and out of slumber. A tiny blinking light accompanied by a rhythmic ticking sound at her window got her out of bed to investigate. As soon as she reached the window, the blinking and ticking stopped. Outside on the ground, an arrow of lights pointed to the maze. This better not be bad news again. She grabbed her clothes and hurried downstairs.

With a lantern in hand, Nagora stood near the rim of the well and looked around at the dragons. Danuka and her young dragons perched on the lintels of the outer ring in the center of the maze. This was the second time she had seen them all on the outer ring. The first was only a few days ago when she discovered Danuka's poisoned son. Nagora cast her gaze on Danuka to talk to her mind-to-mind to confirm her suspicions.

Okâwîmâw, are you leaving for the high flight?

Soon the moon will rise. When you see it from where you stand, then the sun will rise. My young and I will join in formation and leave on our flight.

Mother, is your son well enough?

Ka Peyakot Mahihkan, he is ready, as are my daughters. I must warn you, some dragons might not return. They might pay with their lives to help me reach the height needed to capture the information. It is an unknown to me. You will only know when we return at sunset.

Mother, Lone Wolf understands the importance of this flight for you and for the future of the dragons. It is my greatest hope this journey will be kind to you and to your young. May you return as one family with gifts of knowledge that will help you. I will wait here for your return.

As Nagora finished her words to the mother dragon, Danuka looked down between the lintel pillars beneath her.

Dannor and Sarah came running through the gate. They joined Nagora at the well. Sarah looked up at the dragons. Nagora guessed she was looking for the female who had hatched right after the only male dragon. From her daughter's reports, she was the dragon that helped her connect with the others.

Sarah turned her attention to Danuka. She pointed. "Look, Mum." The moon was full and visible in the sky between the arc of the outer and inner ring lintels from where they stood.

The dragons flapped their wings and lifted off the outer ring. They rose in the sky to join Danuka in formation, the male to her right and the first female to her left. The others followed and took up their positions, flying inland toward the moon. For a moment, the dragon silhouette they formed flashed across the orange sphere and circled back to fly out to sea.

"The sun's rising," said Dannor.

The dragons spiraled upward as they circled back above the maze, gaining speed and climbing higher and higher until Nagora lost sight of them.

Should I tell them some dragons might not return?

As if reading Nagora's thoughts, Sarah reached for her mother's hand. "Let's hope for a safe return for all of them. Mum, later today Dannor and I can take turns watching for their return. We can signal you with a whistle arrow when they do."

Nagora put an arm around their waists and pulled them to her. "You two are as anxious as I am for their safe return with news from your grandfather. I accept your offer. Off to our chores."

Nagora did her morning exercises first. She took the path up to her place on the cliff above their lodge. This morning she used her big skystone blade for the hundred fast repetitions of her exercises from ward off to center balance.

Nagora let the questions that worried her come forward for consideration as she practiced the movements. When will the Dark Twins arrive? What role will Sagora and I play? Will Sagora choose to become a Dragon Talker? Will they arrive before the giant, or after his arrival? What if he arrives first? Will he come this far to kill the dragons? Or do we go to him? How? When? On his terms or ours? Does he kill on his own, or does he lead a force? He's killed dragons elsewhere. How many? Is this even so? Were there witnesses? Will he want others to witness his kill? Who? The Leafers? King Raynhard?

When Nagora finished her exercises, she stared at her reflection on her skystone blade. The many unanswered questions made her feel powerless. Knowledge is power. I do not know this giant, and so I have no power, only my weapons.

Maybe that's all I need. A well-placed arrow to kill this giant as he sets foot on land. Kill the dragon slayer before he even gets to see a dragon. Is that wise or foolish? I've given it so little thought. It's the complete opposite of what Geirador advised. Gather what I learn about the giant along with what Danuka learns on her high flight and consider how to use it. Plan with care.

I'll ask Lars what he thinks.

Nagora found Lars at the table, staring into his bowl of forest tea. The two letters from Moreena, Erin, and Paruline were near his left hand. "Have you eaten? Have you read the letters?"

He gave her his usual warm smile. "I've been waiting for you. Aye, I've read the letters. Young Rogan is spreading lots of joy to those around him. Sit. I'll bring the plates."

Nagora showed Lars Raynhard's letter to Sagora and filled him in on her conversation with her about it.

Lars set the letter on the table. "Hmm. It looks like the king is putting a lot of credence in the Gold Planter's stories."

As he stood, Nagora sat. "I've come up with a simple idea to deal with the dragon slayer."

He kept the fingers of one hand on the table as he looked at her. "Oh? You have?"

Nagora motioned him to go to the counter.

Lars returned to the table with tea, a plate of cheese, bread, and a pot of honey, all of which he set before Nagora. He looked at Nagora as he sat. "A simple idea, you say? From my experience, people usually get them on the spur of the moment to solve simple problems."

Nagora's ears reddened. She told him what it was.

After listening, Lars raised his eyebrows. "It's an idea that needs a plan, and much consideration of what happens if you're successful in carrying it out. Would it harm whatever Raynhard wants to do? Would he have already considered doing what you want to do? If he did, why did he put it aside? Why does he need you? He wouldn't have sent Worsham unless he had a greater purpose. What that is, we don't know. I doubt it's what Worsham stated."

Nagora held her hands out before her. "Lars, I feel so powerless right now. My gut tells me I need to act."

He reached for her hand. "Relax. That dragon slayer is not arriving tomorrow. What we need to do right now is to gather information that will give us an advantage on whichever battlefield we confront this giant.

"We don't know when the Dark Twins will arrive, and we don't know what powers the dragons may gain from them.

"Right now we know nothing. We need information. Therefore, we have to get some that will help us."

Nagora closed her eyes for a moment and shook her head. "I suppose you have an idea." She pointed at him. "If it involves going to Raynhard, before you or I go, you must first convince me it has merit."

Lars sat back in his chair. "I do have an idea. Give me a few days to work out the details. You won't be an easy one to convince."

Nagora grabbed the brown loaf and tore off a chunk. "I can't wait to hear it."

Lars asked, "Do you think Worsham is still in the Land of Skulls? Perhaps even in Skull Bay, knocking on doors and trying to convince people to plant acorns?"

Nagora cocked her head as she looked at Lars. "Are you planning to use him?"

He smiled at her. "Could be." Then his face became serious. "In our excitement to care for Danuka's son, we may have overlooked who tried to poison him. Perhaps someone has been observing the dragons and noting patterns, like which one lands first when they come back from a group flight. The future of the dragons rests with him. That makes him a prime target for whoever wants to kill the dragons. Could that person still be watching the dragons? Would it be in our interest to let Worsham know someone poisoned a dragon and that it might die?"

Nagora shook her head. "We're too late. You had already informed the trainees of our emergency, and then they learned of our success. Word has surely gotten out that he's healthy."

Then Nagora explained what she had learned from the Little People, and how she came to suspect Heqet's involvement, not only in the poisoning, but why she suspected Heqet was, in fact, the Gold Planter manipulating King Raynhard to her ends. "Raynhard's letter to Sagora contradicts the message he had Worsham deliver to me."

"I see what you mean. I'm glad you told me," said Lars.

...

The sun had just set as Nagora approached the well at the center of the maze. Sarah and Dannor sat on opposite sides of the well with their backs against the rim. They were looking skyward. "No sign of them yet?"

Sarah shook her head. Her face showed worry, as did her voice. "Nothing yet. Danuka said they'd return by sunset."

Dannor stood. "Well, up where they are, the sun hasn't set yet. Don't worry, Sarah. Danuka will bring them back, all of them."

"I think your brother is right. Danuka's strong. She assured me her son was feeling stronger than ever. She trained her dragons well. They've gone a long way up. Higher than we could ever go."

Sarah stood and hugged Nagora. "I know Mum, but still I worry."

Nagora held her as she looked to the sky. "It's okay to worry. You care so much for them. We have to trust in them."

Dannor approached and rubbed Sarah's back. "Let's not give up hope."

"Do you two want to go home? I'll stay until they return," said Nagora.

Sarah let go of her mother. "No. I'm staying."

"So am I," said Dannor.

The three of them looked skyward, scanning the twilight.

"Soon there'll be stars. I think I see one now." Dannor pointed.

Nagora spotted the glint. It wasn't white like a star, but had the characteristic iridescent coloring of sunlight reflecting off a dragon's wing. It was a tiny speck, but the changing color gave it away. "That's not a star. Watch it. See the colors change? Soon we'll see it move."

"Mum! You're right! Look at it now! It's growing into a streak and heading inland. Mum! They're coming back!" Sarah grabbed Nagora's arm.

"Wow! See that?" said Dannor. "They're curving back seaward! They're still in formation, and far away, but gliding home. We'll lose sight of them when the sunlight no longer strikes their wings."

He was right. The gleaming speck disappeared.

Nagora followed the trajectory she imagined the dragons would take.

"Mum, we've lost them, and the sky's getting darker," said Sarah.

"Keep your eyes to the sky. Scan wide. We might catch sight of them," said Nagora.

"There!" Dannor was pointing and following what Nagora couldn't see until her eyes caught the silhouette of the formation against a lighter section of sky. It headed inland and would come out against the darker side.

Nagora stared overhead, waiting for them. "Yes! They're gliding seaward again, but closing their arc." She followed it with her gaze. The formation's spiral shortened. Its downward trajectory was clear.

"Mum, they've lined up with the maze!" said Dannor.

"You're right. I can make out each dragon. If I'm not mistaken, they're all there!"

No sooner had Nagora spoken those words, than the dragons broke ranks, each choosing its own homeward flight path and gliding down at their own speed.

"Mum, they'll glide into the cave one after another. Best we let them rest," said Sarah. She clapped her hands. "They're all back!"

Dannor was pointing. "Danuka's holding her flight path above her young. She wants to make sure they all land before she does. She's a good mum."

One after another, the young dragons turned out to sea and then back to land in the cave. Danuka glided down to perch on the outer lintel ring of the maze. She was a shadow against the now starlit sky, with only a gleam from her red eyes lending her life.

"*Okâwîmâw*! *Ka Peyakot Mahihkan* is happy you have returned with all your family." Nagora took hold of the hands of her son and daughter. "We worried as we waited and watched the sky for you. Now you are home. Our hearts are happy."

Danuka spoke to them mind to mind.

Ka Peyakot Mahihkan, our journey was long and difficult. Thanks to the strength of my young, I return with the reward of new knowledge of the Dark Twins. Because Yogari understands their talk, he has sent them to me. They are on their way by sea and will arrive soon. I will share this news with you now so I may go rest afterward.

The Dark Twins are Dragon Talkers like you, but with abilities you do not have. Their power is a gift. They come to transmit complex knowledge to me and my young. It is knowledge of dragons past, of dragons present, and of dragons future. We can receive this knowledge because Dragon Talkers care for us. With this knowledge, we dragons will gain new powers.

Lone Wolf, I must warn you the transmission of this knowledge can only happen under special conditions.

Danuka paused.

Nagora waited for her to continue.

On a night of the first quarter of the moon, the Dark Twin Dragon Talkers, the twin daughters of Yogari, and two other Dragon Talkers of his bloodline will be needed.

"Mother, does that mean Sagora must be a Dragon Talker?"

Dannor and Sarah squeezed their mother's hands.

She felt their anticipation of the answer.

Yes, it is my hope she will choose to join us. Six Dragon Talkers and the Little People will create the relay net necessary for the knowledge the Dark Twins will transfer to me and my young.

The Dark Twins speak one after another to complete a single thought. They are two vessels for the one body of knowledge that inhabits them. Once they have transmitted this knowledge, they will be free of the burden of the dragon knowledge they have carried. Then each will speak in complete and independent thought. The Dark Twins will keep none of the dragon knowledge they carried.

Danuka paused.

Nagora waited. When the dragon did not continue, Nagora asked the question foremost in her thoughts. "Mother, how will the Dragon Talkers and the Little People create the net you speak of?"

Danuka spread her wings, holding her winged talons above the lintel stones at a height Nagora could reach. We dragons will perch on the inner ring of the maze and hold our wings like this. I will lock my talons with my firstborn male on one wing and my firstborn female on the other wing.

Then, starting with the Dark Twin Dragon Talkers standing close to my son and first daughter, each Dragon Talker will link two of the remaining females.

To complete the net, the Little People will come in thousands from the well, spread up the lintel pillars, and cover us all to link us so the Dark Twins can begin the transmission.

Danuka raised her spread wings higher and flapped them to lift off the lintel and disappear seaward beyond the maze.

"Mum, I believe Auntie Sagora will take Danuka's offer and choose to join us. Once she reflects on what she accomplished as a healer, she will find new purpose in life as a Dragon Talker," said Sarah. "She and Umma worked with such assurance to heal the male dragon. I believe Danuka will allow her to continue to work as a healer as well."

"To thank her, Danuka gave her an amulet like she did me in Windhaven," said Dannor. "Wearing it will cause her to reflect on the offer. I believe she'll accept it."

"I hope so," said Nagora, as she led them toward the maze exit gate.

On returning to their lodge, Nagora was intent on telling Lars of the successful high flight and what the mother dragon had learned about the Dark Twins. The small fire in the hearth had burned itself out since having her evening meal alone. Not a candle lantern in the lodge was lit.

"He's not in bed," Sarah called from upstairs.

Hmm. He's not at home. We didn't see him at the training compound in the morning or afternoon. And he didn't show up for the noonday meal at the inn. I speculated he had gone to Skull Bay to find Worsham. That would make sense. He might have a good reason to stay the night. Or he could be on his way back. However, he rarely rides in the dark. Today the moon rose and crossed the sky in daytime. Ha! The bed's all mine tonight.

When Nagora reached the top of the stairs with a candle lantern in hand, she rapped on Sarah's doorframe before stepping through the open door. She rubbed her daughter's back. "I want you to check on the dragons tomorrow. Make sure they're not lacking food. They must be exhausted from that flight, and hungry.

"And if you can, examine their wings and bodies for any signs of wounds or swelling. We don't know what they might have gone through up there. Perhaps the stronger ones had to help the weaker ones. Mind you, if they fly out of the cave and dive into the sea to fish for mackerel, that'll be an excellent sign. Even so, take the time to examine them."

"I will, Mum. Goodnight."

Nagora kissed Sarah's forehead. "Goodnight."

Talk of Plans
Pîkiskwewin Itasiwewin

Late on the fourth night of his absence, Lars snuck back into their lodge without a sound. He woke Nagora from her sleep when he put an arm across her hips and shook her. "I'm home."

Nagora sat up with a start. "Why you … "

She didn't get to finish because he now held her in his arms and was kissing her.

For a moment she struggled, but then his passion overwhelmed her. She submitted to him and matched his fervor. He stopped kissing her only long enough to say: "Don't dare scold me now. Do it tomorrow." Then his lips were on hers again as he pulled her on top of him.

In the heat of their lovemaking, she pushed aside all thoughts of events to come and abandoned herself to their mutual pleasure until they fell asleep in each other's arms.

…

The next morning when they had the lodge to themselves, they came down first to eat, and then to share their plans, as Lars had asked.

With her belly full and the last drop of her forest tea downed, Nagora dared to state: "Well, my man, I was wondering if you had left me for another!"

Lars let the grin on his face spread from one ear to the other. "Not for another, but to plan for a cause, your cause, to help you save the dragons."

Nagora returned his smile. "Well then, let me hear it."

"First, I want to hear what you've been up to and what you've found out. It could have bearing on what I'll share with you."

"Very well then." Nagora pushed her empty bowl closer to the middle of the table and laid her hands flat near the edge of the tabletop. She recited the information Danuka had gathered during her high flight.

"That's it." She sat back in her chair. "Your turn."

Lars stood, picked up their bowls, and brought them to the counter. He returned with a cloth to wipe the table. He tossed the cloth onto the counter before walking over to the hooks near the door. A leather tube with a strap attached hung behind his scrip. It was at least the length of his arm and as big around as his upper arm.

When he returned with it, he set it on the table. "Were you aware Jari went to Skull Bay to find Worsham?"

"No," replied Nagora.

"Well, he did, but the man wasn't there. While he was, Worsham had hired a local trader to translate for him as he spread the Leafers' message. He doesn't speak three words of Skullian. Jari learned he had left two days earlier on a big mare, with a woven basket of bulrushes strapped to his belly. He left a mule with several sacks of acorns with the trader as payment for his services."

Lars then placed his hand on the tube. "Please, before asking a hundred questions about what I tell you, let me finish saying what I have to say so I can keep my thoughts straight. Then you can ask all you want."

Nagora shook her head. "No; first, why did you send Jari?"

Lars smiled at her. "I instructed Jari to tell Worsham that people of the Maze Point are questioning their involvement with the dragons since they've heard rumors about a giant coming to slaughter them. That they don't want to be caught in the middle." Lars pointed to himself. "Especially since I, your husband, have been openly questioning my involvement and, in doing so, I have caused rider trainees to fear for their own safety. And the trainees don't want to put their lives at risk against a giant."

"Okay, so you've told the trainees about this?"

Lars held up both hands. "Don't worry, Nagora. I've spoken to the trainees about my plan, how they'll be involved in it, and the importance of the role they will play. And I've had them swear to secrecy because the future of the dragons depends on it."

Nagora pursed her lips as she stared at Lars. She wanted to know who else from Maze Point was involved.

"Hold your questions. Soon I'll let you ask them before I go on to the next part." Again he touched the leather tube. "We have ninety recruits lined up. The thirty we had handpicked to train as riders are the ones I chose to help me. They swore to keep what they will do a secret, and I gave them the choice to not take part in my plan. But Nagora, all are will-ing."

Lars picked up the tube and unbuckled the short strap that held the cap on at one end. After flipping the cap to one side, he reached in with two fingers and pulled out a rolled sheet of vellum the length of the tube. He stood to set the tube on the armrest on an empty chair before spreading the vellum out on the table. It rolled back up right away.

"Hold on." He hurried over to the windowsill and came back with four of Dannor's war stones. He handed two to Nagora. "For your end." He set his two near the other end of the table before again unrolling the vellum.

With the knobby stones holding the vellum page in place, Nagora stood next to Lars, aghast at what she saw. "This is a map of the maze!"

Lars smiled. "That's right."

Her mouth hung open for a moment. "What are you going to do with it?"

"I'll sell it to Raynhard for a fortune in gold."

Nagora closed her eyes for a count of three as she collected her thoughts. "You will sell it? To King Raynhard? You can't be serious!"

"Think about it. Doing this might give us a clue as to the control the Gold Planter and her Leafers have over the king. Either he's under the control of a witch again, or he's playing along with them for his own reasons. Either way, the Leafers will want the map so the giant, if he has to, can come kill the dragons here."

He held up his hands. "Listen! You know, as I do, that no one can read this map except Dragon Talkers, right? How many times have I followed my finger out from the center and then tried to guide it back in? Too many unsuccessful times to count! It's useless! There's magic that prevents it. However, do the Leafers know that? Will the giant? No, to both those questions. So I ask you: Are you convinced?"

Nagora jabbed his chest. "This is treason! It's sabotage! Raynhard could not ask for a better guarantee that I'll surrender my dragons to slaughter.

"What more have you planned that you're not telling me?"

Lars shrugged. "Details."

"Such as?" She jabbed him again.

"The trainees and I will join the Leafers. We'll bring twelve hundred oak seedlings to plant on the land I will buy on the plain opposite what was once the Isle of Smoke. And we'll be demanding first blood for our oaks, part of the price for the maze map."

"And where are you going to find that many seedlings?"

"There's a forest at this end of Long Lake with an enormous stand of hardwood trees, maple and oak. This is the perfect time to harvest the oak sprouts before deer and rabbits get to them."

"On whose domain is that?"

"The domain of Tankar's father. Our sawyers have purchased cutting rights there. We can take as many seedlings as we want since they'd get trampled in the fall logging. I'll leave with the trainees at sunrise. By noon we'll be there. That's forty sprouts per rider to find, dig up, and pack. We'll camp there overnight and be back the next day."

Nagora grabbed his shirt. "Details, aye? Now those are big details I need to be aware of!"

Lars placed a hand over hers. "That's the whole point of this plan. I'll sell slaying the dragons on the land where we'll plant our oaks. The Leafers will see our commitment and they will have the map as a backup in case you don't deliver the dragons to slaughter. We decide where the slaughter takes place.

"Next, you get to choose the time and day of the kill. It'll be on our terms, not theirs. It gives us the time we need to figure out how best to defeat the giant dragon slayer the Leafers have hired."

Nagora let go of his shirt. Her mouth hung open for a moment as she looked up at him. "Your plan is making more and more sense to me. Still, I don't like the fact they'll have the map to the maze. What if they come here?"

Lars smiled. "If they do, we'll have a backup plan to fight the giant in the maze. I've been working on that too. It came to me while we were in the maze taking care of Danuka's son and the rain was falling."

"Tell me about it."

He shook his head. "Not yet."

"When do you plan to leave?"

"Within five days at the most, the trainees should be ready. That means at least a fifteen-day trip to Windhaven."

"I'll be going to Windhaven too. I'm not sure how soon. While I'm there, I'll visit with Moreena, Erin, and Pare. There are things about this I prefer to tell them in person. If I knew I could meet in private with Raynhard, I would, but he is being watched."

"That means you'll fly there with Danuka," said Lars.

"Aye. I plan to fly at night, to be unseen by the Leafers. How much time do you think you'll spend in Windhaven?"

"Time to request an audience. Two, three days at most, I'd say. If all goes well, the trainees and I will plant our seedlings on our land."

"You're sure of yourself."

Lars took her hands in his. "After seeing his letter to Sagora, I, as your husband, think Raynhard will want an audience with me."

"True."

At the back of Nagora's mind, she knew she too would be in Windhaven with Lars—unseen at the audience.

Lars drew in a lengthy breath as he hugged her to his chest. His free hand rubbed her back. "Work on your plan. Tell me what I need to know. I want to make sure we'll be dancing to the same song."

When Lars released her, he slipped the strap of the scabbard of his great sword over his head onto his shoulder. The handle and crossguard of his sword peeked over it. Then he slipped the strap of his scrip over his other shoulder.

As he stepped toward the table, he said, "I have a busy day. This morning I'll be meeting with my," he raised his eyebrows as he smiled at her, "'deserters' to plan for their trip to the Land of the Danu. I'll fill you in once I've discussed the details with them."

Nagora set aside the war stones to let the map roll up on itself.

Lars picked it up and rolled it tight to fit it into the tube. After buckling the cap in place, he slung its carry-strap over his shoulder. "Don't worry about the riders who'll be with me in Windhaven. The roles they'll play will keep them out of harm's way."

"I'm glad to hear that. Will you need them this afternoon?"

He shook his head. "No. They'll be yours to bash and bruise into combat readiness."

Nagora walked over to the hooks to put on her weapons and scrip. "Ha! I'll try not to break any of them before they desert. Though, if I give them a good enough beating, they just might want to desert for real."

Lars smiled at her. "I know they'll never do that, and I suspect the Leafers might think that too. The trainees have too much respect for you and for the unique opportunity they have. Training with you makes their skills sharper. You force them to focus and practice harder. That's what they've told me.

"Remember, whatever those Leafers think of us, we're not going there to do battle with them, but to gather information. We showing up, just might cause them to show their hand."

Nagora returned his smile. "I'll keep that in mind."

He watched her adjust the holsters of her throwing knives on the shoulder straps of her sheath. "Where are you off to this morning?"

She poked his belly. "A visit to the maze to check on my dragons. I should see you at the inn at noon."

He rubbed the beard on his chin. He seemed to be thinking of what he had to do. "I should be there; but if I can't, I'll be busy organizing supplies for the trip in the guise of taking our trainees on a training mission. I don't want to leave that to the last moment."

Nagora cocked her head to one side. "Training mission?"

Lars smiled. "To scout the trade routes riders will patrol with their dragons. They'll be doing that on their way to Windhaven, and not just deserting."

Nagora stood with a hand on her hip. "So I'm not to let on to anyone that I know about your desertion?"

Lars caressed her cheek. "That's the idea. To you and everyone else, we're off to scout the trade routes we'll patrol soon. How long will it take for word of our declared desertion in Windhaven to reach Maze Point?" He shrugged. "Your guess is as good as mine."

Not a single dragon was in the cave by the time Nagora reached the entrance at the sea cliff. She looked out over the waves to the horizon and then to the sky. Danuka must be on the lookout for the Dark Twins. Now she knows more about why they are coming and how they'll transfer the knowledge to her and her dragons. For now, I don't have good news for her concerning Sagora.

Just as she finished that thought, a shadow flashed across the cave entrance and veered out to sea. Danuka! You heard my call.

The dragon made a slow turn that would take her back to the cave entrance. Nagora rushed back twenty paces and over to one side of the cave. She hugged the wall with her back and waited for her dragon to glide in.

For a moment, the dragon disappeared from her sight. Then Danuka rose with spread wings on a slow glide to land just past the lip of the cave.

Danuka stepped forward and folded her wings to her body. When she came to a stop, she set her wing talons on the floor ahead of her as her tail wrapped around her.

Nagora stepped away from the wall to stand facing the dragon. Speaking with her thoughts, she first thanked her.

Kinanâskomitin, Mother. You heeded my call.

Ka Peyakot Mahihkan, you come with news and questions.

Aye, Mother, I do. Nagora told the dragon what she knew of Lars's plan.

Your man will learn information that will be helpful. I hope my dragons and I gain new powers from the knowledge the Dark Twins will bring. Should you have to battle the giant in the maze, we might help. That Lars is planning for that possibility reassures me.

Have you any more news of the Dark Twins?

The Dark Twins are getting closer. I believe they bring hope for the decision Sagora will make. Many forces are in play to help Sagora. We might not understand them at first. Often, the path to good takes strange turns. The reasons for those turns are not always clear. Lone Wolf, hope is always on the side of those who are truthful and work for good. Keep hope with you on this path and question what you see as it might hide the truth.

Okâwîmâw, I will heed your words.

Danuka leaned her neck back further over her back. Lone Wolf, you have more questions for me.

Aye, Mother, I do. Will you be able to fly me to our secret cave in the Land of the Danu four days from now, so that I arrive there by midday? And if King Raynhard is not there to meet me, can you fly me to Windhaven the next day?

Danuka brought her head forward and stared at Nagora.

To the secret cave, I can fly you there. To Windhaven, I will not. Not even under the cover of darkness. The Leafers' giant approaches the shores of the Land of the Danu. We are not ready to confront that danger.

Mother, I understand. That is why we gather information and make plans to fight him on our terms. It will give us time to prepare. I seek to meet with King Raynhard to find answers that will give us an advantage over the giant and put an end to the danger he is.

At a later time, Mother, in ten or twelve days, can you fly me to Dromester, where Moreena lives?

Under the cover of darkness, yes, I can fly you there.

Kinanâskomitin, Mother.

Danuka's tail unwrapped from around her as she pushed herself up with her wing talons to turn toward the opening of the cave. After a few steps to the edge, she spread her wings and pushed off into the air. She dropped out of sight for a moment, until she rose skyward with the powerful beat of her wings.

Lars hadn't shown up at the inn for the noonday meal, leaving Nagora to eat a light meal by herself before riding over to the training compound.

To Nagora's surprise, the thirty trainees greeted her with their finished goads. Not all seemed pleased with their goads, as they had compared them to others. Still, she gave each goad a careful inspection. She made sure the loop from the wrist strap, tied to the goad, slid from one end to the other and she could not pull it off. She complimented some trainees for their obvious attention to detail and gave pointers to the others whose goads needed more work.

In the training ring, the first group of six volunteer attackers huddled. That could be trouble for me. Had she waited to read their intent, they could have defeated her. Instead, she took the attack to them, vaulting with her staff to take out two attackers when her feet landed on their chests.

As the remaining four made their move, Nagora spun and struck the staff of the nearest one with all her might, disarming him. With three left to contend with, she attacked, striking out at the nearest with a series of blows he parried well.

Then she retreated, luring the trainee to her and forcing him to parry her low strikes until she wedged her staff between his legs and upended him.

The last two spread out, each to a side, one with the staff held low, the other with the staff chest high. Nagora looked left and then gazed right. A quick poke with her staff to his midsection made the trainee with the raised staff bring his stick down onto hers. She had lowered the other end of her staff to the ground. On contact, she pulled and rolled back, throwing the trainee at the other attacker, who had to back off or be taken down too.

One-on-one, Nagora faced the last determined attacker. *Bring it to me. Let's see how much stamina you have.* She let the young woman attack repeatedly. Nagora fended off her blows and stood her ground while keeping her eyes on those of her opponent. *You're getting tired and desperate. I see your anger grow.*

The attacker ran at Nagora, throwing her entire body into a final blow of desperation. Nagora parried with her staff held vertical, pivoting with it until her opponent was at her side. Nagora released one hand from her staff as the other lifted it horizontal. In the next instant, she stood behind her challenger, holding her staff against the young woman's windpipe. The attacker dropped her stick and surrendered.

After discussing what the trainees had observed, Nagora offered them a choice. "We can do more combat training, or I can teach you a series of exercises I do every day."

The trainees chose to learn the twelve exercises.

Nagora showed a series of twenty-five repetitions of the exercises done fast with her staff.

Then with her skystone blade, she led the group in a series of twenty-five repetitions of the twelve movements from ward off to center balance. They did them slowly with their hardwood training blades.

"If you can find a secluded spot and practice there each day, it will be easier for you to adopt the exercises as part of your daily routine."

Two days later, after her evening meal with Sarah and Dannor, Nagora walked to the stable to wait for Lars's return from harvesting the seedlings. She expected him before sunset.

On the way, Nagora met Jari and Jenni coming out of one of the garden plots. "You two look exhausted!"

Jari smiled. "Aye, we just finished seeding." He pointed to the first plot closest to the stable. "Celery should do well there this year. We added extra manure and straw to the soil to hold the water seeping from the little stream that feeds the stable well. Next, two plots up we have leeks. Then we're into the carrots and parsnips for three plots."

Jenni took over when Jari paused. "Them three big plots are cabbages. These two here are rutabagas." She stopped to point back up the slope. "The rest are onion. It can rain now. We're done with the hardest work."

Nagora pointed to the slope past the stable and barn. "Do you think we'll see our first apples this year? The trees will blossom soon."

"Aye, we should. Our bees will be all over the blossoms," said Jari.

"Just like they were on the catkins of our young hazelnut trees three weeks ago. Those should bear plenty of nuts this year. Last year we only had a handful, but this year we're hoping for bagsful." Jenni smiled. "They're in the right spot. Sun most of the day. Soil's well drained. That's if the dragons don't get to them."

"Don't worry. We'll warn them to forage for hazelnuts in the forest."

Jari pointed. "Here comes your Lars."

Nagora looked at the couple she admired so much for their dedication. "The hard work you two put in amazes me. Enjoy your meal. You've earned more than a good night's sleep today."

Nagora ran toward the stable.

Lars had dismounted and was holding Shimana's reins, ready to lead her into the stable. He waited for Nagora to arrive. As soon as she did, he put an arm around her and pulled her to him. "I will miss you. We're leaving tomorrow."

She stood back from him. "So soon! That's earlier than planned."

"Aye, but we will bring eight mules to carry the seedlings, supplies, and grain for the horses. They'll slow us down. An earlier departure won't hurt. The trainees are ready. What brings you here?"

"I was waiting for you, but since you're leaving tomorrow, now I have another reason. First, have you eaten yet?"

"Aye. Why?"

"Unsaddle Shimana. We'll each take a lantern. I want to take you to the maze to show you something."

"What?"

"You'll see."

While he took care of his mount, Nagora climbed the ladder to the hayloft for the two napping blankets she knew were up there.

In the center of the maze, Nagora took Lars to the other side of the well, opposite the exit gate. "When's the last time we watched the stars come out together?"

"Many years ago."

Nagora spread a blanket on the flat maze stones and made a makeshift pillow with the other. "Lie down." She pointed to the sky. "It won't be long before they show themselves."

He obeyed, and when she lay down next to him, he leaned up on an elbow. "I tell you what. So I don't fall asleep, you keep an eye on the sky and I'll keep my eyes on you." He took her in his arms and kissed her with passion, right there under the darkening sky.

They tore at each other's garments to expose their ready desires. The fervor of their lovemaking built to a frenzy. Their hands and mouths fought to cling to each other as sailors to their vessel caught in a squall at sea. They did not let go until the passion of their storm subsided and allowed their limbs to relax.

Resting her head in the crook of his arm, Nagora turned her attention to the sky. Her man's breathing told her he had fallen asleep. She recalled the star stories her uncle had told so many times as she was growing up in his care. That those stories were his way of telling her secrets he could not reveal to her for her own safety at the time still fascinated her.

She found *The Twins* in the sky and wondered if somewhere up there a star story for the Dark Twins was hiding. If she found another set of twin stars, would she, someday, be the one to tell that star story? She knew a small part of it.

That part held both comfort and foreboding. Comfort in that the Dark Twins would bring helpful knowledge to the dragons. Foreboding in what will happen if they cannot transmit the knowledge.

They too are warriors. Will they fight at my side to protect the dragons? Is that another reason for their coming? If they bear this gift for the dragons, what gift can the dragons give them in return? Is a gift required? Danuka said they'll regain their ability to speak their own individual thoughts. What gift can I give them other than to play my part to make this transmission of knowledge happen? Will I survive to tell their story? This last thought made her body shiver, raising the hair on the back of her neck.

She nuzzled Lars as he snored. I better take him home to his bed. She jabbed him in the ribs.

"What?"

"It's best we go home now."

As they dressed, Nagora said, "I should bring you here more often."

Lars kissed her. "Whenever you want. Do you think you can lead us out of here?"

"Of course. Hold my hand."

...

Like two giddy, young lovers, Nagora and Lars snuck into their lodge and tiptoed up the stairs to their bed.

When Nagora awoke the next morning, she was alone in her bed. It was daylight. Raindrops covered her window. The lodge was quiet.

They let me sleep.

At the table downstairs, she found a cloth-covered plate next to her bowl. Beneath it, fresh pan bread, goat cheese, and a jar of honey awaited.

The copper pot for boiling water hung over the dying embers in the fireplace. She touched the water. It was still warm. It won't take long to boil for forest tea. She placed a few sticks of kindling and two small logs over the embers, stopping to fan them until the small sticks caught fire.

While the water heated, she opened the lodge door. Outside, the rain had stopped; though black clouds threatened more would come. No one was near the stable and barn.

Have I missed Lars's departure?

She returned to the table to prepare two pieces of bread with cheese smothered in honey. She added a few leaves to her bowl and then reached for the pot of water on the fire. It had just boiled.

She stood looking out the window as she ate, stopping only to take a sip from her bowl of tea which she had set on the windowsill. I'll do a hundred fast repetitions of my exercises and then go to the stable.

She left the unfinished tea on the table before slipping on her weapons and her heavier waxed and woolen sweater over them.

...

At the stable, Sarah and Dannor were just finishing up their chores.

"Has your da been gone long?" asked Nagora.

Dannor nodded. "Aye. Just as we came down, he was about to leave. He asked us to be quiet and not wake you."

"Did he tell you he was leaving with the trainees?"

"Aye, Mum, he did," said Sarah. "He said we'd see them ride by. We've been keeping an eye to that window," she pointed, "but they've not come into view yet."

"That's a lot of horses and people to get ready," said Dannor. "At least the rain has let up for now. They'll get a good soaking on the trail. Da will have them make camp in the forest halfway to Blood River."

Nagora glanced out the window. "That makes sense." She turned to face her son. "I'll saddle Storm and ride out to meet them."

In her mount's stall, Nagora was preparing to cinch the girth strap when Dannor put a hand on her shoulder. "You can take the saddle off Storm. They're not stopping. It's raining hard now. Come see."

At the window, she saw the last dozen trainees ride by in the distance with rain capes flying as if fleeing for their lives.

"Da wants the horses warmed up in this rain. He'll push them hard while he can on this terrain."

Nagora leaned her hands on the windowsill. "You're right. I missed them. Just as well I not slow them down."

The night before her planned flight to meet with Raynhard at their secret cave, tiny lights appeared at her window as Nagora prepared for bed. Outside, more pinpricks of lights in the shape of two arrows pointed to a spot on the trail that led to the maze. Do they want me to go there, or to the maze? Either way, both are on my way.

With a lantern in hand, Nagora walked to where the arrows still pointed. The closer she got, the dimmer the lights became, until none were visible. She stopped and waited.

"Dragon Talker, listen well." The voice was a whisper.

She guessed it came from a place near her left side. She turned in that direction. "I hear you *Mêmêkwêsiw*. I am listening."

"Do not go to meet with the king. He has not received your letter."

"How do you know this?"

"These times are troubling for us, as they are for you and our dragons. We have cast our net lines from the Land of Skulls to the Land of the Danu to relay information in both directions to help you and the dragons, and us. Today, we completed our lines of communication. We can now relay information that is no older than one day as long as the information carrier can reach a transmission point to relay the message."

"How can you do this? Is it magic?"

"It is complicated and long to explain. I will try to say it in a way that is easy for you. You have seen us as tiny points of light. Unlike candles, our light does not produce heat unless layered to do so. Instead of heat, in a long string of points, we can relay information from one light point to the next. We can make shapes with our light points, as you have seen many times. The information we relay pulses from one light point to the next, so fast you cannot see the light pulse. This allows the messages we relay to travel great distances."

Nagora was nodding as she realized the value of what she was learning. "Thank you. That is enough information. To me, what you do is magical. That means you have eyes and ears with the king."

"And with others who have a stake in these affairs," said the voice.

"Why did Geirador not deliver my message to the king?"

"They watch the king day and night. Leafers who watch his every move and hear his every word report to the Gold Planter."

"Is the Gold Planter Heqet?"

"We are not sure yet, but we suspect she might be, because she is never the same person in the night. We have not found where they go in daylight."

"Do the Leafers prevent the king from going where he wants to go?"

"He can go where he pleases, but always in the company of one of the Head Leafers."

"Do you have eyes with Lars and the trainees he leads?"

"We do. Tomorrow at first light, they ride and if all goes well, they will cross into the Land of the Danu in the afternoon. The mountain passes await them."

Nagora had ridden and walked Storm through those passes six times and guided mules. The difficulties on those steep, stony trails were part of the travel experience. "Did Geirador deliver my missives to my friends?"

"To his daughter and to the two red-haired sisters, he did."

"*Mêmêkwêsiw*, can you deliver messages from me through your network?"

"So far, other than with Danuka, we can communicate only with Geirador."

"Is Danuka aware I will not need her tomorrow?"

"She is."

"Little People, can I call on you to learn information?"

"Dragon Talker, we will signal you to report what will help you."

Nagora thanked the Little People. "*Kinanâskomitin*, I am grateful you have shared this with me. May your work help our dragons."

The wind picked up as Nagora walked back to the lodge, bringing more rain. If the trainees have been riding through this since leaving, their spirits are being tested. Thanks to the network the Little People had established, she was thinking of the possibilities this new line of communication afforded her. It means I can better plan when to leave for Dromester and keep my flights with Danuka to a minimum. No flight to the cave, and one less flight to Dromester. That means I don't have to sneak into Windhaven to meet Raynhard at Olen's place.

However, I will be at the audience Lars will have with Raynhard.

Do the Little People have an eye on Sagora? They must, since they have a stake in the successful transmission of the knowledge the Dark Twins bring. It will help them too. More and more, I believe my sister will want to help the dragons.

For the next four days, Nagora joined Sarah and Dannor to help Jari and Jenni control the rainwater accumulating along the seeded rows in the garden plots. In their wisdom, Jari and

Jenni had made sure the garden plot rows were perpendicular to the downward slope of the terrain.

Jari took it upon himself to manage the water at the bottom celery plot, where the tiny leaves of the seeds had pushed through the topsoil. More water would help them, but only if the rain didn't wash them out of the soil. His was an ongoing battle, from daylight to darkness.

On the sixth day, sunlight broke through the clouds. The harried gardeners finally had some respite. It was time to assess the damage.

By afternoon's end, Jari and Jenni reported they had to reseed a third of the rows altogether. If the sun held, they would wait three days before repairing and reseeding the rows. It would be a full day's work if they all pitched in.

"When you're ready, give us our orders. We'll help you," said Nagora.

The grin on Jari's face showed he was happy with her offer. "Good. We won't say no."

The sun held. On the fourth day, they repaired and reseeded the garden rows, as planned.

That night, the Little People signaled Nagora they had news to report. They delivered the brief message at the same spot as the last time. "Dragon Talker, Lars and the trainees will reach Windhaven in four days."

Nagora's reply was brief as well. "*Kinanâskomitin, Mêmêkwêsiw.* Please tell Danuka to come at nightfall tomorrow at my stable. I will wait for her. She will take me to Dromester."

...

The following day, Nagora and her children carried their willow branch baskets of clothes, cloths, and bedding from their lodge to the stream for the overdue washing chore. Armed with bars of tallow soap and brushes for the more stubborn stains, they each attacked their wash piles.

Nagora knew that to wash and talk would make the task go by faster, so she started. "Tonight I'll be leaving for Dromester with Danuka."

"How long will you be gone?" asked Sarah.

"I'm not sure. Five days, perhaps seven. I'll try to meet with Raynhard and speak to him in private to find out what his plan is. And I have something to look into with Moreena's help. And I want to visit Pare."

"How will Danuka know when to return for you?" asked Dannor.

"Don't worry. We're not the only ones preparing to fight this threat to our dragons. The Little People contacted me. They've set up a land network that stretches from here to the Land of the Danu and relays information back and forth that can help us. The news we'll get will be a day old at most."

"Do you mean they'll be spying for us?" asked Sarah.

"They also keep Danuka informed. Since they'll be in Dromester and in Windhaven, in addition to watching me, I can ask that Danuka meet me at a specific place the next night."

"That fast, Mum?"

"Aye, Sarah. I won't try to explain how they do it. I just accept it as their skillful magic."

Dannor pointed at his mother. "Mum, you and the Little People will be spies in Windhaven. Chances are the Leafers could be on the lookout for you near the places they know you have friends. You'll need a disguise. Something more than folding the edge of your hood over your brand, like you did three years ago. Da and I were with you. We had your back. You will be alone this time."

"True. I've been thinking of making myself into an older version of Tars," Nagora said, referring to the character she had created as a disguise for her hundred day mission while banished from the Cairnmase training group.

"Like you did when you were on your mission for The Cause? Mum! That's a great idea!" said Sarah. "But times were more difficult back then when you carried the chain to loyal smiths. As Tars, you fit in. These days, he would stick out, wouldn't he?"

"And you were younger then. You could pass as a scruffy-looking lad. Now there's no way you'd pass as a man," said Dannor.

"That's true too. I could dress as a hunter. Wear a head-scarf to keep my hair from catching on branches in the forest. I could wear my older leather leggings with my hooded leather shirt. It has the sewn-on bracer on the left sleeve. It's taken a lot of wear, but it's still serviceable. My sheepskin vest is showing its age. I could wear it over my shirt. My old quiver is well worn too."

"And wear your archer's cap! Its pointed brim keeps the sun out of your eye without impeding your drawn bowstring. It'll fit over the headscarf and help hide part of your face if you tilt it down. And wear your old gloves," said Sarah. "I bet your old boots are still comfortable."

"Aye, excellent ideas, Sarah! My kit is coming together."

"Mum! Jari has at least a half-dozen black-tailed ermine pelts from the ones he trapped over the last two winters. He worked hard traveling to the rivers and streams near where they make their dens. If you pay him a good price for them, you could tie them to the saddle of a horse you ride, or to your scrip if you're on foot. People's eyes will be drawn to the white fur and black tails. Right away, they'd mark you as a hunter/trapper. And he has other pelts too, rabbit and seal-skins," said Dannor.

"Adding pelts is a good idea. They'll make for more things to carry, but they'll also complete my disguise."

"And I could do this too." Nagora reached into the stream bed and pulled up a handful of small stones. She fingered through them until she found one half the length of her little finger and as big around, with a slight curve to it. "This is smooth enough." She opened her mouth and placed it above the gums of her teeth on the left side of her face, just below her left nostril. "Well, how do I look now?"

"Wow! It not only changes your appearance, but the sound of your voice too!" said Sarah.

Dannor was smiling. "Aye, Mum. You've lost your pretty face. That'll work with your kit. Just don't swallow the stone."

"I bet your friends won't recognize you in disguise," said her daughter.

"That'll be the test, won't it?"

"Why don't the Little People speak to us?" Sarah pointed to Dannor and herself.

Nagora paused before answering. "I wish I could tell you why. They must have their reasons. I think it has something to do with trust. Something in their history caused them to lose trust in people.

"But since we built the maze and the dragon eggs hatched, they have been present more often, and in greater numbers. They show up in times of need without my having to call them with the dragon coin tied to my skystone blade.

"Both of you, as Dragon Talkers, come and go in the maze with no problems. You've seen their forge room and the wagon room with the stone boats, and so has Lars. You saw how they helped us take care of Danuka's son, but you haven't spoken to the Little People. You've told no one of what you've seen in the maze or below it; just as I've not told you of all my encounters with them. Only that I met with them, and I showed you samples of what they can make for us.

"But think on this. You know what is coming when the Dark Twins arrive. If Sagora becomes a Dragon Talker, she'll join with us and the Little People. That will be your second encounter with them. Believe me. It will be memorable. And you'll keep it to yourselves because if you tell someone what you saw, they won't believe you."

As if reading her thoughts, Dannor spoke. "Well, we're better off leaving stories of what the Little People do run their own course rather than add to them. Heck! People in the village are aware something is going on, and if they try to figure out what happens at night, nothing gets done. When they let things be and fall fast asleep, they wake up to all the benefits. They accept that as good luck. No sense in trying to ruin that. They're better off counting their lucky stars before falling asleep, and leaving it as that."

Nagora smiled at Dannor. "Well said, my son."

Sarah was nodding. "I agree, but I sure hope the Little People will come to trust us too and contact us if ever we need them, or they need us."

Nagora looked at her. "Sarah, you're right. It could happen sooner than you think.

"I don't know about you two, but the clothes on my back need a good scrubbing too. And so do I." Nagora stripped off her clothes. "Sarah, will you help me wash my hair?"

"If you help with mine, I will."

"But first we have to finish our piles," said Dannor.

"Of course," said Sarah. "Scrub away!"

After their evening meal, as Nagora prepared her scrip and a bigger bag she would tie to Danuka's saddle, Dannor and Sarah approached the table. "Mum, will you have room for these?" asked Sarah, as she held out a circular maze puzzle. It was made of wood, the size of a plate, and with a simple maze path. The player would have to tilt it this way and that to move the little round stone to its middle hole. "Rogan might be a wee bit young to play with it now, but soon enough he should enjoy it."

Nagora took it and examined it. "You made this yourself? When?"

"Aye, after we read the letters from Erin and Pare, we made gifts. I made the puzzle in Jari's workshop at the barn. He showed me how to use his carving chisels. The hardest part was smoothing it and applying the finish."

"Sarah, Rogan will love this toy. Your work is impressive!"

Dannor was holding ermine and rabbit pelts, and a small pair of sealskin boots he had made. "They'll be too big for him now, but he'll grow into them. Jari says you were generous in your payment for the pelts."

Nagora tied the pelts to the strap of her scrip before holding up the little boots to view their sides and bottoms. She reached her fingers inside one. "Next winter, his mum will be so happy Rogan has these. I love the ones you made for me when you were on the whaler. They're so warm." She smiled at Dannor and Sarah. "Luckily, I have room for your gifts in my bag."

Nagora reached into her scrip and pulled out a cloth-wrapped package. She unfolded it to show its contents. "Remember when I knit this last winter? It should fit Rogan this coming winter." It was a blue and white wool hat with ear-flaps. She had lined the flaps and the inside of the hat with rabbit fur. The flaps had braided hand-woven wool laces to tie under the chin.

"That's just like the one you made for me when I was young," said Dannor.

"Mum, could you put on your archer's cap and the stone in your cheek so we get to see the new you before you leave?" asked Sarah.

"Oh, all right." She found the stone in the pocket of her leather shirt, fit it in place, and pulled the archer's cap from her scrip. "I removed the feather." The leather cap fit snug over the headscarf. She struck a pose.

"If I didn't know it was you, I don't think I would have recognized you," said Dannor.

"Same for me, Mum. Still, be careful," said Sarah.

"I will."

"And hug everyone for us. Hug Rogan twice!"

Nagora put away the stone and cap. "I will."

...

At the stable, Nagora brought out Danuka's saddle. Sarah held the bridle and reins in one hand and the rider eye mask and gloves with her other. Dannor carried his mother's bag and a candle lantern.

Danuka had landed nearby in the last moments of twilight. Nagora approached, and the dragon lowered her body to spread a wing for the Dragon Talker to climb on. Nagora set the saddle at the base of the dragon's broad neck where it spread onto her back.

Sarah held out the bridle for her mother.

Danuka lowered her head so Nagora could slip the bridle over her snout.

Mother, I know you are not fond of the bit. It is necessary for me to tell you what I want you to do when I react faster than I can think. It is for our safety.

Yes, Mother, I will instruct the riders to use the reins like I do. At other times they will use their goads.

When Nagora finished tying the bridle buckles, Danuka raised her belly off the ground so her Dragon Talker could crouch beneath to fasten the girth straps. With that done, Nagora put on the eye mask and gloves before taking the reins back from Sarah and climbing onto the wing.

Dannor handed his mother the bag, which she tied to the back of her saddle before climbing onto it.

Nagora leaned forward and patted Danuka's neck. "*Okâwîmâw*, I am ready."

Dannor and Sarah waved. As her dragon stood and spread her wings, Nagora waved back.

Close Friends in Dromester
Nitôtemak Dromester

With a few flaps of her wings, Danuka was airborne, climbing higher and higher as she gained speed. Soon the lights from Maze Point vanished behind them. Nagora's eyes adjusted to the darkness.

She pictured the embroidered map on the skin side of her sheepskin vest as the dragon flew over the many mountain tops. She spoke to Danuka in her mind.

Okâwîmâw, you are flying the shortest route to Dromester.

Over the mountains is the straightest and shortest course, Lone Wolf.

That means we will not fly over Stone Stander Plateau.

That is so. After the last tallest mountain neighbor of the Stone Standers, we fly lower over the hills to Dromester. Many years ago, for your safety, you left the road after Twin Rivers to travel those hills.

Nagora did not try to fathom how Danuka knew that. Back then on her mission for The Cause, she had no idea her dragon was connected to it. She didn't know Danuka existed and that she would become a Dragon Talker, but she was aware of the strange yet familiar words that came into her mind. She was sure she understood them when the voice spoke them to her in her head.

In addition, at the time, she guessed it might be her amulet revealing its power to her. That mysterious black stone, encased in a tight web of woven cat sinew, contained a blood-red crystal visible from two of its sides. When she held it up to the sunlight, a pink filament seemed to float within the crystal.

Nagora used to argue with her uncle and pester him with questions about the amulet. She would accuse him of keeping something he knew about it secret. Her uncle's words to her on her twelfth birthday after she had stopped yelling accusations at him came back.

†

"I'll tell you this, child. There's power in the stone. If I tell you what it is, you'll not believe me. Trust me on what I tell you. You'll only discover its power when you have complete trust in yourself. How you go about finding that, I can't say. That's when you'll learn its true power, all on your own. I won't be the one to reveal it to you. It'll reveal itself. So stop asking."

†

He had been right. When the amulet revealed its power, she had trouble believing it. She thought she was losing her mind. Now here she was, on the back of her dragon on another mission to gather information to save her and her young.

The mountain peaks were speeding past her like when Danuka had once taken her on a night flight over the waves of the sea. Nagora carried Sarah in her womb on that flight. It was only months afterward that she realized Danuka had taken her to where she would rebuild the dragon maze.

What will I learn on this mission? There are so many unknowns I need answers to so I can build a plan.

Before she could continue her questioning, the dragon dove down the mountainside of the last high peak. The lights visible below had to be the hamlet of Foot of the Rapids and to the right, in the distance the town of Four Corners.

No sooner had those lights disappeared, then those of Gallanford ahead and to her right came into view. Next would be the lights of Twin Rivers.

From there, it would be on to Dromester. Windhaven's many lights would be to her right.

Danuka landed near a line of trees in a field on the outskirts of Dromester. Nagora removed the eye mask and gloves, folding them before placing them in her scrip. She left the reins fastened to the handhold saddle loop.

After untying her bag from the back of the saddle and slipping its straps over her shoulders, she stepped off the dragon's wing. Nagora spoke to the dragon with her thoughts.

Kinanâskomitin, Okâwîmâw. Dannor will unsaddle you when you return.

Ka Peyakot Mahihkan, I am grateful for what you try to do for me and mine.

Mother, it is my duty. I will do it as best as I can.

Nagora stepped away, closer to the trees, and watched Danuka fly away as she put on her cap and set the small stone in place against her gums above her teeth.

…

Once past the trees and on the cart track, the walk to Bardas's forge was only a count away. Nagora wondered if there was another access to Moreena's home other than through the back door inside the blacksmith's shop. It was not that late, but she didn't want to pound on the big doors of the shop and rouse the neighbors.

On arriving at the forge, Nagora was in luck. Erin and Joni were coming out of the shop. Their boy, Rogan, was asleep, his head resting on his father's shoulder.

"Hello, Erin."

"Do I know you?" She held her lantern higher.

Nagora spit the stone into her hand before pulling back the headscarf and cap and leading Erin back into the shop. Joni followed.

"Nagora! What a surprise!" Erin hugged her. "We were just heading home with Rogan. We live not two hundred paces from here." She stood back to look at Nagora. "My! Nagora! I didn't recognize you. You must have an excellent reason to wear a disguise."

"I do. I've come seeking information in these parts, but I don't want the Leafers to recognize me," she hesitated, "if you know what I mean."

"Aye, do I ever!"

Nagora grasped Joni's proffered hand. "I'm pleased to meet you. We only saw each other from a distance once at," she paused as the image of her standing next to Raynhard flashed in her mind, "my wedding."

He nodded as he turned to show Rogan's sleeping face. "Wait until you meet this one when he's awake."

Erin took Nagora's arm. "Come. Da and Moreena will be so happy to see you! I'll show the way."

Erin and Moreena had married the Konen brothers, Joni and Jani. They worked for the smith, Bardas, father of the sisters they married. Jani, like Moreena, was blind.

Erin led Nagora and Joni through the smithy and past what used to be the back door leading to the yard. Now, it was the pots and pans workshop. Erin held the lantern high to light a long table as they passed. "Look. See those square copper sheets? We press pans from those. Then we rivet on handles. Some have wooden pieces added to make holding them easier."

Joni pointed to the other end of the table. "We're assembling hinge pieces with metal pins. Those almost-full cases are for one of Harri's shops."

"Come." Erin waved Nagora to the door at the other end of the shop.

It led outside to the space that separated the shop from Bardas's door, only twelve paces away.

Erin opened the door and stepped inside. "We're back! Guess who we found outside!"

As Nagora stepped in behind Erin, Bardas, who had been sitting at the table with Moreena and Jani, stood and turned to look at Erin.

"By the stars! Moreena, can you guess who?" He stepped over to Nagora motioning, her to come take his hand. "Come with me. Come!" With a finger to his lips, he led her toward the table and his elder daughter, who was now standing. "Moreena, you have one guess."

Nagora held back her tears as she watched the blue eyes of her red-haired friend try to focus. Her smile was tentative. She took a deep breath and straightened.

"Nagora!" Now Moreena moved along the table toward Bardas. The backs of the fingers of her left hand trailed along its edge.

When Moreena's right hand reached out, Nagora stepped forward, took it, and pulled her dear friend in a warm embrace. The unforgettable fragrance of Moreena's soft, curly hair brought back the images she treasured of their first encounter and the tender moments they had shared.

Moreena pushed back and her two hands reached for Nagora's face, letting her fingers explore its features. She closed her teary eyes when touching the three converging scars of the Tiwaz brand on Nagora's forehead.

Then she hugged Nagora to her and whispered in her ear. "I think of you every day."

Nagora hugged her tighter. When she released Moreena, Jani was standing at her side.

"Welcome, Nagora. You bring great joy to my father-in-law and my wife. How did you come here?" He held out his hand.

Nagora took it and shook it. Before she could answer, Moreena did. "She flew here on her dragon. I can smell Danuka's scent."

Jani looked in his wife's direction. "Is it the mix of leather and spices I smell? Spices I can't identify?"

Moreena nodded. "Aye, and there's an oil that must be from Danuka that binds the scents together."

Now Jani was smiling. "I can only imagine what flying a dragon is like. To do that makes you a special person."

"Jani, Nagora is a Dragon Talker. You know how special she is to us," said Erin.

"Aye, I do. Little Rogan, because of his name, reminds us of Nagora every day."

Nagora looked to the child, who was still asleep on his father's shoulder. "Speaking of your little man, I have gifts for him." She slipped the straps of her leather bag from her shoulders and placed it on a chair at the table so she could unbuckle the flap.

She pulled out the maze puzzle and set it on the table. "From my daughter, Sarah."

Next came the sealskin boots. "From my son, Dannor."

"And from me." She set the knitted wool hat on the table.

Erin reached for the hat to examine it. "Did you make it?"

"Aye." Nagora pointed to the other gifts. "We made them for Rogan."

Erin hugged her. "Thank you so much. Be sure to thank Sarah and Dannor. Your gifts are so thoughtful."

Joni held up the boots. "Thank you, Nagora. Rogan will be set to play outside come winter."

Erin passed the hat to Moreena and the maze puzzle to Jani.

Bardas put his hand at Nagora's back. "Come, we'll sit at the table and talk. You didn't come all this way only to deliver gifts." He motioned to Erin and Joni to sit.

Moreena placed the hat on the table. "I'll make tea. Are you hungry, Nagora?"

"I'm not hungry, but tea would be good." Along with her weapons, she lifted her bag from the chair and brought them over to hang on a hook near the door.

Bardas asked, "Have you come to join Lars? We heard from Geirador he would go to Windhaven to meet with the king."

Nagora moved her head from side to side. "In a way, I am. What I mean is we're both gathering information we hope to put together in a final plan. What that will be, I can't share with you now since I don't know myself. That's why Erin found me in disguise outside. Because I fear the Leafers may be on the lookout for me, I prefer not to be recognized. If I were, I imagine the Leafers would chase me. I thank you now for keeping my identity secret.

"But you are right, Bardas, I haven't come just to deliver gifts. After I visit Windhaven, I will need to speak to you in private." She looked at the others around the table. "Later, you too will learn about the information I seek. Right now, for your safety and mine, the fewer who know it, the better."

For a moment Bardas's demeanor became grim.

"We respect that, Nagora," said Erin. Joni nodded in agreement.

"Of course we do," said Moreena.

Her father's smile returned.

Moreena brought bowls for the tea, and Jani brought the pitcher and a plate of biscuits. "We baked these this morning. Rogan loves them," said Moreena.

Once Moreena and Jani had taken their places at the table, Nagora reached for her friend's hand. "When I read the news of your harp, I was heartbroken for you."

Moreena squeezed Nagora's hand. "I know you can keep this a secret. Da, we can tell her, can't we?"

Bardas nodded. "Aye, tell her. She'll be happy."

"It's in hiding, Nagora. You know where."

"Oh! Moreena! I'm so relieved!" She touched her friend's arm.

Moreena placed her hands over her heart. "There's no way I'll let anyone destroy mother's harp. It means so much to me. Everything about the Leafers has to do with dragon gold. Of course they knew of my harp.

"I knew they would come knocking and inquire about it, like in Queen Raganora's time. I didn't want to relive a situation like that again. To protect the harp and our family, Da and I came up with a plan. If the Leafers wanted the harp, we would sell it to the king on condition we destroyed it and melted it into gold ingots. Da had the idea of creating an illusion.

"On Geirador's advice, Da asked for an audience with the king to tell him of our intention. He was fortunate to speak with Raynhard in private. He assured Da if ever the Leafers set their sights on my harp for whatever reason, he would help us with our illusion.

"Sure enough, months later, the Leafers came up with the idea to have a big gold oak leaf set on a spire above their assembly hall. What better gold than from a harp made of dragon gold in the image of a dragon?

"After making the arrangements, King Raynhard came with the Head Leafer from the Community of the Leaf in Windhaven. They saw Da cut pieces from my dragon harp. He showed the pieces to them, weighing them until he had the right amount to melt to make an ingot. It was the first of thirty-six ingots to be used to cast the final big oak leaf.

"They stayed to watch Da melt the pieces and cast the first ingot.

"The finished oak leaf the Head Leafer saw on the day we delivered it wasn't made of gold. Da had cast it from melted bronze pieces. Da and Joni helped to install it on top of the spire on the same day they delivered it."

Nagora still wanted to know how the illusion worked. "The harp they saw you cutting pieces off of was a replica?"

Moreena was smiling. "Da made part of it into a replica. The piece at the base, where the dragon's claws rest, comes off. It allows access to the eyelets at the bottom of the sound-board through which the strings pass. Da made a replica of that part out of bronze mixed with a few gold coins.

"The Head Leafer saw Da cut pieces off that replica part as Joni held my harp on the low worktable. In the time he was here watching, he realized it would take days to complete the work. He and the king only stayed until Da finished casting the first ingot."

"Well done, Bardas and Moreena! Where do you keep your wooden harps?" asked Nagora.

Erin shifted Rogan to her other shoulder. "Since the Leafers took over the Center for the Dragon Arts and made it into the Assembly Hall of the Community of the Leaf, we've not played there again. Occasionally, we played outdoors in the square near the hall. Our harps were at Olen's then. We've since brought them to my place."

Bardas touched Nagora's arm. "What are your plans for tomorrow?"

"I was planning to go to Windhaven to visit Pare if she's there. Who can I pay for the use of a horse?" asked Nagora.

Bardas nodded and looked at his son-in-law. "If you're not in a rush, Joni and I have the pieces of a wrought-iron gate, three kegs of nails, and six cases of hinges to deliver to Olen tomorrow. Those items are destined for Harri's shop in Twin Rivers. He'll pick them up at Olen's on his way there. It saves us a trip to his shop at the harbor. And it saves Harri unloading and reloading those goods.

"Tomorrow morning, as soon as we finish adding the pins to the hinges, we'll load the wagon. We could have you at Olen's well before noon. He'll be glad to loan you one of his mares for the time of your stay. It'll only cost you feed and the time you give it the care it needs. How long do you plan on staying?"

Nagora did a quick count in her head. "Four or five days, or longer. It depends on what Lars and I find."

Joni looked at his son in Erin's arms. "First thing in the morning, this little man will be wide awake. We should be on our way to get some sleep so we can keep up with him tomorrow." He stood and reached over to pick up Rogan, who was still sound asleep.

Erin stood and gathered the gifts to her. "Thanks again, Nagora. We'll see you tomorrow. If you would like to stay with us for a night or two, we would be glad to have you."

"Thanks for the offer. I might take you up on it," said Nagora as she stood.

Bardas led them to the door to show them out.

Nagora helped Moreena and Jani clear the table.

Then Moreena found Nagora's hand and led her to the wall across from the table. "Da made this fold-down bed so Erin could rest when nursing Rogan. Just pull out the two end legs before pulling the rest of it down. I'll get you bedding to put on it."

The bed was a simple, sturdy frame with ropes woven tight across its sides and ends, creating a taut net to sleep on. Hinges fastened one side of the frame to the wall. The two pull-down legs fit inside the ends of the frame. Nagora pulled them out as far as they would pivot to the corners of the frame. Then she pulled the frame down. "This is perfect! I'll be comfortable sleeping on this bed."

Moreena returned with blankets and a pillow from the linen cupboard next to the door. "Erin lies on the heavy blanket."

"Thanks. I'll be fine with these."

The next morning, Nagora found her friend busy in the kitchen, just around the corner from where she had slept. "Moreena, do you miss having dogs?"

"Aye, I do, and so does Jani. Da has been on the lookout for a pair so we can raise and sell the young from the litters. We had two couples since Keng and Quinn. Da wasn't happy with their temperaments, so he sold them. He wants hounds like Keng and Quinn. He's put word out to the traders who dock in Windhaven and has asked Harri and Pare to keep an eye open for hounds.

"Pare told us about Lars's dogs, Aydan and Lyam. I love those names. That's why I remember them. She told me Aydan's story. Da and I figured Lars's dogs must have been from our Keng and Quinn. Aydan was the red-haired runt. The trader took him just the same, hoping to sweeten the sale of one dog by including the runt at no cost. And the time was right too."

Images of the good times with their two hounds flashed through Nagora's mind, especially the first time Aydan sat at her feet. She also recalled the story of how Lars had brought the scrawny runt to her mother, Tagnyoriva, to seek her help to nurse it back to health. "I figured the same thing back then when I met Lars and his dogs in Skull Bay."

After they had finished their morning meal at Bardas's table, they heard a tentative knock at the door. Bardas smiled and winked as he mouthed the words: "That's Rogan." In a booming voice he called out: "Who goes there?"

They heard Rogan's giggle from the other side of the door, and then the child answered in a voice, trying to imitate his grandfather: "Rooogan!"

"Come in, Rogan!" boomed Bardas.

The door opened and in came Rogan, running to his grandfather's open arms.

Erin and Joni followed behind their son. Erin held the maze puzzle. When she stood next to Bardas, she tapped the puzzle and pointed to Nagora. "Rogan, this is Auntie Nagora. She's the one who brought the gifts for you. The hat with rabbit skin inside. The seal-skin boots. And this toy."

"Hello, Rogan," said Nagora.

Rogan gave Nagora a shy glance, and then reached for the puzzle. He showed it to his grandfather. Bardas helped the boy hold it and set the ball in motion. Rogan was smiling. He glanced up at Nagora now and then.

Joni said, "Wait till he comes around. He won't be so shy." He nudged Bardas's shoulder. "Shall we start our day so we can get Nagora to Windhaven?"

Bardas stood, keeping the boy in his arms. "Let's go make a nail, you and me."

Rogan nodded.

...

It didn't take long for Joni and Bardas to finish setting the pins on the hinges. While they did, Erin showed Nagora the three sizes of pots they made and explained how they riveted the handles on. Rogan took part in the explanations and even allowed Nagora to carry him so he could see what his mother was explaining.

The biggest pot had a curved handle attached at opposite ends to hang over a fire.

They also made lids for the pots and three sizes of pans. The biggest pan had a small curved handle held in place with two rivets opposite the long handle on its other side. Jenni would like that, I'm sure, thought Nagora.

Rogan held up the table cutlery they made: a big spoon, a fork, and a knife. "We make these with wooden handles too, but buyers in the shops prefer without the wood," said Erin. "Our big metal cooking spoons, forks, and knives have wooden handles. And we make big cooking spoons and flat pot and pan scrapers out of hardwood."

When Joni brought the wagon around, Nagora, in her disguise, helped the men load the gate.

Old Friends in Windhaven
Kayâsi Otôtêmimâw Windhaven

Nagora spent the ride into Windhaven with Bardas and Joni, talking about dogs and young Rogan. He was the joy in the life of both his father and grandfather.

Nagora shared how old age had taken its toll on their faithful hounds, Aydan and Lyam. Lars had brought them to live out their last days with Black Jack, the charcoal maker and lumberyard guard, on the outskirts of Skull Bay.

She wanted to ask Bardas to keep two of the first litter of his hounds should he ever find another breeding pair. However, something in the back of her mind told her to wait until the coming ordeal was over.

As they approached Windhaven's tall stone wall, Joni guided Bardas's horse to the line of delivery wagons waiting to go through the gates. Carts not delivering anything had to park outside the gates in a field set aside for that purpose.

Nagora could see the helmets and the padded shoulders of the guards nearest to the outer wall as they walked by. On her first visit years ago, Bardas had told her the wall archers could march four abreast at the top of the rampart. Today, as she sat on the wagon bench between these two men, it was just as impressive.

The wagon line moved forward at a reasonable pace. The two efficient guards, who inspected the wagons at the gate to make sure they were only delivering and then leaving, kept their questions and scrutiny to a minimum.

When Joni pulled the wagon to a stop, one guard asked, "Where to, and for how long?" while the other looked at the contents of the wagon.

"Delivery to the smith, Olen, on Stables Way, and then we leave."

The other guard slapped the side of the wagon twice. He backed away and waved them through.

Now Joni had the horse go slowly on the cobblestones as they passed through the shadow of the main gate on the other side of the tower. Nagora looked up along the wall of buildings on the street, eager to see the spire with the oak leaf at its peak. She glimpsed it momentarily above a smaller building.

They soon came to Stables Way, where Olen's stable was six doors down. Joni parked the wagon in front of the closed stable doors. "I'll wait here while you get Olen to open up."

Nagora went in by the smithy entrance adjoining the stable. Bardas followed.

Inside and to the right, a passage opened onto the stables. They stepped through it and walked past the twelve stalls to the inner courtyard, where Olen was spreading straw beneath the hooves of his three mares.

"Hello, Olen!" said Nagora.

His face wore a questioning look, as he obviously had not recognized the voice and the one who stood before him.

Nagora showed herself like she had with Erin the evening before.

Olen's face turned into a cheerful smile as he recognized her. "No whistling this time to announce your arrival? Had you not shown yourself, I might have been inclined to give you the same treatment as on that day." He laughed.

Nagora smiled. "I'll never forget that first time we met. Do you still whistle the same tune when cleaning the stalls?"

He pointed to her and then to Bardas. "Moreena's song that I like so much. Nagora, you're in good company. I'm happy to see you." He gave her a quick hug, and then stepped over to Bardas and shook his hand. "What do you have for me today, my friend?"

"Goods Harri will pick up to deliver to his shop in Twin Rivers: a wrought-iron gate, three kegs of nails, and six boxes of hinges. Joni has the paperwork for you to sign. You know Harri. He keeps a record of everything delivered, sold, repaired, or traded."

Olen grinned. "Aye, that's him all right."

After Bardas and Joni had left, Olen let Nagora choose which of his three mares she wanted to borrow. Since she might travel back and forth to Moreena's place, she chose the young brown mare shod with the lighter shoes, like what a hunter would ride.

"Excellent choice. I'll give you a work saddle to go with your outfit. I got Bonnie from Geirador last fall. He fully trained her."

Nagora looked to Olen in surprise. "I didn't know he was training horses again."

Olen smiled. "As soon as he returned to Cairnmase, horses were back in his life."

He pointed to Bonnie's feet. "Stay away from the steep streets with cobblestones. If you're headed down to the docks, stay on Stables Way. At the castle stable, turn right and then left on Castle Way. It continues past the castle where it becomes a gravel slope track. It'll be easier on Bonnie's legs, but it's the long way to the harbor."

"Good. That's what I'll do. Listen, Olen. Don't worry about me. If on some days you find Bonnie here without me, it means I'll be back for her. The stars only know where my business will take me over the next few days. For some of it, I might be better off on foot."

Olen nodded. "Good to know." He pointed to her. "If you need a place to stay the night, you're always welcome to knock on my door."

"Thanks, Olen. I appreciate your offer."

A guard raised his hands to block the way as Nagora came onto Castle Way, which crossed Castle Square. "Sorry to stop you," he pointed in the square's direction, "as you can see, it's busy. Market day today. They have ordered me to ask riders to walk their mounts across the square."

Nagora nodded and dismounted. "I'm headed to Castle Way on the other side of the square."

The guard pointed. "See the line of tents straight ahead? If I were you and in a hurry, I'd lead my horse behind them."

"Thanks, I'll do that."

Passing behind the vendor tents, Nagora stopped to glimpse two men wearing silver-leaf medallions, standing above the crowd. She guessed they were likely standing on boxes or steps. They held small scrolls of vellum in the fists of both hands that they agitated to incite people to approach and join those already waiting to listen to them. Leafer recruitment is alive and well out in the open. How many will buy their promise?

On Castle Way, well past the noise of the square, Nagora realized she was riding past the original small parcels of farmland. They must date back to before the castle was built. Most of the farm buildings were of stone and in excellent condition. The farmers lay out their gardens along the slope like those of Jari and Jenni. The stone fences with cedar rail gates stand proud around their plots. Connecting cart trails crisscrossed the homesteads. Most of the barns that housed small animals had outside enclosures for them. Hens, goats, sheep, and rabbits were in abundance.

One thing that caught Nagora's attention was the footwear the farmhands wore. A young couple walking alongside the road confirmed what she had guessed. They were wearing shoes carved from wood. The girl wore hers barefoot; the boy, with heavy wool socks.

Only days ago she had worked in soggy boots, finally preferring to discard them and work barefoot like Jenni. The wooden shoes struck her as a clever alternative. Nagora wanted to know how they were made. It was something she'd look into before leaving Windhaven, if she had time.

Lower down along the road and closer to the bay as the slope leveled out, apple orchards in full bloom came into view. The smell of the blossoms reached her nose, and Nagora spotted dozens of beehives in the orchards. Their season is well ahead of ours.

The road curved to follow the shore of the bay, where fishing huts of all sizes spread along it. She only spotted the occasional curragh like the ones she and her Uncle Dangor used to make at their beach hut on Sandy Hook Bay. Most of the wooden skiffs were plank-on-frame and equipped with two pairs of oarlocks. The bigger ones had two tall masts and a small stern mast. Their little "bum whackers," as her uncle called the small sails on the stern ends, kept the fishing boats pointed into the wind. When the mainsails were furled and the crew worked the nets or hook lines, those little sails were like an extra crew member.

Castle Way's gravel section ended at the bottom of Castle Hill Way to become Harbor Way, a cobblestone street. "Easy on these stones, Bonnie. Good girl."

Nearby, Nagora had witnessed the ultimate fate of the captured young rebels, Matton and his sister Ilma, acquaintances she had made while on her mission for The Cause. Prince Acindor had sentenced them to trial by barrel from his carriage in Castle Square. If they survived, it would prove them innocent, and if they didn't, guilty. It was not a trial, but a horrible death sentence.

Now if the possibility that Acindor were still alive proved to be true, she would again place him on her list of those on whom she had promised to serve justice.

At the sight of the busy throng, Nagora dismounted to lead Bonnie. The street along the harbor front was busy with dock workers. Some pushed hand carts loaded with goods, while others were loading or unloading wagons pulled by mule teams. Traders, on boats tied up at the wharves, were hawking their wares to passersby. People in need of goods were searching for the shops that sold them.

Here too Leafers stood on boxes, trying to sell their promise to those who stopped to listen.

Among the activity, the aroma of freshly baked goods, soups, and roasted meats filled the air. Now and then, her nose caught a whiff of stale ale. Nagora came to a merchant who sold all sizes and kinds of baskets woven of branches and rushes. He also sold hemp rope and twine in any length and thickness to suit a buyer's needs.

She stopped to look up at the pulley that hung from the rail protruding from the top of the shuttered stock window. With it, the merchant could hoist goods up there and haul them into the second floor storage area.

I released my arrow from that window, on that fateful day. It cut the rope from which Matton and Ilma hung and sent their corpses into the bay. That's how I became the most wanted outlaw in the land. Acindor offered a thousand gold coins for my capture. If he's alive, he'll wish his mercenaries had captured me.

...

Nagora found Harri's shop further along on Harbor Way. On the wall above the shop door hung a long wooden panel. On it were many oversized decorative and standard hinges, locks and keys, nails, and cutlery arranged to spell "KONEN BROTHERS" in big letters.

She tied Bonnie to one of the corner hitching posts in front of the shop.

Three steps up from the street was a wide landing that stretched from one shop window to the other. Between the windows, the shop door was open. Nagora stepped inside. She heard humming from the back of the store. *I know who that is. She used to hum that tune when baking something. Does she have a fireplace back there?*

Without making a sound, Nagora walked toward the open door at the back. There was a hint of smoke in the air as from a newly lit fire. The crackle of kindling confirmed it. She stuck her head past the doorframe to peek inside.

Like the dozen that lit the shop, four lamps hung from the ceiling, lighting what, to Nagora's eyes, was a kitchen like the one at Olen's place. Paruline was at a counter, her back to Nagora. She was kneading bread dough. *How many times had she watched Pare do that in Cairnmase? Often, it was their time to talk about all kinds of things.*

Nagora hummed along with Paruline as she stepped into the kitchen.

The woman froze for a moment, stopping her push on the dough. "Nagora?" She turned to confirm her guess. "Who are you?"

Nagora showed her face.

"It is you! No one else ever hummed that with me except you!" She wiped her hands on her apron and stepped to Nagora with open arms. "I was just thinking about you!" They held each other tight until Paruline danced Nagora around in a circle. "When Da brought your letter, I was so happy! And now you're here like you promised." She stopped and held Nagora at arm's length to look her up and down. "You're in disguise. I can guess why. You don't want the Leafers to know you're here." She then touched Nagora's cheek. "You're on another adventure. Beautiful as ever, and just as strong. You never change!"

Nagora pressed Paruline's hand to her cheek. "As I watched you, I thought the same thing. My beautiful big sister is still baking. I can't count how many times I watched you make bread or recalled all the things we talked about!"

She took Paruline's hand and led her to the counter. "This dough still needs your attention."

Paruline wiped her hands on her apron and pressed the heels of her palms into the dough. She pushed it, pulled it, and then folded it over on itself before giving it a half turn and repeating the kneading motions. "If I recall, back then many of those conversations were about boys."

Nagora laughed. "That reminds me! I had Rogan in my arms for a better part of this morning as Erin gave me a tour of their workshop."

Paruline stopped kneading for a moment. "Oh! Isn't he a little charmer? I love that red hair of his. He's such fun to be with."

"It didn't take him long to win me over. He's a loveable lad."

Paruline looked at her friend. "Did you fly there on Danuka?"

"Aye. I had business with Bardas, and I wanted to visit Moreena and Erin. And I wanted to call on you. I came here with Bardas and Joni to make a delivery to Olen's stable. Harri's goods for Twin Rivers are waiting there. Olen gave me the loan of one of his mares, Bonnie. I tied her out front. Did your father talk to you about what we're facing?"

Paruline nodded. "He did. He gave me a full account of his visit with you and everything you shared with him. Nagora, we're both worried. I haven't shared the details with Harri. No need for him to know them yet."

"Where is Harri now? Are you alone here at the shop?"

Paruline waved her hand. "Harri's gone to haggle with a trader about an order. I don't know when he'll be back. And I'm not alone here at the shop. Our hired help, Matti, has gone out to buy something to eat. He should be back soon. Few people come in at mealtime. He's knowledgeable and trustworthy. When Olen did carriage repairs, they worked together. He recommended Matti to us. He enjoys selling to a customer's needs. If he judges they are serious, he offers them custom-made work. Then he arranges for them to meet with Harri."

"Pare, can I trust Matti to not speak to anyone about me being here?"

"Just like you trust Olen. I'll remind him, and Harri too. But you didn't come to Windhaven just to visit me. I know Lars is on his way here. Will you be meeting with him?" asked Paruline.

"Aye. I'm looking for information that will help me put together a plan. Lars has his own. When we meet, we'll see how we can mesh them together."

Paruline took a knife and cut the dough in two. She formed both pieces into balls, wrapped them in floured cloths, and then placed them into woven straw baskets to rise. "Come see where I'll cook them."

At the fireplace, Paruline pointed to the sturdy rectangular grate. It stood on four feet, keeping its row of ribs off the hearth floor so burning logs could rest on them. On the left side of the grate, centered between its two feet, rose a metal post. Set perpendicular on the post was a rectangular, flat metal plate the same size as the base of the grate. It was obviously designed to cook on. Paruline could pivot it outward on the post, away from the main flames of the fire, as it was positioned now.

Paruline picked up a big, oval copper pot with handles on each end and set it upside down on the pivoting metal plate. She pushed the plate over the fire on the grate. "When the bread is ready to cook, I'll put it under the pot and let it cook covered for two counts, and then uncovered for one count. Da loves the crust on the bread cooked that way. So does Harri. He had Da make the grate with these parts. Now we sell them in the store with the pots. I can set the plate at different heights on the post to control how close to the fire I want to cook."

Voices came from the shop. "Sounds like Harri and Matti," said Paruline. "Put on your disguise."

...

Harri was in an animated discussion with Matti. Nagora understood part of what they said. " … and they think they can take up the whole wharf for themselves. The traders are not happy. They're protesting. Those vessels invited here by the Community of the Leaf can anchor and wait their turn, or when one docks, tie shoulder to it."

"What's going on?" asked Paruline.

Both men looked in Paruline's direction. "Her? She? Not Olen? When I saw Bonnie outside, I was expecting to find Olen in here. Right, Matti?" Harri tapped his shoulder.

"Aye," said the bald-headed man.

"Meet our good friend, Nagora. She's come a long way from Maze Point in the Land of Skulls," said Paruline.

As she had done with Erin the night before, Nagora showed her undisguised face. "Hello, Matti. Pare was just telling me about you moments ago."

He smiled at Nagora while pointing at her. "I know you as Edana."

"True."

"Matti and Harri, you two listen up. Nagora is in her disguise on important business. She doesn't want the Leafers to find her. Not a word to anyone that she's here."

"Count on us," said Harri.

"Just another customer." Matti pointed around the shop. "If there's anything you need in here, I'm your man. I know where everything is, and if I can't find what you need, I can get Harri Konen to make it for you."

Paruline laughed and held up a hand. "If she wants a tour later, I'll send her to you. Did you eat?"

He patted his belly. "Sure did."

Harri came over and hugged Nagora. As he did, Paruline repeated her earlier question.

He pointed to the kitchen. "I'll tell you in there. I didn't eat yet. Did you, Nagora?"

She patted her scrip. "Moreena gave me biscuits, and cured boar belly she sliced up and put between two pieces of bread."

"I'll boil water for tea. We have soup, Nagora, if you want some with your," she paused and smiled, "rations."

"I won't say no to your soup, Pare."

As soon as Nagora removed her weapons and Harri had her sit with him, he described the situation. "Remember the boat that anchored at the mouth of the bay yesterday evening?"

Paruline nodded as she stirred the pot of soup. "Aye."

"Two Leafers rowed a skiff to that boat this morning. When it came back to shore, the Leafers had news. The boat is from a unit connected with the Leafers. Other vessels will join it in the next few days. They want the entire wharf space for themselves to offload all their people, horses, and other animals. The rumor is that one vessel coming will bring a giant the Leafers sent for. Nagora, you must have heard about him. Apparently, he's a dragon slayer!"

"That's one reason I came here, to see if that rumor is true," said Nagora.

"It's supposed to be an entire group that travels together. They say they won't have it any other way," said Harri.

He held up both hands. "Well, you can imagine how the traders who are already tied up and doing their business feel about that. Their livelihood is at stake!" He shook his head. "My meeting with the trader got interrupted with that news.

Right now, the harbormaster is beyond himself trying to sort this out to accommodate everyone.

"He's supposed to call a meeting tonight for the traders who are docked, and those waiting on moorings for their turn. He wants their input so he can set clear conditions for those other boats to come in at daylight on the tide. They'll tie up at the docks, offload, and then leave with the next tide. If they need to reprovision or what have you, they can go to the moorings, or drop anchor to wait their turns."

Paruline gazed over her shoulder. "The traders would lose a day to accommodate those boats. To me, that sounds reasonable. To a trader, it might not. Are you going to that meeting?"

Harri pushed his hand through the hair on his head. "You know me. I like to get my information firsthand."

He then slapped a hand on the table. "That's the thing, though! We're always accommodating the Leafers, always! If it were up to them, we'd all lose a day of work once a week to go tend the oak trees we planted had we joined them." He waved a hand in dismissal, obviously trying to contain his anger. "I'm glad I'm not one of them!"

Paruline set a bowl of soup in front of her man and winked at Nagora. "You're next."

The bowl of soup with a piece of bread and cheese seemed to have calmed Harri. However, no sooner had he finished, he was off again to see if he could still talk business with the trader.

"When not traveling, we're here in Windhaven. It's often like this. He would need three of himself to do everything he wants to get done," said Paruline, as she cleaned off the table.

Paruline placed a few small logs on the grate before uncovering the two loaves that had risen. With mitts, she set the big pot on the floor. Next, she set the woven straw baskets on the floor near the fireplace. One at a time, she turned the baskets over to empty the loaf onto the iron plate.

Then she placed the big pot over the two loaves. "There. We can tour the shop while the bread cooks. Matti will show our wares if he's not busy with other buyers." Paruline removed her apron and held out her hand to Nagora.

Matti was busy with a customer. Paruline guided Nagora around the shop, pointing out the hardware they sold, which smiths made the pieces, and how long they took to complete special orders. The aroma of the baking bread took them back to the kitchen, where Paruline removed the pot to show the pale, crusty loaves. "They'll brown more for a count. I'll show you our rooms while they finish."

Paruline lit a candle lantern to show Nagora the pantry room behind the kitchen. "It's not as cool as the one Da has in Cairnmase. I don't keep as much produce in the floor bins since it would spoil because we travel often enough. Besides, we can buy fresh from the sellers at the markets and even from traders."

"Where do you get your water?" asked Nagora.

Paruline led her through a small door in the pantry into what she called the water room. She pointed to a framed, square hole in the floor filled with water. "All the streets that run across the slope of Windhaven have a basin at each end. Those basins connect to the water rooms of all the buildings."

The hair on the back of Nagora's neck stood. Now she understood how easy it had been for the witch, Hag, to poison the water supply of Windhaven. Her mother and Sagora had trained people to disinfect the wells, not only those of Windhaven, but in other towns and villages in the land.

Now she worried what might happen if the Leafers, under Heqet's influence, put something in the water to control the population. Has the king thought of this vulnerability? If I can meet with him alone, I'll discuss it with him.

Paruline held her arms stretched out, the lantern in one hand and the other hand cupped like a bowl. "The two big basins control the level of the water in all the water rooms. It can't overflow, but the level can run low in hot, dry spells."

Paruline pointed to a post that ran down the corner of the square hole. "It's hollow inside. Upstairs, we have a cistern with a pump at the end of this pipe. Once a week, we pump the cistern full. I'll show you when we go upstairs."

Paruline blew out the candle and pointed to the skylights above. "I wouldn't live up here without daylight."

To the left of the stairwell was a drawing table. Around it were sketches and drawings of hinges and implements with labels, arrows, and measurement notations around them. "It's where Harri works on custom designs and ideas for new products. It's messy right now. When I work on my designs, instead of disturbing his papers, I work at the table in the kitchen."

Paruline walked over to the door next to Harri's desk and opened it. "Come look."

Nagora stood next to Paruline as she looked at the storage area lit by six skylights, three on each side of the low-peaked timber roof. A stout wooden rail with an attached carriage of metal wheels hung from the roof's center beam on big, forged metal hooks. A low-sided framed cradle of woven metal bands hung from chains attached to the carriage on the rail above.

Paruline noticed Nagora examining it. "We call that our sky wagon. Da set it up for us. It makes anything we lift from a wagon in the street below easy to move to where we want to store it up here."

Wooden boxes and crates were spread in orderly fashion across the floor on each side of the sky wagon's lane. "Those boxes contain items we have a demand for, especially from traders."

Nagora pointed to the stock window doors at the other end of the rail. "You must have an excellent view of the bay when those doors are open."

Paruline nodded. "Aye, depending on the ship docked out front. We rarely have an unobstructed view. Only in the coldest months of winter. You should see the fishing huts that get hauled out onto the ice."

"As I rode down Castle Way past the fishing village area, I spotted a section of beach with at least a hundred of them. They were lined up in rows, shoulder to shoulder, above the high-water mark," said Nagora.

"That would be them. When on the ice, the fishers fly their own little flags so they can find their huts.

"Do you want to look out the stock window?" asked Paruline.

Nagora stepped back. "I'd like that. We'll come back later. Your bread should be ready."

Paruline put on her mitts, picked up a loaf, and held it up to Nagora's face. "There's no fragrance that says home like freshly baked bread!"

Nagora inhaled the aroma. "I'm with you on that!" How many times had she caught a whiff of Paruline's bread before stepping into their lodge in Cairnmase? It was the smell of home, her second home with Paruline and Geirador.

Paruline set the loaves on the counter to cool and pulled off her mitts. "Come, we'll take the stairs from the shop up to the stock window."

With the wooden doors pulled back, Nagora peered past the mast rigging of the docked boat. She pointed to the only vessel at the mouth of the bay, its sails furled and riding on an anchor rode. "Is that the ship Harri talked about?"

"Aye. The fishing boats that raced to sea early this morning are sailing past her on their way back in. They look tiny next to her."

Nagora touched Paruline's arm. "If I'm still in Windhaven when it and the others that will join it come in to dock, I'd like to watch them."

Paruline held up a thumb. "Sure. You can even stay with us while you're here. I have a cot you can sleep on. We can set it near the kitchen fireplace for you." She laughed. "Or even right here, in front of this open window. You're not planning on loosing arrows, are you?"

Nagora shook her head no. "I did that once. It put a price on my head and earned me a new name and a reputation." Though, at the back of her mind, it was still an option.

Paruline put an arm around Nagora's waist. "But you gave new hope to the people of this land. Knowing you, you'll do what you have to do. Be careful."

"I will." Protecting the dragons at all costs was at the forefront of her thoughts. Two essential questions bothered her: How will I defeat the one who seeks to destroy the dragons? And is there anything I can do that will help Sagora choose to become a Dragon Talker?

Wanting to hear what Harri would learn from the harbormaster's meeting, Nagora accepted Paruline's offer to spend the night. News came late, five counts after sunset, when Harri returned to find the two women sitting at the kitchen table in conversation.

"I thought you would be in bed by now. I'm glad Nagora has stayed to keep you company," said Harri, as he prepared to light the pantry lantern.

Paruline stood. "Don't tell me you haven't eaten since we had soup?"

He shrugged. "There was just so much happening."

Paruline took the lantern from him. "Let me get you something that won't keep you up all night."

Nagora looked at Harri. "You don't seem pleased with the outcome of the meeting."

He pulled a chair from the table and sat. "Too many people talking at once. People needing translators because the trader's tongue doesn't account for such disputes."

Paruline stepped back into the kitchen. "Wait for me. I want to hear what happened too."

She had a wax-sealed jar in one hand and the lantern in the other. She set both on the counter and reached for one of her loaves in the breadbox.

Paruline sliced up half of it, putting the slices on a plate and bringing it and the jar to the table. "Pickled herring. This isn't only for you, Harri. Nagora and I will have some too. Go on about the meeting."

Harri was already trying to remove the wax lid of the jar with his fingers. "The short of it is the traders are willing, but they want compensation from the Leafers, in coin—gold coins! They say they won't move their vessels unless they get paid in gold coins!"

Paruline was putting water in a pot to boil on the fire. "Were members of the Community of the Leaf present?"

Harri set the jar down, using the fingers of his hands to help answer. "Oh! Aye! Not only the two from the skiff this morning, but ten others from the Assembly Hall of the Community of the Leaf. Those twelve manage the operations and events that take place in the hall. Counting the traders from the ships at the moorings and at anchor and those docked, they outnumbered the Leafer lads five to one. Add mead and ale to the mix, and spirits get lively and insults fly. Lucky the harbormaster had brought a dozen guards to keep the peace."

Paruline set three plates, spoons, and bowls for tea on the table. She grabbed the jar before Harri could pick it up again. Back at the counter, she popped the wax seal with the tip of a small knife.

Harri nodded. "Thank you, dear." He held up his hand and set the jar within reach of the three of them. "I need my sleep for the meeting tomorrow morning. I can't wait to see if the Leafers will pay the compensation."

He pointed to the jar of cut pieces of herring and onions in spiced-vinegar brine. "Nagora, please help yourself. They are so tasty."

That night, Nagora lay in her cot before Paruline's fireplace, watching the flames of the last two logs on the grate die and turn to red, glowing embers. Suddenly, the flames hopped back to life, jumping from one charred log to the other.

It was enough to stir Nagora from her drowsiness. She leaned up on one elbow to watch and listen. Two flames came together, producing a single, tall bright one that undulated; and then she heard the voice. "Dragon Talker, before sunset tomorrow, Lars and his trainees will set up camp outside the walls of Windhaven. Go to him under the cover of darkness."

The undulating flame died. "Thank you, *Mêmêkwêsiw*." Nagora lay back and stared into the darkness above the cot. A day early. How soon will you seek an audience with Raynhard? Knowing you, you'll not waste time. Surely by morning the next day. An invisible shadow will follow you. She closed her eyes.

The next morning, Nagora and Paruline had a light meal with Harri before he left in search of the latest news. Nagora, in her disguise, walked with Paruline to the large stable further along on Harbor Way, where she had left Bonnie for the night. Paruline and Harri rented a wagon and horse there when needed.

At the door next to the stables was a blacksmith who worked for the stable owner. Next to the smith was a cooper who not only made barrels, but wooden shoes. He had Nagora try on a pair that fit her, and while she walked around in them, she questioned him to learn the details of how they were made.

In his opinion, the ideal wood was willow. "Carve the shoes as soon as possible after you cut the tree down. Then leave them to dry completely in a warm place before using them. When they dry, the wood tightens up and the shoes become hard and light on the feet."

That information, and seeing his set-up for carving them, was worth the price she paid for her pair. She would provide Jari with details and an example to work from.

Nagora fit the shoes in her bag.

Outside in the mid-morning sunlight, Paruline said, "Be careful if you ever wear them on cobblestones, especially in the rain."

Nagora smiled. "Where they're headed, that won't be a problem."

On their return to Paruline's place, they saw Harri enter the shop.

"Could the meeting be over already?" asked Nagora.

"We will find out."

Harri was talking to Matti when they entered the shop. He turned to Paruline and Nagora. "I was just telling Matti here about the meeting. Two Leafers showed up with a document for the traders to sign, including those docked, those on moorings, and those lying at anchor. One of the Leafers, by the name of Lanken, was assigned to work with the harbormaster and deal with the traders.

"He, Lanken, established three sizes of trader vessels by the number of masts they carry. A gold coin was offered per mast and per day of delay caused by the Leafer ships that will come to dock. It was a take-it-or-leave-it offer.

"Any trader signing the agreement must show their vessel's logbook indicating the name and description of the boat. Lanken will then sign and date a blank page in the log and place his seal on that page, along with the number of masts as described in the trader's book.

"Oh! And Lanken confirmed the rumor. Those are the giant's ships. After they have docked and departed, traders who present their logs with Lanken's signature and seal will receive payment according to the agreement."

Paruline looked from Nagora to Harri. "The traders accepted that with nothing in advance?"

"Aye. Most of them know damn well it'll take more than a day for those vessels to offload. Maybe even up to three or four days or more. There's only so much space along Harbor Way, and only so many mules and wagons available."

Matti rubbed his hands together. "I'd be happy to sign that if I were a trader."

Harri waved a finger. "But most small traders don't have log books. They're scrambling to make their logs. The harbormaster will have to approve the logs once he has inspected their boats. Only then will Lanken sign and place his seal."

"Any news when those other vessels will arrive, and how many there will be?" asked Nagora.

Harri was nodding. "Lanken said they were expecting twenty vessels, twenty-five at the most. He said if the winds were favorable, in four or five days they would drop their anchors in the bay."

How will I use my time until then?

Matti pointed in the direction of the bay. "If they're the size of the one out there now, they won't all fit along the wharf here. Some will have to wait their turn. I bet when the traders learned that, they were glad to sign on."

"Exactly!" said Harri.

Matti smiled. "If I were a betting man, I would wager a bag of coins on the parade of boats at the docks lasting for over a week."

Harri laughed. "The traders are thinking the same thing. Some of them with smaller goods are making plans to bargain with fishers so they can tie their skiffs to their docks and do business from over there."

Nagora guessed something was bothering Paruline. She was frowning as she bit on her lower lip. Nagora touched her friend's arm. "What's on your mind?"

Harri stopped laughing and looked at his wife.

Paruline looked from Nagora to Harri and took a deep breath. "Horrible images came into my mind."

Harri took a step toward her and reached for her hand. "Of what? Tell us."

Paruline shook her head. "You'll think I'm worrying for nothing."

"No!" Harri placed his other hand over Paruline's.

She looked from Harri to Matti, and then to Nagora. "What if the Community of the Leaf doesn't pay the traders?"

In the silence that followed, Nagora realized she wasn't the only one who let play out the many possibilities that could result. She shuddered at one vision. Windhaven was on fire. It started with the buildings on Harbor Way, and the wind carried the flames uphill. The massive brazier consumed the rest of the town.

Both Harri and Matti were shaking their heads. Harri waved his hand. "The Leafers wouldn't dare think of doing that. Those signed agreements have to mean something."

The three of them looked at Paruline.

She pursed her lips as she nodded. "You all pictured the worst situation. Why? Because it's a possibility. I'm not saying they won't pay the traders. However, these Leafers made a bright shiny offer and have given nothing upfront but signed agreements.

"Are they worth more than the vellum they are written on? Where will the gold coins come from? From the vessels that will dock? Or have they already accumulated such wealth from their oak trees?"

Nagora crossed her arms. "Watch in the coming days when the traders get over being blinded by this bright, shiny offer, as Pare calls it. They'll start to think along the same lines and ask for hard guarantees they'll get paid. 'Show us the coins, where they are kept, and who vouches to hold them in trust for payment due us.'"

Nagora uncrossed her arms and pointed at Harri. "Here's something else the traders will most likely think about: What about other trader ships that arrive and drop anchor before those of the giant? They'll be delayed and want to be paid too. The coffer that holds those gold coins has just gotten bigger."

Paruline took hold of Nagora's arm as she stood next to her. "Harri, before those boats arrive, why not sow these seeds," she pointed to Nagora to indicate the words her friend had spoken, "among your trader friends? It might help prevent a lot of needless worry."

Harri held his chin and nodded. He seemed to give serious consideration to what Nagora had said. He held up his thumb. "I'll see you later. I have important business to attend to." In several long strides, he was out the shop door.

Matti smiled and pointed at the two women. "Looking at things away from the action can be a good thing. Which reminds me, I'll go eat something, if that's fine with you?" He winked at them. "And listen to what the gossipers are saying."

Paruline returned his smile. "Enjoy your meal. We'll take care of the shop while you're away."

She was about to lead Nagora to the kitchen when Nagora stopped her. "Listen Pare, I have business to take care of with Olen this afternoon, and I expect Lars will arrive before the end of day. I'll eat a bowl of soup with you and then be on my way."

Paruline hugged her. "But you will come back when the giant's boats dock?"

"Oh! Aye! I don't want to miss that."

Time to Act
Nayihpayin

After riding to Castle Square, Nagora dismounted and took her time walking Bonnie across the square. It wasn't as busy as on market day two days earlier. The vendors came to set up their tents and wagons every seventh day. Today, the shops from around the square had samples of their wares outside on display tables and shelves next to their doors.

A few vendors, pushing carts of baked treats, had staked out their locations on the square. One played a flute to get attention; another juggled balls.

Nagora wanted to locate feasible hiding places to avoid bumping into people when wearing her invisibility armor. She scouted for recesses and doorways to stand in along building walls, and for barrels and crates to crouch behind.

Will Lars seek an audience on his own, or will someone go with him? Which street will he take to the castle, Stables Way or Castle Way? Stables Way is the shortest. I'll walk Bonnie along Castle Way to the hall, just in case, and then ride Bonnie back along Stables Way.

...

Castle Way ended where it met Main Gate Way. Nagora stood on that corner, looking across at what had become Assembly Hall Square. On her first visit here twenty years earlier, it bore the name Temple Square because of evil Queen Raganora's Temple of Fire. Originally, it was called Center Square after the Center for the Dragon Arts.

The eight tiers that rose to the hall's walls were of equal height and depth. Comfortable sets of steps up to each tier were located ten paces from one another. The tiers gave the hall its prominence in the square.

Now, the latest incarnation of the towering, eight-sided gray stone building was the Assembly Hall of the Community of the Leaf. It stood two hundred strides from Nagora. Three of its eight sides were visible: the main entrance side and the next two walls to its right.

The slanted roof of the hall covered the surrounding seating area inside, leaving the center stage open to the sky. On each wall beneath the roof eaves, tall stained glass windows pointed skyward. A single, heavy, windowless wooden door stood beneath each window, except for the two big doors at the primary entrance.

Nagora wondered if the Leafers had changed the central stage area inside.

She looked up at the spire that rose skyward above the hall. It was made from the trunks of three tall trees, most likely spruce or pine, stripped of their bark and branches, shaved smooth, and stained black.

At the spire's peak, where the three poles met, the big bronze oak leaf sparkled in the sunlight. It faced the main entrance.

Two body lengths down from the base of the oak leaf was a small platform, built on sturdy frame pieces that crossed from one trunk to the other. Beneath the center of the platform, Nagora spied a big shackle suspended where three metal bars came together from their separate attachment points on the platform's frame pieces.

To hang a bell to call Leafers to assembly?

That made Nagora wonder how the poles had been attached to the roof since it wasn't originally designed to hold a spire.

Maybe that's why its three sides are not covered. If they were, a powerful wind might topple it. Open like that, wind can blow through. Still, that platform will catch a fair amount of wind. It's the Leafers' problem.

Her eyes traveled down to the stained glass window above the main doors. The lines of lead, which held the pieces of glass together, allowed her to discern the outlines of the scenes on the panels. Seen from inside in daytime, the painted details and colors of the glass would be amazing.

The scene still depicted her as the warrior, Edana, frozen in a moment in time, standing at the top of the steps of Queen Raganora's infamous Temple of Fire. Edana held her bow in one hand and her other high in the dragon-chord salute. A flaming arrow was stuck in the door frame, another on the open door.

Inside the temple behind Edana, the scene showed a young sacrificial virgin hanging from her arms, tied to the metal bar, ready to be lowered into the furnace.

The background scene behind the girl showed the burning curtain that Nagora's fire arrow had set in flames. The foreground scene displayed the crowd below the main entrance steps, returning Edana's dragon-chord salute.

Nagora's memory of that moment was clear.

†

Nagora stood before the main entrance just as the carriage driver whipped the horse to urge it forward. She raised her bow in the air and looked out over the people.

She raised her right hand, her fingers splayed as they would be if they were to play the dragon chord. Finally, the carriage lurched across Main Gate Way onto Castle Way. Hag, we'll meet again someday.

The crowd became quiet. They were waiting. Some raised their hands like hers.

"Who are you?" It was a lone voice from the crowd.

Nagora placed her splayed-fingered hand over her heart. "I have a message for you." Then she raised her hand high in the air. "Dragons will fly here again! Edana will return. Believe me! Dragons will fly again! Edana will return!"

†

Nagora shook her head. That's how I got the name Edana. When I spoke that name, I was referring to the virgin girl I saved from sacrifice that day, not myself. I didn't want to identify myself. However, when the people returned my salute, they yelled: "Edana! Edana!"

Raynhard unveiled the new Edana window to me the night we wed in the Center for the Dragon Arts. Except for the window of the dragon on the wall opposite the main entrance, he had the six other windows remade to their original scenes.

Years before, Raganora had all the stained glass windows destroyed and boarded up, except for the dragon window. She wanted to destroy it only after she had Danuka killed.

What fate awaits those windows now that the Community of the Leaf has made the building its Assembly Hall in the Land of the Danu? Are the Leafers waiting for their dragon slayer to kill my dragons before they act?

Not if I come up with a plan.

Nagora led Bonnie across Main Gate Way to Assembly Hall Square. Should I tie her to a hitching post and then go look inside the hall? Without a leaf medallion, I most likely won't be welcome there.

Instead, Nagora walked the horse around the remaining perimeter of Assembly Hall Square until they arrived at Main Gate Way. Stables Way was a brief walk away. She climbed back into the saddle and took Bonnie for a slow walk along Stables Way to the castle stable.

Nagora's eyes continued to scan the way ahead as she patted Bonnie in front of Olen's stable doors. "You thought I was taking you home. It won't be long. We'll come back soon." No one seems to be watching Olen's place.

As she rode along Stables Way, Nagora registered the places and objects that would give her cover when following Lars, if he took that direction. Being invisible on a crowded street will be a challenge. I'll see who's in the way, but they won't see me dancing to avoid them.

After Nagora had led Bonnie to Olen's inner courtyard, she knocked on his door.

"Back so soon? I figured you'd be away longer." Olen waved her inside. "Sit. Sit." He pointed to a chair at his table.

Her nose caught the aroma of something cooking in Olen's fireplace. "I'm taking you up on your offer. If I can, I'd like to spend two or three nights here. If you don't mind, maybe more."

He sat. "Not at all! Not at all! What do you have going on?"

Nagora looked at her hand and then at Olen. "I expect Lars and his group will arrive before sunset. The weather's been good. I figure those young trainees have taken to life on the road and are now making up for earlier lost time when it rained."

Olen nodded as he listened.

"Do you know where such a gang as his would set up camp outside the walls?"

Olen pointed. "To the right, as you leave the gate where the wagons park, there's a line of trees at the end of the wagon lot. On the other side of the trees, there is a field with place for a hundred tents to set up. There's a brook for water, though I'm not sure about firewood. The gate guards could tell you."

Nagora smiled. "That's not far away. It's a quick ride. I could even walk there."

"Aye, a simple walk." He pointed at her. "They might arrive sooner than you think. I mean, setting up camp with dark coming on them is not a good idea. Why don't you go for a look before dark? I'll be eating soon." He pointed to the covered pot that hung above the coals in his fireplace. "Rabbit stew has been simmering since this morning. I baked bread yesterday. I'll be happy if you join me."

She had guessed right. "I'll not say no to your stew, Olen. It smells delicious."

Nagora pointed at him. "Olen, there's news you should know."

His smile grew wider. He rubbed his hands together before leaning his elbows on the table. "I'm listening!"

Nagora informed him of everything she had learned while at Paruline's: the coming of the giant's boats; the Leafers demanding all the dock space for his boats; the traders' protests; and the agreement offered the traders. She told him of her and Paruline's speculation about the agreement not being respected.

When she finished, Olen leaned back in his chair and whistled through his teeth. "That's news to me. I don't see the Leafers being able to pay the traders. But I see the king as the only one who can guarantee they will be paid."

"Olen, do you know of a Leafer by the name of Lanken?"

"Aye, he's the one in charge of the young Leafer cell that runs their Assembly Hall. He takes orders from the Head Leafer, Kiviran. He's the Leafer who's almost always with Raynhard."

"Do you still have someone in the castle who can report what's going on?"

He frowned and shook his head. "I did until the Head Leafers arrived."

"Head Leafers? There's more than one?" asked Nagora.

He nodded. "I'm talking about the Head Leafers from the various towns in the Land of the Danu, the ones who founded the first Leafer cells in those places a long time ago. Many are in residence at the castle. They've come with members of their cells. Those members have taken over the kitchen and housekeeping duties in the castle. They serve the Head Leafers their meals.

"The locals who've kept their jobs in the kitchen never go to other parts of the castle. The former maids only work scullery and laundry duty, serving the Head Leafers in residence and their members. They only come and go to those rooms. The Leafer members share the barracks with the castle guards."

Nagora raised her eyebrows. "What you're telling me is the Community of the Leaf has control of the castle, and the Head Leafers are keeping a close watch on the king."

Olen was nodding. "Aye, they watch his every move, especially Kiviran."

"Even when he has an audience with someone concerning state or business affairs?"

Again, he nodded. "It seems so. Moreena must have told you about the Head Leafer going with the king to Bardas's forge."

"Aye, she did."

"That was Kiviran, the Head Leafer from Windhaven."

If I can make it into the castle with Lars, I'll have a privileged view of those whose eyes are always on Raynhard. Is he professing to believe in their promise until the Gold Planter reveals the secret to a higher yield of gold? Does he take part in their assemblies at the hall?

Olen leaned closer to the table. "What are you thinking?"

"Does Raynhard go to the assemblies in the hall?"

Olen shook his head. "He doesn't need to. He has a small hall in the castle. They call it the Leaf Room of Light."

Nagora cocked her head at what she had just heard. "Where in the castle?"

Olen laughed. "Where else? In the maps room." He pointed up. "Light from the skylight shines down on the potted oak that sits in the middle of the round table, like the bigger one in the Assembly Hall of the Community of the Leaf. Rumor has it that the oak waits to be fed the blood of dragons."

Nagora shook her head. "It's ironic. My dragon, who they want to kill, broke through that skylight and pulled me from that room right after Sarah and I killed the witch. I thought Raynhard would explain my disappearance as a death casualty from fighting Alizarine. He could have had a funeral for the one he had married and crowned queen that same day."

Olen smiled at her. "Aye, but the good king didn't let his heroine die. He wanted her to keep her promise and return with the dragons. That's how he explained your disappearance."

"But Olen, do you truly believe he wants me to return with the dragons to have them slaughtered?"

Olen shrugged. "By all appearances, he is a Leafer. That could be his plan."

"Tar piss! It's been three years since I've seen Raynhard. A lot has changed in the brief time since the Leafers have manifested their existence.

"When I witness those who believe in their unproven promise, I wonder about the king, and I worry about the future of the dragons. This is the Land of the Danu, the Land of the Dragon. Has Raynhard forsaken the vision his father, King Bernhard, had for the people of this land? If the Leafers' dragon slayer kills the dragons, I fear for our land's reputation. What name will this land then bear? They'll change it to what? The Kingdom of the Leaf?"

Olen crossed his arms as he sat back in his chair. "Nagora, I wish I could tell you he has a definite plan, and it's not to kill the dragons. I just can't fathom he would do that. I listen to you talk about your fears for the dragons on the one hand. Then on the other, if the king has called you to him, I'm certain he's calling on the right person. You, Nagora, are the person who'll do what's best for the dragons and for the people. The king knows Edana will keep her promise. Most people in the land know that."

Nagora dropped her gaze to the table. I want to do my best, but I don't have a plan, only part of a plan. I need more than that, because I feel helpless right now. I need more information to advance my plan.

She looked up at Olen. "Can you do me a favor?"

Olen placed his hands on the armrests of his chair, as if about to stand. "Of course." He waited.

"At dusk, can you go check if Lars and his trainees have arrived and set up camp?"

He nodded. "Aye, I can. Do you want me to give him a message?"

"Aye, tell him I want to meet him at the tree near the bridge where I met him and our son the last time we were in Windhaven. He knows where. Tell him to go there two counts after sunset, alone. I'll be waiting for him."

Olen stood. "I can do that for you. Let me get bowls for the stew. It's ready; we can eat."

Nagora left the stable on Bonnie well before Olen departed. Her plan was to ride past the tree, cross the bridge, and scout the land on the other side of the brook. She wanted to find a spot on high ground that would give her a view of Lars's encampment. If it was there, that would confirm his arrival, and she would wait to meet with him.

If there was no encampment, she wouldn't wait past darkness at the tree. She'd return to Olen's and change into her dragonskin armor to scout access to the castle.

On the road from Windhaven, Nagora rode toward a timber bridge that reminded her of Edana's Victory Bridge that Godomor had built in her honor in the Land of Skulls. This one had the same design, except the two center posts at its side trusses did not have skulls sitting on their tops. The bridge was wide and strong enough for two heavy wagons and a mounted rider to cross it side by side. She slowed Bonnie to a walk and crossed the bridge, looking ahead for a spot to cross the ditch. She found one that took her down the embankment to the brook near the bridge.

Nagora guided Bonnie along the brook until she came to the edge of a field. From there, she rode to a small hill in the distance that she hoped would give her a view of the trainee encampment.

Once on top of the hill, Nagora spotted the small one-man tents of Lars's group. They had set up, campaign style, an outer square with five tents on three sides, side by side, and one side of four tents. The inner group of tents also formed a square with two sides of four tents, one side of three, and one of two.

Four cooking fires, one to a side between the two groups of tents, were burning with trainees gathered around them.

A hundred paces from the brook, two trainees were on watch at the horse lines. Nagora guessed Lars had scheduled five rounds of watch duty for the night. Four of the six on a watch rotation would take up positions at the corners of the camp, with the remaining two at the horse lines. Everyone would have a turn.

Nagora patted Bonnie's neck. "Let's go wait for Lars at the tree."

It was twilight by the time Nagora reached the tree. She dismounted, strung her bow, and nocked an arrow before doing another slow scan of the area. Satisfied she was alone, she leaned her back against the tree. She didn't have long to wait.

Lars showed up on time. He took Nagora in his arms and was about to kiss her. "What happened to you?"

She spit the stone into her palm. "It's part of my disguise. Let's try that again." She put her lips on his.

When he let her go, he said. "Clever. For a moment, I was worried. It's been a long haul, but now the trainees have settled into the routine. So much so that we've arrived a day earlier than planned; in good part, thanks to help from Labrys's team in guiding our mules over the steep mountain passes, and also the improved conditions of the trade route."

"Not saddle sore, I hope?"

He grinned. "No. I had them bring salve."

She poked his chest. "I hope you had them bring soap too. You could use a good bath."

"Until Olen showed up, that was my next order of business."

"Are you going to seek an audience with Raynhard tomorrow?"

"Aye. First thing after we've eaten, we'll ride into Windhaven."

"All of you?"

"Four will stay to guard the camp. We hope that our twenty-four trainees carrying oak seedlings will help us get an audience."

"All of you together?"

He chuckled. "Oh! No. Just Trowan and I, if we get the call. The seedling carriers will stand in formation in the square."

"Olen won't have place for all your horses. Will you leave some at the castle stable?"

"We'll all ride to the castle stable and tie up there. Two trainees will stay to guard our mounts. From there, we'll march in formation to the castle gate to lend importance to our request. We hope the king will not just consider our request, but accept to receive us."

"Oh! I learned Kiviran is the name of the Head Leafer from Windhaven. He's the one who's always with Raynhard."

In the dark, Lars's hand searched for and found Nagora's hand. "How long have you been in Windhaven?"

Nagora told him all: when she had arrived, who she had met, where she had gone, and what she had learned since her arrival. She did not tell him how she had learned he was arriving a day early, nor of her intention of being his invisible shadow at his audience with the king.

"That many ships!" Lars took a deep breath. "A fleet ferrying the Leafers' giant slayer of dragons! With that reputation, he's unlikely to travel alone. He must have an armed force with him. If I can get my audience with Raynhard, I might learn more details. Gaining information like that before the giant arrives could help us."

He squeezed Nagora's hand. "If I get the audience tomorrow, what you've told me will help me."

He hugged her. "It's time I take a bath, or I won't get that audience. Will I see you tomorrow?"

"For sure. If you meet with the king, you'll tell me what happened. Where and when should we meet?"

"Depending on that meeting's outcome, if it happens, I might need to speak with Bardas afterward. I imagine I could be there by mid-afternoon, if all goes well," said Lars.

"And if you can't meet with Raynhard tomorrow?"

"If he turns down our request, I'll leave a message with Olen. We'll meet one way or another."

"I'll tell you what. I'll hide in Castle Square tomorrow morning. Either way, if you're welcomed into the castle or not, I'll meet you at Olen's afterward. From there, we can decide what to do next."

"That's a plan!" Lars hugged her, gave her a quick kiss, and then held her shoulders. "I want to warn you about how you see me act with Trowan tomorrow. It's all for show, so don't jump to conclusions."

More details, aye? I won't press you for them now. I'll be the judge of what I see. "Okay."

Nagora let Lars mount his horse and ride to his camp before she returned to Windhaven.

Back at Olen's kitchen, Nagora conferred with him about Lars's plan and hers for the next day. He sat across the table from her and confirmed what she had learned from Lars.

"Don't worry about me if I'm not here when you get up tomorrow morning, or if I don't show up before Lars returns. I want to make sure I'm not seen anywhere near him outside of your stable."

Olen held up a thumb.

Nagora pointed to the big pot near the fireplace. "Olen, can I warm some water in that and get a bucket of water from your cistern? I could use a quick bath."

And be early to bed. I'll be rested and alert when I rise early to scout access to the castle in my dragonskin armor.

He stood. "Sure, I'll put wood on the fire. Fill the bucket, and then pour what you want heated into the pot. Soap and washcloths are in the first room upstairs. It's yours. You know where to empty the bucket in the morning."

Nagora stood to check on the water. "This will be fine." She emptied the pot into the pail and touched the water. "Just right!" She smiled at Olen and picked up the pail. "Good night."

Invisible to the Castle
Namoya Nôkwan Kihci-Okimâwikamik

The next morning, in the lantern light, Nagora stood before the mirror in the guest room. She combed her hair back, pulling it into a tight bunch and tying it with a leather lace.

Next, she combed out the tail, separated it in three, and braided it tight. With the braid done, she rolled and wove it into a bun at the back of her head. A turn of the leather lace around her head and tied to the side of her forehead would hold it in place until she put on her armor.

Nagora crossed the inner courtyard to the stable. She lit one of the stable lanterns that hung from a hook. She chose the empty stall next to Bonnie to empty her scrip so that she could to reach the tab of the false bottom under which she had hidden the small scrip that held her armor. After removing the armor and setting it on the stall shelf, she refilled her scrip and stripped naked. She folded her clothes and stuffed them and

her scrip into her saddlebags that hung next to Bonnie's saddle.

When she took the armor from the shelf, she let the fine
mesh of Danuka's dragonskin scales unravel before her. Her
fingers found the hole in the front. She stretched the hole to
first squeeze each leg into it, followed by each arm, after
which she pulled the skin up over her shoulders and head so it
covered her whole body.

The hole folded closed into a tiny seam over her belly. The
armor clung to every bump, curve and indentation of Nagora's
skin, but not in a restrictive manner. It was part of her, like
another layer of skin that was transparent, seamless, and as
comfortable as her own skin. She looked at her hands. The
fine mesh of dragon scales was impossible to detect in the
lantern light.

Once inside it, the essence of the Dragon's Kiss, as Nagora
called it, enveloped her body. It made her remember the last
time she stood before her dragon in Raynhard's secret cave.
On that day, Danuka ended her apprenticeship as a Dragon
Talker.

Prior to that day, the essence had overpowered and controlled Nagora in a way she never imagined. She could not
resist it. She had to submit to it.

And that thought made her reflect on how different her
children's apprenticeships had been, seemingly without the
sacrifices she had made. Yogari, my father, trained Sarah as
the Dragon Talker to replace him while on his quest to find
the king's gold. Being younger, she was probably easily sus-
ceptible to Danuka's will.

Danuka rewarded Dannor with a dragon-tear amulet for
getting back her egg with the last male hatchling from Aliza-

rine. She did not use her essence to control Sarah and Dannor like she did me. Perhaps my being their mother made it unnecessary.

Now, as a Dragon Talker wearing the armor, it made all the muscles of the limbs of her body come alive. Danuka's skin seemed to multiply their strength tenfold. I can take on any challenger. No one can harm me.

Like the last time she had put it on, the dragonskin wrapped her in strange warmth. An even wave of heat pulsed over every part of her body with each beat of her heart. In the armor, each heartbeat was a distinct echo.

Before heading to the door at Olen's forge, Nagora blew out the flame of the candle and returned the lantern to its hook. As she stood at the door that opened onto Stables Way, she willed the armor to make her invisible.

In dawn's early light, Nagora walked up Stables Way to the castle stable, to the spot she had chosen to wait for Lars. She crossed the first drawbridge to the way that ran along the other side of the moat. The way was forty paces wide from the edge of the moat to the castle wall where the first set of big stable doors stood closed.

Two big, curved, wedge-shaped stone projections from the castle wall stood on each side of the closed doors where they could be hooked open. The rounded edges of the projections protected the open stable door from passing wagon wheels and their axels.

The space between the projections and where the open door hooked was big enough to allow Nagora to stand and have a view along Stables Way. If she peeked past the projection to her left, she could see to where Castle Way opened onto Castle Square.

From this spot, she could choose where and when to make her move to fall in behind Lars.

It was early. Nagora wanted to be in position when the doors opened so she could scout the inside of the stable. There she would look for a door to take her inside the castle to the barracks, the armory, or the kitchens.

From her past visits to the castle, she did not recall ever seeing a supply wagon in its main courtyard. Nor did she ever see cooks, maids, or other castle workers come and go that way.

To her, the logical way in and out for workers and supplies was a separate entrance, and it would be from somewhere in the stable. She wanted a way out of the castle, even if guarded, should she not be able to follow Lars out.

It was sunrise when Nagora heard a stable hand open the first set of enormous doors. She followed him along the wall to the other set and then inside. He turned right and walked up the way to where the stalls were.

Nagora noted the entrance twenty paces from her. The two four-handled barrows leaning against the wall and the wheelbarrow full of kitchen scraps next to them told her it must be the way into the kitchens.

She walked past the parked manure wagon to go to the other end of the stable. This is the way wagons come in to park near the kitchens to unload.

A door like the one to the kitchens stood ajar. Nagora listened and heard voices from inside. When she stepped closer to look in, a heavy, latticed timber gate blocked the entrance. Access to the kitchen at the other end is probably set up just like this. Beyond, the passageway was clear. To the right, six paces away, was an open door. The voices came from there. A guard room? Her nose caught the smell of gruel and warm bread.

Where the hallway ended a dozen paces away, a young man walked by, carrying a tray with bowls and chunks of bread on it. I've seen enough. I have two outs from the castle. Back to my post outside.

Nagora waited. The stable hand held the reins of the two horses, pulling the manure wagon out of the stable. A farmer along Castle Way will probably receive the manure.

Another wagon arrived, carrying cages of chickens, cabbages, and rutabagas. The vegetables were most likely from a farm's root cellars, and the chickens from its coop. The driver had time to unload and leave before the manure wagon returned.

A procession of young men wearing silver-leaf medallions crossed from the square in front of the castle to disappear on Castle Way. They walked two-by-two with brisk steps. They must be going to Assembly Hall.

Nagora saw movement in the distance on Stables Way. As soon as she caught sight of the man with the crossguard of a big sword visible over his right shoulder, she knew it must be Lars.

…

The trainees rode across the drawbridge in pairs. Over their woven hemp shirts, they wore sleeveless brown leather vests laced up the front. A green oak leaf was embroidered on the left side above their hearts. Like Trowan, their unstrung bows tied to their quivers and the feathers of their arrows peeked over their right shoulders. They wore stern looks on their faces. In place of their saddlebags, baskets of tiny seedlings hung from behind their saddles. If they're carrying all the seedlings, that means twenty-five per basket.

Lars had his trainees line up along the castle wall between the two entrances to the castle stable. The two riders nearest the wall dismounted first and strung ropes from iron rings further along the wall to make a horse line. Then the first group of riders with seedling baskets dismounted. They set their baskets on the ground near the wall before bringing their mounts to the line.

With the way clear, the second group did the same.

When the two who would stay signaled they had tied all the horses, the other twenty-four trainees slung the straps of their seedling baskets over their necks so they hung in front of them, at waist level.

Lars called another order. As one, the trainees formed three lines, facing in Nagora's direction. Lars walked along the right side of the group, Trowan on the left.

Trowan did not wear her long black hair pulled back tight behind her head in a single braid as she usually did. Instead, she wore it loose on each side of her face where she had gathered and tied it just below her ears with leather laces. Two tails of thick, shiny hair fell over the straps of her blades and quiver and onto her breasts. She looked younger, wearing her hair that way.

The archer walked with an easy, confident, unhurried stride, with her broad shoulders held back, chest out, and with a relaxed swing of her muscular arms. She wore an arm guard over the shirtsleeve of her left forearm and an archer's glove on her right hand. Over her laced leather vest, the straps of her quiver and scrip crossed between her breasts, drawing attention to the strong, proud archer she was.

Lars and Trowan now stood facing the group. Lars had tied the leather tube that contained the maze plans to the scabbard of his sword. Have the trainees ever seen him draw it, or show how he fought with it? It's an impressive weapon. I've yet to see a sword bigger than his.

Nagora watched the faces of the trainees as he spoke to them. "We're counting on you to perform as well as you did in practice. Today is for real. There'll be many eyes on you. Take your time. Execute one formation at a time. Obey any reasonable orders from the castle guards. When at rest, stay together.

"If asked to leave the square, march back here to the horse lines. Set the seedling baskets on the ground near the wall. You know what to do if we don't return. Don't worry. News will find its way to you.

"You two," Lars said to the trainees guarding the mounts, "be polite when asking stable hands to fill the leather buckets from their water supply. Don't accept to fill them in the moat. Use the Danuian phrases I taught you. Be patient for our return."

The trainees were mostly young men and three young women. None were older than Dannor. That Lars had prepared them for these many possibilities seemed to reassure them. They were on a mission. They had a role to play. Their leaders were counting on them. This trip had surely brought the trainees closer to each other, and to their leaders.

Lars and Trowan turned to lead the group across the drawbridge, marching in step. The trainees followed ten paces behind. Nagora fell in behind Lars and Trowan. After crossing the drawbridge, the group headed for Castle Square.

It wasn't market day at the square. It was still early, and not all the businesses around the square were open. After turning into the square, Lars signaled a halt. Trowan raised her hand, showing four fingers. The three lines of eight formed up into four lines of six.

Nagora stood on her toes, looking around to keep her distance and be ready to move out of the way if she needed to.

Lars signaled the march forward.

The group stopped in the square just in front of the rising way that led to the castle gates. Four-by-four, the trainees lowered their seedling baskets to the cobblestones and turned to line up behind the others. When done, the forty-eight baskets sat together, forming a small forest of oak seedlings.

Nagora followed Lars and Trowan. The way narrowed the closer they got to the moat and castle drawbridge. Eight soldiers standing abreast could cross the bridge. On the other side of the bridge, the huge outermost castle gate blocked the way. It was built of wooden beams forming a grate, strapped together with strips of iron. Three soldiers guarded the heavy, latticed timber door set within the gate to allow a single person through. It stood open. Nagora stepped past Lars and Trowan to stand closer to the gate, several paces from the guard who had stepped forward with a frown on his face.

Lars spoke first. "We request an audience with King Raynhard. We bring information of utmost importance to him."

The officer of the guard looked them over and then past them to the trainees in the square, who stood still behind their seedlings. "Who do I say requests an audience?"

"Lars Marraden and Trowan from Maze Point, in the Land of Skulls." Lars reached into his scrip and pulled out something Nagora didn't recognize right away until he spoke. "Show this to his majesty. Tell him it belongs to his queen. He wore one just like it on his wedding day. The king can keep it if he'll see me today."

Nagora felt her jaw drop. *Another bloody detail you didn't tell me about! When did you take that from its pocket in my scrip? You better have a damn good reason.*

He handed the ring to the guard and then put an arm around Trowan's waist and pulled her to his side.

Trowan leaned her body against Lars's side, placing one hand on his shoulder and the other on his chest. She looked up at his face and smiled in admiration.

Nagora swallowed. *You warned me! Still, this better be for show. If it isn't, Lars Marraden, I'll drag you by your balls all the way to Maze Point. Those nights away from home! You better have been planning and not in her bed.*

The officer looked from them to the ring and back. He smiled and turned to walk through the door in the gate. The other soldiers, armed with spears, stepped in front of the doorway and took a wider stance, holding their spears with both hands.

When the officer returned, he motioned Lars and Trowan in.

Nagora followed, unseen.

Inside the courtyard, eight guards had assembled in two lines leading to the door opposite the gate they had just come through. The officer stopped them just before arriving where the guards stood. He signaled with his hand. Four of them lined up, two by two.

Then he spoke to Lars. "Follow these four. We'll follow behind you to a room where you'll leave your weapons."

Lars nodded.

Nagora stepped aside, waiting to follow the escort. *If I recall well, I know where they're going.*

Nagora followed the group inside along a wide corridor. Most of the doors were on the left-hand side. The only door to the right stood open next to the single door at the end.

That one on the right leads to the throne room.

The group walked through the last door on the left.

Nagora walked ahead and stepped inside the high-vaulted throne room.

Like the first time she had entered with Lars and Dannor, the room was sparsely furnished with the throne of carved wood resting on a dais at the far end to her left, two long tables standing on each side of the dais, and the semi-circle of twelve empty chairs behind the table to Nagora's right.

Again today, as Nagora looked around, the beauty of the windows impressed her. Three sets of three stained glass windows, each bearing different scenery, decorated three of the chamber walls two thirds of the way up. The forest, mountain and lake, and coastal scenes all contained animals. People and dragons were absent.

On each wall, two taller windows separated the stained glass scenes and shed light into the throne room. Glass rondelles interconnected the clear glass panels of patterned squares and rectangles. The dark grey lines of lead holding these panels together, and the rough texture of the glass, gave a distorted view of the sky.

The escort led Lars and Trowan into the throne room. The officer showed where they were to stand before the empty throne. Four of his men stood on each side of the couple.

When the officer appeared satisfied everyone was in place, he turned to walk past the throne.

Trowan, with a slow rotation of her body, took in the windows on each wall. Lars leaned close to her and whispered something in her ear as he touched the leather tube which he carried on his shoulder. She nodded.

Nagora watched the officer as he walked toward the door of the maps room. It was behind the throne, twenty paces away. On it hung a banner of sky-blue cloth with an embroidered green oak leaf. Where had Lars learned what color badges his trainees should wear? From Geirador? Most likely. And on the top of the doorframe was a medallion like the one Worsham wore. Was it nailed there?

The officer knocked on the door. It opened. He entered, and the door closed behind him.

Nagora counted. She had almost reached one hundred when the door opened, and the officer came back out. He was carrying something covered with a sky-blue cloth. Four armed soldiers followed him. King Raynhard came next, dressed in simple garments all of black. He wore a golden oak-leaf medallion on a gold chain around his neck. Four more guards followed.

Behind them, twelve old men wearing golden oak-leaf medallions emerged from what Olen had called the Leaf Room of Light. Some of them had placed the stems of the leaf medallions in the pocket on the front of their robes, probably designed to ease the weight of the medallions hanging from the gold chains around their old necks. Several of the men walked with canes. As usual with old people, Nagora had trouble guessing how old they might be. She surmised they could be from the original founding Leafer cells of the communities they came from. Their slow, deliberate procession took them to the semi-circle of chairs where they sat.

The officer took a position far to the right of the throne and watched as the king's escort took their positions on each side.

King Raynhard climbed onto the dais and stood behind the throne, carved into the shape of a dragon. The armrests were the wing talons. Folded-back dragon wings formed the throne's backrest where Raynhard had just placed his hands. The dragon's back was the seat of the throne. From there, the neck of the dragon curled down, under, and back to the front so the dragon's chin rested on the surface of the dais. The king's feet would rest on each side of the dragon's head if he sat on the throne.

Once the guards were in place, the officer walked to the nearest table, to the right of the dais, and placed the cloth-covered object on the center of the table.

Next, he walked to the other table to the left of the dais and pulled open a drawer. He took out four smooth, rectangular bars. Nagora guessed they had been made from molten glass. He placed two at each end of the table.

Then the officer returned to where he had been standing. He looked toward the Leaf Room of Light.

Raynhard waited, his eyes on Lars and Trowan. He kept his face expressionless.

Until now, this was not how Nagora expected the audience to go. Are they waiting for the Head Leafer?

As if in answer to her question, a man several years older than the king stepped from the former maps room, wearing a golden oak leaf. He gazed at those assembled before walking to the semi-circle of old men where he stood in the middle, with them at his back. Their eyes were upon him.

The Head Leafer looked at Lars and Trowan for at least a count of thirty while the fingers of one hand caressed his golden medallion.

He must be Kiviran.

He glanced at Raynhard and nodded once to him.

Nagora kept her eye on the king as she moved to stand near the end of the table where the officer had set the glass bars.

The king remained standing behind the throne, and for the first time smiled at Lars and Trowan. "Lars, it's been a long time. I don't believe I know your companion."

Lars put his arm around Trowan's waist and pulled her to him. "Your Majesty, meet Trowan, a renowned archer and warrior from the Land of Skulls who has won my heart."

My man, you make it sound so true. It better not be so.

Trowan took a step forward and bowed.

Raynhard bowed his head. "Trowan, welcome to the Land of the Danu. I take it your journey here with Lars has been interesting so far."

Trowan nodded and smiled as she pointed to the windows around the room. "Beautiful! Not enough words to describe."

Had Lars taught her those words in the Danuian language? Most likely.

Raynhard smiled. "They are scenes from our beautiful land."

His eyes shifted to Lars. "Apparently you've traveled here with a force of sorts of your own, archers carrying oak seedlings." Raynhard raised his shoulders as he spread his hands open before him. "What's this all about? What is of utmost importance?"

Lars stepped forward to stand next to Trowan. "Your Majesty, forgive me. You'll probably find what I have to say long-winded, but you'll understand why I've requested an audience."

The king waved his hand. "Call me Raynhard. Go ahead. Say what you need to say. You have my full attention."

Lars took another step forward and Trowan, a step back. He continued. "As you know, I come from Maze Point in the Land of Skulls, where the Dragon Talkers care for the dragons that hatched in the maze. I'm not a Dragon Talker. I don't speak the dragon tongue. Without a map, I can't find my way into the maze. I never could without one, even after I helped build it."

He paused and pointed to himself. "My son can." He pointed to Raynhard. "And your daughter, Sarah, can. Like I said, aye, I helped build the maze, but I know next to nothing of its workings. I know there's a well at its center and two dragon-perching rings made of stone lintels resting on pillars."

Raynhard held up a hand.

Lars stopped.

The king pointed to the officer and motioned him to the table with the covered object.

When the officer reached the table, he looked to Raynhard, who stared back at Lars. "What about this?" The officer pulled the cloth from the object.

Nagora recognized the stone boat as the one Alizarine had brought with her when Sagora kidnapped her and brought her to Windhaven three years earlier.

Lars pointed at it. "It's only a stone seat for a hatchling egg, like the egg Alizarine cherished so much. When an egg heats and the dragon breaks free, the molten gold from the egg collects in the depression. Then the Little People take it. Where? I don't know. Your guess is as good as mine."

Raynhard's mouth twisted as he looked at Lars. "You say you are not one of them. What, then, are you?"

Lars took a deep breath. "I'm tired of tending sheep to feed the dragons, of seeing that stone maze every time I set foot outside my lodge, of having to be led into the maze blindfolded when asked to help there, and of being led around by the nose on my face by a woman I thought I once loved."

Even if it was an act, the words of the last phrase he spoke struck Nagora's heart.

He pointed to his bare ring finger. "Nagora came back to me with the ring I wove for her from a willow branch, but not the one she wed you with. It's not a ring of value one could offer for exchange, but it's one tied to my heart. For almost three years it ate at me. Whom did she truly love? You, King, Raynhard, or me? Has she always wanted to be your queen? Now that ring has become the symbol of the love I lost."

Nagora wanted to speak to defend herself. I had no choice. Just listen! He's acting! Don't ruin his plan!

"Finally, I took it as a sign I best seek my fortune elsewhere," he pointed back at Trowan, "with the one I love now, instead of living in service to the dragons."

Lars stepped back to stand next to Trowan. "We are deserters. We are warriors. We want to build a life of our own choosing."

Lars pulled the leather tube from his shoulder and held it up. "To that end, we stand here before you today with a plan to make our lives worthwhile," he pointed to the king, "and yours too! We want what you want—gold! We know we are late in coming to join the Community of the Leaf, but we know we stand a chance of increasing the gold yield of our oaks if we act now. Our intention is to plant the biggest, best-tended oak forest in the Land of the Danu," he held up his hand, "and they will all get to drink the blood of dragons. Not a drop will be wasted."

He pointed to the seated old men. "Like you, we know the ancient legends of how, long before men like us came to these shores, dragons lived freely in this land in numbers greater than can be imagined. The dragons laid their eggs wherever they wished. The gold from their eggs seeped into the ground where the young dragons hatched. We too, like you, want to harvest that gold."

Lars walked to the table with the glass bars. Trowan followed and stood at one end of the table. Nagora could have reached out to touch her. Instead, she stepped back a full pace as Lars set the tube on the table.

He turned to face Raynhard. "Before I show you my plan, let me tell you more about it first. Then I'll tell you what you can do to help make it happen."

Lars pointed to the officer. "The captain of your guards has told you of my force of trainees standing in the square with baskets of oak seedlings, only twelve hundred of them so far, and of the maneuvers they've been practicing to draw attention to the seedlings. They are twenty-four of the thirty people chosen to become dragon riders." He held up his hand to prevent an outburst from the Head Leafer.

Lars, like Nagora, must have had an eye on Kiviran, watching for his reaction. The movement of his head and eyes showed the Head Leafer's alarm at the words Lars had spoken.

"King Raynhard, I want to assure you, these trainees, like me, have seen the light and heard the message of the Community of the Leaf. They, like me, no longer want to live their lives in servitude to the dragons of the maze. They have followed me here of their own free will. I assure you: We have all deserted the dragons."

Is Kiviran buying Lars's words? If his eyes were hot coals, they would burn right into him. Lars placed a hand over the embroidered symbol on his vest, looked to the ceiling, and closed his eyes. "We solemnly hope when word of our desertion gets back to Maze Point, the sixty others who enrolled to become dragon riders will come and join us. We hope they too will not want to risk their future lives by living in servitude to the dragons of the maze."

Lars held up both hands, palms out to Raynhard. "Please, allow me to say this: It is no secret, even in the Land of Skulls, that a champion dragon slayer hired by the Community of the Leaf heads to these shores. Word is he is the biggest, strongest armored knight to have ever lived, and he comes with his unique dragon-killing lance."

"The people of Maze Point do not want to be caught between the dragons and the giant in the bloody battle they know will come. The trainees either. They signed up to be trained as dragon riders who would patrol coastal and inland trade routes to deter outlaws and pirates, not fight giants."

Lars paused and pointed to Raynhard. "I see a major problem and a major benefit to the giant coming here. The major problem will be the amount of dragon blood the giant will shed when he kills the dragons. Think how precious every drop of dragon blood is to the Community of the Leaf. Think of all its members, old and new, who will clamor for their share."

He looked each of the old men in the eye. "Aye! I think you see my point. I'm sure you've already thought of it. Dragon blood will have its price, won't it? How will you decide it? In what quantity will you sell it? Will the supply be limited or unlimited? How can you ensure an unlimited supply? I have the answer to that last question."

Kiviran looked to Raynhard and then back to Lars. "What major benefit will the giant bring?"

Lars took a deep breath as he stared at Kiviran. "He'll be the deciding factor to make Nagora surrender her dragons to slaughter." He raised a hand. "But not to any slaughter, especially a bloody one by the giant. He'll cause her to surrender the dragons on her terms, meaning she'll decide who will kill them, how they'll be killed, and when. She's been told," he turned his gaze to Raynhard, "that the Community of the Leaf wants her to become their dispenser of the blood of dragons."

My man, do you truly think their greed for gold will make them buy that possibility?

Lars looked at the floor and made a motion with his boot, as if he were crushing a spider. "Honestly, I don't see her accepting that position." He looked at the king. "Raynhard, I'm willing to bet you don't, either. She would rather die than dispense the blood of her dragons. That's where the giant comes in. If he can kill dragons, he can surely kill Nagora, the Dragon Talker. All it will take is for him to challenge her."

My man, how well you use the words they preach to your own ends.

Raynhard's eyes blinked as he bowed his head.

Nagora wondered if the king was trying to hold back tears.

Lars stepped to the table to take hold of his leather tube. Trowan picked up one of the glass bars as he pulled the plans from his tube and set them on the table.

"Wait!" It was Kiviran, as he and Raynhard were on their way to the table. "You seem certain that's how the Dragon Talker will act."

Lars held up his hand with fingers spread. He pointed to each finger in turn, as he stated his arguments. "When the others who signed on for training as dragon riders desert and join me, when the people of Maze Point realize their personal security will be compromised if the giant shows up, when those people stop working to feed the dragons and leave Maze Point, and when my son, Dannor, comes to join me."

This last phrase about her son took Nagora by surprise.

"And when Nagora and Sarah realize they can no longer care for the dragons by themselves," his fingers had folded into his palm to form a fist. Lars slammed it on the table.

Then, with greater force, he struck the table with his other fist. "When Nagora learns the giant has the map to the maze, I promise you, that's when Nagora will surrender her dragons!"

Lars leaned on both fists as he stared into the Head Leafer's eyes. "I'm certain my son will join me. His sister will too. That's why he is not with me today. He's still trying to convince Sarah it's the right thing to do, the safe thing to do."

He stood straight and took a deep breath. "Nagora is a Dragon Talker. Danuka, the mother dragon, chose Nagora at birth to serve and protect her. Nagora is a lone wolf warrior." He waved a hand. "On her own, she cannot protect and care for fifteen dragons. She can't hide them in the maze forever. The Dragon Talker knows eventually the giant will come, most likely armed with ballistae, to strike the dragons from the sky. Nagora fears the giant knight in armor with his drag-on-killing lance!"

Lars crossed his arms. "What choice is she left with?"

He looked from the Head Leafer to the king. "One, to fight for the dragons. If she makes that choice, she knows it will be a fight to the death. Not only of her dragons, but her own death.

"Two, to surrender her dragons to slaughter. If she makes that choice, she knows she could survive, but not as a dispenser of dragon blood."

Lars uncrossed his arms. "I think she'll surrender the dragons, but she will come to discuss the terms of their surrender."

He held up a thumb. "She'll want to choose the day. We can give her that."

Then his index finger went up. "She might want to choose the place. We won't give her that. If she brings it up, we won't even discuss it. The battleground has to be to the giant's advantage."

He showed his third finger. "Knowing her, she'll want to have a say in the kill. I will not be surprised if she wants the first kill. She'll want to kill Danuka first, gently, with a dagger to the mother dragon's heart. If we don't give her that, there's no telling what she might do."

Lars looked at his three digits and then let his hand drop to his side. "She might want to discuss other terms. What they could be, I don't know."

Raynhard looked from Lars to Kiviran. "We'll let her come to us. There is no rush when we can have her on our terms in our land. To go to the maze overland would be a waste of time, energy, and resources. Would Godomor the Terrible allow us into the Land of Skulls? That would require lengthy negotiations, even if Nagora were to choose to fight for the dragons there. Our champion, the threat to her dragons, will be here. If she chooses to fight, she must come to him."

Raynhard scratched his bearded chin as if reconsidering what he had just said. "Then again, while she decides, we'll negotiate with King Godomor for safe passage to Maze Point. Skull Bay is the nearest port. We'll get his permission to allow the giant to land there with his fleet. Our aim will be to attack the maze, to kill the dragons. No harm will come to the citizens of the Land of Skulls, and their coffers will be fuller with the gold we'll offer in compensation."

Now you too, Raynhard, are getting in on the act, taking your lead from Lars. Godomor will never allow that unless it's to our advantage. Lars, you must explain to Godomor how we'll fight the giant in the maze, if it comes to that.

The king spread his arms and raised his hands. "Either way, she'll have no choice but to surrender the dragons. If she does so without a fight, I will make her my queen again!" He lowered his arms. "How I look forward to that day!"

You know I would never betray my dragons for a throne next to yours. Are your words a ruse? If they are, they might make it possible for me to speak to you in private.

The Head Leafer bowed to the king. "Good fortune has brought these messengers to us this day." Kiviran turned to Lars and bowed to him and Trowan.

They returned his bow.

Good, Lars, it looks like you've bought us more time. We know where we'll do battle. I have to think with care on the terms I want.

"Now show us your plans," said Kiviran.

Lars unrolled the vellum page. Trowan took hold of an edge and placed a glass bar near one corner and then the other. Lars placed the glass bars on the other corners. He set the tube on the floor beneath the table.

The king and Head Leafer stared at the page as Lars pointed. "As you can see, these are tripods three times as tall as the spire on your Assembly Hall of the Community of the Leaf. They are equipped with a system of pulleys, ropes, poles, and hooks. I call them butchering stations. After the giant kills a dragon, we'll suspend it from the hooks on that pole and raise it to the apex of the tripod.

"Then we'll bleed the dragon, collect its blood, and transfer it to secure containers for storage and transport.

"Next we'll skin the dragon before butchering it for its meat and organs."

Lars stood straight and looked over at the old men. "Later, you'll want to come and have a look at the plans. I'm sure your king and the Head Leafer are now considering the logistics of setting up such an operation. Not only that, but the profit they can make from the sale of items made from dragon skin, not to mention the talismanic and medicinal value of the dragon organs and other body parts. Imagine the fortune to be made there! Some of those organs just might have anti-aging properties. Wouldn't that be a boon for you good men?"

For the first time, they were talking amongst themselves. Nagora could imagine the lecherous thoughts of these greedy coots who'd been eyeing Trowan since they sat, especially the one who played with the clasp of his medallion, hooking and unhooking the S-hook to the O-loop on the chain.

Lars now looked to Raynhard as he pointed to the page. "Obviously, this is where you can help. You can quickly put together the laborers and the resources to make this happen. My trainees and I will help, but only if there's something in it for us."

"What do you want besides gold?" asked Kiviran.

"Land for the oak forest we will plant to harvest our share of dragon gold from the ground."

Kiviran looked at Lars. "You said it would be the biggest, best-tended oak forest in the Land of the Danu. Where, exactly, will you plant those seedlings of yours?"

"Not only those we have brought, but the thousands more that will come here for us to plant. We'll plant them on the plain opposite to what was once the Isle of Smoke. Think about it."

Lars pointed to the plans again. "What better place to set up a battleground for the giant and his force, along with the space to set up the tripods nearby to collect the blood of freshly killed dragons?

"Imagine the crowds such a spectacle will draw. How many among them will pay to be closer to the action and witness the slaughter with their own eyes? The giant could stretch this out for days. You could sell cooked dragon meat on the site.

"If you take the time to set it up properly, it will make your Majesty richer than you can imagine. It'll be a once-in-a-lifetime event people will not want to miss. Do you want to miss such an opportunity?"

Lars pointed to himself and Trowan. "All we want is the land and the first of the fresh dragon blood for our oaks."

Raynhard looked from Kiviran to Lars. "How can we get an unlimited supply of blood?"

Lars smiled. "I was waiting for you to ask. Part of the answer is inside this tube. As you most likely suspect, it is the map of the maze. For all I know, by now Nagora has discovered that it is missing. Not that she or the other Dragon Talkers need it to navigate the maze. However, should the giant ever need it, you will have it as a backup plan provided you pay me for it. And if you pay me, I can provide you with the other part."

"What is the other part?" asked Kiviran.

"You'll need two dragons, one male and one female, to produce eggs that will hatch to create other eggs, like chickens in a coop. The maze will be the coop. My son, Dannor, and the king's daughter, Sarah, both Dragon Talkers, will manage the flock, so to speak, and sell you the dragons for their blood, and for all those other items I mentioned earlier. The Community of the Leaf will have an extra line of business."

Raynhard was shaking his head. "But the dragons will not accept that."

My king, you're right about that! Neither would Dannor, nor Sarah!

"They will, as soon as the mother dragon is out of the way. The dragons are young. My son and your daughter can train them for this. The young male has bonded with my son. Its sister has bonded with Sarah. Both dragons are ripe for this opportunity. My son and your daughter will grow rich doing this. And so will the Community of the Leaf. Send thirteen to slaughter and keep two in the maze for an unlimited supply. With Dannor and Sarah, the breeding couple will be safe in the maze. No one else will get to them without the map."

Lars pointed to the tube. "It's in the interest of the Community of the Leaf to buy the map and hold it in a secure place in the unlikely event it is ever needed."

"Nagora would never allow her son and daughter to do that," said Raynhard.

You're right on that, over my dead body.

"True," said Lars, "if she's alive. However, if she dies in a valiant fight against the giant, her children will definitely mourn her passing. Afterward, they'll be grateful to have a dragon couple to manage, rather than see all the dragons killed. For them and for you, it will be a win-win situation. They'll grow rich, and the Community of the Leaf will have an unlimited supply of dragon blood to satisfy the demand and not end up with a revolt on your hands."

That would be a sad star story for my son and daughter. May this never come to pass.

Trowan picked up the tube and pointed to it. "The map to the maze is here. Do not play us for fools. If you harm us or prevent our free movement in the land," she pointed to Lars and continued to speak with slow assurance, "his son will poison all the dragons and send them to die in the sea. You will have no dragon blood. That is the blood pact this father has made with his son. I am witness to their pact. If you not want to buy the map, we have another who will."

The old horse trader's trick to get the buyer to ask to see the animal and then make them an offer they think they can't refuse.

"It's your call," said Lars, as he looked from the king to the Head Leafer.

Kiviran turned to look at the old men. They were nodding.

He faced Trowan and pointed at the tube. "Show me the map."

She held the open end toward Lars, who pulled it from the tube and placed it on the table.

Kiviran helped Lars place the glass bars on the corners of the map. He leaned over it, studying it. "There are so many twists and turns. How do I know it's the real map?"

Lars shrugged. "You must take it on my word. I drew it up with Nagora's help. I warn you though, it's magical. Don't draw on it, whatever you do. Make a copy to draw on. I'll give you a hint. Start from the middle and work your way out. Once you've made it out, the first few times you won't be able to make it back in. Be patient. It requires study, but I assure you, you'll get it. Won't he, Trowan?"

She nodded and placed her index finger in the middle and, with many twists and turns that took her back closer to the center several times; her pointer finally came to rest outside of one of the four maze entrances. Trowan then held Kiviran's gaze with her expressionless face.

Ha, the bugger will never admit he can't do what she just did.

"Like I said, it requires study. Trowan has spent many counts with the map."

"What's your price?" asked Raynhard.

Lars did not hesitate. "Three thousand gold dragons, delivered three days from today when we deliver the map."

Trowan rolled up the map and put it back in the tube, leaving the tripod plans on the table. "My family and my friends from the Land of Skulls, warriors like me, will escort us when we deliver the map. Prepare the payment coins so we see them all and tally them fast. I warn you again. No foul play or you will never see a drop of dragon blood," said Trowan.

Warriors from the Land of Skulls. That's an interesting detail that might come in handy. They must be camped separate from the trainees, waiting to join them if the payment happens.

...

The sound of footsteps rushing into the throne room from the side entrance caught not only Nagora's attention, but that of the others in the room. A soldier led a young Leafer to the officer and whispered in his ear. The officer whispered a reply and pointed toward the Leaf Room of Light.

Straight away, the soldier led the Leafer past the throne to the room. The Leafer stepped inside. The soldier stood next to the door.

In the meantime, the officer strode over to the king. After speaking to Raynhard in a hushed voice and bowing to the Head Leafer, he returned to where he had been standing.

Raynhard looked to Lars. "If you'll excuse us for a count, we have urgent business to deal with. It should not take us long."

Nagora didn't hesitate. She followed Raynhard and Kiviran to the adjoining room. There was a sense of urgency in their stride.

Nagora made it past the door before the soldier pulled it closed. She noticed the big key was in the door lock. The last time she had seen it was when she held it in her hand. It weighed as much as a Stone Stander war stone. She had locked the door and taken the key from the lock so the child witch, Alizarine, couldn't escape the maps room. Then, as today, the pyramid-shaped skylight of clear, leaded glass panes, three floor levels above her head, formed most of the room's ceiling. Nagora had hurled the key with all her might so it broke through a pane and fell on the roof. Alizarine couldn't get her hands on it.

Raynhard and Kiviran stood side by side, facing the slim messenger. He held his silver-leaf medallion as he spoke.

"Twelve of Golgotha's ships have anchored in the bay. He sent a message ashore. He wants the wharf free of trader vessels so his can dock tomorrow morning at first light."

The messenger ran a hand over the close-cropped hair of his head before continuing. "Leafer Lanken, along with the harbormaster, issued the order to free the harbor docks, but the traders tied up there refuse to move unless we pay them now. And because this order comes on such brief notice, they are asking for double the agreed-upon amount to move their vessels today. Then they will accept the daily amount after Golgotha's ships leave."

The messenger bowed to Kiviran. "Leafer Lanken wants to know what we should do."

Raynhard looked to Kiviran, who crossed his arms and gave his orders. "Tell Lanken to calculate the total payment needed today to meet the traders' demands. Tell him he is to return with the number in his book of notes. Then we'll prepare the coins and an escort for him to bring the payment to the traders. Also remind him he is to note proof of this double payment in their ship logs and his book of notes upon paying the traders. Without such notes, we will make no further payments."

The messenger stood with the palms of his hands pressed together and his index fingers resting on his chin. The slight movement of his lips suggested he was reciting Kiviran's instructions so as not to forget them.

Kiviran looked to Raynhard. "Do we have any other choice?"

The king cast his eyes to the floor for a moment and shook his head. "No." He looked back at the Head Leafer. "Our champion must come ashore as soon as possible."

Kiviran bowed his head and returned his gaze to the messenger. "Repeat my instructions."

The Leafer clasped his hands together and repeated the instructions.

"Very well. Go now! Run!"

As soon as he left the room, Kiviran turned to Raynhard. "Not a word of this out there. When Lanken comes for the coins, we'll make sure his book of notes is in order and that he understands how to follow my instructions to the letter. If I have the slightest doubt, I'll go to the traders myself."

Nagora returned to her position near Trowan at the table. The leather tube with the map of the maze hung from her shoulder.

When Raynhard and Kiviran returned to the table, Lars bowed. "I have a question."

"Speak it," said the king.

"When will the giant arrive?"

Raynhard looked to Kiviran, and then to Lars. "Any day now. Why do you ask?"

Lars pointed to the plans on the table. "We are assuming you will consult the giant on the choice of the battlefield we proposed. If he is agreeable to the place, and expresses how he wants to set up his encampment, we expect you will have a team of surveyors and builders bring the tools and labor to stake out what goes where on the plain. We realize it is a lot of planning. Still, we would like to be informed so we can plant our seedlings away from the event activities. Also, as stated earlier, if you would like our help, we are pleased to offer it."

Raynhard pointed to Lars. "If I were to put you in charge of this project, what would you need beyond our champion's consent, his encampment requirements, and his notion of the ideal battlefield?"

Lars crossed his arms and leaned his head to one side. He seemed to make quick calculations. "Ideally, I would need a detailed plan with dimensions of what your champion wants. Then I'd need a team of surveyors and wagons for their measuring chains, axes, pickets, ropes and other instruments.

"It's almost a day's travel there with wagons. Then there's deciding on the encampment site; measuring and staking it out; plotting the battlefield and butchering area; building viewing stands and the tripods; and establishing access points to the site to control the crowds." He paused and nodded, as if confirming his thinking to himself. "If the weather is favorable and everyone works hard, I say we have at least five days of work there, and another to return here. That's a minimum of seven days. If you send cooks and a few extra attendants to take care of us, we might do it in that time."

Raynhard looked to the Head Leafer.

Kiviran nodded.

Raynhard looked back to Lars with a smile on his face. "A campaign kitchen unit will go with you. They'll bring food and water and feed for the horses. You have thirty-two mounts?"

"Aye, and eight mules," said Trowan.

"If we have time to consult with the giant before you come to deliver the map, we'll let you know where we are in our planning, and if our people want your help. You seem to know how you'd get the job done. In the meantime, if you wish to plant on the periphery of the plain, you may do so. Any other questions?"

Lars and Trowan bowed. "Thank you for receiving us to-day," said Lars. "We have no further questions."

Kiviran returned to the group of old men and led them back to the maps room. Raynhard picked up the plans from the table and followed them.

The officer gave a signal with his hand. The soldiers of the escort turned to march to the side door of the throne room.

Can I make it back to Olen's before they do?

As soon as Nagora made it into the hallway, she ran to the door that led into the courtyard. She opened it a crack to peek out. Two guards paced in the courtyard below the steps. She slipped out and closed the door.

Down the steps and past the guards to the gate, she found the door ajar. On the other side, half a dozen paces away, an officer and two armed soldiers stood watching the maneuvers of the trainees with their seedlings. She had no problem getting past them. Instead of crossing the bridge into the square, she stayed on the way along the moat that took her to the stable.

From there, she ran across the drawbridge and onto Stables Way, which was not crowded.

Nagora stepped through Olen's forge door and then through the door leading to the stable. She rushed to her saddlebags to take out her scrip and her clothes before wishing the armor to make her visible.

...

Nagora crossed the inner courtyard, knocked on Olen's door, and opened it. "Olen! I'm back!"

He came out of his room. "You left early this morning. They must have gotten in. Are they on their way back?"

Nagora shook her head. "I saw them go in. Then I watched the trainees practice maneuvers, but tired of that. It held the attention of Leafers passing by. I figured they'd be coming back soon, and I felt naked without my weapons. They're in my room. I'll go get them."

Olen sat at his table. "When you come back down, I have news for you."

"Well, what's the news?" asked Nagora as she hung her quiver and blade holsters on the hook near the door.

When she sat, Olen said, "The ships of the champion dragon slayer dropped anchor in the harbor this morning."

"Oh! That's what people were talking about. Not everyone, mind you, but I noticed people pointing in the harbor's direction when stopping to talk to others. I wasn't near enough to make out what they said. After Lars stops by, I'll ride down to visit Pare to see if I can learn more about this champion."

Olen leaned back in his chair. "Word is he's a giant."

Just then, the door opened after a brief knock. "Olen! Nagora! Trowan is with the trainees outside," said Lars.

"You got in! Good for you!" said Olen.

Lars smiled. "Aye, and it went better than I thought. Olen, if you'll excuse me, I'll ask Nagora to come with me. I don't want my riders blocking the way any longer than they have to."

Olen waved Nagora over to Lars. "Give him the news I gave you in case he hasn't heard."

"I will." She put on her weapons and left with Lars.

Outside, Lars turned to Nagora. "I'll be going to Dromester on my own to meet with Bardas. Are you coming with me?"

She shook her head and explained the giant's ships had arrived in the morning, and she was on her way to Paruline's to learn more about him. "You seem happy about the meeting. I know you're in a hurry. Without giving me all the details, just tell me what will help our plans."

He placed his hands on her arms. "Nagora, we've got more time to plan. You can set the date when you surrender the dragons. And they've accepted my idea to plant oaks on the plain opposite the Isle of Smoke. That's where the champion and you will slaughter the dragons."

She didn't like that he used those words and let her face show it.

He waved a hand in dismissal. "You know what I mean. Soon as the king meets with the giant to get the details of his camp set up, we stand a good chance of working with the king's surveyors to plot the giant's encampment and battlefield. We'll be away at least seven days if we go."

He tapped the tube tied to his scabbard. "We'll be getting three thousand gold dragons for the map."

She smiled and hugged him. "Just having extra time will make all the difference. I don't think I'll be able to see you until you've returned from surveying. When I do, I'll most likely have lots more news for you."

...

Trowan stepped into the courtyard from the stable. She smiled. "He tell you the news?"

Nagora nodded. "Did you like the throne room?"

Trowan held up an arm and waved it in a slow circle. "Tall windows, beautiful, many colors!"

Then she looked to Lars. "Wagons waiting to pass."

Nagora walked with them until Bonnie's stall. "Be safe. Both of you."

Trowan smiled. "I watch him for you."

I believe you will.

Lars kissed Nagora's cheek. "You too." He looked her in the eye. "Find out as much as you can about the giant."

"I will."

Enemy Arrival
Nôtinâkan Takosin

Nagora found Harbor Way even busier than two days earlier. Walking Bonnie to the stable was slow going. She noticed crews on the trader boats were readying to leave their berths at the wharf. Most had their skiffs on deck to bay side. Their oars were tied to the seats, and they each carried a big coil of tow line. Sailors had tied one end of the line to the boat's bow and the other to the skiff's stout transom post.

Skiff and dock crews would work together to pivot a boat's bow away from the wharf. If there was no wind, the skiff would haul the boat to an anchorage in the bay. If the wind were favorable, a portion of hoisted sail could help the boat ghost to its new location on a mooring.

Close to the stables was the harbormaster's building. Benches had been set out in front of it. Nagora counted six men on the benches with books resting on their laps. The Leafer who had brought the news of the giant's arrival stood on the top step of the landing in front of the harbormaster's entrance. He was looking along Harbor Way.

He must be waiting for Leafer Lanken to arrive with the promised payment.

Nagora walked into the Konen Brothers' shop just as a customer was leaving. When Matti saw her, he rushed to her. "Pare and Harri aren't here right now. I'm sure they won't mind if you wait for them. I don't know how long they'll be gone."

She pointed to the stairs leading up to the storage area. "Do you think they would mind if I wait up there? I'd like to open the window and watch the harbor-side activity."

"Not at all!" He touched her arm. "You picked a good day. Did you hear who arrived?"

She nodded.

"His boat is the one with all the flags flying. We can't make them out from here, but according to a fisher, they're flags of the dragons he killed."

That sent a chill down Nagora's back. He's a proud executioner.

"Go on up. Make yourself at home. You'll find a ship's hammock up in the corner by the window. There are at least three sets of hooks to hang it from. Choose the one that gives you the best view."

"Thanks, Matti. I'll do that."

"Oh! And if you're hungry, you know where the kitchen is. I had an early meal. Harri said they would eat at the Harbor Way Inn."

Nagora smiled at him. "Thanks again."

• • •

After opening the wooden shutters, Nagora stood back out of view and removed her weapons. She strung her bow, checked the string and along the bow shaft. Satisfied they were in good working condition, she unstrung her bow.

Then she pulled three arrows from her quiver. She chose the sharpest broad-tipped hunting arrow. Her uncle Dangor had long ago taught her such an arrow would most likely not penetrate metal armor nor even good quality leather armor backed with layers of woven linen.

Her uncle said that an arrow with a long, narrow, three-sided, hardened-metal tip that tapered to a point would do the job, and only if shot with a powerful war bow. The armory only issued such bows and arrows to the king's biggest and strongest archers when needed. She had neither a war bow, nor the required arrows.

Those bows were taller than the archers, and the arrows were almost double the length of a hunting arrow. She wouldn't have the draw length nor the strength to loose one like that. Hers was a hunting bow. The broad-tipped arrow she held would penetrate living animal hide or human flesh.

Nagora replaced the other two and then examined the feathers of the sharpest one. Satisfied she would remember it, she set it so it rested on the other arrows in her quiver. She leaned her quiver in the corner below the hammock, along with her sheathed skystone blade. Who knows what tomorrow brings?

Happy with the hooks from which she had hung the hammock, Nagora settled into it. With the heavy woven linen canvas wrapped around her, she grabbed two of the ropes strung through the riveted eyelets along that end of the canvas and pulled to adjust her position. Now she could look out into the bay at the giant's ship in the distance with its many flags flying.

Voices yelling orders, the sound of a splash, and more orders being yelled woke Nagora. A blanket covered her. The daylight outside told her she must have slept for most of the afternoon. Who covered me? Pare? She would do that. Where's the giant's ship?

After struggling out of the hammock, Nagora took the stairs down and hurried through the shop to the latrine next to the kitchen door. She closed the door and sat just in time.

Nagora found Paruline in the kitchen. Bread was baking, and her dear friend was stirring a pot that hung over the coals at the other end of the grate in the fireplace. "I'm awake."

Paruline looked over her shoulder. "That you are! I wondered how long you would sleep." She brought the long wooden spoon to her lips and tasted. "I think you'll like this."

"I smell lamb stew," said Nagora.

Paruline dipped her spoon into the pot again and brought it to Nagora. "Tell me if you think it's ready."

She licked the spoon, cleaning off every drop of sauce. "Pare, it's ready, and I'm starving! I haven't eaten since last night."

Paruline took back her spoon. "Soon as the bread has finished baking, we'll eat."

She pointed to the shelf with the bowls and plates. "Set the table for two. Harri's somewhere along Harbor Way, keeping his eye on all the activity. His scrip is full of scrolls that have our shop's name on them, just like our shop sign. Traders look for those things. He figures we'll see business from the giant's boats."

Paruline filled a kettle with water and hung it in place of the pot with the stew. She sat the pot on the fireplace floor next to the grate and then placed two small logs on the coals beneath the kettle.

Paruline pointed to a chair. "Sit. I know why you've come back today. Tell me what you've been up to."

After Nagora told Paruline what she had learned about Lars's audience with the king, and they had eaten, Harri burst into the kitchen. "Guess whose ship is about to dock out front! Oh! Hello, Nagora. Not exactly in front, but," he made a motion to the left with both his hands, "that way. Its back end will be in front of us, our shop, and the rest that way."

Paruline was smiling at him. "I'll guess. The giant's ship?"

Harri rubbed his hands together and pointed at her with a broad grin on his face. "You, my lady, have guessed correctly! Come! Come see!"

With arms crossed and an intense look on his face, Matti stood on the landing just outside the shop door. He hardly took notice of them as they too looked to their right in the direction of the giant's ship. "That will most likely be the biggest ship to dock here ever."

Harri pointed to the edge of the wharf. "That's what the harbormaster thinks too. The water along the wharf here is the deepest. Though, he won't guarantee the Gethsemane won't touch bottom come low tide tomorrow morning."

Nagora counted the flags. Fifty-nine. Where did he kill all those dragons? Why? Are Leafers in other lands wanting dragon blood? I don't see the sense in that. What do I know? I'm only a Dragon Talker. Maybe Danuka will have answers after the Dark Twins transmit the knowledge of dragons past, present, and future.

The Gethsemane was still too far away for Nagora to make out the details on the flags fluttering in the wind. When it's closer.

The ship was riding on an anchor rode from its stern. An eight-man crew rowed a skiff hauling a light line toward the wharf. It was most likely tied to a much heavier docking line at the boat's stern.

Wharf hands, under the supervision of the harbormaster, waited alongside the wharf's mooring posts. Some held gaff hooks at the ready to retrieve heaved lines that might fall short.

A second skiff, towing a light line from the ship's bow started in the dock's direction. A crew member of the skiff heaved the light lead line ashore. The stern line from the other skiff followed moments later.

Dockhands pulled the lead lines to bring the boat's bigger docking lines ashore. The ship's crew then began the slow process of raising and dropping anchor as they paid out on the docking lines. At the same time, dockhands hauled on the docking lines to control the ship's approach to its berth at the wharf.

Along the dock, as the few remaining trader ships left their berths, skiffs from the giant's other ships maneuvered to deliver lead lines.

Harri pointed. "They're not all as big as the giant's. At this rate, it'll be well into night by the time they're all docked. Whoever or whatever is coming off the giant's boat will have to do so at low tide. Even then, any ramp they put to shore will be steep."

"They've probably done it many times before. I can't imagine the giant killed all those dragons in one country," said Matti.

As wharf hands pulled the giant's ship closer, Nagora could make out details on the flags. Often they showed the armored giant on his horse, hooves rearing over a bleeding dragon trans-pierced with the lance. Each standard had three words embroidered beneath the gold-colored leaf at the bottom of each scene. The words, in another language, meant nothing to her.

Those dragons are all small. I see none the size of Danuka. Those images can't be to scale. They're made to exaggerate the giant's ability to kill.

The Gethsemane had just dropped a stern anchor. Its crew and the dockhands worked the docking lines to pivot the boat, bringing its side to the dock.

Nagora touched Paruline's arm. "I'll watch from the window above."

Paruline made a sign for her to wait, and then spoke into Harri's ear. He nodded. Then she nodded to Nagora and followed her.

Up in the storage area, Paruline took Nagora's arm. "Come with me. There's an empty crate over there. We'll load it into our sky wagon and pull it over to the window. Then we'll have something to sit on as we watch."

With the hammock out of the way and the crate set near the edge of the sill of the stock window, Nagora and Paruline watched the big ship's final approach. Crew members had hung big bundles of heavy woven cords to cushion the side of the ship against the wharf timbers.

Even from her new vantage point, Nagora couldn't see the ship's deck, so high were its sides. From what she could see, none of the crew was of extraordinary size. Where is the giant? Is he not curious about the next place where he will slay dragons? Or does he stay out of sight because he is vulnerable without his armor?

What if I snuck on board in the dead of night, invisible to those on watch? I could strike him a fatal blow in his sleep with a weapon I find at hand. Then another thought occurred to Nagora. Perhaps he's not on this vessel. It could be a lure to protect him from such an attack.

Once dockhands had secured the vessel to the liking of the harbormaster, Paruline stood. "I've seen enough. If you want to stay and watch, do so. I will make fresh tea."

"I'll join you soon."

With evening's approach, the wind was dying. One of the last flags Nagora glimpsed was of the giant holding a bloody sword with two hands. One of his armored feet rested on the dead dragon's neck, and the other stood next to the dragon's severed head. The blade of that sword would have to be more than sharp to off Danuka's head.

Nagora wondered if the scenes on those flags were nothing but unreal depictions of slayings that never happened. Were they from made-up stories like the unproven promises of rewards the Leafers told? Show me the dragon's severed head, and I might believe such a story.

Nagora leaned out the window for a last look both ways along Harbor Way. She counted seven boats that had berthed. Harri was right. It'll be night by the time they're all secured at the wharf.

Nagora was sipping from her second bowl of tea when Harri came into the kitchen.

Paruline looked up at him. "Have you learned anything new?"

He rubbed his eyes and yawned. "Aye, I have. For one thing, the ships have to dock in a specific order. That has slowed down the process."

He placed his hands on the table to ease his backside onto his chair. "Tomorrow morning, we will see a procession of all the giant's attendants and servants, musicians, jugglers, and flag bearers set up on Harbor Way."

Harri turned to Paruline. "Apparently he has his own traveling kitchen, stable, and two smiths: one for his horses, the other for his armor and weapons. Oh! And his own chicken coop. And he has his own tent, a big one, and his own personal guards. Along with the tents for all the others who travel with him wherever he goes."

"Where will they go?" asked Paruline.

"From what I heard, they'll be marching all together up to Castle Square where they'll set up camp," said Harri.

Nagora tried to imagine that. "They'll be taking over the square and spilling out of it if there are that many setting up tents."

Harri shrugged. "Again, from what I overheard, they have a specific setup they need to respect. You're right, Nagora.

Most won't fit into the square. I mean, life around the castle still has to go on."

He shook his head. "Maybe the giant can pitch his big tent in the castle courtyard. Someone said he doesn't like to stoop to go through doorways, so if he sets up there, they'll have to raise the gate."

Paruline laughed. "The moat will stink something awful if it's used as a latrine by all those people. Or do they have that figured out too?"

Harri smiled. "Well, you know how it is. Guests send all the information about their needs, but when they show up, they have more than you planned for. You have no choice but to adapt. That's what they'll be doing at the castle tonight, changing their plans to adapt to the reality of the giant's visit, depending on how long he and his retinue stay."

Nagora winked at Paruline. Looks like for a week at least. I'll let her tell Harri.

Harri stood up and placed his hands on his lower back. "It's been a long day standing on my legs. I'm off to bed. Good night, ladies."

"I'll join you soon," said Paruline. She looked to Nagora. "The cot near the fireplace, or the hammock?"

Nagora smiled. "I slept a good part of the afternoon. Give me another blanket and I'll sleep in the hammock."

"Do you want a lantern?"

"No, my eyes will adjust, and I imagine with all the activity going on, there'll be more than Harbor Way lamps lit."

"I'll give you one, anyway, just in case. If you have to come down, I don't want you to take a tumble in the dark on those stairs."

...

Nagora's night vigil yielded two things.

First, she received a visit from the Little People. For a moment, the lantern she had hung from one of the hammock hooks lit and then died as a voice whispered to her. "Tomorrow, three counts after nightfall, Danuka will meet you in the field near Dromester, where she had left you. Be there."

"Thank you, *Mêmêkwêsiw*." She wanted to ask a question, but had the impression they would not answer.

Second, she slept a sound night until dawn. When she awoke, it was low tide, and the preparations were underway to offload the docked vessels.

Nagora made a quick trip to the latrine and then returned to her window.

With the low tide, the deck of the giant's ship was visible. Crew members were untying the hold-down lines covering the cargo hold. Twelve men on two sides of the cover slid it open.

A huge metal hook hung from a series of ropes and pulleys and was attached to a chain strung between the two masts above the hold. A team of crew members lowered the hook into the hold. Another group of men joined them.

When the man watching the hold gave the signal, the two teams began hauling on the stout rope. A cage with an opening on one side emerged from the hold. A wooden ramp with cross pieces nailed to it leaned out of the cage. Four separate planks rested on top of the ramp.

When the cage was above the edge of the hold, a deckhand jumped inside the cage next to the ramp. From there, he pulled and fed the planks one by one to the two deckhands waiting to grab hold of them. The men positioned each plank diagonally across a corner of the hold in the space beneath the cage.

When the hold watcher gave the signal, the teams lowered the cage onto the planks, supporting it above the hold.

Then four deckhands, two on each side of the ramp, slid the rest of it out of the cage opening.

With the help of four more men, the group carried the ramp to the edge of the ship's offloading rail.

There, dockhands on shore waited to take hold of the shore end of the ramp. That done, the deckhands positioned the ramp, hooking it in place, and securing it with rope.

Meanwhile, other deckhands had hoisted the cage once more, slid aside the corner planks and lowered the cage back into the hold.

When the teams pulled the cage up again, a saddled horse dressed in an armor of leather and metal stood inside it. Holding its bridle, reins, and a coil of rope, a groom stood beside the horse. The leather armor made up most of the skirt that hung around the animal to just below its knees. A molded metal plate covered its forehead from between its eyes to its nostrils. Three others covered the back of its neck and one on each side of its rump.

The groom's hand that held the bridle was well above his head, leaving only a slight bend in his arm. Nagora guessed the horse to be over twenty hands tall. Until now, she had never seen a horse that tall, so powerfully built, and with such huge hooves.

Once the planks were in place and the cage lowered onto them, the groom led the horse out.

...

The groom stood at the edge of the ramp and waited. Two more young men, dressed like him and with coils of rope slung over their shoulders, came running across the deck. From each side of the horse, they tied a rope end to the upright hand-hold loop at the front of the saddle. When they finished, they backed away, ready to follow the horse down the ramp.

The lead groom stepped onto the steep ramp. He patted the horse's neck and appeared to speak to it while he coaxed the horse to place its hooves on the plank's first cross member, and then onto the next. Finally, with its four hooves in place on the ramp, the horse followed the groom down to the dock. The two with ropes followed.

The lead groom placed a treat in the horse's mouth.

Next out of the hold came a platform with four steps attached. Deckhands brought it down the ramp and placed it near the horse.

By the time they had climbed back on deck, the teams were raising the same cage again. A full-faced, shiny metal helmet with black and red plumes sticking up from its top appeared first. The helm had a single finger-width eye-slit from one side to the other.

I can't imagine how he can see through that opening.

Another slit, half as long and the same width, was at mouth level.

Tar piss! What caught Nagora's eye dismayed her. Attached to the bottom of the helm was a collar of dragon teeth, pointing outward and down.

Then the rest of the giant in his full body armor came into view. Another single line of dragon teeth ran across his upper chest from one shoulder to the other.

The bastard wears his trophies!

Tar piss! He will have to stoop like his horse did to walk out of the cage.

Two men, dressed in red and black, stood one to a side of the giant. The tops of their heads were at the height of the giant's elbows. One man held a heavy lance at his side. The blade's tip resembled in shape and in length that of a long sword, but with a finer point. His dragon-killing lance! The other man held a sword in its scabbard.

Tar piss! It's way bigger than Lars's!

Twelve soldiers, dressed in black and red leather armor with matching helmets, marched along the deck with swords and spears in hand. There must be a door I can't see on that side.

Then twelve archers followed, dressed in black and red garb with jackets of what Nagora guessed to be quilted layers of linen. Their quivers were made of leather, stained black and red. After they filed down the ramp, they took up defensive positions around the horse. The archers each nocked an arrow, while the other soldiers held their spears and swords at the ready.

After the deckhand team had set the cage back onto the planks, the aides bearing the giant's weapons handed them off to two waiting deckhands. They carried the weapons down the ramp and waited with them near the horse.

Then the giant's aides each took hold of his forearms to steady him as he placed one foot ahead of the other and bent his knees and middle to crouch through the opening. The collar of dragon teeth spread from the front, across his shoulders at the back, and met between the shoulder blades. From there, two rows of teeth ran down the middle of his back to his hips. One aide steered the plumes of the helm past the opening of the cage.

Once the giant's feet were on the deck, his aides guided him toward the ramp.

The giant placed a tentative foot forward and began his descent of the ramp with his aides at his sides, lending him support.

Thoughts rushed through Nagora's mind. My arrow won't pierce his armor. That my arrow makes it past the eye-slit is slim. It could take out one of his aides, and then the giant, already off-kilter, might trip and fall down the ramp and break his neck. No, his guards would be onto me in no time. Trying to do either would put Pare and Harri in danger. Don't do it.

The aides led the giant to the platform next to his horse and helped him climb the steps. One aide grabbed a rope tied to the saddle hold as the giant took hold of it with a gloved hand.

His other hand waved slowly. Nagora guessed the giant might be speaking to his horse to reassure it.

Once the giant had both hands on the saddle hold, the other aide helped him swing his right leg up and over the back of the saddle.

The deckhands handed the weapons to the aides. One attached the sword's scabbard to the left side of the saddle. The other aide stepped down the platform steps and walked to the other side of the horse. He held up the lance for the giant to take and helped guide the heel of the lance into its holder next to the giant's right foot.

The head groom handed over the reins to the giant's left hand. He made sure the giant had a secure grip on the reins before returning to the rope that hung from the bridle. He picked it up and coiled it, keeping a comfortable length between him and the horse's head.

The head groom stood in front of the big, docile animal and looked to the other grooms. They held up the coiled-ends of their ropes. He held his up and spoke to the giant.

The perimeter of guards behind the giant opened up. The driver of a mule-drawn, flatbed wagon guided it to a stop two mule lengths from the giant's horse. Deckhands and the giant's two aides carried the platform to the wagon and lifted it onto its bed.

One aide rushed to the giant, letting him know all was ready.

The giant raised his left hand.

Trumpets blared and drums beat a slow cadence. Nagora leaned out the window to look past the plume on the giant's helmet to the assembled groups that Harri had described the night before.

Your back would be such an easy target for an armor piercing arrow. To carry such a bow around would be like waving a flag. Guess what I'm hunting? No, we have a plan that's building. Even if I could draw such a bow today, I wouldn't loose such an arrow and risk the lives of my friends.

...

The giant raised his hand again and the massive line of people, horses, and mules moved forward along Harbor Way. Nagora watched the front of the line move. They were not taking Castle Hill Way up. The cobblestones on that hill would be treacherous for the giant's horse.

Nagora looked down. Paruline, Harri, and other people she did not know were watching the procession. Nagora whistled a bird song signal to get Paruline's attention. She looked up. Concern covered her face as she pointed in the direction the procession was coming from.

Nagora hadn't watched the activity at that end of the wharf. When she looked, her jaw dropped. Tar piss! They would pass her window.

Five units of soldiers armed with swords, spears, and shields bearing the oak-leaf symbol of the Community of the Leaf marched four abreast in lines of five.

Behind them followed three ballistae pulled by teams of two horses. Each ballista had an armed escort of eight soldiers. The ballistae were as big as the one that had killed her uncle on the Isle of Smoke Bridge nineteen years ago.

Tar piss! Dannor was right. How are we going to fight them? Have we just set a trap for ourselves? What conditions can I ask for that might give us an edge?

I need to warn Lars before he leaves. He might figure a way to render the ballistae useless.

Wait. Why did Lars choose the plain? Was this a possibility he considered and planned for? He mentioned ballistae when speaking to Raynhard and Kiviran. Is he somehow gaining an advantage by staking out the battlefield? What would it be? The high ground? If I recall, there's not much high ground on the plain itself, only closer to the forested hills. I'll ask him.

The more she thought about it, the more the blood rushed to her head and her jaw tightened. Raynhard! What have you done? Tar piss! Now what'll I do?

Nagora looked down at Paruline, who held a hand to her mouth and shook her head. She wanted to hold her and say: Pare, don't you give up hope. You've always supported me in the darkest of times. I don't know how, but I'll find a way.

Nagora bit her lower lip as she watched the ballistae go by. How many bolts do those cases on the back hold? Two, maybe three dozen? Tar piss! She swallowed.

What can I do? Ask Godomor for volunteers again? Even if he agrees, before the counselors meet and relay the request to their vassals, time will be eaten up. Then volunteer warriors would have to prepare and provision for the journey here. That'll use up more days.

And Raynhard? Would he even approve of Godomor's warriors coming here? Not likely. To all appearances, he has sided with the Leafers. He has to maintain that impression.

Wait! What about The Guard? Would they be leading a secret force Raynhard has organized? That could be!

A spark had just lit the wick of the smallest candle of hope in the otherwise dark tunnel she feared she was heading into.

And if Raynhard has such a force, he'll surely call upon the Stone Standers to come with their slings. Grim had led three hundred of them to the plain nineteen years ago.

I want to believe that, but I have no way of confirming it. Would the Little People know? Why wouldn't they? They serve the dragons too. It's in their interest to help protect them. Why haven't they given me this information?

Her fists clenched and her jaw locked. Breathe. Think. Anger won't help. There must be reasons they're keeping plans from me. Too many things I can't control.

Nagora rubbed her face with both hands and took a deep breath as she recalled what her uncle had told her in the past when she felt like this.

✝

"Remember, last year you had similar feelings. It's what I call 'the feeling of war.' I've felt it many times. It's the feeling of not being in control of all these events going on about you."

Uncle Dangor had pointed a thumb at his chest. "How do I deal with it? I don't, because I don't control those events, but I have control over some things. I focus on those things. In my case, it's my weapons. I make sure my bow and all my arrows are in perfect working condition or that my blades are perfectly sharpened. I focus on my task, not the big picture. I let the leaders worry about that. You did that last year. You completed your task, and much more. Do that until you're called upon to lead."

✝

His words are still true. That's what I felt then, and now I feel it even more. Is Raynhard's call for my help also a request for me to lead? If doing my part makes me a leader, so be it. My weapons are ready. As a Dragon Talker, I have to focus on what I can control, or at least try to.

I need Sagora, and my dragons need her. Danuka will take me to her tonight. The arguments I have will convince Godomor and Gabe to allow me to see her.

. . .

Nagora closed the wooden doors of the stock loading window, put on her weapons, and brought the blankets and lantern downstairs with her.

Paruline stood at the foot of the stairs. "I was about to go up." She pointed toward the street outside. "We weren't expecting this. And more ships are on their way. We don't know if they'll bring more soldiers. Nagora, what are you going to do?"

Despite sensing Paruline's worry, Nagora smiled at her. "I'll put away these blankets for you, and this lantern. Then I'll boil water to make tea to have with a piece of your delicious bread, and I'll cover the bread with honey from that jar in your pantry."

She nudged Paruline. "And you, big sister, will you join me so I can tell you all the reasons not to worry about me?"

Paruline blinked away the tears that had welled up in her eyes and forced a smile on her face. She grabbed hold of Nagora's arm. "Those are the words I want to hear. Let's go."

It was almost three counts later. Nagora had shared with Paruline her thoughts on what the king's greater plan might be. She did so even though she could not confirm it. And she told Paruline what she would do for the rest of the day.

Now Nagora was having another bowl of tea with her dear friend. Her optimistic view of the whole situation seemed to have lifted Paruline's spirits. That's when Harri came into the kitchen.

He sat at the table opposite Paruline. "Well, the procession has disappeared up Castle Way. It will be total confusion in

Castle Square. I'm glad to not have a shop up there. I've never seen anything like this. Who could have guessed that many people would be with this giant, Golgotha?"

Paruline stood. "First things first, like Nagora says. You must be hungry. She had two big slices of bread with honey and goat cheese."

Nagora reached over to touch his arm. "I would have eaten all the cheese, but I left you some."

Before he could answer, Paruline spoke. "Nagora thinks Golgotha will set up camp in the castle courtyard."

Harri nodded. "She's right. A Leafer confirmed that just a short while ago. The question is, where will his soldiers set up camp? Word is his personal guards usually set up their tents around his. Space in the courtyard will be scarce. The hundred and twenty-eight others will be a problem. They will overrun the castle. Maybe they'll turn the throne room into a barracks."

Harri waved a hand. "Unless they have tents. Then they could camp in farm fields up on Castle Way, not far from the castle. Whatever crops growing there will take a beating."

Nagora interrupted him. "That wouldn't be a good idea. Outside the main gates, beyond where wagons park, there's a field for a hundred tents. Lars occupies part of it now with his trainees. The giant's soldiers could make camp there and in the wagon field."

"True," said Harri. "I didn't think of that. It's best to protect the crops."

Paruline set two plates in front of her man. "Tea's on its way. Go ahead."

"Harri, I want to bring Bonnie back to Olen. Pare says Castle Way is not the only way up that's on gravel. How can I get to it?"

He placed a slice of bread on his plate. "Easy. Walk Bonnie up Main Gate Way to the second way that crosses it. Turn left onto what we call 'Lonesome Lane,' because of the, err, hospitality let's call it, sailors can find there. The actual name is Walker Way because past that disreputable part, the road is narrower and it winds its way around enormous boulders and trees. It's fine on foot or on horseback, but not to be taken with a wagon."

Could the inn where Worsham recovered have been on that way?

Paruline set a bowl of tea next to Harri's plate. "But where does she go from there? I mean, where does it lead to?"

He was pouring honey onto his bread. He set the jar down and licked his thumb. "Soon as you see Windhaven's stone wall ahead of you, you have two choices."

He licked his thumb again. "Either you go to the wall, turn right and follow it all the way to the main gate in the wall."

He spread the honey with the back of his spoon. "Or you take the first way you come to on your right. Follow that. It will bring you to Main Gate Way. Turn left. Go up. The next way you come to on your right is Castle Way. Assembly Square is across from it on your left. I take it you know how to find Olen from there."

That'll be my route. No sense in drawing unnecessary attention by riding along the wall alone.

"Thanks, Harri. I'll take your second suggestion," said Nagora. "I told Pare I'll be leaving Windhaven today, and I can't say for sure when I'll come back. Thanks for allowing me to drop in and out on you like this. I think I'll be on my way now." She stood and leaned to kiss Harri's cheek.

His mouth was full. He nodded and held up a thumb.

Paruline helped Nagora put on her weapons and adjust her disguise before walking her to the shop door.

She hugged Nagora close. "You be careful. No matter what you've told me, I'll still worry about you."

Nagora hugged her back. "I will. Thanks again."

This time it was Olen who had news for Nagora. He was in his stable when she brought Bonnie in and exchanged greetings.

She was telling him what she had seen earlier in the morning from the stock window above Harri's shop, and that she would warn Lars.

Olen's jaw shifted before he answered. "No need to. Leafers already warned Lars the giant's soldiers would take over the field where he had set up camp and that they'd occupy the entire wagon parking area too. They'll park their ballistae and other wagons there."

"So Lars had to move?"

"Aye, he had his trainees move their camp to the field on the other side of the brook. It meant clearing some scrub brush growing over there. He didn't put up a fuss when given the order to move. He said it would allow him to observe the giant's troops, taking their measure to see what he'll be up against."

"Lars told you this himself?"

"Aye, he came to tell me so I could warn you. He told me to tell you not to go to him day or night. If you want to meet with him, it'll be in Dromester. I'll give him the message if that's what you want.

"Oh! And he said he had the feeling if he gets the call to help set up the battlefield on the plain opposite the Isle of Smoke, he'll have the company of the giant's advisors. He figures some of the giant's troops and the ballistae will head there too."

"Did Lars seem preoccupied or worried about that information?"

Olen shrugged. "He seemed to take it in stride. You know him. Big grin on his face." The smith made the motion. "Reaches over his shoulder, taps the crossguard of his big sword and says, 'The more, the merrier.'" He laughed. "Your man didn't look worried to me."

Do I take that as a good sign? My man's not one to back away from a necessary fight. Though I've yet to witness him get his blade wet, as I've heard him say.

"Do you want me to bring him a message?"

"No. He seems to know as much as I've learned."

"Are you headed to Dromester right away?"

Nagora shook her head. "No, I'll walk up to Castle Square to see what happens when the giant's procession arrives."

Nagora wasn't the only one wanting to see the giant arrive. Castle soldiers had cleared the square of people, pushing them back into the streets leading into the square. She was well back among the crowd on Castle Way. She wanted to see Golgotha ride into the square. Right now, the crowd blocked her view of those on foot in the procession.

Flags and the sound of trumpets and drums entering the square had the crowd jostling for a view. From what she could see, a single drummer followed a single flag. Two flags marched by, and two others stopped in position. When one flag waved, a single drum played.

I know what they are doing. They've done this before. They're guiding the units from the procession to their places in the square.

While the flags and drums did their work, word from people in the crowd with a view on the square made its way back. The square was filling up with the various groups from the procession. Each group was marking its position in the square, showing discipline and order. The castle gate was being raised.

When many trumpets and drums began to play, Golgotha came into view. The crowd murmured in awe of him in his shining armor with lance in hand on his big, armored horse. The sound of the trumpets and drums faded. They must have led Golgotha into the castle courtyard.

Then shouts of "Make way! Make way!" caused the crowd on Castle Way to move toward Assembly Square. Nagora stayed with the flow, crossing Main Gate Way to take up a position on the highest tier of the building opposite the main doors of the Assembly Hall. Onlookers like her filled the tiers surrounding the square.

Looking back along Castle Way, Nagora saw marching formations of soldiers, followed by three ballistae and a dozen wagons.

The soldiers marched into the square and surrounded the Assembly Hall, while the ballistae units turned onto Main Gate Way and parked. A dozen camp wagons stopped on Castle Way.

Twelve young Leafers stepped out of the main door of the Assembly Hall of the Leaf. From what she could see, seven of them spread out along the top tier, each standing at one of the other doors of the hall. The five at the main door raised their oak-leaf medallions three times and then clapped in unison. The seven others joined in, clapping in time with the five. Lanken shouted a command. The clapping stopped. All twelve raised their medallions.

The soldiers drew their swords and slapped them against their scabbards in unison. The spear carriers joined in, pounding their spears on the cobblestones. Leafer Lanken raised his hands. The soldiers stopped their noise.

Then Lanken led them in a chant. "Dragon blood for our oaks! Dragon blood for our oaks!" The other Leafers joined in leading the chant, building it louder and faster all around the hall until it became a shrieking battle cry.

On Lanken's signal, they all stopped. The people around the square looked on at the force assembled before them, obviously waiting to see what they would do next.

Lanken signaled again. As one, the soldiers raised swords and spears high above their heads, shaking them and chanting: "Blood! Blood! Blood!" On his third signal, the swordsmen returned their swords to their scabbards and the spear carriers stood at attention.

When a commander yelled an order, the formations marched in step around the Assembly Hall of the Leaf and then onto Main Gate Way, ahead of the waiting ballistae and wagons.

The crowd left the square. Nagora swallowed the lump in her throat as she watched the force march out of Windhaven's main gate. Anger, mixed with fear, unsettled her stomach.

They'll only get the blood of my dragons over my dead body. I'm the last line of hope for the dragons. The battle has yet to begin. What did the onlookers think? Might is right? That remains to be seen!

How busy will it be at Olen's stable as the giant's guards take over the castle stables?

Along Stables Way, as far as Nagora could see, empty wagons stood parked one behind the other. Their tongues and neck yokes were tied to stand up in the air instead of being left to rest on the ground.

The doors to Olen's stable were open. The men inside were taking care of their mounts, some still removing saddles, and others brushing the horses. Those who had finished were rubbing their silver-leaf medallions while they waited.

Nagora waited for them to leave before going in. She leaned against a wagon, out of sight and away from the open stable doors.

When the procession of twelve Leafers left the stable two-by-two, she crept in.

Olen was walking along the row of stalls, inspecting the mounts. He saw Nagora. "They know what they're doing. It shows they are well trained."

Nagora nodded. "The soldiers impressed the onlookers in Assembly Hall Square. You could have heard a mouse fart after their chants. Did any of those twelve Leafers talk to you?"

Olen held up a finger as he continued along the stalls. "Only one. Just to confirm they were at the right place. Not a talkative bunch, that's for sure. Not happy to give up their stalls at the castle stables. Tell me what you saw in the square. The chants echoed here."

After telling him what she had seen, Nagora joined Olen in his kitchen for a bite to eat before retrieving her bag from her room to head for Dromester.

In disguise again and ready to leave, Nagora thanked Olen for his hospitality. "It's time for me to go. Bonnie will get me to Dromester before sunset."

"Tell Bardas there's no rush to bring her back. Upon his next delivery will be fine," said Olen.

She gave Olen a quick hug. "I'm sure I'll be back here soon. Take care."

The Key to the Curse
Âpihkokahikan Mayasowasowewin

That evening at Bardas's, Nagora had an eager audience for the news she brought. She answered questions Moreena and Jani had. They were happy that she had been their eyes at the harbor. When she finished, Bardas said, "The number of those who join the Leafers will grow. Such displays of power impress people. You can bet the Leafers will make the most of the giant's stay in Windhaven to recruit new members into new cells for the Community of the Leaf."

Nagora inhaled. "And increase the call for dragon blood."

She looked around the table. "Excuse me. Moreena, I need to speak with your father in private. Bardas, can we go to your shop now?"

"Aye." He stood and showed Nagora to the door.

In the shop, Bardas lit two more lanterns. "How can I help you?"

Nagora removed her quiver and sheepskin vest to pull the straps of the holsters of her blades from her shoulders. She had made a leather sleeve to fit over the sheath of her big sky-stone blade, into which she fitted the golden-handled dragon dagger. "I have something to show you. I will tell you about it and then ask your permission for something, but only after you've heard me out."

She set the dagger in its scabbard on the table next to Bardas's hand and told him the story of how it had first come into her possession. Bardas listened and examined the weapon with great care. She also told him of her past uses of it and how the king's messenger, Worsham, had recently delivered it to her.

When she finished, Bardas looked at her, still holding the dagger. "Do you believe it's cursed?"

Nagora replied just like Godomor had when she had asked him the same question. "Bardas, if, instead of letting you take and hold the dagger, I showed it to you and told you the blade is razor sharp, would you believe me or want proof?"

He grinned. "I'd want proof."

"Worsham said that I am blind to the curse of the dagger." Nagora pointed at it. "That I will only see the destiny it holds when I truly see as only the blind can see, not before." She took a deep breath. "Bardas, I ask your permission to let me show the dagger to Moreena. Since she is blind, perhaps in her way of seeing, she can tell what the curse is. I want you to know that if, for whatever reason, you don't want me to show it to her, I will respect that decision and respect you."

Bardas looked from Nagora and back to the dagger, examining it again. He held it up so it pointed at his face, allowing him to sight along the blade. Without a word, he set the dagger down, stepped back, and leaned over to take a scrap of lambskin vellum that lay on the table. Holding the dagger in one hand and the vellum in the other, he pressed the tip of the blade into the vellum. After pushing the vellum along the symmetrical blade to the crossguard, with the nail of his thumb, he pressed hard on the lambskin on both sides where it rested at the juncture of the blade and crossguard. This left visible crease marks on the vellum. He pulled it off the blade and set it on the table. "Are your throwing knives sharp?"

"Aye. They are." She handed him one.

Bardas bent and cut along the crease lines with repeated, precise stabs. When he finished, he held up the piece of skin to show Nagora. The hole, like the cross section of the blade where it met the crossguard, was symmetrical, with two little details she had never noticed before. Each long, curved side of the hole had a corner bump that stuck out.

"Just as I thought. I know where I've seen a hole like this before." Bardas picked up the dagger. "This, I'm willing to bet, is the key to a mystery I've pondered for many years. The mouth of the dragon on Moreena's harp has a hole exactly like this. Nagora, you have my permission to show the dagger to my daughter after you insert it into the dragon's mouth. I'm sure it's a key that either does something to the harp or un-locks something on the harp."

Nagora pointed to the piece of vellum. "This shape tells you that?"

"Not only that, but something Moreena's mother had said about the harp a long time ago. That within it, it held secrets for the king and queen, secrets she had assumed were the songs or music she could play on the harp for them."

Nagora's mind raced as she took in what Bardas had just told her. "My dragon will come soon to bring me to Skull Bay. If Moreena comes with me, Danuka could fly us both to the cave where she hides her harp. The dragon knows the way. She flew me there with my daughter, Sarah, three years ago. It wouldn't take long. I would return with Moreena within six counts at the most."

"I trust you, Nagora. It's a good plan."

As she donned her weapons and vest, Nagora said, "She'll have to dress warm."

"Let me speak with her. If she agrees to the plan, I'll take you two to meet the dragon; then I'll await your return."

Returning from the shop with her father, Moreena rubbed her arms, as if fighting off a chill. Bardas led her to face her husband.

"Jani, I'm about to embark on a short adventure with Nagora." She reached out to find his hands. "Don't be afraid for me. Nagora is going to fly me to my harp on the back of her dragon. I know that I'll be safe with her."

Before Jani could speak, Erin and Joni approached to reassure him.

Jani pulled Moreena into a hug, nodding all the while before finally saying: "Go with Nagora. I trust she'll bring you back safe, and that you'll tell me all about your adventure."

As soon as Danuka alighted, Nagora climbed onto her wing and tied her bag to the back of the saddle as she spoke to her dragon, mind-to-mind.

Okâwîmâw, the giant dragon slayer of the Leafers has arrived in Windhaven.

Ka Peyakot Mahihkan, this news came to me today. I have just seen the fires of the encampments outside the walls of Windhaven. Think of what you witnessed today so my knowledge of the enemy will be clearer.

Mother, before I do, will you fly my friend Moreena and me to the cave on the mountain nearby where you brought me with Sarah three years ago? Let me tell you why.

When Nagora finished explaining, Danuka agreed to the flight. Lone Wolf, your friend might help you learn useful information.

Nagora signaled to Bardas. He brought his daughter over to the dragon's wing. Nagora helped Moreena climb onto it and guided her to the saddle. "That's it. Hold on tight to the handhold. I'll sit behind you. My arms will be around you as my hands hold the reins. I'll not speak to you until we land. It won't be long."

Nagora climbed onto the saddle and reached around Moreena to take hold of the reins. "Are you ready?"

"As ready as I'll ever be! I feel both frightened and excited! But definitely more excited!" said Moreena.

"Trust me. You'll be fine." Mother, we are ready.

Danuka flew into the night sky to their destination as Nagora recalled the day's events. What she had seen of the giant at the harbor and her later visits to Castle Square and Assembly Hall Square played out in her mind for the dragon.

When they landed, Nagora helped her friend to the ground. "That wasn't frightening, was it?"

"My heart's still hammering from the excitement! My legs feel strange to be back on the ground."

"That's normal. It's from the motion of the flight, like after being on a boat at sea when you come ashore. You'll be fine soon. Wait while I go get the lantern from the bag."

"I'm glad I've been here before. Otherwise I wouldn't be able to find the entrance," said Nagora.

Moreena had her hands on the enormous stone's surface, feeling their way along it to the crack. "Now I know where I am. We sit here to go in."

Nagora followed with the lantern, going down the hole on the carved footholds with the heel of one hand and her bum.

"Come this way around the seam in the rock wall," said Moreena.

Inside the major section of the cave, Moreena had found the candle lanterns and set them on the small table. "I'll let you light them, Nagora."

She lit them and hung one from the ceiling just before it sloped upward above the firepit. She hung another on a wall hook near the bed frame, and left one on the table. "Shall I make a fire, Moreena?"

"No, I'm eager to learn what the dagger will do to the harp." She was already at the side of the rack that held blankets and skins for the bare wooden bed frames with their woven-rope sleeping surfaces. Moreena pulled the harp out from its hiding place behind it. Once she had it out, she looked in Nagora's direction. "Do I have it pointing toward the table?"

"Aye, you do."

Moreena lifted it and walked toward the table, counting her steps as she approached.

The harp still fascinated Nagora, like when she had seen it for the first time twenty years ago. The proud dragon was all made of gold, from its rearing head down along its neck and belly to its clawed feet. The dragon's golden wings spread back and joined along their pointed tips, extending to the top of the long wooden sound box. Gold strings were strung from the edges of the wing tips to the harp's box. The harp could stand on its own on a smooth, flat surface, but not on the cave floor. Moreena would set its clawed feet on a cushion stool and then rest it on her shoulder to play it.

"Hold it while I get the cushion and a chair."

After Nagora helped her set it on the stool, Moreena sat and rested the harp on her shoulder. "Do you see the hole in the dragon's mouth?"

Holding the lantern from the table, Nagora inspected the slight opening of the mouth. "It's exactly as your father described. No one would notice it unless they examined beyond the opening. Let me retrieve the dagger."

"Okay, but first let me play the dragon chord. Perhaps the dagger does something that affects the sound."

As the wondrous sound filled the cave, Nagora's entire body shivered like the first time Moreena had played the chord.

"Go ahead," said Moreena, when the sound had faded.

With the lantern in one hand and the dagger in the other, Nagora aimed the tip at the mouth, lining up the blade to go straight into the dragon's muzzle. The blade slid along the bottom of the gold opening as far as the crossguard permitted.

She heard a first click followed by nine more in sequence, slow enough to count, and then came a brief snap.

"Over here! On my right! I felt something brush against my knee."

Nagora held the lantern to light the side of the soundbox. A panel had popped open. "Moreena, it's a hidden door! Behind it are two carved-out spaces with words carved beneath them. One space, with the word 'REX,' holds a dagger identical to the one in the dragon's mouth. The space with the word 'REGINA' is empty."

"The words mean king and queen," said Moreena. "You must have the dagger destined for a queen."

Nagora reflected on her experience with the dagger. King Raynhard gave it to me. I cut my thigh with it, thinking I had failed in my duty to my king. Sarah and I killed Alizarine with it to fulfill one witch's curse on another. "I think you're right. That makes sense."

Nagora reached for the dagger marked REX. "I'm taking the other one out of its holding place. I'll hold your harp while you take the dagger in your hands. Tell me what you feel."

Moreena moved her chair back and extended her hands.

Nagora laid the sheathed dagger across her friend's palms and watched as she manipulated it.

Moreena rested it on her lap. The fingers of both hands traveled over the surfaces of the dagger, taking in every detail. She placed her right hand on the handle and pulled the blade from its scabbard. The fingers of her left hand glided over the blade. She was careful of the edges as she tested them for sharpness. "It's beautiful, a masterpiece, a gift for a king."

"Do you have any images or feelings that come to mind as you hold it?"

"Other than its appearance in my mind, nothing, no feelings or other images." With a deft hand, Moreena returned the dagger to its sheath and handed it to Nagora. "Will you show me the other one?"

"What did your father tell you about the dagger when he brought you to his room to ask if you would come with me?"

"Because of the shape of the dagger's blade, he wanted to know if it's a key because of what my mother once told him about the harp. And that you would ask me to hold and touch the dagger to see if it gave me images or feelings. Just like you did with that one."

"Did he tell you why I want you to do that?"

"No. He said you would tell me all about it."

"Moreena, do you want me to tell you before or after you examine it?"

"After. That way, what you tell me won't influence me."

"Let me put this one back before I give you the other one."

"Wait, Nagora! Let me play the dragon chord again to listen if the harp makes an unfamiliar sound." Moreena pulled her chair closer to the harp and reached for the strings. She plucked the strings, and the wondrous sound resonated once again.

To Nagora's ears, there was no change in tone. "Well?"

"No change. I was expecting the empty dagger holders to make a slight difference. But there's none that I could hear."

Nagora bent to replace the dagger in the space marked REX and then stood to pull the other from the dragon's mouth. When she did, the snap sounded followed by ten slow clicks, the reverse of when the panel had opened. She looked. The panel had closed. "Moreena, did you close the panel?"

"No. I heard it shut. Would that mean at least one dagger must stay outside the harp to open the panel?"

"That's my question too. Could they take turns being outside the harp, but are never together within it? For what reason?"

"Perhaps it depends on whoever will rule the kingdom."

"That could be, Moreena. How will we ever know?"

"Give me the other one. Maybe it will give us an answer."

Nagora placed the sheathed dagger across her friend's palms.

Again, Moreena rested the dagger on her lap. The fingers of both hands studied the surface details. As before, she placed her right hand on the handle and pulled the blade from its scabbard. The fingers of her left hand glided over the blade, first on one side, then the other. Her index finger stopped near the crossguard. "This one has a different etching than the other. It's likely difficult to spot in poor light because the symbol was most likely intentionally etched lightly. You would see it if you tilted the blade in sunlight. Father taught me to use my fingers to detect poorly etched initials and numbers on the pan handles, knife blades, and cutlery pieces we make. It happens when the acid we use loses its strength. He wants our numbers etched lightly so as not to detract from our handle and blade designs. The symbol etched here is extremely light."

"What is the symbol?"

"A simple circle with a cross beneath its lowest edge, representing a woman sitting at her mirror."

"And on the other?"

"Again, a simple circle but with an arrow pointing off its upper edge at a slant to represent a man standing behind a shield holding a spear."

"So the etched symbols help tell the daggers apart."

"That makes sense, Nagora. I won't guess it's for any other reason."

Moreena's fingers tested the edges of the blade for sharpness. When her index reached the tip, her right hand trembled, causing her to prick her finger and draw blood. She held the dagger away from her as her arm shook.

"Drop it, Moreena! Let it fall!"

Moreena shook her head and grabbed onto the seat of her chair. The shaking subsided to a tiny tremor that appeared to come in waves from her shoulder to her hand. Moreena's eyes closed as her head tilted back, and she spoke. "A dagger cursed to a line of queens. They shall in turn, knowingly or unknowingly, carry with it life and death, mother to daughter, and daughter to mother, until dragons fly no more, and Heqet rules as queen forevermore." Moreena's eyes opened as she sat straight facing Nagora.

"Moreena, are you well?"

She nodded and placed the dagger on her lap. "Did I understand well, Nagora? Is that a curse or a riddle?"

"I fear it's a curse hiding within a riddle that names the players and states the outcome. The question is: How does one prevent such a curse from unfolding?"

"Nagora, I remember you telling of Heqet's curse on Alizarine. And then we learned how you carried it out with your daughter, Sarah, and this dagger." She pointed to it. "What has changed about it?"

Nagora told her how the king had sent Worsham to deliver the dagger to her and what he had said to her about not being able to see its curse. "Moreena, I thank you for what you've done to help me, but I still don't see how the curse relates to me. That's why I call this a riddle open to many interpretations, except for the outcome. Perhaps I will have to become blind to see it. Perhaps, for the sake of the future of the dragons, I won't have a choice."

"Don't, Nagora! You'll regret it. You might learn how you're involved in the curse, but at the cost of losing your eyesight? No! Don't!"

"Moreena, I hope it doesn't come to that. All I want to do is protect the dragons. You've given me much to speculate about, and you have an answer for your father. Do you want to play one of your songs before we go?"

"Nagora, I'm tired, but I want to give you hope. Let me play *As Dragons Soar* for you. Do you remember when I played that tune?"

"I do. You played it twice: once in a practice session, and next on the night Dannor switched Alizarine's dragon egg. Please, play for me."

As the last notes faded, Nagora spoke to herself the same words as the first time she had listened to the song: *Okâwîmâw*, will you be the last dragon to soar in our skies? Let it not be so. I must not despair. "Thank you, Moreena. You've given me hope. I'll bring you back to your father. He'll be waiting to take you home."

With slow flaps of her wings, Danuka alighted in the field near the trees where Bardas waited. Nagora led his daughter along the dragon's wing to him. "Thank you again, Bardas.

You guessed right. I'll let Moreena tell you." She hugged her friend. "Thank you, Moreena. Because you have a place in my heart, I'll not lose hope. Until we meet again."

She hugged Nagora. "Thank your dragon for taking me with you. I'll never forget this night."

Nagora put on her eye mask and gloves, climbed into the saddle, and waved to her friends. *Okâwîmâw, I am ready. Take me to King Godomor's lodge in Skull Bay.*

Danuka spread her wings and pushed off with her powerful legs to begin her ascent to the starlit sky above Dromester.

Nagora held on, closed her eyes, and let her thoughts speak of what Raynhard's plans might be; what Lars had achieved at his audience with the king and the Head Leafer, and what he might do in the coming days; what she would warn Godomor and Gabe about; what she had just learned about the dagger's curse, thanks to Moreena; and how she planned to meet with Sagora.

Danuka's reply was brief. *If the fair winds hold, the Dark Twins arrive tomorrow before sunset. We dragons will need them if we are to survive to soar in the sky, as in the song your friend played.*

The news caught Nagora by surprise. *I knew they were coming. I wasn't expecting them so soon.*

A Sister's Choice
Nîtisân Nawasôh

On this night, as Danuka flew over the wall of Skull Bay nearest its harbor, Nagora caught sight of the greater number of sentinels standing near small braziers. *Okâwîmâw*, the guards have signaled our approach. Their fires dot the wall of Skull Bay from one end to the other.

Ka Peyakot Mahihkan, you will learn why tonight.

Mother, I trust you.

Once her dragon had landed near Godomor's lodge, a complete contingent of the king's guards, armed with bows and spears, greeted Nagora. One of the guards entered the lodge. Before she climbed down from Danuka's extended wing, Gabe stepped past the open door and walked to greet her. Has something happened to Godomor? Gabe was smiling. That's a good sign. What's he doing here at this time of night?

"Nagora, you're a welcome sight. We were just talking about you. Come, my father will be glad to see you."

"Is the king well, Gabe?"

"He's fine. It's the events of the past two days that make us wonder what is going on. We're hoping you'll be able to give us an answer."

"I will, if I can. I bring important information for both of you."

"Come in." He held the door open for her.

Before following her in, Gabe spoke something into the ear of a guard.

Inside, Godomor was adding a log to those on the grate in his fireplace. He smiled at Nagora as he straightened and walked over to the table, motioning her to it. Two lit lanterns sat on the table, and two more hung from overhead beams. Nagora removed her weapons and hung them on the hook near the door.

Gabe pulled a chair from the table and pointed her to it.

Nagora waited for the king and the prince to sit before she did. "Thank you for seeing me at this time of night. I feared I would find you asleep. All of Skull Bay seems on alert."

Gabe turned to Godomor. "Father, Nagora said she had important information for us. Should we let her speak it first?"

Godomor nodded and leaned back in his chair.

Nagora spoke in Skullian. "I'll start with what is most pressing for you to know. If favorable winds hold, the Dark Twins arrive tomorrow before sunset. I just found out from Danuka. She said without the Dark Twins, she and her dragons might not survive. Let me tell you about the high flight she took with her dragons." Nagora explained the details Danuka had learned about how the Dark Twins would transmit the knowledge with the help of the Dragon Talkers and the Little People. She emphasized the necessity of Sagora becoming a Dragon Talker.

Godomor looked from Nagora to Gabe. "We will welcome them. My son will see to their protection. He will choose trusted warriors to guard them while they are here. I will have no choice but to announce their arrival tonight. Because of your arrival, I am sure many curious folk have assembled outside."

Next, Nagora summarized what Lars had achieved at his audience with King Raynhard and the Head Leafer, Kiviran. Then she warned them of envoys who would come to negotiate on Golgotha's behalf, seeking permission to dock his boats and safe passage to Maze Point for his force. If granted, the envoys would offer Godomor gold to guarantee no harm will come to the people of the Land of Skulls.

Godomor sat straight. "Nagora, many forces are at play. Certain members of the Community of the Leaf in the Land of the Danu have been planning in secret to bring about these events. Their greed has made them shrewd and rich, hoping to become even richer by preying on the greed they find in the hearts of so many who will believe their unproven promise. Though, the one you suspect to be a witch with unimaginable powers will soon reveal proof of that promise. Then word of its revelation will spread like a grass fire. The call for dragon blood will be strong. We must be ready for them. When I say 'them,' I mean the Leafers and the witch. My feeling is Heqet has been playing the Leafers to her advantage all along. If you can expose that, the advantage will be yours."

That remains to be seen. What if her proof is irrefutable, even if their promise defies all logic?

"Lars has informed us of his plan to battle the giant in the maze. Should something happen to him," Godomor looked to his son, "Gabe has the details. With the help of the Dragon

Talkers, he will prepare to flood the center of the maze for such a confrontation. Nagora, it is unnecessary for you to know those details now. With some thought, you can surely guess how."

It may be unnecessary, but it's unnerving to realize my man shared his plans in the event something would happen to him. Nagora swallowed.

Lars shared more thoughts of his mission to Windhaven with Gabe and Godomor than with me. Why? To give me less to worry about? Has what I've done been a futile waste of my time? Still, I learned a lot. I should tell them about it.

Before she could speak, Godomor continued. "As for collecting the gold for the sale of the map, yes, a dozen warrior archers from the family of Trowan and her friends are in the Land of the Danu to help, but Lars has no trust that payment will come. He is certain the Leafers will make excuses and delay. The enemy, like Lars, is buying time. The Leafers are waiting for you to show your hand, and the giant wants to learn about you, just like you want to learn about him."

"Speaking of the giant, let me tell you what I saw at the harbor in Windhaven when the giant's ships arrived." Nagora gave them a complete account, including what she saw in Castle Square and at Assembly Hall Square.

She finished with how she learned about the mysterious riddle of the curse of the dragon dagger thanks to the help of her blind friend, Moreena. Do I ask them now for permission to speak to Sagora, or wait? If I can speak to her alone, I'll tell her about Danuka's high flight and the Dark Twins' arrival tomorrow. That should influence her decision. And I'll ask her if she executed Acindor or knows who did. I want to know if that puzzle piece is in place or not. No, I'll wait. They want answers from me about something.

Nagora looked from Gabe to his father. "I hate to admit it, but all this information is coming at me and I have yet to make up a plan of my own that gives me confidence in what I must do."

Godomor leaned toward the table. "Nagora, you must focus on what you need to do next, not on the future battle with the giant. Do those things well. Information will come to you one piece at a time. Put only the necessary pieces together. With time, your plan will build. To worry about many things at once does not clear your mind to think."

He's right. I need to focus on the task at hand.

Gabe cleared his throat. "If you have nothing else to tell us, perhaps you can answer a question we have about recent events here in Skull Bay. First, we'll let the one who answered some of our other questions explain the situation to you. Sagora, will you do that now?" He looked to the king's room.

Nagora couldn't believe what Gabe had just said.

Sagora tiptoed from Godomor's room with a finger to her lips. Then she put her two palms together and leaned her head onto the back of one, closing her eyes as she mouthed the word "Raean." She smiled as she walked toward the table. "I'm not a Dragon Talker yet, but I can tell the difference between feeder eggs and hatchling eggs."

Nagora was out of her chair and in her sister's arms. "Did I hear you right? Have you decided to become a Dragon Talker?"

Sagora looked from her sister to her husband. "Gabe has encouraged me. He says my attitude has changed since I helped heal the dragon, that now I walk with confidence among the people. Some look at me with pride and compliment me for saving the dragon. A few even asked me to examine their children. Signers whisper fewer insults from the shadows.

"With the witch-influenced danger approaching, Gabe better understands the uncontrollable forces I had to submit to until you had Sarah take me away from the witch in the castle in Windhaven. He says if it weren't for you, I might not have returned to be in his life. Now with Raean, we're together as a family. He wants me to be proud of the work I do. He believes I can be a healer and a Dragon Talker, and that I'll grow stronger from being both. This is what I want too. So yes, little sister, you heard right."

Through teary eyes, Nagora looked at her sister and let her words play again in her mind for her dragon. "You can't imagine what a relief this news is to me and to Danuka! Come and sit. Tell me about the dragon eggs. What has been happening here? Mother Dragon must know, but she did not tell me."

Sagora looked from Gabe to Godomor and back to her sister. "Two nights ago, two dragons flew into Skull Bay and perched on the top landing at the king's Grand Hall. The two guards at the door had a momentary fright, but since the dragons were quiet, they remained at their post and watched.

"One dragon laid six eggs. It nudged the eggs toward the guards until they lined up against the doors. By that time, other soldiers had arrived. The two near the doors made a sign for them to stand down and be quiet. After the dragons flew away, the guards sent notice to the king, who then sent for Gabe and me to join him in the hall.

"Having seen dragon eggs before, I recognized those six as feeder eggs. I could only guess why the dragon had laid them in that spot. I didn't want to leave them out in the open, so I had Gabe and a guard help me bring them into the hall. We put them in the cave behind the throne where our king once lived.

"Last night, the dragons returned. One laid two eggs this time, hatchling eggs with the gold veins on the surface, not just the red and blue veins like on the feeder eggs. I brought those to the cave also and asked Gabe to post two guards there. That's the situation. That's why so many sentinels stand on our wall, to signal the arrival of dragons."

Nagora looked to Godomor. "You want to know why. So do I. Let me ask Danuka." She closed her eyes and spoke mind-to-mind to the dragon. *Okâwîmâw*, why has a dragon laid eggs at the Grand Hall?

Ka Peyakot Mahihkan, my daughter mated and fertilized her eggs. She could have kept them inside her for a long time. I feared that if she did, the transmission of knowledge from the Dark Twins might not work. If the dragon slayer comes to the maze, it will not be a safe place for her eggs. Until that danger has passed, the cave where Sagora put them is the easiest to defend. Of the two hatchling eggs, one is a male. My daughter will return tonight to lay more feeder eggs. If the king does not want them in his cave because he fears for their safety, or that knowledge of their being there could jeopardize negotiations with the envoys of the giant, we will find another place. We will need pouches to move them. We will hide them and tell no one where.

Nagora spoke aloud Danuka's words for the benefit of her eager listeners. Then she said, "King Godomor, Mother Dragon has great trust in you and your people to allow her daughter to lay her eggs here. Still, the decision is yours. Tell me if ..."

The king cut her short. "It will be an honor for my warriors to protect the dragon eggs. They are most precious. I will have pouches prepared should we need to move them to a safer place. The eggs have given me an idea for my announcement later."

Nagora relayed the king's words to Danuka.

"Danuka thanks you, King Godomor. She likes your idea. Now she wishes Sagora to wake her son so he may witness his mother become a Dragon Talker." Has Danuka just listened to Godomor's thoughts?

Sagora stood, blinking back tears as she looked to Gabe. He and Godomor were smiling as they stood.

Nagora followed her sister to the room, watched her put on her weapons, and then bend over her son. "Raean, time to wake up. We have dragon eggs to fetch. Auntie Nagora is here, and Danuka is waiting outside. She has a surprise for you."

At the door of his lodge, Godomor held up his hand. "Nagora, you will come with Gabe and me as I must make a proclamation about twins before two elder witnesses of Skull Bay and those who have assembled outside." Nagora nodded as she put on her weapons.

He placed a hand on his grandson's shoulder. "Raean, watch from the open door with your mother. When your father gives the signal, bring her by the hand to Nagora. You will lead both of them halfway to the dragon. Pay no heed to the signers."

The boy nodded.

Nagora followed the king and his son out the door.

Danuka pushed her belly up from the ground with her powerful wing talons and rested on her hind legs. The light of the tapers surrounded the assembly place in front of Godomor's lodge and subdued the beautiful, iridescent colors of the dragon, transforming her into a darker presence.

Godomor signed to Gabe to wait with Nagora as he approached the two elders standing on the edge of the assembled crowd. He greeted the man and woman, thanking them for interrupting their sleep to witness his proclamation.

As the elders took their places at his side between Nagora and Gabe, the king looked around to all who had assembled, either by duty or out of curiosity. Nagora saw Umma, who smiled and waved. She returned her smile, along with a discrete wave.

Godomor spoke in a deep voice. "To all of you present tonight, known that Nagora the Dragon Talker has brought answers to our questions of why the dragons lay eggs at our Grand Hall. Through her, Mother Dragon Danuka tells us the eggs are gifts of thanks to Sagora and Umma for healing her son, and that she wishes the healers will display them at our next feast in the Grand Hall."

Judging by the smiles and murmurs from the crowd, Nagora guessed the continued recognition shown to their healers pleased most of the onlookers.

When the whispers subsided, Godomor continued. "This night, Nagora has also brought most significant news concerning Sagora. The Mother Dragon wishes to make Sagora a

Dragon Talker, not only because she helped heal her son, but because Sagora is the sister of Nagora by blood in a line of Dragon Talkers from their father, Yogari.

"Since Mother Dragon has chosen to make Sagora a Dragon Talker for her role in healing the male dragon, I lift Nagora's self-imposed banishment from her sister. We, the people of Skull Bay, opened our hearts to the dragons by sharing our healers, and in doing so, the dragons have rewarded us. Let us open our hearts once again.

"Also, sisters from a faraway land will soon come to our shore. They, too, are Dragon Talkers. They bring gifts to the dragons.

"So ends my proclamation this night. Our elders, in hearing it now, bear witness to it as my official announcement, to be recorded at the next council meeting for open discussion."

Ohtawimaw was wise not to mention the sisters from faraway are twins. Now he and Gabe have time to plan how to protect them.

Godomor nodded to Gabe, who signaled to Raean and Sagora to come forward from the doorway of the king's lodge.

Nagora took hold of Sagora's other hand and walked toward Danuka. Raean had them stop at the halfway point, as Godomor had instructed. Sagora squeezed Nagora's hand and then hugged her son before sending him off with his auntie. When they were standing with Gabe and the king, Sagora turned to face the dragon and took a decisive step forward.

The dragon's red eyes focused on Sagora as she stepped closer.

Danuka spread her wings forward and crossed them behind Sagora, resting her wing talons on the ground to envelop the healer in a tent-like space. The only opening was to the light of the stars.

The dragon's neck curved farther back as she lowered her head into the space she had created for Sagora.

Nagora began a slow count as she guessed what might happen to her sister behind the dragon's wings. Will Danuka touch her snout to Sagora's forehead? Will she let my sister keep the dragon-tear amulet she gave her? Will she speak to her mind-to-mind and give her the gift of the Language of the Dragons?

Surely, she'll look inside Sagora like she did me and learn her deepest thoughts. There is no way to resist her when she does. Even now, I can hide nothing from her when she looks inside me.

Sagora, if you are truthful and submit to Danuka, you will become stronger.

Nagora had not yet reached one hundred when the dragon's head rose. She opened her wings to pull them back to her sides so her talons rested on the ground on each side of her belly.

Sagora remained kneeling on the ground with her backside resting on her heels as she stared up at the dragon, clutching the amulet Danuka had rewarded her with for helping heal her son.

You submitted to *Okâwîmâw*. She looked inside you and learned your most secret thoughts. Now she knows you like no other. You spoke with her, yet you can't believe you did. Did she give you a name? She called me *Ka Peyakot Mahihkan*. I won't ask you. It's yours to keep secret. Sagora, while you, Lars, and Sarah know it, Godomor is the only other who calls me by that name.

One leg after another, Sagora stood and backed away to join her family.

"Mum, what did Danuka say to you?"

"*Onâtawihowêw, kinanâskomitin kese isihcikewin.*"

"What does that mean?"

"The dragon said, 'Healer, thank you for your decision.'" Sagora held out the dragon-tear amulet that hung from her neck. "*Niya isihtwawin asici kanawisimowin.*" She smiled at her son and Gabe. "Mother Danuka gifted me not only with this amulet, but with the powers of a Dragon Talker, and the gift to speak to her in this language I now speak as if I always have."

"Danuka is happy with your choice. So am I, and so is Da!" Raean said, as he looked up at his father's face.

Gabe smiled. "So am I, Raean, so am I. I'm proud of your mother's decision. Look! The signals! Best you go with your mum to see the dragon lay feeder eggs."

Umma crossed over to Nagora and Gabe. She reached out to take their hands. "I am happy for both of you! This is great news! It will be a fresh beginning for Sagora. Excellent news for the mother dragon too!"

"Thank you, Umma. I'm happy for Sagora," said Gabe.

Nagora was nodding. "It is significant news for all of us! Umma, will it be possible for me to spend the night with you, since the Dark Twins arrive tomorrow?"

"Of course! I have plenty of room at the infirmary."

"Good! Thank you so much."

Nagora touched Gabe's arm. "If I don't see my sister, please tell her where I'll be. Thank you for encouraging her. You won't regret it."

She turned to Umma. "I will get my bag from Danuka's saddle. Then I'll join you."

Okâwîmâw, we will bring the Dark Twins to the maze as soon as we can. I will ask Gabe to give us an escort. Dannor will remove your saddle when you return.

Ka Peyakot Mahihkan, I will fly back with my daughters. Keep the Dark Twins safe.

I will, Mother.

Dark Twins
Kaskitewiyâs Nîsotewak

The next morning at first light, Nagora awoke in the infirmary. She slept in the bed in the room she had long ago shared with her sister. She hadn't been able to fall asleep right away. The riddle of the dagger's curse had kept her awake as her mind grappled with it, asking questions and finding few answers.

She had simplified the curse to its essentials. A line of queens carries life and death, mother to daughter and daughter to mother. What line would that be? Julianna, King Bernhard's queen; Raganora, King Bernhard's queen again; me, Nagora, King Raynhard's queen. Where are the daughters in that line? I see only Sarah. Where are the other daughters? Julianna had a son, Raynhard; and Raganora had a son, Acindor; only I had a daughter, Sarah. Who carried life and death with the dagger? Julianna? Life to her son. Death to her husband at the hand of her jealous cousin, Raganora. Raganora? Death to King Bernhard. Life to Acindor. And I? Life to Sarah. Death to Alizarine, with Sarah's help.

Wait! Who, other than me, had the dagger in their possession? Raynhard said his father had left it in the cave. He was young when his father told him about it. A dagger of that value, the queen's dagger. Did he hide it there for a reason? To help his queen escape a curse? Did she? Or did she not? Then why tell his son of its existence? That would have been around the time Hag began her quest to rid the Land of the Danu of its dragons. Raganora wouldn't have had the dagger. I did, and I still have it. Mother to daughter? Did my mother ever even touch that dagger? I touched it, and so did Sarah. Perhaps those other queens had daughters I don't know about.

Don't start over on that. Focus on the task at hand. What will the Dark Twins need when they arrive? They will have traveled a great distance by sea. They'll have missed bathing in fresh, warm water; eating meals other than what they ate on board; wearing freshly washed clothes; and sleeping in clean beds. And they'll need clothes for our climate. I think we can give them most of those.

The sound of Umma starting a fire in the nearby kitchen had Nagora out of bed and dressing for the day.

"Good morning, Umma. I noticed you didn't sleep in my mum's old room."

"No, I sleep in the saddle room. No more weapons there. Just my bow and arrows. And my saddle. It is near the back door. If people need me at night, they know they can knock there.

"The Dark Twins can sleep in Tagnyoriva's room, or in the sick room at the front. I have six cots there. No sick or injured needing my care."

"I suggest we let them choose," said Nagora.

"Yes. After we eat, I will go for food, and then we will cook. Chicken soup will be good."

Nagora enumerated the things she thought the Dark Twins would need.

"Yes, we will heat water for a bath and to wash clothes for sure." Umma pointed to the wooden door at the far corner of the kitchen. "Bring the butter and cheese from the wet box, and fill the pail with water. I have enough in the pot for our tea."

Umma had just left when Sagora arrived with a guard. "Gabe insisted, just in case some signers decide to act up. 'Be safe, not sorry,' he said." Sagora pointed to the doorway on the right. "Let's talk in the medicine room."

Nagora followed. "Did Raean enjoy seeing the dragon eggs?"

"Did he ever! The dragon laid eight last night. He couldn't believe how warm they were, and how heavy. He felt privileged to help bring the eggs in the cave, and to see and touch the hatchling eggs. Now he dreams of becoming a Dragon Talker like his mum."

"I'm so happy for you, and for Raean and Gabe. And for us! Look at us! I can't believe we're together—alone!"

Sagora touched Nagora's arm. "Let's enjoy it while we can. Gabe thinks his father went out on a limb with his proclamation last night, wording it to give us time, at least until the next council meeting. He thinks there will be signers standing in line to petition him to add their grievances to the meeting agenda. Anyway, let's just keep our eyes open for any troublemakers."

"We didn't hear a peep out of them last night."

"I think they were afraid of Danuka," said Sagora.

"Aye, and when she's far away, they'll call for her blood for their oak trees. Hypocrites!"

"Let's talk about other things. Were you able to meet with Raynhard?"

"No. From what I heard of Lars's audience with the king, and from what Bardas and Moreena have told me, Lars seems to play the role of a convinced Leafer." Nagora paused. "I have a question I want to ask you. I hope your answer will give me one less thing to worry about."

"Ask."

"Did you execute Acindor?"

Sagora took a breath and for a moment looked away from Nagora. "If you want to call it that, yes, I did. I didn't think the skystone blade could take the head off a man, but it did in a single swing. He didn't think I would do it. To tell the truth, I didn't think I would either. Then I asked myself what you would do. I didn't hesitate when he dared me. He was the first and only man I've killed. In that moment, I felt I belonged to Godomor's Hundred Best."

A brief smile crossed Sagora's face. "It was easier to carry his head back to Raynhard than have Simana and Tremon waste their energy to bring him along, kicking and screaming."

"You never told me," said Nagora.

"Some warriors like to boast. The dangerous ones never brag. They just do it. If you want more details, ask Simana. She leads a unit of Skull Bay's wall archers. I'm sure she remembers."

"I believe you. Now I don't have to worry about Acindor. Thanks for doing it. He deserved it."

Nagora pointed to the shelves that held the bound pages of her mother's medical notes. "Sagora, do you think Mum's recipe for the healer's secret is in her notes?"

Her sister shook her head. "Over the past three years, I've read through them several times. I didn't come across it. If I had, I'd remember." Sagora walked over to the shelves and took a bound volume of notes. She set it on the table near where Nagora stood. "There's a pattern to mum's notes. She arranged them in order of time. So there's a mix of recipes for medicines," she said, turning pages to show Nagora, "and treatments of patients; descriptions and drawings of medicinal plants and their uses; and actual plant samples pressed between pages.

"Because Mum bound the pages of all these volumes between two boards tied with ribbon, I was thinking of classifying the pages into groups that would be easier to refer to. Volumes of recipes, volumes of treatments, volumes of pressed plant samples, you get the idea. But tell me, why do you want that recipe?"

"Well, for another weapon I might use against the giant."

Sagora shook her head. "The only vial of that I'm aware of is in Mum's medical scrip. Remember, I showed it to you?"

"Aye, right here at this table," confirmed Nagora. "We were preparing the medical scrips for the campaign with Godomor's Hundred Best. You explained how Mum intended it to be used. If ever a warrior suffered so much from wounds she judged were fatal, she could give them a drop of this to allow them to fall asleep and go peacefully to the stars."

"That's right, and I also told you she was the only one to make that decision." Sagora put the volume back on the shelf.

"True."

"Enough talk of poison, little sister. Let's go to the kitchen to prepare for Umma."

"Godomor told me you spend a lot of time here," said Nagora.

"Aye, this has been my refuge. It was my home with Mum for so many years. I know my way around every nook and cranny, where Umma stores everything. She's been like a mother to me since Mum left." Sagora shrugged. "What can I say? I feel safe here. Many haven't forgiven me for what I did to Gabe. That's just starting to change as the facts of the events sink in. For some, it's easier to hate instead of trying to understand with an open mind.

"Godomor has been a great help. He spent a lot of time reasoning with Gabe about what I lived through in Windhaven. I owe him for that. He could have turned his son against me."

It was late afternoon, well after Umma's return. In the kitchen, a big pot of soup was simmering and two more loaves of bread were on the rise. At the front door, the guard announced a messenger.

Sagora brought Raean to the kitchen. "Important news! The lookouts have spotted a vessel under sail on a course for Skull Bay!" said the proud boy.

"Thank you, Messenger Raean!" said Umma. "Are you staying with us?"

"No, I cannot. I'm off to advise the king."

"Very well! Do your duty!" said Nagora.

"It smells good in here." Raean hugged his mother, waved, and left for the front door.

"They won't dock for at least another three counts," said Sagora. "Gabe told me his plan is to escort them here after they tie up at the dock and ready whatever they have to bring ashore. He figures it'll be easier to guard one set of twins at the dock than two. Umma, he'll post guards around the infirmary for the entire time they are here."

"That is good," said Umma, as she stirred the soup.

Sagora took Nagora's hand. "Little sister, are you feeling like I am? Anxious and nervous? These are important guests from far away. I want to do what's right for them."

"I feel that way too. The best we can do is to be ourselves. We're Dragon Talkers, and so are they. We have that in common."

One of Gabe's guards brought a written message. Sagora read it aloud. "'Your guests from the Sea Wolf are the Dark Twins, their two attendants, and Tagnyoriva.' Nagora! Umma! Our mother traveled with them! I can't believe it! She has come home! I can't wait to see her!" Then she finished reading the message. "'Tomorrow afternoon, to avoid threats to two sets of twins moving to the Grand Hall, King Godomor will greet them at the infirmary.'" She hugged Nagora and then Umma. The three had tears in their eyes.

Da remains in the Black Lands. Danuka spoke true. There must be a reason. I can guess, but I'll let Mum tell us.

"Tagnuska returns. When word spreads, many will be happy. I am happy. This will be a wonderful day," said Umma.

...

The sound of voices brought Nagora to a window. The commander of the contingent of archers and spear carriers was instructing the twelve guards on where to take up positions and how long they'd be on watch until relieved. Godomor and Gabe aren't taking any chances. "Sagora, our guests are coming. They've got an escort of fifteen, plus two pulling a cart with sea chests. We will have a full house."

Sagora and Umma joined her at the medicine room window. "I see Mum. Who is who among those wearing hooded coats? All four appear to be warriors. Two have strung bows, and two carry spears," said Nagora. "Umma, you go greet Mum first."

The sisters followed her to the entrance.

Umma opened the door to step outside.

"Umma! What joy I have to see you again!" Tagnyoriva took her dear friend in her arms as four sets of eyes looked on from hooded shadows.

"Tagnuska! Welcome home! You are in my thoughts every day, and I wonder what you are up to. Come in. You must know who waits for you."

"Aye, Gabe told me. First, let's bring in these four women from Kemet."

Umma motioned Nagora and Sagora into the medicine room; and then, with Tagnyoriva's help, she guided the four from Kemet into the sickroom. The two porters unloaded the wooden sea chests from the cart, carried them into the sick room, and lined them up on the floor.

The twins watched as their mother signed to the Kemet women to remove their coats and make themselves at home.

Then she turned in the direction Umma was pointing. She rushed across the entrance space into the twins' arms.

"My daughters! I wasn't sure I would find you in Skull Bay. Gabe told me you were both here!" She held them at arm's length and looked at their faces with questioning eyes before reaching to touch the scars on their foreheads. Tears welled up in her eyes as she pulled them both to her for a long hug.

Nagora felt her own tears build as she pulled back and examined her mother's face. It showed the signs of wear of those who are at sea in every weather. Her face was the color of well-worn leather, with fine crease lines around the eyes from squinting in the sun, wind, and rain. She wore her hair in two loose braids that fell over her shoulders and onto her chest. An abundance of white now streaked her hair.

Answering Tagnyoriva's unspoken question, Sagora said, "It's a long story, Mum. Don't worry. It's turning out for the better. I'll tell you about it later. In case you're wondering, I'm Sagora. I'll be helping Nagora take care of the Dark Twins."

Tagnyoriva brought her hands to her mouth as she looked from one daughter to the other.

Nagora found herself at a loss for words as tears spilled from her eyes. She was trying to calculate the actual time she had spent in her mother's presence. Her mind returned to that day eighteen years ago after reuniting with her. It was late in the evening after her mother had returned from caring for Godomor.

✝

Nagora watched in silence, studying her mother's profile and her hands, willing herself to sear those images of Tagnyoriva into her mind in that place where pictures of one's mother should always be. She waited until Tagnyoriva closed the book and stood to place it on the shelf. Then she stepped into the room.

"Nagora."

"Mum, will you hold me?"

Tagnyoriva opened her arms and took her close.

Nagora held her tight, wanting to feel her mother's heart-beat to see if her own heart remembered it. She breathed in the smell of her mother's skin and the scent of her mother's hair on her neck, searching for the distant memory of those odors. From the lake of tears inside her, which she thought was empty, a flood came. She cried, and Tagnyoriva kept her arms around her until they both stopped crying.

†

Nagora wiped her tears, swallowed, and took a breath. "Mum, how is Da? Is he safe?"

Tagnyoriva wiped at her tears, nodded, and managed a smile. "Yogari is fine. His health is good. He's as strong as ever. He's safe where he is, but there are conditions for his safe return. I'll say like your sister said: 'It's a long story.' First, we have important guests to take care of. Yogari sent a message to you two. The Dark Twins, as you call them, will deliver it soon when the time is right. Come, I'll introduce you. Let me take this off."

Tagnyoriva folded her coat over the back of a chair and rested her skystone blade sheath on the seat. She wore a tunic the color of undyed wool, with a keyhole neck and fitted sleeves that ended below her elbows. Over her tunic, she wore a forest green linen apron that covered her bosom and fell just below her knees.

Tagnyoriva led her daughters by the hand into the sickroom. The four Kemet women had been rummaging through the open sea chests. They stopped to stand, facing Tagnyoriva. Two tall, identical, dark-skinned young women, with long black hair that fell in loose curls down their backs, stepped forward. Behind them stood two younger women with the same dark skin, though they were slightly shorter and had shaved heads. Four sets of eyes darted from Tagnyoriva to Nagora and Sagora.

Tagnyoriva pointed to Sagora's Othala brand over the Tiwaz brand and then to herself. "My daughter, Sagora." Then pointing to Nagora's Tiwaz brand and then to herself, she said, "My daughter, Nagora."

The first two women stepped forward. Tagnyoriva pointed to one and then the other. "Princess Kalhata and Princess Tabiry, daughters of King Nimabaka and Queen Kamenirdis of Kemet, coming from their home city of Napata."

Nagora greeted them with the words: *"Miyoteh ka wisamiht awîyak, nîtisân okimâskwêsis."*

Sagora repeated the greeting.

"Kinanâskomitin," said Kalhata, *"miyoteh ka wisamiht awîyak, nîtisân,"* added Tabiry, completing the thank-you for their welcome.

In alternate turns, Kalhata and Tabiry spoke these words to form a sentence: *"Kîyânaw," "peta," "kiskeyitamowin," "wîcikiya," "paskwaskisiw."*

Sagora translated for her mother and Umma. "Together with you, we will bring knowledge for the dragons."

Tagnyoriva pointed to the women standing at the shoulders of the princesses. "Khensa, attendant protector of Princess Kalhata, and Nefruke, attendant protector of Princess Tabiry."

Those are the two with strung bows, thought Nagora, as the young women straightened and bowed their heads. Nagora and Sagora returned their bows.

When Tagnyoriva bowed, the four women returned to their open sea chests.

She turned to her daughters and Umma. "I don't know how they do it. The princesses speak the Language of the Dragons, but can't speak their own language to talk to their attendants. Yet they understand when their attendants speak to them in the language of Kemet. The entire trip I spent with them, I had to mime instructions and warnings with hand signs and gestures." Tagnyoriva touched the arms of her girls. "Now I'm relieved to have you take over for me. When the four of them communicate, there's no way for me to even try to follow what they're conveying."

"Leave it to us, Mum. We'll take care of them," said Sagora.

"The princesses want to bathe, arrange their hair, and dress their best to represent their parents. From what I understood, they want to be clean before they eat," said Tagnyoriva.

"We have water on the fire for them. When they are ready, we will put a basin in your room. We will keep water on the fire for all of you, and we'll keep the pail full with water from the well," said Umma.

"Thank you so much. It'll be a welcome change from bathing with cold seawater."

Tagnyoriva took Umma by the arm and led her to the medicine room. Her daughters followed. She showed Umma to a chair and took one herself. She pulled a book from her scrip. "Umma, it is my duty to bring you sad news today of your husband's death."

Umma crossed the fingers of her hands and looked out the window. "I knew in my heart he would not return. Tell me more."

"Gabe asked me to show you this. It is Henri's logbook for the ProudWynd. In his entries you'll find the story of the sad fate of him and his crew. Gabe wants it back to show Godomor for official notification to the families, and to prepare a ceremony of remembrance for the deceased."

Umma did not reach for the book. "How did you find it?"

"Our search for Raganora brought us to the port of Tanis in the Land of Kemet, known as the Black Lands. The Tanis harbormaster gave it to us."

"But that was not his destination."

"I know. In his log, he recounts how, at the last port of delivery, one of Raganora's mercenary ships had, by fortune, made it to port in their vessel, which was no longer seaworthy. The night before the ProudWynd was to set sail, the mercenaries commandeered it and forced Henri to bring them home to Tanis, promising him they would kill none of his crew if he complied. They forced Henri to ration the food on board. As a result, on arriving in Tanis, he and his crew were weak. They succumbed to the delta fever. None survived."

"Lars's brother, Norbuls, crewed on the ProudWynd," said Nagora. "This will be sad news for him as well."

"Not a one survived?" asked Umma.

"Not one," said Tagnyoriva. She placed the book on the table and reached for Umma's hands. "They've all gone to the stars."

"I will read his book and then tell our son and daughters."

"Are they here in Skull Bay?"

"Ronja is in Charlengon's domain with healer Emma. I sent Noora to help healer Jenna in Oliwer's domain. Jussi is like his father. He loves to be at sea. He is on a trader's boat."

"Do they have children?"

"I am a grandmother to Ronja's boy, Timo, now five. Soon, I will be a grandmother again. Ronja hopes for a girl this time. Noora will return in two months. She is not married. Jussi too is not married. When they are home, Noora and Jussi live in our lodge."

"Umma, you must inform them so they can come to the ceremony King Godomor will organize. I am sure he will try to accommodate all the families who have lost loved ones."

Umma nodded, picked up the logbook, and stood. "Excuse me. I will go read now."

Nagora placed a hand on her mother's shoulder. "It's never easy to deliver such news. Who was skipper of the Sea Wolf on this voyage?"

"Do you remember Mikersen and Pickersen?"

"Aye, are they still sailing?"

"No, but their sons sailed with us, Aarne Mikersen and Curre Pickersen. Aarne was our captain on this trip. Both are capable navigators and seamen, like their fathers."

"Mum, do you want to bathe first? It looks like those four are still choosing what to wear. Nagora and I will take care of them."

"That's an excellent idea. It'll make me feel better before we eat and talk more."

After Tagnyoriva and the Kemet women had bathed and dressed, they sat at Umma's table for the meal of chicken soup and fresh bread. Umma was her usual calm self, but not as talkative, mentioning she would finish reading Henri's log that night.

Sagora suggested that her mother should go join Godomor, Gabe, and Raean tomorrow before they come to Umma's to welcome the Dark Twins. Tagnyoriva agreed. Umma asked her to bring the ProudWynd's logbook to Godomor at the same time.

Sagora asked how Yogari had found the Dark Twins. As her mother spoke to answer the question, Nagora summarized the events in her own mind to tell Lars later.

In Kemet, at the port of Tanis, Yogari inquired about a ship laden with gold coins and carrying a foreign man and woman that might have docked there fifteen years earlier. Yogari was on a quest to find the evil queen, Raganora, to bring her back to the Land of the Danu so King Raynhard could serve justice on her. He also hoped to bring back the gold Raganora and her captain, Grallimdor, had stolen. Since Yogari's inquiries led nowhere, he decided on a different tactic: to follow the gold coins.

Yogari reasoned dragon coins would have to turn up, eventually. Through his interpreter, he met with traders plying the great river inland and the desert routes. He gave each a gold dragon coin, promising a thousand-fold reward to help him recover his king's gold.

Months later, a trader came to Yogari with a gold dragon coin. It was given to the man by a king seeking a foreigner able to show him another such coin. The king had promised the trader a reward of a hundred more gold coins if the foreigner knew the story connected to the coin and spoke the language connected with that coin.

Yogari showed the trader another dragon coin and asked if he knew how the king had come into possession of the dragon coins. The trader recounted the story the king had told him.

A foreigner, guided by a trader who had traveled to that land, was in search of a king in a faraway land to share a gift of value worth its weight in gold on condition the king gave him haven. The gift was a ship loaded with a cargo of rare honey. Bees had made it from the nectar of flowers that grew in no other land, and it tasted sublime, incomparable to any other.

After tasting that honey, and with the promise of a handsome fee, the trader assured the foreigner he knew the King of Napata would give him sanctuary for a share of that honey of such unique sweetness and flavor.

Napata was far up the great river, between the third and fourth cataracts; thus they had to carry the honey overland past three waterfalls, and after each one, place it on a new vessel to continue their journey. Since the honey was stored in wax-sealed amphorae, and each amphora had been packed in a wooden box lined with straw, the honey jars survived unbroken.

Then Yogari asked the trader why the king wanted to meet with the foreigner who knew of the dragon coins. The king had explained to the trader that, the day before the foreigner's arrival, the queen had given birth to twin baby girls. The next day, the king savored the honey and gave the foreigner haven for as long as he desired. So pleased was the foreigner that he placed gold dragon coins, strung on gold chains, around the necks of the baby girls.

The following day, the king's servants found the foreigner dead in the palace guest room. How he died remains a mystery. His death dismayed the king because he wanted to know the story behind the coins.

Being Yogari's only lead of the cargo and a foreigner, and because both matched the time of the events, Yogari asked the trader to take him to the king of Napata. The trader informed Yogari there was no need, since every year the royal family traveled down the great river to spend the summer at their palace in Tanis. At that moment, the king was on his way. Yogari could ask for an audience to speak to King Nimabaka after his arrival. That was when Yogari met the Dark Twins.

It was not until the next day when King Godomor came to the infirmary, and Tagnyoriva introduced the Dark Twins to him, that Nagora would learn more about how her father had found the Dark Twins.

That morning, Sagora helped the Kemet women put order in the sick room to make room for King Godomor's arrival. Then the four women took over Tagnyoriva's room. The attendants spent the better part of the morning combing and arranging their mistresses' hair. When Tagnyoriva's daughters stopped by the room, they took turns answering the questions the Dark Twins had about the dragons and the maze.

When the princesses returned to the sickroom to await Godomor's arrival, they wore hooded robes of woven white wool with keyhole necklines. In contrast, the beautiful features of the women's dark-skinned faces stood out, especially when they smiled, revealing their gleaming white teeth.

The hoods of their robes, each with a single white tassel, draped over their shoulders and down their backs.

A single, long thick braid of black hair hung from the spiraled arrow bands of gold at the backs of their heads. The women wore leather sandals on their feet.

Something Nagora did not remember from her dreams of them was the fine gold chain each wore around her neck. From each chain hung a gold dragon coin pierced with two holes, one on each dragon wing. Those coins are like the one I wear!

Under armed escort, King Godomor arrived with two elder witnesses, Gabe, and Raean, who held Tagnyoriva's hand. Umma welcomed them and showed them into the room. Nagora placed three chairs near the far end of the room to seat the elders on either side of the king.

Tagnyoriva rested her hand on Raean's shoulder and introduced the princesses in a more formal manner than she had to her daughters and Umma the day before.

Still standing, Godomor spread his arms with palms open before him. He looked to Nagora. "Please translate my message for the others in the room." He spoke to the Dark Twins in the Language of the Dragons. "Welcome to my land, now known as the Land of Skulls."

The Dark Twins looked at each other and then back at Godomor with smiling faces.

He returned their smiles, held his hands before him, and continued. "It is a humble welcome that I, King Godomor, offer you today in the presence of the honorable Skull Bay elders," he pointed to the man and woman who sat nearby, smiling as they listened, "who come to witness my greetings to you." The elders stood, bowed, and sat.

"And in the presence of those dear to me." He showed as he spoke: "My son, Prince Gabyndor; my grandson, Raean; his mother, Sagora; his aunt, Nagora; and my healers, Tagnuska and Ummnuska. I owe them my life and will forever be grateful to them."

Godomor turned to Umma. "Today Tagnuska brought me the logbook in which your husband, Henri, Captain of the ProudWynd, recorded, until his last breath, the details of the unfortunate deaths of his crew. My son and I share in your sorrow and promise to inform all the families of the crew of Henri's vessel. We promise to hold a remembrance ceremony for them. May they find welcome places among the stars with their ancestors."

The king looked to the Dark Twins. "Tagnyoriva, I thank you for bringing the Princesses of Kemet here." He gestured toward them. "Fear not, daughters of King Nimabaka and Queen Kamenirdis. Your parents have entrusted you to my care. While you are here, I will ensure your protection. A more deserving welcome by the people of my land is not possible because of old beliefs some here still hold about twins. Please accept my humble welcome."

The princesses bowed to King Godomor.

Tagnyoriva stepped forward. "The princesses wish to deliver Yogari's message. Nagora and Sagora will receive it. Nagora will speak it as she hears it, and Godomor, will you please translate it for us?" Her mother had warned them of this moment. Nagora looked forward to hearing her father's message.

The princesses grasped the dragon coins that hung from the gold chains at their necks and turned to their attendants, who unhooked the clasps holding the chains together. Khensa and Nefruke pulled the chains through the holes of the coins to release them.

Tagnyoriva stepped to the side. "Now Kalhata and Tabiry will transmit the message Yogari sent. My daughters, let them guide your hands. Do not be afraid." Nagora wondered why there wasn't a written message instead. How will this work?

Kalhata and Tabiry reached past each other's far shoulder so their fingers rested on the far sides of their faces. They motioned for Nagora and Sagora to do the same and come closer.

The Dark Twins held up the dragon coins, showing the dragon on that side of the coin. Then they turned the coins over. Nagora couldn't believe what she saw. How can that be? Kalhata's coin bore the Tiwaz symbol in relief and Tabiry's bore Othala over the Tiwaz!

Kalhata placed the dragon coin against the Tiwaz brand on Nagora's forehead and then pressed her own forehead against the dragon side of the coin to hold it in place. Tabiry did the same to Sagora.

Then the Dark Twins joined the fingers of Tagnyoriva's twins with theirs.

"Close your … " said Kalhata.

" … eyes and … " said Tabiry.

" … breathe deeply … " said Kalhata.

" … with us," said Tabiry.

When the rhythm of their breathing matched, Yogari's face appeared in their mind's eye, and he spoke in the Language of the Dragons. "My daughters, for the future of the dragons, these two Dragon Talkers your mother brings to you are vessels of knowledge of dragons past, dragons present, and dragons future. They, with the help of the Dragon Talkers from my bloodline, will transmit the knowledge they carry to the dragons in the maze. The survival of the dragons depends on that knowledge. I know you can make it happen."

For a moment, the image disappeared and then returned. "I have placed myself in guarantee to King Nimabaka and Queen Kamenirdis. I swore their daughters would return on Danuka's back. When they do, I will be free to return with Danuka.

"But Danuka will only be able to make such a flight once she has the knowledge. The knowledge will give her greater strength and the ability to find me because, as a Dragon Talker, I will be her beacon. I will guide her to me by the shortest distance."

Again, the image disappeared and returned. "Sagora, I trained you as a rider. I offered you a chance to become an apprentice Dragon Talker. You refused because you feared how it would change you. Daughter, in my heart, I know you will help the dragons. It is in your healer's heart to do so."

The image disappeared, and the four twins released their hold on each other. The Dark Twins removed the coins which had stuck to their foreheads. Their attendants strung the gold chains onto the coins and reattached them.

Tagnyoriva spoke. "There are two things Yogari did not speak of in his message." She looked down at the floor before continuing. "One, when two female dragons are healthy with eggs, they will fly the attendants to Napata. The dragons will stay there with Princess Kalhata and Princess Tabiry, final gifts from Yogari, for his safe return."

She looked around the room. "Second, there is a time limit for Danuka to fly the princesses home. If she doesn't reach Tanis by then, King Nimabaka will order Yogari's execution."

Nagora translated her mother's words for the princesses.

Why would the king and queen allow their daughters to make such a journey?

Nagora answered the question with a question of her own, one to which she knew the answer.

How can a mother abandon her own daughter only days after her birth? The circumstances that came into play for that to happen will someday be part of my star story. Who will survive me to tell it? Her thoughts returned to the Dark Twins.

Do their parents know about dragons and why their daughters have come this far? They must. Perhaps Mum will get to that part tonight.

That night, Nagora sat with her mother at Umma's kitchen table. The logs on the fireplace grate had reduced to hot embers, displaying dying flames. Earlier that morning, Nagora had heard from Kalhata and Tabiry how they had met Yogari in Tanis; but now, she wanted her mother to tell it.

Tagnyoriva shared her story. "With our dragon coins and an interpreter, we gained an audience with the king and queen three days after the royal family had arrived. The king wanted to know the origin of the dragon coins. Your da explained about the history of the Land of the Danu, its dragons and their gold, and who might have minted the coins: workers in the royal mint, or the Little People in their secret caves."

Nagora smiled. "The part about the Little People must have raised the king's eyebrows."

"It did, but when Yogari told the king that he was a Dragon Talker and spoke the Language of the Dragons, both he and his wife showed greater interest. Yogari felt he was getting closer to the true reason the king was searching for a foreigner with this knowledge. He told the king the story the trader had told him."

Tagnyoriva pointed towards the room where the princesses slept. "The queen explained how, whenever they tried to remove the gold-coin necklaces from their baby girls, they cried, but their crying stopped as soon as they put the necklaces back. The queen expressed their worry about not understanding the language their daughters spoke as they grew older. Though, the daughters seemed to understand each other.

"To the queen's surprise, Yogari suggested their daughters might be Dragon Talkers and, if the king permitted him to speak to them, he could determine that."

Tagnyoriva waved her hand. "The king was eager to know. He called for his daughters, now twenty-year-old women.

"Well, as soon as they stepped into the room and began speaking, your da engaged them in conversation. Those twins seemed pleased. It was like they were meeting with an old friend.

"When he asked to look at the coins, what shocked Yogari were the relief symbols on the opposite sides. He explained to the king that he had two daughters, twins also, and one was a Dragon Talker who wore the Tiwaz brand on her forehead. As for the symbol on Tabiry's coin, that to him was a mystery, considering how long the girls had been wearing the necklaces."

Tagnyoriva reached for Nagora's hand. "Now that I've seen Sagora's brand, it confirms what Yogari learned from the twins."

"What did Da learn?"

"He had looked at each coin. After seeing the symbols on Tabiry's, and while still holding it, he reached for Kalhata's again. While holding both, a voice spoke in a whisper in his ear. It said, 'Two sets of twins, one of light, one of darkness. Both destined to empower dragons, for in light dwells dark and in dark dwells light. One cannot exist without the other. Let the voice of dark bring forth the light of knowledge. Those of your bloodline will make this happen.'"

Nagora wondered how the Little People had journeyed there. When? Why? With the foreigner who died a mysterious death after placing the necklaces around the infants' necks? To protect the honey? The words from Tagnyoriva's telling the night before came back to her: "a gift of value worth its weight in gold." Ha! There was more than honey in the amphorae. The dragon's gold! The Little People followed it! They knew Da would follow it too!

Yet what about the symbols on Tabiry's coin? If they were destined for Sagora, they were a window to the future. When were those coins created? How did they get into the foreigner's hands? By chance? Or on purpose? Could he have seen them as coins not struck properly, lacking the coat of arms of the Land of the Danu? Are there others with the same symbols? Those coins are pierced and fit on gold chains. Will I ever learn the answers?

Her mother squeezed her hand. "You must be thinking about your destiny."

Nagora nodded. "And Sagora's. How did the king and queen react to that?"

Tagnyoriva's eyes widened. "They weren't sure what to believe because your da tried to explain what Dragon Talkers do, and that their girls were Dragon Talkers.

"What truly had them wondering was when Yogari explained why the girls were speaking in turn, one starting a thought and the other completing it. It was because of the amount of knowledge they were holding for the dragons, too much for one to hold. Your da tried to convince the king and queen that their daughters had been gifted with this knowledge. That, with the help of you and Sagora, they could transmit it to the dragons, and afterward be able to speak their own language and that of the dragons."

"How did Da convince them?"

"Well, the king was skeptical that Yogari was even speaking to his daughters. Yogari had the king whisper a command in his interpreter's ear, who then whispered it to your da. Yogari then relayed the command to the daughters. When the daughters carried out the command, the king knew his girls understood Yogari."

Nagora's mother clapped her hands. "That opened their eyes! Afterward, the king and queen spent the rest of the day speaking with their daughters through Yogari and the interpreter. They learned their daughters understood them, but when they tried to answer in their own language, it came out in the Language of the Dragons. It had always been that way since they were young."

"Were the twins eager to come here?" asked Nagora.

"Aye, for the chance to get their language back because that would make them better warriors, able to take command and lead others. Still, Yogari wanted to make sure they were up to the voyage. The Sea Wolf in no way has the comforts of the royal barge that sails the great river of Kemet.

"Your da had the princesses come visit the Wolf with their attendants and an escort to see where they'd spend their days on the voyage. We showed them the kinds of clothes they should wear for the trip and here, given our much cooler weather, as well as the practicality of wearing a scrip to carry useful items.

"Yogari told them his Dragon Talker daughter would give them sets of skystone blades like the ones we wore." Tagnyoriva paused. "That reminds me, who will make those for them?"

"We have smiths at Maze Point who apprenticed with Geirador. He brought them skystone pieces, the recipe for the alloy, and blade molds. They're making some for our dragon riders. I'll have them make the additional sets."

Tagnyoriva continued. "Your da described the stone dwellings they'd live in during their stay, and he told them not to expect royal treatment in the Land of Skulls, where the proud warriors lived simple lives under the rule of a just king. He also warned them of the signers, but assured them the king would protect them."

"They didn't even hesitate?"

"No. They told Yogari they trusted him because, in revealing their destiny, he helped confirm the significance of the dragon coins they wore at their necks. They said they were ready to carry out their duties as Dragon Talkers."

Tagnyoriva leaned back in her chair. "You know the agreement your da reached. This morning, Gabe told me about Sagora's brands, though not in significant detail, because he knows she'll want to tell me herself. And he told me how she became a Dragon Talker. Nagora, the more I think about it, the more I believe in destiny. It's the most mysterious of things that leaves us with so many unanswered questions. No matter how hard we try to grasp it, it eludes us. All we can do is accept it."

Do I have to accept a curse I cannot see? Does destiny tell me I have no choice?

"How did Da give the message to them?"

"The same voice, which had whispered in his ear your destinies, instructed Yogari to place the symbol side of the dragon coins in the palms of his hands, and then press the coins against the twins' foreheads and speak the message from his mind to theirs. Yogari thinks because they are vessels of knowledge for the dragons, this is possible. After they've delivered it, he thinks such mind messages won't be possible."

Nagora recalled the time in Moreena's secret cave with Sarah when she used the dragon-tear amulet to show events from her past.

†

"Come, give me the amulet and lie on your back. It'll be easier." Nagora focused before pulling the leather lace over Sarah's head. Only images from when I wore this amulet. If Sarah wishes I see something from when she wore it, let it be her decision. The amulet hung free at Nagora's neck.

Once Sarah had lain on a hide, Nagora brought the amulet to her lips and closed her eyes. So many events to show you.

Too many. Only enough to give you proof. One at a time. If you want more, I'll call them forth.

She moved closer to Sarah's right side, took her arm, and placed it along her left thigh. "I will place the amulet on your forehead and then lean over and place my forehead against it. In that position, I will show you images of events the amulet witnessed as I wore it. If you wish to hold me, you may. I'll take you from one event to another to show you what you must know. And I'll try to show you my thoughts and feelings at those moments."

"I'm ready."

†

Did the gold coins the Dark Twins wear witness my and Sagora's brandings? They've worn them since birth. Possibly Kalhata's with the Tiwaz, but not Tabiry's with Othala over the Tiwaz. Knowledge of dragons past, dragons present, and dragons future. And unknown powers for Danuka and her dragons. I see only another dragon, or dragons, that could have given the Dark Twins this knowledge to transmit. Why do I try to solve this riddle? I need to focus on the task at hand.

These unanswered questions keep nagging me. "You and Da were searching for Raganora, to bring her back to the Land of the Danu so King Raynhard could punish her and reclaim his gold. In all that time, were you ever able to track and find Raganora or learn what happened to her? And was Grallimdor that foreigner? Or did he go by another name?"

"No, we found not a trace of her. And when we used their names in our queries, we turned up nothing. I don't know if Yogari ever mentioned the foreigner's name. Had it been Grallimdor, he would have. That's why your da followed the coins. It paid off. We found the king's gold. Someday, much of it will come back to Raynhard."

That puzzle piece is still in play. Could Heqet have used Raganora somehow? Let that question ride.

Instead, I'll ask Mum if she still has the healer's secret. If she does and consents to give me some, I'll have one more weapon in my arsenal.

Nagora explained how she had used the healer's secret poison in the past, and how she might use it in the days to come.

Tagnyoriva stared at Nagora. "I destroyed that recipe years ago, but I still have the vial. I'll give it to you in the morning on one condition. If you don't use it, you're to destroy the vial by placing it in a hot fire in a deep outdoor firepit. Promise?"

"I promise, Mum."

The next morning, Tagnyoriva led Nagora into the medicine room. "Be careful when handling the glass vial in here. Stick to our agreement and keep it secret." She handed over the small leather-wrapped box from her medical kit.

"I will, Mum. Thank you."

A short time later, Sagora returned with Raean, who followed her with a handcart that held six saddlebags. He unloaded them while his mother spoke to the Dark Twins. "Tomorrow morning at first light, Gabe will deliver six horses with saddles. Will you need one or two mules with pack saddles to bring your belongings? Or do you intend to travel fast?"

The Dark Twins did not hesitate. "Travel … "

" … fast!"

Sagora smiled. "That's what I thought. Weapons, bedrolls, a change of clothes, and rations for the road tomorrow. Raean, tell your da to have two of his contingent lead the mules that will carry the princesses' belongings. They should arrive at Auntie Nagora's lodge before nightfall."

"Aye, Mum." He was out the door.

Sagora looked around the sickroom and spoke to her mother and Umma. "They'll have to repack all that into their four chests and spread the weight evenly among them. It'll help when we tie the chests onto the packsaddles of the mules. Umma, your sick room will be free again."

The healer smiled. "That will be good."

Tagnyoriva scratched her head. "I'll try to get Khensa and Nefruke to do that and understand that we leave early tomorrow. I think the saddlebags will help."

Nagora hugged her mother. "I'll tell the princesses what you're trying to do. They'll surely help you."

After Nagora had conveyed the message, it didn't take long for the princesses and their attendants to speak with hand signs and gestures as they set about packing their saddlebags and lining up their weapons.

To Maze Point
Natawi Âpihtâwâyihk Miniwatimik

The next morning, the princesses thanked Umma for her hospitality and gave her two silver bracelets.

As promised, Gabe showed up with six saddled horses and a dozen mounted archers. Sagora, and to Nagora's pleasant surprise, Raean rode with them. Nagora noticed he was wearing not only a bow tied to a quiver, but Gabe's small scrip made from the skin of a bear's paw. He wore the narrow strap like his father had, across one shoulder so the claws of the scrip rested on his opposite thigh. When Gabe wore it, it rested on the scars left by the bear that had attacked him when he was a boy. Thanks to Geirador, Gabe survived. Is it an amulet to protect his son?

Two of Gabe's men arrived, each leading a pack mule. Umma pointed them to the back door of the infirmary where the sea chests of the Kemet women waited.

The group mounted and waved to Umma. She extended her hand in the dragon-chord salute as they left her corral.

...

On their ride out of Skull Bay, Gabe led them to Godomor's lodge, where the king wished them a safe journey. From there, the group rode in silence. Except for a few signers, most onlookers were quiet. Nagora wondered if they had ever seen two sets of twins at the same time. She guessed the curious lining the streets and road wanted to see the four dark-skinned women from away, since two were Dragon Talkers bringing gifts of great knowledge to the dragons who had days before gifted them with eggs. The coats, hooded shirts, and woolen hats the women wore to keep off the morning chill only afforded the bystanders a view of the women's faces and hands.

The group made good time, stopping only for trail rations and to stretch their legs at noonday. Nagora figured they would arrive at Maze Point by the end of the afternoon, well before the evening meal.

When the group rode up the last grassy hill, Raean called out, "Dragons! I see the dragons!" He was right. High in the sky, fifteen dragons circled in the air.

Nagora pointed up, and in her mind she spoke to Danuka.

We are home, *Okâwîmâw*. The Dark Twins are with us. Four Dragon Talkers to complete the six you need. Tagnyoriva is with me. Gabe and Raean have come with escorts.

By the time the riders reached the top of the hill, the dragons, led by Danuka, flew by in a slow glide, displaying the multiple shades of their sparkling, iridescent colors.

Nagora stopped to let the group admire Danuka and her brood as they circled back, this time in a formation Nagora had never seen them fly. It was the Tiwaz, with Danuka at the point. It made Nagora's heart ache as she swallowed the lump in her throat.

The four from Kemet sat on their mounts with mouths wide open as they watched the fifteen dragons. They rose higher in the sky and curved back until they were over the maze where they split up and flew off in every direction. Then, as one, the dragons climbed in the sky in a spiral until they followed one another. Then they broke apart and flew toward the group, slowing the flap of their wings until they were gliding again. They skimmed so close over the group that the surrounding air moved as if from a great gust of wind. The riders' horses whinnied and pranced.

When the dragons flew out to sea, Nagora pointed to her lodge in the distance, just below the big stone bluff. "*Kîyânaw kiwe.*"

The Dark Twins repeated her words. "We are … "

" … going home."

Nagora glanced at Raean and Gabe. Both looked proud.

"Will Dannor be at home?" asked Raean.

Nagora smiled at him and then glanced at her mother. "We'll find out soon. Let's go!" Nagora had told Tagnyoriva about her son, even how he had entertained Sagora's boys in those strange days in Windhaven. Mum too can't wait to see Dannor.

Dannor had just finished helping Jari and Jenni weed the garden crops. He was on his way back to the stable from the tool shed next to the barn.

Raean spotted him and rode ahead to greet him.

...

As the group drew closer, Tagnyoriva said, "By the stars, Nagora! He looks just like Lars! The girls around here must be falling over themselves for his attention." Dannor was leading Raean's mount and looking up at him in cheerful conversation.

Kalhata and Tabiry said, "The Golden … "

" … Boy!"

"See what I mean?" said her mother. "Look at those four. They're completely taken by him and they haven't even met him yet." The eyes of the four girls from Kemet were wide open in admiration of Dannor. It was as if they were watching someone they could never have imagined or dreamt of.

Dannor waved and, like his father, smiled a grand, winning smile. He let go of the bridle and ran toward the group. "Auntie Sagora! It's good to see you again! Gabe! How are you? Thanks for bringing Raean! Each time I see him, he has grown."

Nagora had dismounted.

Dannor hugged her and looked to Tagnyoriva. "Don't introduce this woman. She has to be my Grandma! Now I'm certain from whom Mum and Auntie Sagora get their beauty." He helped her dismount and hugged her. "Welcome to Maze Point, Grandma Tagnya! I've heard so much about you, and now I get to meet you." He hugged her.

Tagnyoriva held his shoulders as she looked up into his face. "If I didn't know who you were, I would swear right now I've been taken back in time and Lars Marraden is standing before me." She stepped back to look him over. "I can't get over it!" She reached out to hug him again. "My grandson, Dannor! I'm so happy to meet you."

Nagora placed a hand on her mother's shoulder, and the other on her son's. "What did I tell you? He's just like his da!"

Sagora laughed. "That's true! He's a replica of Lars in more ways than one." She stepped toward Dannor to take his hug. As he held her, he whispered in her ear.

Nagora didn't hear it, but when Sagora whispered back in Dannor's ear, he held her tighter.

Then he looked from his aunt to his mother. "Now you two will be on my case."

Raean laughed. "Don't worry, Dannor! I'll be on your side!"

Dannor gave the boy a thumbs-up and then shook Gabe's hand. "Prince Gabyndor, I can guess why you came with an impressive escort." He looked to the four from Kemet. "Will you introduce me to these ladies?"

Gabe smiled. "It's the least I can do. As for introductions, I'll leave that to your mum."

The four women had dismounted and removed their hats. The attendants stood a pace behind their mistresses, yet from places where they could observe Dannor.

Nagora and her mother led Dannor before them. Pointing to her son, she spoke in the Language of the Dragons. "This is my son Dannor," and then, pointing to the Dark Twin to her right, "Meet Princess Kalhata and her attendant, Khensa."

Dannor bowed.

She pointed to the Dark Twin to her left. "Meet Princess Tabiry and her attendant, Nefruke."

He bowed again.

"They are the daughters of King Nimabaka and Queen Kamenirdis, and they have traveled from the faraway land of Kemet to carry out their duties as Dragon Talkers."

Dannor then spoke in the Language of the Dragons. "Welcome to Maze Point." He motioned to his mother and Sagora to join him and the Dark Twins. As they did, he pointed in the maze's direction. "My sister, Sarah, is at the maze right now. She should be back soon. When we are together, it will be our greatest pleasure to help you carry out your duty. Our dragons are as anxious as you for this event. Thank you for journeying here. We will do our best to make your stay here memorable."

Her son's polite welcome impressed Nagora.

Kalhata and Tabiry stepped forward and reached out to Dannor. Each twin touched his hair and his face and pointed to his eyes. "He is truly the Golden Boy … " said Kalhata.

" … who visits in our dreams," said Tabiry.

I dreamt of them, and they dreamt of my son? Why? How? There must be a reason. Is this to be another unknown?

In a whisper, Dannor said, "Mum, they're so beautiful."

Tagnyoriva said, "Yogari said the same thing when he met them."

When the princesses stepped back, Gabe and Raean came forward.

"Nagora, it'll be safer for the women from Kemet to stay here rather than at the inn. It'll be easier for Raean," he placed a hand on his son's shoulder, "and me, and the escorts, to guard your lodge. We'll set up a temporary barracks in your barn loft. A kitchen wagon and another with our food and feed for our horses should arrive before nightfall, along with the pack mules carrying the sea chests of the Kemet women. The guards have a rotation schedule for watch duty. I'll advise your farmhands we'll be guarding them too and how we're setting up in the barn. They won't have to worry about chores. We'll be glad to have something to do when not on watch."

"That's an excellent idea. I'll worry less. You'll find places for some of your mounts in the stable, and for others in the barn." Nagora rubbed her chin. "I'm not sure how our guests will fit in the lodge!"

Dannor reached for her hand. "Not to worry, Mum. Give your room to the princesses. You can take the bed on the top floor. Auntie Sagora and Grandma Tagnya can have Sarah's room. The attendants can have mine. Sarah and I can sleep on cots near the fireplace."

Nagora shrugged. "That's settled, then." I get to sleep in the little room where Alizarine slept.

Dannor pointed. "Here comes Sarah!"

As soon as Sarah crossed the stream bridge, she rode Kimmo at a gallop toward the group. She was quick to dismount. "Danuka told me! I'm so happy to see you!" Sagora and Raean ran to her. The boy arrived first and hugged her. She held him at arm's length. "Raean! My! You just keep growing! Give me another hug!"

Sagora in turn gave Sarah a hug; after a quiet moment between them, Sagora withdrew and said, "Raean missed you the last time you visited in Skull Bay. Since he wanted to come visit you and Dannor, his father decided it was time for him to take part in escort duty."

"I'm pleased you've joined us, Bowman Raean," said Sarah.

The lad smiled.

Gabe approached and hugged Sarah. "We've brought important guests."

Sarah looked to her grandmother and the Dark Twins. "I can see that!" She waved as she strode toward Tagnyoriva, pulling Sagora and Raean with her. "Grandma Tagnya! What a happy day! It's been so long! You look good!"

"Oh! Sarah! How I've missed your hugs!" She held her granddaughter in a warm embrace. When Sarah released her, Tagnyoriva held her forearms. "Girl, you're a woman now! And so beautiful!"

Dannor approached with his mother and the princesses and their attendants. "Come, Sarah! I want to introduce you to our guests. It'll help me remember their names." Holding hands, his sister, grandmother, and Sagora joined the Kemet women, as did Raean and Gabe.

Raean reached for the hands of Khensa and Nefruke as they looked on, waiting to be introduced.

Following the introductions, Sarah spoke in the Language of the Dragons. "I have a message from Danuka. Mum, please translate for Grandma Tagnya, Raean, and Gabe."

Nagora nodded. Sarah didn't include Sagora in her list, so she surely knows of her aunt's decision to become a Dragon Talker. Sagora must have whispered it to them when she hugged Dannor and Sarah earlier.

Sarah continued. "Danuka wants the six of us Dragon Talkers to meet with her today on the cliff above our lodge, one count before sunset. If all goes as she hopes, she will have instructions to prepare us for tomorrow night. Best we walk up to the lodge now. We have to settle in and prepare a meal."

The Dark Twins squeezed Nagora's hands. I'm as eager as they are. Sarah led the way, with Tagnyoriva and Sagora and Gabe. The others followed.

After their evening meal, the six made their way up the hill, past the big stone bluff, to meet with Danuka. Dannor led the way, holding the princesses' hands. Nagora couldn't make out what they were saying, but the laughter of the twins told her they were enjoying her son's company.

Standing at the top of the cliff with their backs to the sun, the six looked out to sea and waited. The strong afternoon breeze had died down, and the waves had lost their whitecaps.

The princesses and Sagora will be in for a surprise. Danuka rises in a slow glide from below the cliff, as if appearing from nowhere. She will spread her wings wide. With the sun shining on her, they won't believe their eyes. Until she lands, all the iridescent colors of her dragonskin scales will be on display.

Then she will fold her wings forward to rest her wing talons on the ground before her. Her long tail, with its bulbous red tip with top and side fins, will wrap itself around her as she lowers her belly to the ground.

Will they be frightened when she stares at them with her red eyes? I have warned them. And Da must have told them about Danuka.

The dragon appeared at the end of her glide up above the top of the cliff. Her wings held her in place in the air. Her long tail undulated, and her neck swayed from side to side as she looked at the six. The rays of sunshine appeared to ripple outward in iridescent waves from her chest to her wing tips.

Danuka spoke to them mind-to-mind in the Language of the Dragons, staring at each Dragon Talker in turn when she named them.

Dragon Talkers, tomorrow you must prepare. You will need a ladder to climb to the lintels of the inner ring. You will need shelters beneath the outer ring, bedrolls, food, and water.

Before you come to the maze, you shall bathe in the stream so you will stand clean, without clothes and without weapons, on the inner ring.

Before we dragons come to the maze, we shall bathe in the sea.

In the maze tomorrow at midnight, when half the moon is in darkness and half is in light, I shall gather with my young and you, my Dragon Talkers.

First, we dragons will perch on the inner ring, facing each other. I will lock my talons with my firstborn male on one wing and my firstborn female on the other wing. The six remaining pairs of females will take their place in order of birth to my right and left.

Then, starting with Kalhata and Tabiry standing next to my son and first daughter, each Dragon Talker will take hold of two of my remaining daughters and face the outer ring. Dannor and Sarah will move the ladder for you to climb to your dragon pair. Dannor will be the last to climb the ladder to his pair.

To complete the net, the Little People will come from the well in the thousands and spread up the lintel pillars, covering us to link us so Kalhata and Tabiry can begin the transmission. On my signal, they will transmit the knowledge of dragons past, of dragons present, and of dragons future.

Kalhata and Tabiry will be exhausted after they transmit the knowledge. You other Dragon Talkers will be tired and need sleep. The safety of Kalhata and Tabiry must be your first concern when you bring them down from the lintels. Once they are secure in their bedrolls, it will be time for you to rest.

My dragons and I will also need to rest. We will sleep in the caves below the maze. Do not disturb us. Once we have rested, we will return to the sky.

After conveying her instructions, and with a last intent look at each Dragon Talker, Danuka flew seaward.

Dannor approached with the princesses and spoke in the language they understood. "We will have a busy day tomorrow."

Sagora held out her amulet. "Dannor, I still can't believe it! *Niya isihtwawin asici kanawisimowin.*" She laughed. "Mother gifted me not only this amulet, but this language I now speak as if I always have."

Dannor pointed to his amulet. "I'm still amazed I can speak it!"

"After tomorrow, we too will … " said Kalhata.

" … speak the language like you," said Tabiry.

Sagora smiled at them. "Yes! Each in your own complete thoughts! And then we will speak and laugh together with ease."

Nagora reached out to gather them in a circle. "We are the keys to the future of the dragons. May what we unlock serve them well."

…

On their return to the lodge, Nagora unpacked the wooden shoes she had bought in Windhaven. After Sarah tried them on and they fit, the others wanted to try them. They fit Khensa and Nefruke, but no one else.

Nagora placed the shoes in Sarah's hands. "Tomorrow morning when you and Dannor go to the stable to check if Gabe needs help with the chores, give these to Jari. Tell him that later I'll share what I learned from the shoemaker about how to make them.

"Explain to him and Jenni that we have guests. Ask Jenni if she could bake extra bread for us, and a big pot of her smoke-cured venison stew that's so tasty. Tell her we'll be eleven at the table, and that we'll cook our own meals after that.

"Then find Gabe and invite him and Raean to come for the evening meal with us. And let them know how busy we'll be at the maze tomorrow."

Tagnyoriva and the attendants, Khensa and Nefruke, wanted to help at the maze the next day. Nagora warned her mother she could get lost in the maze if she tried to go in or out on her own. If she did, Danuka would find her. The princesses gave the same warning to their attendants.

Nagora was curious if her sister and the Dark Twins could find their way into the maze center on their own. She had them lead the way on the first trip in when everyone carried something to help set up camp.

Finding their way to the center was effortless. Tagnyoriva could not get over the uniform fit of the stones along the maze walls. "Yogari won't believe you and Lars built this over fifteen years, even if you had the help of the Little People. It's huge! The thickness and the height of these walls! So much work has gone into this! I have trouble believing it myself. And Lars can't find his way in?"

Nagora laughed. "Not even with the map. Though, he knows of another way."

First, they hung ropes from the lintels of the outer ring. Then they tied them to the pillars. With a few support poles, they fashioned waxed canvas tarps from the stable and barn into comfortable shelters where they hung lanterns and water-skins. Dannor carried in the small ceramic stove he had brought the last time. With it, he brought a big bundle of kindling wood tied with twine.

They would bring the food on their last trip in, after bathing.

Raean and Gabe arrived at the lodge for the evening meal. Raean was proud to be on watch duty with his father. Sagora warned them the Dragon Talkers might not return until after they spotted dragons in the sky. She answered Raean's questions as best as she could based on what Danuka had told them. She held Raean in her arms. "I promise to tell you everything I can remember from this experience. It is new to all of us. We can't say for certain we'll remember anything."

For their baths, Nagora had prepared baskets with bowls, bars of soap, and linen cloths. Tagnyoriva and the attendants accompanied them to the stream, carrying changes of clothing for themselves and the princesses. After the Dragon Talkers had finished, they too would bathe and then return to the lodge with the baskets and clothing that needed washing.

Dannor hung a lantern in the bathing hut and gave the women first access while he carried the food rations into the maze and stored them in the shelters.

Knowledge and Power
Kiskeyitamowin
Mâmatâwihikowin

The Dark Twins, carrying a single lantern, led the other Dragon Talkers into the maze. Dannor followed the group with another lantern. Then they waited, with eyes to the sky, for the dragons to arrive.

At first, their distant silhouettes appeared as shadows on the half-lit moon. "They're coming," said Sarah. "Danuka is leading them. They'll be here soon. Best we undress now."

The mother dragon landed first, followed by the others in order of birth with such precision Nagora wondered if they had practiced it.

Dannor and Sarah placed the ladder in position for Kalhata to climb up first. Once she was standing and holding the dragons' wing talons, they held the ladder for Tabiry, and then Nagora and Sagora. With Sarah in position, Dannor moved the ladder to where he would stand with the dragons.

When Nagora's son took hold of the talons, a slight glow of light illuminated the space between the inner and outer rings. The area beneath the inner ring brightened, and soon the lightest of touches traveled up the back of Nagora's legs and then around to her front. The sensation spread up across her back, over her belly and up her chest, onto her shoulders and out from there onto her arms.

From the corners of her eyes, all Nagora could see on her arms were countless pinpricks of light. They flowed out from her arms onto the outstretched wings of the dragons, covering them in a layer of lights. The surface of the lintels became a carpet of lights.

Soon they covered her head, and she had no choice but to close her eyes. The sensation was like floating on gentle sea waves. Nagora relaxed, and the network of tiny lights supported her. How many can there be? It would be like trying to count the stars in the sky. Where had the Little People all come from?

Danuka spoke to the Dragon Talkers, and her words came into Nagora's mind.

Soon you will sense the heartbeats of Kalhata and Tabiry. Your knees will bend and straighten to the rhythm of their heartbeats. Let your body move with the beat. Fear not, the Little People have bound you to the dragons you hold on to and will not let you fall. Your mind will clear. You will have no notion of time. Once the beat moves you and takes complete control of you, you will no longer be aware of it. Once the beat controls all of us, the transmission of knowledge will begin.

When the transmission is done, you will only regain awareness of your surroundings when Dannor touches you to help you climb down from the ladder.

Nagora wondered if it would be like sleep, but without dreams to remember.

The next thing Nagora remembered was Dannor placing her hands on the top rung of the ladder. Tiny pinpricks of light illuminated the ladder from top to bottom. Sarah was standing at the bottom, holding the ladder. When Nagora looked around, the dragons were gone, and the remaining Dragon Talkers lay on the lintels covered in blankets of lights.

With feet and legs heavy as if carved in stone, Nagora descended. Sarah helped her down the last two rungs and placed an arm around her mother's waist once she was standing next to her. "Are you feeling well?"

Nagora took a deep breath. "Like waking from a deep sleep and wanting to go back to bed."

"It won't be long, Mum. I felt like you just a few moments ago."

Dannor moved the ladder over to Sagora's position on the lintel.

"Do you think you can help us with Auntie Sagora?" asked Sarah.

"Aye. I'll hold the ladder," said Nagora, as she walked over to it.

As soon as Dannor stood next to his aunt, the ladder became illuminated once again. He helped Sagora onto it like he had his mother.

Once Sagora was on the ground in Nagora's arms, she shook her head. "You and Danuka told us what it would be like when the Little People came. Your words didn't come close to describing what I felt."

Nagora pointed to where Dannor and Sarah had just placed the ladder. Sagora blinked as she watched it light up. "Come, we must help."

"Mum, you and Auntie Sagora hold the ladder," said Dannor. "Sarah will follow me up. She'll stay on the ladder right behind Tabiry to guide her down after I help her climb on."

Once Tabiry's hands were on the top rung, lights from the rung and the rails wrapped around them, tying them in place. With Sarah's help, Dannor placed Tabiry's feet on the rung. This time, the lights secured her feet to the ladder.

Dannor knelt on the lintel next to the ladder. "She's not awake. As I move one of her hands down to the next rung, do the same with her foot on the same side. We'll do that for four rungs. Then I'll get on the ladder and bend to her hands. With the Little People helping like they are, we'll bring her down safely."

After the descent, Nagora and Sagora placed Tabiry's arms around their necks and walked her to her shelter. Once tucked away in her bedroll, they returned to help with Kalhata.

They brought her down in the same manner and put her to bed next to her sister.

Dannor pointed up. "The half moon has crossed the sky. Soon it will be out of sight, and so will I. I bid you all goodnight."

"Goodnight, my son. Thank you for your help." Nagora turned to her sister. "Can you check on Kalhata and Tabiry to see if they have a fever? Just in case."

"Aye. I'll do that."

They were sound asleep with no fever.

...

It was early morning twilight when tugging on the leather lace around her neck awoke Nagora. Her lethargy did not want her to wake up, but then a voice whispered in her ear, causing her to blink her eyes open. "News for you, Dragon Talker." When Nagora propped herself up on one elbow, she glanced over at Sagora. The voice continued. "Do not worry. She is sound asleep.

"Today, Lars will return to Windhaven. The giant grows eager for you to appear before him and the king to bargain the terms of surrender of the dragons.

"On the instructions of the dragon mother, this night we measured the Dark Twins. We will make invisibility armor for their return trip home. We made a saddle with bags, bridle, and reins the mother dragon can will invisible. These are necessary for their safety, and for the safety of Danuka."

"Thank you, *Mêmêkwêsiw*."

"Go back to sleep, Dragon Talker."

Nagora let her lethargy overtake her.

The next time Nagora awoke, it was because of the hunger in her belly.

Am I the only one awake? With her linen-wrapped packet of rations and a waterskin slung over her shoulder, she crept out of her tent, leaving Sagora still fast asleep.

She peeked into the princesses' tent. They too slept.

Dannor and Sarah were not in their shelter.

Nagora looked around the outer ring and past the inner ring. She spotted her children's heads on the other side of the well. They must be sitting there and talking.

Nagora crossed under the lintel of the inner ring to the well in the middle.

Dannor looked up and waved to her.

Nagora found them sitting crossed-legged with their rations spread on the cloths they had wrapped them in. Sarah had hazelnuts in her hand. Dannor was biting on a strip of smoke-cured venison. He pointed to the sky. "No dragons yet. It's past midday."

"If they're like us, they'll be hungry," said Sarah. "Before you arrived with the twins, Danuka had us prepare cured sheep meat in nets. The dragons flew the meat into the cave. We spent a day spreading it out and stacking it, like we do for their shedding. They have plenty to eat to help them regain their strength."

Nagora joined her children and opened her folded cloth packet. "How do you feel today?"

Sarah pointed to her brother. "We were just talking about that. It's something we'll never be able to forget, and it's something no one else will ever believe if ever we try to tell them."

Dannor was nodding. "It must have felt different for each of us. I was telling Sarah, when the rhythm of the heartbeats overtook us, I sensed my entire body was being carried away to a place where I danced and danced. After, I had the floating sensation Sarah described."

Sarah held out her arms. "Because the Little People were supporting us. What I remember most is the sensation of lightness, as if I weighed nothing. Mum, what was it like for you?"

"For me, it was like floating in the sea, but not cold. Wrapped in warmth and supported, as you said." Nagora looked at her son. "Perhaps, because you're a man, you felt something different."

Dannor shrugged. "Also, we wonder what the dragons will get out of it. We've been told it's supposed to be knowledge. What we're curious about is how it will change them. Are there lessons from the past that will help them? What if they learn of other dragons living elsewhere? They'll no longer be alone."

Sarah held open her palm. "What will they know about the future? I mean, when you think of it, how would knowing the future make you feel? Perhaps dragons don't experience feelings like we do. They just accept whatever is to come and deal with it. Or they have more ways of doing that. It brings up so many questions. Can the future be controlled? Can it be changed? To answer those questions requires knowing the future. Wouldn't knowing the future be a terrible burden? Maybe not for dragons. For them, it could be a gift."

With one finger, Nagora rolled the small hazelnuts to one side of her palm and the dried berries to the other side. "Sarah, those are deep, worthwhile questions you're asking. Here's my opinion." She glanced up at her daughter. "I don't know what the future holds. I'm sure Danuka, until now, has had some knowledge of the future. What, I can't say, except it involved me, her, and her brood. All these years, she has had control of my future. She put me on this path for a reason—to protect her and her young, from the time they were eggs to the present. Every step of the way on that path, I've submitted to her will, no matter the cost.

"Is that what being a Dragon Talker is all about? To be in total submission and service to dragons? To not have a say in what you want to do or be, but only to accept, and to try to be happy in that acceptance?"

Dannor was staring at his mother. He pointed at her. "Mum, when you were twelve years old, you argued with your uncle, Dangor, about the amulet you wore around your neck. At the time you had no idea it was a dragon-tear amulet. Correct?"

"Aye."

"What did Dangor say to you? You've told me the story before, but I want to hear you say it again." There was an edge to her son's voice.

To speak her uncle's words from that day twenty-five years ago, Nagora let the image of his face surface in her memory.

†

"I'll tell you this, child. There's power in the stone. If I tell you what it is, you'll not believe me. Trust me on what I tell you. You'll only discover its power when you have complete trust in yourself. How you go about finding that, I can't say. That's when you'll learn its true power, all on your own. I won't be the one to reveal it to you. It'll reveal itself. So stop asking."

†

Again, Dannor pointed at her. "Mum, be honest when you answer my next question. If today you had the choice to go back to that moment, what would you do? Rip that amulet from your neck to throw it away? Or leave it on and relive your life up to this moment?"

Nagora stared back at her son. "I never thought of it that way. I had that choice, didn't I? I could have ripped it from my neck and chosen to become a curragh maker. Or a curragh maker's wife with a slew of kids, the two and four-legged kind to take care of.

"Instead, I chose the unknown. I chose to see what power the amulet would reveal. I took what destiny offered me, even if I didn't know a dragon awaited me."

She took a deep breath and glanced at Sarah before looking back at Dannor. "I would leave it on and relive my life just to have you two be part of my star story."

Out of nowhere, a gust of wind blew over them. They reached down to keep their open ration packets from blowing away. Then Danuka appeared on the lintel of the inner ring where she had perched the night before.

The three of them stood.

Danuka's voice came into their minds.

This is one of the new powers we dragons now have. We can will ourselves invisible for as long as we want.

She disappeared and then only her neck and head reappeared near the ground, just below where she had perched. Then they disappeared, and only her wings appeared.

An inkling of a new part to her plan flashed into Nagora's mind. *What if we give the dragon slayer something he has never seen? A many-headed dragon!*

Danuka reappeared completely once again, her belly resting on the ground before them.

Another new power we have is to make parts of us visible and other parts invisible.

The dragon looked at Nagora.

Ka Peyakot Mahihkan, come. I must speak to you.

· · ·

The dragon enfolded her Dragon Talker in her wings and lowered her head inside them to within an arm's length of Nagora's face. Her red eyes looked deep inside her.

Now Lone Wolf, share how you will confront the giant dragon slayer, even if you lack details. Do this so I can help you.

Okâwîmâw, how can I plan for what I do not know?

Trust those who glimpse the future.

That would be you, Mother, and your dragons, and the Little People. I trust all of you.

That is why you must share what you know so far—to confront the unknown. I will give you a glimpse into it.

The dragon placed her snout on Nagora's Tiwaz brand. After a few moments, Nagora fell to her knees.

Okâwîmâw, have I no choice in this other than to trust you?

Trust me.

Okâwîmâw, I trust you. I will prepare. Here are my plans so far given the information I have. I will set the terms of surrender that I have yet to decide with Lars. On the day of the battle, you will fly me to the battlefield and land a safe distance away from danger. I will confront the giant and call him to honor the terms. If he does so, you will return to the spot where you landed with your belly to the ground and your head at my feet. I will bend to ask you to roll onto one side to expose your heart. When you do, I will lodge the dagger behind your scales in the appearance of stabbing you. You will drop your raised wing to the ground, pretending to be dead. The next dragon will land, and when the giant moves to make the kill, I will attack him with my skystone blade before he can even get close.

But Mother, I do not expect he will respect the terms. He will attack me first to eliminate me. Before he does, this is where you, with the help of your dragons, if they are willing, will appear as a single dragon with three heads to fly over the giant at great speed, out of his striking distance. Your appearance as a three-headed dragon will be brief, in three blinks of an eye, enough to distract and frighten the giant so I may strike at him. With your powers to make parts of you visible and invisible, if you see I need your help to distract him, you could fly over him from two other directions. You and your dragons will only do this if you are certain you will be safe and not putting yourselves at risk.

When Nagora finished, Danuka lifted her snout from the brand and spoke to her mind-to-mind.

Today at sunset, meet me at the cliff above your lodge. I will wear a special saddle covered in dragonskin the *Mê-mêkwêsiw* made. Wear your armor. Bring your disguise, your scrip, and your weapons. You will place them in the bag behind my saddle. I can will the saddle and the bag invisible to hide whatever is in it. You can too, if the bag touches your dragonskin armor. In the bag, you will also find a belt with a pouch in which you can fit the golden-handled dagger. I had the Little People make it for your safety. If you wear the pouch next to your armor, you can will it to make the dagger invisible. I will fly you to a farm field on Castle Way in Windhaven. Near the field is a tree where you can hide the bag and its contents.

Let me warn you, *Ka Peyakot Mahihkan*. I fear for your safety. You are equipped to defend yourself with your armor, your weapons, and your experience. But you must not let your guard down. Be careful. Do not trust the words of this giant. If he can get to you before he faces you in battle, he will. Believe what I tell you.

From the field, go to the castle. With the help of the Little People, you will gain entrance by the stable and kitchen doors. Inside, seek the king. Get answers to your questions. They will help you focus on the actions you must take.

Then go to Lars. Tell him Dannor will not join him as planned because I fear for his safety. I must protect him at all costs, as he will accompany me on the journey to Kemet. I will inform Dannor of this and his other duties as a Dragon Talker. He must hear these things from me.

Confirm to Lars that more reinforcements are on their way. They travel in secret to the forest on the far end of the plain where he has planted the oaks. The Guard has sent one hundred archers. The Stone Standers sent sixty volunteers with slings. Twenty archers from The Guard and ten Stone Stander slingers have already joined Lars, posing as trainees from Maze Point. On our way, I will fly over his encampment so you can find Lars.

The Little People spy to learn information to protect you. They will warn you if you are in danger, but they cannot learn all the secret dealings that go on behind Leafer doors. Be vigilant. Do what you must protect yourself.

Tomorrow, return to the castle. Bargain the terms of our surrender.

Yes, *Okâwîmâw*, but first I have to meet with Lars to clarify what the terms will be. He will surely have suggestions, based on what he has learned.

That is true, *Ka Peyakot Mahihkan*.

After you bargain the terms of surrender, leave Windhaven. Ride to the edge of the forest where the oaks of the king grow. The Little People will meet you there. Leave your horse to them. They will make sure it returns to its stable. They will have something to show you. Be invisible when they lead you to it. After, I will come for you where you met them.

Remember, your battle with the giant must happen within the next ten days. I must return the Dark Twins to their parents within twelve. I give myself two days to fly them home, and two days of rest before returning with Yogari.

Mother, are you aware of the plans Lars has made to flood the center of the maze to fight the giant and his force, should that ever become necessary?

I am aware. *Ka Peyakot Mahihkan*, we dragons are prepared. I will discuss elements of your plan with my dragons. Keep in mind your strategy will likely change with what you learn. You must share that with me, and I will inform you of what I can do to help you.

Before her eyes, her dragon disappeared again. It gave Nagora an eerie feeling.

Has the dragon slayer ever seen a dragon disappear before his eyes? But more so, she realized Danuka was taking a more active and decisive role in her and Lars's plans. One thing worried her: the safety of the trainees. Will they be fighting alongside the archers of The Guard and the Stone Stander slingers? Lars said I wasn't to worry about the role they would play. Is this why I've heard no talk of other defections from Maze Point? And Dannor will go with Danuka to Kemet, and he'll have other duties as a Dragon Talker. Will those duties have to do with the Dark Twins calling him the Golden Boy? I'll wait for Danuka or Dannor to tell me.

When I find out what Lars has been up to, I'll better be able to assess our chances of beating the dragon slayer.

"Mum! That was strange! If you ask me, that's the solution to save our dragons. They just have to remain invisible. The slayer can't kill what he can't see!" said Dannor. He could barely hold still where he stood.

Sarah reached for his arm. "Maybe, but them being invisible doesn't remove the giant as a threat. He's not just going to leave because the dragons have vanished. He'll want proof. What he wants are his kills."

"Sarah's right. I've seen the flags on his ship. They show how he killed those other dragons from away. How would he put 'I scared them away,' on a flag? He wants their blood. He wants their teeth for his armor. And the Leafers want the blood of the dragons.

"King Raynhard called me to duty to deal with the giant—to end the threat to the dragons. End it I will, even if it kills me. That our dragons can become invisible at will for however long they want gives us possibilities in how we'll fight the giant. And fight him, we must!"

Nagora put her hands on their shoulders. "Danuka is bringing me to Windhaven tonight. Now, I'm going to get my mother and Khensa and Nefruke. I'll bring them here to help you care for our two sleeping beauties and your auntie. When I come back from Windhaven, I'll fill you in on my plan and tell you what Lars and Raynhard are up to."

Invisible to the Castle Again
Namoya Nôkwan Kihci-Okimâwikamik Mina

This time, the flight to Windhaven was quicker. Nagora wondered if it was because she was wearing her armor and sitting in the dragonskin saddle. Perhaps the dragonskin did not slow the flow of air over her like her regular clothing, or maybe this was another new power Danuka had gained from the knowledge transferred by the Dark Twins, giving her greater strength. Also, Nagora wasn't cold on the flight. As always, the armor wrapped her in strange warmth. An even wave of heat pulsed over every part of her body with each beat of her heart. Is heat from Danuka's body also spreading through the saddle to me?

True to her word, Danuka flew over Lars's encampment in the field on the other side of the brook. From what Nagora could see, less than half of the giant's force now occupied the designated field, and the ballistae were nowhere in sight, no longer parked as Olen had reported. Could they already be setting up on the plain?

...

After landing invisible in the field, Danuka showed the tree where Nagora was to hide the bag containing her scrip, weapons, and disguise. *Ka Peyakot Mahihkan*, the *Mê-mêkwêsiw* will guard them for you. Go now to the castle.

Nagora's next challenge was to cross Castle Square, where most of the giant's followers had set up camp. However, when she arrived there, it was obvious most had left except for the giant's entertainers performing in the square. They will go with the giant on his way to the plain. Those who left must be setting up over there. From Castle Way into the square and to the main entrance of the castle, guards had little work to do to keep the way open for supply wagons bringing goods to and from the castle, like the empty manure wagon a hundred paces ahead. If I run, I can catch up to it and follow it. It must be headed to the stable.

As the wagon crossed the moat bridge, Nagora took a quick peek back into the square. Members of the Leafer community were in the middle, standing on boxes and calling out their promise of future riches to passersby. Few stopped since they had come to see the giant's acrobats, jugglers, fire eaters, and musicians. Olen had said they were part of the giant's circus, and Golgotha was the main attraction.

On the other side of the bridge, the wagon turned left and followed the moat way along the castle wall to the open stable door. Once inside, Nagora ran past the wagon before the stable hand parked it.

The outer door giving access to the kitchens was closed. How will the Little People get the guards to open it? She stood and waited. From inside, she heard pots and pans clatter, followed by shouting.

The outer door opened, and the inner door was open enough for Nagora to squeeze past it. Right after the outer door closed and the latch slipped into place on its own, she closed the inner door and slid its two heavy latches in place.

"Thank you, *Mêmêkwêsiw*," Nagora whispered.

Behind her, the noise from the kitchen continued. From what she could gather, two guards were chasing a cat that had caused the commotion in the kitchen. The hallway ahead was empty.

Past the doors to the guardroom and the kitchen, Nagora came to the laundry room. The smell of soap was heavy in the air. She stepped in for a quick look. On a table, she found a big basket with garments waiting to be sorted and washed.

Wearing a robe from the basket to visit Raynhard in his room crossed her mind. No, best I go unseen. I can find something from a shelf in his clothes room.

Where to from here? To the throne room. From there, I'll take the stairs up to the third floor where Raynhard's room is.

The last door to her left in the corridor opened onto another hallway. This one was familiar. She now had her bearings.

On the third floor, the hall to her left led to two rooms. Nagora recalled the first one had been Sagora's, the last one Raynhard's. Why are there no guards up here? No one to guard? Could all the Leafers be in what was once the maps room? The skylight was lit when we flew overhead. Or are they with the giant in his tent in the courtyard? Do I risk going to the courtyard? First, I'll check the king's room and then go to the roof for a look into the yard. I counted only five soldiers up there, one near the skylight and the other four at the corners.

Nagora took a last look in the direction she had come, then slipped into Raynhard's room. She felt her way to where she hoped a lantern still hung on the wall next to the head of his bed. As Nagora reached for it, the candle's flame came to life. Thank you, *Mêmêkwêsiw*. With the lantern in hand, she walked to the curtained doorway of the small clothes room across from the bed.

In it, she chose a nightshirt and set it on the back of the chair near the row of boots to her right. Do I wait here in the dark or go to the roof? As if in answer to her question, a voice spoke in a whisper. "Return the lantern to its place; the king will retire to his room soon."

In a count, a young man wearing a silver-leaf medallion at his neck and carrying a lantern entered the room, inspecting it and the clothes room before leading the king in. The attendant lit two lanterns and turned down the covers on Raynhard's bed before leaving with a simple bow to the king.

Nagora pulled the nightshirt over her head and willed her armor to make her visible. She stepped past the curtain and spoke in a quiet voice. "My king calls me to duty once more."

Raynhard twisted in surprise on the edge of the bed to look at Nagora in disbelief. "Nagora? How did you get in here?"

"For now, that will be my secret. You have some questions to answer. I warn you I have many, so you better answer quick and true."

"Na … "

She held up her hand to cut him short. "Answer my questions first, and then you can ask yours."

He stood and took a step around the corner of the bed.

Again, she raised her hand. "Stop where you are. Sit and listen."

He sat on the big oak chest at the foot of his bed, placed one hand on a knee, and motioned for her to speak with his other.

She began. "Why did you choose Worsham to carry your message to me?"

"The Gold Planter ordered me."

"You take orders from others now?"

"As a Leafer, I sometimes have to," replied Raynhard.

"When did she give you that order? Daytime or nighttime?"

"It was nighttime."

"Was that the first time you met with her?"

"No, I've met her many times."

"Always at night?"

Raynhard nodded. "Always."

"Was her appearance the same or different each time?"

"Of necessity, she disguises herself each time."

"How do you know she is the same person?"

"By the knowledge she speaks."

"You sent the dagger. Since when have you known it is cursed?"

"Since the Gold Planter told me."

"And you believed her?"

"When she told me all Hag had done to find the dagger to destroy it to be free of the curse it held for her, and knowing you killed Alizarine with it, I believed her."

So many things at once made sense to Nagora. That's why Hag wanted to destroy all the golden dragon harps. Not only did their music beguile her, but one of them held a dagger, cursed to put an end to her life.

That's why Hag gave Pug the poison I asked for to kill the king's baby in my womb, so it wouldn't become a princess to carry out the curse with her mother.

That's why Alizarine did not fear me in the cave when I held the dagger. The curse required two to kill her.

And that's why Heqet spoke her curse again to Alizarine to change her into a child infatuated with a dragon egg until the princess grew of age to help the queen carry out the curse.

Alizarine wanted eternal beauty at all costs. Instead, she got a stay in her execution. Heqet and Alizarine were battling each other. What does Heqet want? It has to be more than the death of the dragons.

Nagora's mind grasped at something she felt she needed to understand, but couldn't. Why would Heqet spend all those years in a frog's body as Alizarine's pet? Had Alizarine cursed Heqet, turning her into a frog? When and why?

And what connection is there to the curse the dagger now holds that I cannot see? Will the present curse on the dagger benefit Heqet? Raynhard doesn't have the answers to those questions.

The king moved to stand, attracting Nagora's attention.

She shook her head and motioned with her hand for him to stay seated. "Do you still stand by the story your father told you about leaving his dagger in that mountain cave?"

"I do."

"Did he ever give you a different reason for leaving it there?"

Raynhard shook his head. "No."

"Did he ever speak to you about a curse connected to that dagger?"

"No."

Nagora pointed at him. "Do you know who the Gold Planter is?"

Raynhard took a deep breath before answering. "She is the most knowledgeable of all the members of the Community of the Leaf, the one who discovered the capacity of the oaks to attract dragon gold from the soil."

Nagora placed a hand on her hip and tilted her head as she stared at the king. "Do you know where she lives?"

"No."

Holding out her hands and leaning forward, Nagora asked, "Have you ever tried to find out?"

Raynhard bit on his upper lip before answering. "She told me not to."

Nagora pointed at Raynhard and then to herself. "Why do you question my loyalty to the dragons?"

Raynhard looked to his reflection in the mirror before answering. "I've been told by the Gold Planter that you've been planning to destroy all the dragons since you started rebuilding the maze."

Nagora rolled her eyes. "She did, did she?"

A smile etched itself at the corner of Raynhard's mouth. "You talk in your sleep, Nagora. Those who've heard you have listened. And they have spoken. Your words of treasonous intent traveled far."

Until this moment, no one has ever told me I speak in my sleep. No doubt a lie told by Alizarine's frog.

"What do you think, my king, in your heart? Do you believe I would concoct a plan to kill my dragons?"

"I do, because you told me so yourself."

Tar piss! I'd hit you if it would knock some sense into you! "In my sleep, I suppose!"

Raynhard shook his head. "No! You were wide awake in my cave and about to kill Danuka. 'Damn you, Raynhard for what you did to me. The last dragon is going to die and so is her last egg.' Those were your words, Nagora."

He jabbed a finger in her direction. "You can't deny that! You just postponed your intentions until now to fulfill your destiny!"

"I don't deny my words." Nagora squinted as her gaze bore into his. "Do you remember anything after that? What I did? What I explained to you?"

"Only that I fled from that cave because I had seen enough of your carnage!"

Aliza must have struck him harder than I thought. Unless Heqet caused him to forget from that moment on in the cave. I see it now. He was wearing the amber ring, and Hag was in her beautiful younger body, as Aliza. Who controlled the ring that controlled Raynhard, Aliza, or Heqet?

I once thought it was Alizarine, but now, in hindsight, I see Heqet as the one pulling the strings, playing her long game at the child witch's expense. When Sagora kidnapped Alizarine and brought her to the castle, that must have been Heqet's doing through the ring my sister wore. Even then, Raynhard, you did not recognize Alizarine, nor did you know Sarah was your daughter. I remember when you introduced us on our arrival at the castle.

†

Raynhard stepped forward. "We must not forget Sarah, Sagora's eldest. And of course, you know this dear strange child, Alizarine, brought here well in advance of the wedding. Needless to say, Alizarine has adopted us, as is clear in how she has chosen to address us. I'm sure you understand."

We understand, but do you?

†

We thought we understood, but now I see it was Heqet all along who had brought us together in Windhaven. My mission was to convince Sarah she was my daughter, and that she had to help me carry out Heqet's curse. Doing so would eliminate Alizarine as a threat to the dragons, or so we thought. But no, the true threat of Heqet's plan remained hidden. With the dagger, we had done part of her work for her.

"Besides that, Raynhard, do you have any other proof of my scheme to eliminate the dragons?" asked Nagora.

"I do! Just two days ago, Worsham reported you had attempted to poison the only male dragon in the maze. You even admitted as much to Sagora when she let you read my letter to her."

How does he know this? From Sagora? Or had Heqet returned to the scene of her crime to witness what she hoped would be an important death? By my count, that was twenty-six days ago. That would have been something to report, and she would have struck a major blow for her cause. Instead, she left with a false report of attempted murder on my part.

He's not wearing a ring now, but he is wearing a gold oak-leaf medallion. And he speaks his beliefs with conviction, contradicting what I've learned from Geirador and Moreena, and his own words in his letter to Sagora: that he was seeking information to prevent me from harming the dragons. If he is the one who professes to others to be on the side of the drag-ons, why do I feel no love from him? He's not himself. Is he Heqet's puppet once more?

When was the last time I saw him as the lucid man I once knew?

The answer came in images from her memory of her coro-nation as queen after she married the king at the Center for the Dragon Arts. She, posing as Sagora, had convinced Raynhard to wed her with woven willow-branch rings instead of the amber rings she knew the witch Alizarine had cursed. Raynhard had removed the cursed ring and was clear-headed when crowning me.

†

As Sarah removed Nagora's shawl, Raynhard's eyebrows rose. He was staring at the dagger that hung from her left hip. His voice was a whisper. "Did Nagora give that to you?"

She smiled at Raynhard and held his gaze. "The one you gave it to stands before you. She is your wife. Will you make Nagora your queen?"

Raynhard's eyes grew wide as they searched her face. He's trying to make sense of the events. What will he do? His eyes went to her hands, and his astonishment held him until he gazed at the crown in his hands. Slowly, Raynhard raised it until his eyes were again looking into Nagora's.

Raynhard's eyes brightened as the smile on his face broadened.

†

You had always wanted me to be your queen. Free of the control of the amber ring that day, you were happy to crown me your queen. You were lucid enough to remember who Sagora's sons were and that she would return for them, so you crowned them to be honorary princes of the Land of the Danu until their mother returned.

And you had the sense to have me crown the princesses, Sarah and Alizarine. I did not lie to you on that day. I, as Edana, Queen of the Land of the Danu, crowned Sarah, the daughter of King Raynhard and Queen Edana, Princess of the Land of the Danu, with all the power and recognition she inherited with that title. That's when you realized I had not killed our child in the cave.

Finally, I crowned the child witch, Alizarine, Princess of the Land of the Danu, for that day only and without power or privilege.

But today, you believe the lie I told you in the cave about killing Danuka and her last egg. On our wedding day, you were happy to learn Sarah was our daughter, and that I had lied in the cave about killing our child.

To me, this is proof that Heqet once again controls you. My poor king, what do you truly expect of me? I fear your answer will be one to suit Heqet's purposes.

Nagora pointed to the medallion on his chest. "The Community of the Leaf sent for a giant to come slay the dragons. Do you truly believe that I will surrender the dragons to slaughter to become the dispenser of dragon blood for the Leafers?"

He held his hands out to her. "Nagora, you don't have a choice. It's your destiny. It's the destiny of the dragons. And you know it. Otherwise, why would you have given Lars the map to the maze to make sure we can find the dragons there if we have to?"

Nagora shot back. "I didn't give it to him! He took it without my knowing! You must be happy to have it."

Raynhard shook his head. "We don't need it. We have someone who will lead us in."

The frog witch, Heqet, no doubt learned the way thanks to Alizarine.

"In that case, I want it back!"

Raynhard waved a hand in dismissal. "Ask Lars for it. He's been trying to sell it to us."

"I'd like to, just so I can tell him to his face that his son will not be coming to join him! Dannor and Sarah are staying with me! And no one else from Maze Point will desert the dragons to come plant oaks for him!"

The king stood, holding the gold oak-leaf medallion in his right hand as he took a step toward her. "Don't you see, Nagora? All you have done to keep the dragons safe has been for this moment. You will have a place of honor among all the members of the Community of the Leaf.

"Not only will they grow rich with the dragon gold their oaks will reap for them, but so will you with the blood you will dispense to them to increase their yields. It will be long overdue payment to you.

"The true meaning of the stained glass windows in the Assembly Hall of the Community of the Leaf will stand as homage to what you promised years ago. On the day of the hall's inauguration, you will feed dragon blood to the oak we planted in the center of the hall. It will pull dragon gold from the ground as it grows to heights above the hall, a symbol of the prosperity of our great Community of the Leaf."

Whose great community? Heqet's? Its greatness lies in the fact that she has built it on unproven promises and taken control of the minds of those who believe them.

"I've heard your Gold Planter will soon give proof that the blood of dragons will increase the yields of gold the oaks will produce. Mark my words, Raynhard. If I hear from those who witness proof that they are sure beyond any doubt of her promise, then I will surrender my dragons. I'll make that clear tomorrow, along with my other terms. Have Lars bring me my map tomorrow."

Nagora held up her hand as he moved to take another step toward her. "But I warn you, I'll only do so on my terms. My first one is that you guarantee my safety tomorrow when I meet the giant. Be warned: Should anything happen to me, you'll not see a single drop of dragon blood. My son and our daughter will poison all the dragons and send them to sea to die. Know, Raynhard, that the blood pact my son made with his father holds for me too."

Raynhard appeared to force a smile. "Of course, Nagora, on your terms."

She placed her hands on her hips. "When and where will the Gold Planter give her proof?"

He pointed skyward. "On the night of the next full moon. Where, I don't know. The members the Head Leafer invited to attend are here in the castle and will follow her to that place on horseback. We leave three counts after sunset."

You just lied to me. You know where because you told Geirador before you were under Heqet's yoke. He told me.

Four nights from this one, she'll lead you to the royal circle of oaks. It's near here, in the forest on the hill overlooking Windhaven and this castle. I'll be there to witness Heqet show her proof.

Nagora held up a finger. "I have a last question. On all the giant's standards just below the golden oak leaf on his flags are three words: '*nam mater mea.*' What do they mean?"

"For my mother."

Nagora frowned. "He kills dragons for his mother? Do you know why he chose that motto?"

Raynhard shrugged. "He didn't say."

Didn't, or won't say? If I were one to place a bet, I'd put all my coins on Heqet being the giant's mother. Why do I believe that? Is intuition telling me this?

Nagora stepped back into the clothes room, pulling the curtain across the doorway. As she removed the nightshirt, she willed her armor to make her invisible.

Raynhard followed, pushed the curtain to one side, and looked around in dismay, bending and then standing on tiptoe to search the shelves.

Nagora slipped past him into his room.

He came out, holding the nightshirt she had let fall to the floor. He gazed around the room before checking under the bed. When he opened the door to the room and stepped into the hallway, Nagora snuck past him to leave the way she had come in and return to the tree where she had hid her bag.

Now visible in her disguise, Nagora scanned along Stables Way before opening the door to Olen's forge. From the stable's passageway, she saw Bonnie in the inner yard with two other mares.

...

When Nagora met with Olen in his kitchen, he informed her Lars had returned from the plain in the late afternoon. It confirmed what the Little People had told her. "Good. I'll borrow Bonnie again to go see him and then come back here to spend the night. Olen, my plan is coming together, but with so many details still in play, I don't dare share it with you yet. I can tell you I'll need Bonnie tomorrow when I go to the castle to negotiate with the giant my terms to surrender the dragons."

Olen reached for her arm. "Best you keep all that to yourself. I don't need to know it, not even your terms. I know you'll do what's best for the dragons and for the people of the Land of the Danu."

His words made Nagora realize the weight of her actions. The people of the kingdom will be judging me.

Olen then shared what his sources had reported: King Raynhard was spending most of his time entertaining the giant in his tent in the courtyard. The smith patted his belly. "He likes to eat. He has his own cooks and has brought his own animals. Word is he butchers them himself. Anything he eats or drinks doesn't touch his lips until his tasters try it."

Olen placed a finger across his lips and delivered his last words in a whisper with the wink of an eye. "Rumor has it the giant has only one eye in the middle of his face."

As Nagora rode out of Windhaven, she tried to imagine a face with only one eye in the middle. That's so unusual. Would that be frightening to see? I can't imagine an advantage one eye might give him. In the middle? Was he born that way? Or does he come from a people in a land of one-eyed giants? Perhaps the answer is so obvious, I don't see it. Another unknown. I can remember the times I've been glad to have two eyes. Dust or a grain of sand in one until I got it out was bad enough. At least I could still see with the other. With only one eye, a single grain of sand could disable him. If it's true he has only one eye, that information could be useful. It would be a weakness.

After crossing the timber bridge in the light of the hump-backed moon, Nagora left the road and guided Bonnie the long way around toward Lars's encampment. She tied the horse to a bush on the far side of the knoll, out of sight of those on watch for the giant's troops on the other side of the brook.

She climbed the knoll for a look at Lars's tents. Their layout impressed her. Now two of the camp's four outer sides had wagons parked in defensive positions. They must have their own camp kitchen and supply wagons of food and tools, as well as feed for the horses. If the Stone Stander volunteers are armed with their slings, and the volunteers of The Guard their bows, any force attacking this camp will suffer major casualties.

Nagora went there on foot, confident in her disguise as a hunter.

At the camp entrance, the slings and war-stone pouches the two on watch wore labelled them as Stone Standers. "Password!" they said in unison.

Nagora looked at them. "I have no password, but I bring an important message for your commander, Lars Marraden. I'll wait here while one of you goes to fetch him."

...

It didn't take long for Lars to arrive. He thanked the one who had notified him and turned to Nagora. "You have a message for me?"

"Aye. Where can we talk in private? Everyone is in such tight quarters here."

He led her back in the direction she had come. "Let's walk away from the camp." As soon as they were out of sight of those on watch, he took her in his arms. "I miss you so!"

She savored his embrace.

He pointed back at the encampment. "We limited the brush we cleared in this barren field since we stayed only two nights, and then left for the plain with the king's surveyors and a contingent of the giant's force."

She interrupted him. "Without the fortune you hoped to get for the map."

He chuckled. "Aye, without the fortune I knew I wouldn't get for the map. It's been one excuse after another. I'm sure they'll come up with more." He shrugged. "We did our thing over there, offered to help, but the giant's team didn't want our help to set up his ... well ... let's call it a circus battlefield. He likes to kill for a crowd. By how they were setting up, they're expecting many onlookers to show up. Those who want to get close to the action will have to pay. We just came back today."

Why do I feel I'll be walking into a trap? While walking further away from the camp, Nagora said, "Tell me about the battlefield."

Lars stopped. "Give me your hand. It'll be easier to explain. Hold it palm up, fingers together." He touched her fingertips. "This end of the field faces where the Isle of Smoke was. It's not roped off. The other three sides are.

"Along this side," he ran a finger from the tip of her index all along it to the big knuckle joint on her thumb, "the giant's support tents will be set up. Anything he wants fixed or needs can be found in them. When we left, only two tents were up, but his team had staked place markers for eight more between those two."

From the thumb knuckle, he moved his finger in a straight line across the heel of her hand to the corner of her palm. "On this short side of the field you'll find a viewing stand they built for about twenty people.

"In successive areas behind it," he drew several lines across her wrist and forearm, "are Golgotha's big tent, his stable tent, and the three ballistae with the tents of the units who operate them.

"Beyond those is another big tent with a flag flying a golden oak leaf."

"I can guess who that's for. Is there a tent for the king?"

"If there is, it wasn't set up when we left. Mind you, on our way back, we passed a half dozen other wagons on the road headed that way."

Lars moved his finger from the corner of her palm to the base of her little finger. "On this side will be tents for musicians, flag bearers, and entertainers. Like on the other side, they had only pitched two and placed markers for four additional tents."

His finger then traveled the length of her little finger. "Along this part is a big, roped-off, square area for those willing to pay to see the action up close."

"Ha! It might be worth it for those near the edge of the field, but not those at the back, unless the action moves off the field." Nagora touched the middle of her palm. "I'm worried about the trainees. Where will they be?"

"Palm up, put the tip of the little finger of your other hand against the tip of this index." She did. "Where your thumb is on that hand is where they'll be, far from the giant's circus. Don't worry about them."

"Why did you choose that spot?"

"For two reasons. First, our camp will be at the base of that slope. Six archers from The Guard and six of the Stone Stander slingers who joined us will hold the high ground in the forest at the top of the slope with Trowan and her people."

Nagora was about to interrupt until she remembered Godomor telling her Trowan's twelve warrior archers from her family and friends had joined them to help guard the gold Lars hoped to get from the sale of the map.

"Should we have to retreat there, they will protect our trainees, and will only join our attackers if they have to. That will be on my signal only. Our strike force will engage only if the giant orders his troops to action."

Nagora reached for Lars's arm. "Oh! I don't want to forget. Danuka told me to confirm that more reinforcements are on their way. They travel in secret to the forest on the far end of the plain. The Guard has sent one hundred archers, and sixty Stone Stander volunteers with slings are on their way."

"That is excellent news!" Lars gave her hand a squeeze. "Now that we outnumber Golgotha's force, I'll double the archers and slingers on the high ground."

"What if something happens to you on the battlefield?"

"It'll be Trowan's call."

"I hope it doesn't come to that. What's your second reason for choosing that spot?"

"When the giant arrived, we heard he was particular about his armor, wanting to keep it shiny and free of rust to reflect the lines of dragon teeth on it and give the appearance of an abundance of fangs. He also won't fight or hunt a dragon in the rain. That gave me the idea that we might use shiny shields to blind him for you at an opportune moment."

Nagora touched his arm. "You're like me; you know he'll fight dirty."

"No choice but to plan for that, right? On the day before we left for the plain, I rode to visit Bardas to ask him if he could make thirty shields using the square copper sheets he uses to make pans. I told him I didn't need combat-strength shields, only ceremonial ones built on light wooden frames with carry straps. They'll be ready tomorrow. One of our wagons will go pick them up."

"That's a lot of sheets!"

"Aye, they'll knock his supply down by more than half, but I paid him well with coins from our war chest, the one we thought we'd never have to use."

"Turns out you were right in convincing me we should have one. How will you use the shields?"

"While we were at the plain, we planted heavy stakes in three lines on the slope, where we set three level rows of squared-off logs. They have measured angle lines on their tops to show where the shields are to rest in different positions. That gives us three tiers of ten shields per tier. Our thirty trainees from Maze Point will control them so they work in unison as one big mirror." Lars spread his arms and rotated his chest slightly from side to side before continuing.

"Later, I met with the giant's circus leader and offered having us flash the shields to welcome the giant and Raynhard if they arrive before sunset. And to flash with the drumbeats used to signal the giant's arrival on the battlefield. Or to be in the parade he's supposed to have after he kills a dragon. Since we'll be so far from the action, except for the parades, he didn't object. My feeling is he doesn't trust us."

He pointed at Nagora. "All I need from you is a signal when you want the shields to reflect sunlight on the giant."

She raised her arms. "I'll clap my hands above my head, like this."

Lars nodded. "That'll work."

Nagora reached out to touch his arm. "I'll use it, but only if it will help me."

He appeared to consider her words for a moment. "It'll be your call, Nagora."

"Lars, I'm glad you've thought this out, but won't blinding the giant be enough to trigger Golgotha's troops into action?"

He shrugged. "Aye, that could happen. If it did, our rein-forcements around the field and Trowan's archers on the high ground will make them think twice."

Again, Nagora's hand went to his arm. "Will that be your call?"

"It will. I'll be there to decide," Lars confirmed, placing a hand over hers.

"Who'll be watching for my signal, Trowan?"

"Aye, she'll be with the trainees, keeping an eye on you."

As Nagora leaned against Lars, she weighed the options she might have to choose, depending on the outcome of her fight with the giant. Do I stay and fight if our force clashes with the giant's troops? Or do I seek the high ground with the trainees and join in the fray with them if Lars makes that call?

Lars's next words brought her back to the moment. "If you've run out of questions, perhaps you have news for me."

Nagora said, "Guess who returned on the Sea Wolf with the Dark Twins."

Lars cocked his head to the side. "Yogari?"

She shook her head. "No."

"Your mother!"

"Aye!" Nagora said, smiling.

Lars's eyes lit up as he hugged her. "I'm happy for you. I can't wait to see her. How is she?"

"She's well. Lots of white hair now. She brought unpleasant news for Umma, and for you."

He held her shoulders as she described how Tagnyoriva had given Umma the ProudWynd's logbook that Henri had kept on their forced voyage to Kemet. "When you return to Skull Bay, you'll be able to read the log entries. Godomor will plan a remembrance ceremony. He'll advise you when it will be. Lars, I'm sorry for your loss."

Lars held her in his arms. "I had so little time with him. I was looking forward to doing things with him if he ever came back. Now I have nothing to look forward to. All I have to remind me of him is this brand on my forehead." He sighed and took a deep breath. "Such is life. May he smile down on me from the stars until I join him.

"What other news do you have?"

Nagora began with how Sagora had become a Dragon Talker. Next, she shared her mother's telling of how Yogari had found the Dark Twins. She followed that with how the Dark Twins had transferred the knowledge.

Nagora paused before giving Lars the next piece of news.

He must have sensed she had more to tell him, because he took hold of her hands. "What is it?"

"Dannor won't be coming to join you on the plain. Danuka insists on protecting our son at all costs, since he will accompany her on the journey to Kemet with the Dark Twins. Danuka will inform Dannor of this herself and explain his other duties there as Dragon Talker."

Lars hugged Nagora. "That's great news! I want to know more."

"So do I. I promise I'll do what I can to have Dannor tell you himself before he leaves."

"What an adventure our son will have! I'm happy for him, Nagora!"

"So am I, and proud."

Finally, she shared her plan to use the dragons when delivering them to slaughter on the battlefield, and she gave him a full account of her earlier encounter with King Raynhard.

After listening to her, Lars took her in his arms again. "It remains to be seen if the dragons will perform such a display on the battlefield, even if they now have the powers to do that. Still, it could be at great risk.

"One of your terms should be that the giant's ballistae not be armed, since that contingent will target them. The giant might agree to that.

"As for his archers, they'll remain a threat. They might aim to wound the dragons and leave the kill to their commander. With the archers of The Guard and the Stone Standers slingers present, they just might stand down and keep the fight fair. Though, my feeling is that you'll know soon enough if he will play by the rules."

"Do you have other suggestions for the terms I should ask for?"

"Insist the giant come out of the castle to bargain the surrender. When he does, you'll get a better idea who you're up against."

He placed a hand on her cheek. "Making me give you back the map as one of your terms was an excellent idea. It confirmed Heqet knows the way into the maze and gives them an excuse not to pay me."

Nagora took his hand in hers. "Lars, do you think you'll be in danger when you do?"

He chuckled. "Not if I show up on my own and hand it over to you, like an obedient Leafer. Though, they'll worry about me being on the plain, intent on seeking revenge for not getting the gold. Why would I risk that when I'm supposed to get first blood for my oaks?"

She squeezed his hand. "For your sake, I hope they see it that way."

"Are you spending the night at Olen's?"

"Aye."

Lars held up a finger. "Be careful when you go in. Look both ways. If you see anyone suspicious, keep moving. The Leafers are most likely on the lookout for you," pointing at her, "even if you warned Raynhard. If he's under their control like you say he is, then he's not in charge of things; though, they may allow him the appearance that he is."

"True. Tomorrow, I'll set the day of surrender to four days hence. That'll be the day after I witness Heqet reveal the effect of dragon blood on the amount of gold the oaks can yield."

Lars crossed his arms on his chest. "That should work. Adding some pressure won't hurt. It'll take the giant and what's left of his circus here in Windhaven at least two days to travel to the plain, and then another day to set up camp at his surveyed site. That's better than a thirty-day march to the maze in the Land of Skulls. Besides, he wants to see you face-to-face."

"And I want to see his one-eyed face!" said Nagora.

"If that rumor is true, it'll help if we flash the shields to blind him. Four days will suit him. The sooner, the better. He's been waiting for this. Where's your mount?"

Nagora led him to Bonnie. Lars hugged her before she climbed into the saddle. "Sleep well."

"I love you."

Olen was waiting for Nagora when she arrived. "I bet you feel the tension in the air. It's been building since the giant arrived. His people work hard to spread the news of the coming slaughter of the dragons. He wants a big crowd to attend his circus."

"You're right. I feel it. And I think he would prefer that I not be part of his show. Golgotha wants the glory of the kill all for himself. If I can get out of Windhaven alive tomorrow, I'll have a few surprises for him on the battlefield.

"Remember when you lent me an old coat to wear those many years ago?" she asked Olen.

"Aye. It was big for you, but long enough to hide your strung bow and a few arrows beneath it when you went to save Erin. Would you be needing another one like it for to-morrow?"

"I would, but not to hide a bow and arrows. I'll tie my unstrung bow and quiver to the saddle. The coat will help hide the weapons I'll wear on my back. I don't trust the Leafers. Maybe I'm being cautious because I've been told to be careful by more than one person."

"I think I have what you need. Let me go get it."

A coat like that just might help me if I get chased. Tomorrow, I'll wear my armor. My blades, scrip, and leggings will be in the dragonskin bag slung across my back under my long hooded shirt. I'll wear the dragonskin pouch belted to my waist, but with the dagger over it. Skin on skin, I'll will the bag, pouch, and belt invisible.

I'll go to the castle on horseback, bargain the terms of surrender, and then leave. If I get chased and can't get away, I can easily shrug off the coat, shed my shirt, kick off my boots, and then vanish before their eyes. Edana the legend will live again. I'll use that as a last resort. I wouldn't want the giant to know I can do that.

Terms of Surrender
Miskosihcikew Pakiteyimowin

The next morning, Nagora rode Bonnie across the moat draw-bridge, stopping before the guard at the castle gate. "The king is expecting me. Have him send the giant out here to negotiate the terms of surrender of my dragons." She didn't wait for him to reply. Instead, she remained in the saddle and guided her horse back to the other side of the bridge, wondering what the people in the square must be thinking. She wasn't wearing her disguise. Her brand was visible. What do they feel for Edana now? Is she truly going to do this? Is she letting us down? Are the Leafers winning? Were they wondering why they stood by, watching the spread of the Leafers' promise take hold of their neighbors, friends, and family members without questioning the truth of the promise of future wealth? And now Edana is surrendering her dragons. What will they do? What can they do? It's inevitable now, isn't it?

Nagora turned Bonnie around so that her front hooves rested on the first floorboard of the bridge.

Movement on the wall above the gate caught her eye. Two dozen archers spread out above the gate. They had their bows in hand. Two officers stared at her. Are they gauging the threat I pose?

Below, a guard on the inside was closing the gate's heavy, latticed timber door and sliding its half-dozen bolts in place to lock it shut. When the guard stepped away, the windlass creaked as it took up the slack in the chain attached to the gate.

Nagora heard the first slap of the crank gear mechanism drop into place. The heavy gate rose. When the gate was halfway up, a dozen of Golgotha's personal guards, armed with spears, ran out and took up positions along the moat near the drawbridge. A dozen of his archers followed with strung bows and nocked arrows.

The archers at the top of the wall nocked their arrows.

Next came a parade of standard bearers, carrying the flags Nagora had seen on the giant's ship. They spread out along the castle wall on each side of the gate that was still rising.

When the gate was fully opened, Golgotha appeared, dressed in his shining armor studded with the teeth of dragons. He was dragging something with one hand, while his other held his dragon-killing lance. From its widest part, the width of her hand, the long blade tapered to a fine point. The giant walked with a slow, deliberate step, planting the heel of the lance ahead of each stride. The blade of the lance wobbled each time.

Nagora focused on the tall, red-and-black plumes of his helm. They swayed with each step the giant took. She tried to spot his single eye through the top slit of his helm as he passed through the open gate. It was just a black slit.

When Golgotha set his feet on the wooden drawbridge, he raised his hand to show what he was dragging. Its length ran from the bridge floor up to his shoulder. Nagora wasn't sure what she saw.

The giant twisted his gloved hand. He had thrust two of his armored fingers through the nostrils of a dragon's snout. Its toothless mouth hung open at a grotesque angle, showing the damage done to the jaw from pulling its teeth. Its eye sockets were empty and its ears had been torn off.

Below the dragon's head, its severed neck had been stabbed too many times to count. Nagora imagined how the giant had tormented the dragon, jabbing at its neck with his lance so many times until it fell before him, bleeding. She wondered if, in his cruelty, the giant could have made the dragon beg to have its neck cleaved from its body with a single stroke of his lance to end its misery. How sharp the blade must be.

Golgotha swung his arm back and flung the dried-out scarred remains onto the bridge not ten paces from Nagora. "Last dragon I kill."

Nagora clenched her teeth to hold back the bile that wanted to spill from her throat. I won't give him that pleasure.

"Where is Raynhard?" Nagora's question came out with a hiss.

The giant pointed up and back.

Nagora looked up. Raynhard stood above the gate next to Kiviran. She walked her horse as far as the dragon's head.

To make sure they heard her, she raised her voice, speaking slowly and pausing with each phrase. "In four days at noon, I will surrender the dragons on the plain opposite the remains of the Isle of Smoke.

"Here are my terms: If those who witness the Gold Planter's proof that dragon blood increases an oak's yield of gold and report that they are sure beyond any doubt her promise is true, then I will surrender my dragons.

"Should anyone try to stop me from leaving Windhaven today, the dragons will disappear forever, to never return to the maze or to this land.

"Lars Marraden must return the map of the maze to me.

"You must not arm your ballistae on the battlefield.

"I get first kill. It will be the mother dragon. The giant will have the next kill. Then the next kill will be mine again until we kill the fifteen dragons. I will kill eight. He will kill seven.

"I will collect the blood of the dragons and store it under my protection in a place of my choosing. I will have the honor and privilege of distributing it to the members of the Community of the Leaf for my sole gain.

"Those are my terms."

Golgotha raised a hand and took a step forward, and slapped his chest. "Agree. If rain that day, we kill next day with sun in sky."

I doubt he speaks for the Leafers. They'd never agree to that last term. The giant has no intention of respecting any terms except his own, to protect his armor. Does it rust that easily? Could be. That condition works for us too. Invisible dragons would be visible in a downpour, though not recognizable as dragons.

"If it rains, I agree with that."

The giant took another step forward and pointed at Nagora. "Weapon you kill with? Show me."

Nagora reached into her coat at the waist, grasped the golden-handled dagger, and pulled it from its sheath at her belt. She held it up before her. "I will kill my dragons with this dagger."

Golgotha laughed, slapped his hip with his gloved hand, and shook his lance, making its thin blade ripple. When he stopped laughing, he pointed at her. "You lie."

Raynhard's voice came from above and behind the giant. "She does not lie. I saw her kill a dragon with that dagger."

Nagora couldn't believe her ears. Why is he lying for me today? Is he not wearing the gold oak-leaf medallion?

Not looking at the king, the giant waved his hand in dismissal. "How?"

"My dragons will kneel before me and offer me their hearts so I may give them a swift death with a single thrust of my dagger."

Golgotha waved his hand. "When I see, I believe." He turned and strode back into the castle courtyard as his armed guards and archers closed ranks and backed in behind him.

When the standard bearers re-entered the courtyard, the gate closed with a rattle from the chains of the windlass that had lifted it.

Raynhard was pointing past Nagora. She turned in her saddle to look. Lars was standing alone on the bridge. She turned Bonnie to face him. "You took the maze map! It's mine! If you want your newfound friends to get a single drop of the blood from my dragons, you have no choice but to give it back! Now! And for your information, our son is not coming to join you and your deserters! No one else is deserting Maze Point! Even after the dragons leave! The maze will become a shrine to them!"

Without a word, Lars slipped the strap of the leather tube from his shoulder and walked to her horse. As he handed it to her, he stared past her. His face was expressionless. She guessed his eyes held the king in their gaze.

Nagora freed the cap to check that the map was inside. Satisfied that it was, she hung the tube from her shoulder and rode Bonnie past Lars onto the cobblestones of Castle Square. The people watched in silence. A little girl who held her mother's hand let go of it, formed the fingers of her tiny hand to make the dragon-chord salute, brought it to her heart, and then held it high in Nagora's direction.

Nagora fought back her tears and returned the salute. *What happened to the hope I gave them?*

Little People in the Oak Forest
Mêmêkwêsiw Mistikominâhtik Sakâw

From Castle Square, Nagora rode Bonnie towards Main Gate Way, wondering if she would make it out of Windhaven despite the terms of surrender she had set. She crossed the way and rode to the far side of Assembly Hall, where fewer people gathered. She shoved the leather tube into the bag alongside her blades and placed the dagger in its pouch before taking a moment to glance back to see if anyone was following her. If they are, they'll be on the other side of the hall. As she rode back onto Main Gate Way, Nagora wondered if the gate would be closed. If I have to climb the wall to leave, I will.

To her relief, the portcullis was open. Will the archers up on the wall have orders to loose arrows at me? Bonnie, if they don't and if troops from the giant's force aren't waiting to greet me, as soon as we're out of sight, we'll be on our way to the king's oak forest.

...

At the crossroads, instead of continuing on to Dromester, Nagora turned right on the road leading to the Isle of Smoke. Her mountain destination was in view. Soon she would leave the road to her left and then take a farm track that would take her past hay fields to the edge of the forest. The night before, Olen had said it was the shortest way there.

Nagora stopped at the trail that led into the forest and dismounted. As soon as she did, a voice spoke in her ear. "Roll the coat and tie it to the back of your saddle. Put your clothes in the bag, and then will it and your armor invisible. We will take care of your horse. Take the trail a hundred paces in. One of us is waiting for you." She obeyed without a word, knowing further instructions would come when needed.

From the tracks Nagora saw on the trail, it was obvious mule-drawn wagons had traveled that way, but only one had returned. Several horses had come and gone along it as well. "Follow the tracks," said the voice she had been expecting. Nagora climbed the easy slope of the mountainside for about a thousand paces to a small plateau where she found a parked wagon.

In it were shovels, picks, axes, pry bars, and a big posthole auger, all covered in dried out soil. Near the tools, in a pile, were chains, ropes, and two pulleys. Someone had come to work. What did they do? "Go to the plateau beyond the wagon," said the voice.

Within fifty paces, the first small stone circles that surrounded the oak trees came into view. Nagora stopped to scan ahead. The stone circles spread up the slope to her left and down it to her right.

"Continue along the plateau."

She passed more of the oak enclosures, noticing the trees within them were bigger. I must be nearing the big stone circle of thirteen oaks, the first ones planted.

So this is where workers used the tools from the wagon. Nagora stopped to take in what she was seeing. They had erected a big spruce post next to an oak in the big stone circle and tied it to the tree's trunk, lower down and higher up. Also, they had rigged ropes along with a series of pulleys from the high point on the post to the two oaks outside the big circle. The ropes came together at the Y intersection of a chained-lever hoist attached to the oak ahead of Nagora.

I see it now. With this setup, and with the help of mules or horses, the workers will pivot the oak to uproot it. Its roots will be visible to those standing within the circle of oaks. "*Mêmêkwêsiw*, when did the workers set this up?"

"Two days ago."

"And they have left no one to guard their work?" asked Nagora.

"No," replied the voice. "Worsham told the workers to re-turn in three days for further instructions."

"That's when the Gold Planter will prove the increased yield of gold," said Nagora.

The voice spoke again. "But the workers know nothing of the gold, only that they will uproot two trees.

"Dragon Talker, now we will reveal the trick of her proof. Go to the other side of the oak in the big circle. We will ex-plain."

As Nagora climbed over the stone-circle fence, she imag-ined the old Leafers doing it. Perhaps someone will install a fence ladder to help them.

...

On the other side of the oak tree, the voice spoke again. "Look on the ground around you. Watch the old leaves." A half dozen turned up to reveal holes in the ground big enough for her to stick three fingers in. "There are many more like these all around the tree."

"Do you know what or who made them?"

"Last night, Worsham came with his basket. He set it on its side on the ground. A snake with a gold nugget in its mouth slithered out and pushed among the dead leaves. We guessed it was looking for a soft spot in the soil. The snake disappeared into the ground and then resurfaced to take another nugget from the basket."

"Would that have been Heqet in the body of the snake?"

"We think so. When Worsham left, we found these." A leaf flipped over, revealing two small gold nuggets. "These are not real gold nuggets as we find them in the land. We know because we have mined gold for centuries, especially ancient dragon gold, the purest of gold. It is why we care for the dragons."

"But how can you tell the difference?"

"They all contain the same purity of gold as that found in minted gold coins. These nuggets are made from melted coins. And they are all similar in size."

"Did you go see where the snake placed the nuggets?"

"Yes, among the root of the tree, near their tips. It is easy for us to reach them."

"*Mêmêkwêsiw*, you have given me an idea, but I don't dare ask if you can do it."

"Ask. We will answer in one of two ways."

"Can you replace all the gold nuggets the snake planted with gold coins?"

"A simple task. We have the coins, golden dragons with your Tiwaz on the other side, ready for release when dragons return to Windhaven as you promised. If it is your desire, we will place them there.

"Also, do you want us to replace the nuggets of the oak with the lesser yield, the tree supposedly not treated with dragon blood?"

By the stars! I feel honored that they are willing to help, and this will change so many things.

"Where is it?"

"It is the one opposite, on the other side of the circle of oaks."

Nagora turned to look. She hadn't noticed the ropes wrapped around its trunk. They must have rigged that oak for uprooting like this one. "It is my desire! Please replace all the nuggets of both trees! It will be my trick on the Leafers. Did Worsham leave with the snake?"

"Yes, in the basket."

"Do you know where he brought the snake?"

"With him; but somewhere along the way, it either escaped or changed into the frog that is now in the basket."

"I gather you have not found how Heqet takes on the body of the Gold Planter?"

"Alas, not yet, as she has only returned recently with Worsham. He lives at the Oracle Inn on Walker Way. We are watching. When we know, we will inform you."

Hmm … That way is also known as "Lonesome Lane." Could that be the same inn where two women nursed Worsham back to health? Its name matches his description of it.

Could one of them have been Heqet, the one who read palms and predicted the future of patrons of the inn? Another piece to my puzzle?

Nagora walked around the tree to examine the post tied to it. In her mind she could see how, when the post reached the stone wall, it would act as a fulcrum, raising the tree's roots clear above ground. "That's a big oak to uproot. It won't be easy."

"Easier if the soil was soaked with water, but they will do it two days too soon."

"What do you mean?"

"A big storm is coming. Four days from now, it will rain all day and night. The next day, the ground will be soaked—the best day to uproot the tree."

Nagora smiled. That will delay our battle with the giant by a day. This coming rainstorm is giving me new ideas for my plan. I'll ask Danuka if the dragons can make that happen.

"Little People, do you have anything else to show me?"

"No. Your dragon waits for you."

"Thank you, *Mêmêkwêsiw*. You have been a great help."

Nagora's mind did a quick calculation as she hurried down the trail. Thirteen acorn planters stood in that big stone circle, and then for twelve successive years each of them planted an oak. That's one hundred and fifty-six oaks plus the first twelve, for a total of one hundred and sixty-nine oaks. What will I ask the dragons to do with them? They can find many others in the land, if that's not enough.

When Nagora came off the trail, her dragon was nowhere in sight. *Okâwîmâw*, where are you? I don't see your shadow.

A dozen paces in front of her, the special saddle appeared, along with the wing Danuka had lowered for her to climb up on.

Lone Wolf, now that I can will my skin to make me invisible for as long as I want, it bends light around my body to prevent a shadow from forming, like your dragonskin armor does when you will it to make you invisible.

Why have I never noticed that before? How often does one look at one's shadow? I'm ready, Mother.

The dragon took to the air, speaking to Nagora mind-to-mind. I will take you to the battlefield. Perhaps seeing it will give you more ideas from what the Little People showed you.

They covered the distance in moments only. Danuka flew past the plain and out to sea, where she circled back on a straight flight path that took them over the remains of the Isle of Smoke and onward toward the battlefield in a slow glide.

Ahead, Nagora saw the big rectangular field that had been roped off as Lars had described it to her. What he hadn't located for her were the three big tripods, standing to the right of the open end of the battlefield. No one will butcher a dragon of mine on one of those.

He hadn't mentioned the tall poles flying the giant's kill flags that now lined the three roped-off sides of the field. Seeing a newly built platform like the one the giant had used at the harbor confirmed which tent was his stable tent.

Three hundred paces beyond the Leafer tent, some of Golgotha's troops were setting up their tents within a marked off perimeter.

Beyond the performers' tents, a row of tents facing the forest on that side of the plain was being set up. Curious onlookers would settle along that edge of forest. She could only imagine what those tents would offer for sale, as behind them, near their wagons, people were setting up fire pits with roasting equipment.

Danuka circled back, gliding closer to the perimeter forest around the plain. Nagora searched for the three rows of logs where the trainees would stand with the copper shields. They were on the slope, well away from the battlefield, as Lars had said.

Before leaving the plain, her dragon flew over the temporary pens stocked with farm animals to feed Golgotha's retinue. After seeing the layout of the tents and spaces, Nagora guessed the giant's circus master, as Lars had called him, had plenty of experience setting up for such events.

Nagora could only imagine how much the Leafers paid for Golgotha's services. That bothered her, because deep inside her she knew there was a greater scheme in the works than to just kill the dragons for their blood. Heqet, as Moreena revealed in the riddled curse of the dagger, will rule as queen forevermore. What troubled Nagora was how the witch would make that happen. She knew the answer was in the dagger's hidden curse and, if she wanted to uncover the curse, Danuka told her she had no choice but to trust her. *I'm battling more than this giant. I'm fighting a witch and her curse. If I lose sight of either, I fear I will die. How can I fight them both if I am blind? Is that the curse I'm burdened with?*

Preparations for Battle
Wawîyewin ohci Nôtinikewin

Nagora's invisible flight home in daylight gave her a fresh perspective of the terrain they flew over and of the speed they traveled.

Once Danuka had landed on the cliff above Nagora's lodge, she became visible and spoke to the Dragon Talker mind-to-mind.

Remove your armor. Then we will talk.

After dressing and donning her weapons, Nagora placed the golden-handled dagger in her scrip before fastening the dragonskin bag to the back of her dragon's saddle. Thank you, *Okâwîmâw*, for having the *Mêmêkwêsiw* make this bag. It was most useful, as were the belt and pouch for the dagger. I have left them in the bag for another time. Thank you for bringing me home.

Then she stood before her dragon.

Ka Peyakot Mahihkan, do you have new plans to share with me?

I do, but they will depend on whether your dragons have the strength to carry out the mission I imagined.

Speak it. With the extra strength we have gained, we may be able.

Do you think a dragon has the strength to pull an oak tree from the ground where it grows and fly it to the battlefield or to a place in Windhaven?

That will depend on the size of the oak. If one cannot, two or three together can. Flying such a tree any distance would require as many dragons, using ropes to allow them flying distance from each other. Tell me more.

Three nights from now, the Gold Planter, whom I suspect is the witch Heqet, will show the Head Leafers proof of the increased yield of dragon gold the oaks can harvest from the ground if tended with dragon blood. The Little People showed me the oak the Gold Planter will uproot to reveal the gold nuggets harvested by it.

The dragon interrupted. The *Mêmêkwêsiw* told me of the trick to dupe the Leafers, and of your trick to embarrass the Gold Planter. Where do you want us to bring that oak?

Okâwîmâw, drop that big one on the battlefield with its roots facing the viewing stand. And if the dragons can uproot smaller trees and fly them there to scatter them over the bat-tlefield, leaving me enough space to walk among them to the viewing stand, I will then confront the Head Leafers about their doubts concerning the promise of the Gold Planter. If they are honest, they will know they have not met my first term of surrender, and that means they will not meet my last term as well. I will tell them I will not surrender the dragons. Dragons will no longer be the main attraction of the circus of Golgotha. He and the Leafers will lose face, but because I will show up, I expect he will challenge me to fight him, to make me, as Dragon Talker, the attraction. His intention will be to eliminate me so he can hunt the dragons.

When will you want us to do this?

The Little People said that in four days, it will rain day and night. If that is so, the dragons should wait until the rain soaks the ground, making the trees easier to pull. The dragons should be invisible when they drop the trees onto the field. Rain and the cover of darkness will help protect them. Also, the dragons could first hit the ballistae with oaks to destroy them, or at least render them useless.

You mentioned Windhaven. Where do you want us to deliver the oaks?

Drop them onto the ship of giant, the Gethsemane, to damage it almost beyond repair, but not sink it. Then fill the Assembly Hall of the Leaf, Castle Square, and the castle's courtyard.

Lone Wolf, this tells me your battle with the giant will not be over before I leave with the Dark Twins.

That is true, Mother, but you will have plenty of time to bring them to Kemet, rest, and then return with Yogari. I will do my best to defeat the giant on his field, or at least strike a blow as best I can to wound him and enrage him even more because he will have no dragons to kill. He will come after me to fight me in the maze. I doubt he will trek overland to the Land of Skulls and risk having his force decimated on the way. He will want to sail there. Before he does, I will have time to prepare. Golgotha will have to come ashore. King Raynhard will not fund his quest. He'll not have any Leafer funds to offer King Godomor in some form of negotiations. Godomor will do all in his power to stop the giant.

Also, Mother, if I can find where Heqet is hiding, I will have another weapon to use against the giant, one that will sting his mind. Because of the three words on his flags, 'for my mother,' I believe he is the son of Heqet. When I learn the secret curse of the dagger, I will know how to strike at her. And when I do, Golgotha will become blind with rage. His rage will be his downfall when I fight him in the maze.

Ka Peyakot Mahihkan, you know what your choice means?

Okâwîmâw, I do. I will do it for you.

If you do, I may help you regain your sight, but I make no promises.

I understand. Dragons do not make promises.

Lone Wolf, I spoke at length with my young of your plan to create the illusion of a three-headed dragon. We must keep them safe at all costs. And I, at all costs, will keep myself safe. Two of my young and I can create the deception you want. We have been practicing it, but, given the significant risks of performing it on that battlefield, we have decided against it. Should you battle the giant in the maze, I will ask my young to reconsider the risks. Until then, we will continue to practice the maneuver.

Okâwîmâw, I respect your wise decision. All I ask you is to bring me to the plain, a safe distance from the battlefield. If the dragons carry out my mission with the oaks, I'm not sure there will be a confrontation with the giant. Though I could be in the heat of a battle between our strike force and the troops of Golgotha. Or I will reach the high ground above Lars's encampment and go to the cliff on the seaside of the forest up there. If Lars does not need the trainees, I will call to you.

Ka Peyakot Mahihkan, the Dark Twins are warriors. They wish to help, to go into battle with you. This I will not allow. We must keep them safe at all costs. I must bring them back home unharmed. At most, I will allow them to witness it.

Okâwîmâw, do not allow them to witness it. Remove that worry. Tell them it is my fight, and that I too will not allow them to watch.

Tomorrow, you and Dannor will help them and their attendants take their first flight on me, and then on two other dragons.

Danuka moved her head closer to Nagora's and stared into her eyes.

Thank you for doing your duty to protect us from the dragon slayer. We and the *Mêmêkwêsiw* will do our best to help you. The only one we want to fear us is the cruel slayer. Scattering the oaks on his battlefield will give him second thoughts about our powers, even if he is not aware of our oath to not harm your kind. Today, you saw the work of Golgotha on a dragon unfortunate to live without knowledge and without the protection of a Dragon Talker. I know you will not let that happen to us.

Remember, Lone Wolf, people have one gift they share with dragons. It might help your kind survive. That gift is the hope that truth will prevail. The seeds of hope are sown in the reality of the present. It is the one gift you and your people can offer one another in hard times. However, if your people cease to offer hope, they will lose it forever.

As Danuka disappeared before her eyes, leaving behind a momentary trace of the gust and sound of the beat of her wings, Nagora thought: I still cling to hope.

...

As Nagora trudged down the slope to her lodge, she wondered if she might be lucky enough to strike a fatal blow to the giant. Then she'd only have to worry about Heqet. Will the witch be on the battlefield waiting and watching for her son to kill the Dragon Talker? I have no proof the giant is her son, only what my gut and the words on his flags tell me.

Lars has helped set the stage for that battle. If the dragons can do what I ask, the battlefield will change and influence the outcome. Can I warn him? Perhaps Danuka can fly to the seaside cliff above his encampment at dusk on the way to see the uprooting of the two oaks. If I can't, will he and the strike force be able to assess the new situation I've created?

On watch at her lodge door, Gabe and Raean greeted Nagora. "I have a report for you, Auntie Nagora. A Maze Point smith delivered four sets of skystone blades this morning. Other than that, all is quiet here. Did you see the giant?"

"Aye, Raean, I did. Golgotha is his name. If you were standing straight on Uncle Lars's shoulders, he would be that tall. Rumor is he has only one eye in the middle of his face. I can't say if that's true or not, as I've only ever seen him in armor. His helm has only two narrow slits. One for the mouth and the other for," she crossed her eyes, "his eye!"

The boy laughed. "Are you afraid of him?"

"Aye, I am. He's a cruel dragon slayer. He showed me what he did to the last dragon he killed. I'll not tell you because it'll make your stomach turn, and mine again. Something I don't want to happen because I'm so hungry." She pointed to the door. "Can I get something to eat in here?"

Raean nodded. "Mum and Grandma Tagnya have been cooking lots of tasty food." He pointed to his father. "We're hungry too. They invited us to have some. Soon we'll be off duty, and we can go in for our meal."

Nagora looked to Gabe. "I need to speak to you later, in private."

"When you can, send whoever is on watch for me. Though, I might go to you before you send someone for me."

Inside, as Nagora hung her weapons on the hook next to the door, the warrior women from Kemet greeted her, eager to show her the sets of blades they had received. They put them on. "Now we are warriors like you," said Kalhata.

Then, as soon as they removed their weapons, they had more questions than she expected. They spoke them all at once, causing her to hold up her hands. "Feed me, and then I'll answer your questions. I'm starving! Raean said two talented cooks work here. Have Dannor and Sarah given you any help?" She looked from her son and daughter to her sister and mother.

"They've been great help," said Tagnyoriva, who stirred the pot on the fire. "We're almost ready to eat."

Sagora and Sarah brought bowls and spoons to the table. "Thanks to them, we know our way around your larder. Dannor's been showing the Kemet women how we make bread."

"If there's any left, I'll have a piece. I'll wash my hands first," said Nagora.

"Coming, Mum! Slicing it now," said her son, as he worked the knife on the fresh loaf.

Nagora bent past his shoulder to look at the pile of slices on the plate. Two other loaves sat nearby on the counter. "Those look good! Dannor, you're an excellent teacher."

...

They were eleven crowded around the table once Gabe and Raean joined them. Tagnyoriva seemed most pleased to have her grandson sitting next to her.

With a hot bowl of rabbit stew and a plate of bread within reach, Nagora began the long round of answering questions. Sarah translated for Tagnyoriva, Gabe, and Raean, and for the Kemet women when her grandmother asked a question. The Dark Twins took turns translating for their attendants. It became a meal with continual conversation in three languages.

Each princess, with her attendant, sat on either side of Dannor. They wanted to know who the players were on the side of good and on the side of evil.

Nagora described the actors involved on both sides. First she described who King Raynhard was and gave a brief history of her relationship with him, placing him on the side of good, but clarifying that presently he was under the control of the Leafers.

Next came her descriptions, in historical context, of Raganora, Acindor, Worsham, and the witches, Hag and Heqet; their relationships; and the various names and titles they wore. She described her and Raynhard's interactions with those five over time, placing them on the side of evil. Acindor and Hag were now out of the picture, and possibly Raganora also. That left Worsham, Heqet, and Golgotha as the three remaining foes, with Heqet most likely being the Gold Planter and the giant's own mother.

As she painted the opposing sides, Nagora brought the dragons into the picture, explaining their oath to not harm humans. She followed that with the arrival of the evil witch, Hag, and how and why she sought to destroy the dragons.

Nagora then put the maze in historical perspective, telling how Godomor had helped explain that the scars of the cuts she had made on her thigh were the key to the map of a maze that would protect the dragons when laying their eggs; how that allowed her and Lars, with the help of the Little People, to rebuild it even with the child witch, Alizarine, at her side; and how Heqet's curse led to the witch's demise. From then to the present, Nagora told how she learned of the coming of the princess twins from Kemet and their vital mission for the dragons.

Then Nagora spoke of the imminent threat from the Leafers' dragon slayer and explained how Lars had created the desertion ruse to set in place the surrender of the dragons; how that allowed her to pick the day and set the terms of surrender; and how her plan was developing with the new pieces of information she had learned.

That brought Nagora to the hoax Heqet, as the Gold Planter, was playing on the Leafers, and how, with the help of the Little People, she would trick the Gold Planter.

She then described the battlefield, how Lars and the trainees would support her in her attempt to strike at Golgotha, and the mission she had given the dragons to wreak havoc on the giant's plans. Nagora explained how, if she were not lucky enough to strike a fatal blow to the giant on the battlefield, he might come to the maze to fight her. She stressed that by then, the women from Kemet would have returned home, and that Yogari would have returned to Maze Point with Danuka.

"He'll have ideas to help you fight that dragon slayer," said Tagnyoriva. "Will Lars have time to return with the trainees?"

"I think he will. If the giant tries to come overland, I'm sure Lars, along with The Guard and the Stone Standers, will dog his troops all the way to pick them off one by one."

Nagora ended the explanations of her plan with the words: "And that is where we are today. The unknown is present in such battles. I can't plan for it. I'll deal with it in the moment."

Kalhata and Tabiry wanted to know more about the witch, Hag, also known as Alizarine.

Sagora surprised Nagora when she offered to explain Alizarine's influence from her point of view, since she had been under the witch's spell. All the while, she held Gabe and Raean's hands. Tagnyoriva held her grandson's other hand as she listened to her daughter speak.

The Dark Twins sat next to Dannor, often leaning against him and taking hold of his hands. She wondered how he felt about their obvious display of affection for him. So far, you're not shying away from it. Khensa and Nefruke too seemed taken by her handsome son. They seldom took their eyes off of him as the twins took turns translating for them.

When Sagora finished, Raean stood and announced he wanted to tell about his experience with the witch, Alizarine. He had everyone's attention. He told how she had killed his twin brother, Baerik. My nephew is a brave young man to speak of that.

After Sarah and Dannor had recounted their encounters with the witch, Tagnyoriva suggested they have more tea to drink.

Nagora was expecting Sagora to bring up a question about the present curse on the dagger. She had most likely overheard what I told Godomor and Gabe since she was in the

king's bedroom, where Raean was sleeping. Since Sagora didn't ask, Nagora didn't offer any information on it. In her mind, she went through a list of those with whom she had discussed it: Worsham, Lars, Godomor, Gabe, Bardas, Moreena, and Raynhard. I discussed the original curse with Sarah three years ago when I proved to her she was my daughter and informed her we had to fulfill it. My sweet Sarah, I fear the dagger's present curse is in your destiny. Deep inside me, I feel I must keep it away from you. How will I thwart destiny?

With that question in mind, Nagora gazed around at the faces of those she loved, realizing that soon she could never look at them again. From then on, will the sound of their voices bring up images of them in my mind?

Nagora nudged Sarah. "What have the dragons been up to?"

Dannor took over as translator.

Sarah placed her hands on her knees. "Well, we seldom see them fly. What I mean is they're flying, but they're flying invisible most of the time. Yesterday when we saw them, it was just before darkness. Some are practicing a special flight formation. We're guessing it's connected with the plans you've shared with us."

Nagora explained the three-headed dragon illusion, but that the dragons had decided not to use it over the battlefield given the risk involved; but perhaps, if the giant ever comes to the maze, they would reconsider using it.

Kalhata spoke. "When will we learn to fly the dragons?"

"Is it difficult?" asked Tabiry, who translated for the nodding attendants.

Nagora looked from her daughter to her son. "As my children can tell you, as Dragon Talkers, it will be easier than you think after you overcome your first fear. It will be like riding a horse for the first time. Except, you can tell the dragon where to go with your mind; but keep the reins in hand, for, as when riding a horse, our bodies react faster than our minds can think what to do. There will be times when you want to use the reins to protect yourself and to protect the dragon you ride. Can you wait until tomorrow for your first ride?"

"I can," said Tabiry.

"I can too!" said Kalhata.

"More tea, Mum?" asked Dannor as he leaned over the table to take away her plate.

"No, thanks. I'm done. My compliments to the cooks. I feel better."

When her son returned to the table, he bent to her ear and asked, "Can we talk in private? Outside?"

At the same moment, Gabe and Raean stood. "Once again, thank you for the meal." He placed a hand on his son's shoulder. "We're off to make the rounds of our troops. We'll see you tomorrow." Sagora hugged them both.

Nagora stood, pointing to Dannor. "Now would be a good time. Can I take this man from his chores for a while?"

His grandmother waved him away. "I think he'll be glad to go out."

Mission Preparation
Nitawi Natonikewin Wawîyewin

Outside, Dannor led Nagora to the other side of the lodge, away from the guards posted at the door. "Mum, I have something to tell you. Danuka said that for now, I could only share it with you."

Nagora touched his arm. "I'm listening."

"Last night, Danuka told me she had informed Kalhata and Tabiry that I was to bring Khensa and Nefruke down the well to the drawing of the dragon to meet with the Little People. Mum, I did. We had to lie naked on the floor so the Little People could measure us. They will make special armor for us to wear on a journey we'll be taking. Danuka said she would tell me more when she was certain that the journey was possible. Mum, Khensa and Nefruke will return to their home on dragons that will stay in Kemet. Will I be on that journey too? I mean, Danuka said: 'we' and 'journey,' not 'journeys.' If I am, how will I return? With Grandda?"

Nagora bit her lower lip. "Danuka's right, don't share this with others yet. As for the trip, I too want answers to your questions. I'll ask her before it gets dark."

Dannor's look became bashful. "It's funny, Mum, but since coming back from down there, those two, whenever I go near Kalhata and Tabiry, they laugh and point at me and say something in their language. When I ask the twins what it means, they dismiss it."

Nagora smiled and shrugged. "Most likely they're teasing you. Before you go back in, I have a question. Can I borrow your sling and two war stones, ones with no chips on them?"

"Of course. I'll find two like that in the buckets at the stable. There's another sling in one of them. It's in perfect condition. You can have it. Are you planning to use those on the giant?"

"Well, let's just say I've been giving it a lot of thought. Depending on how things turn out on the battlefield, having a sling as a first strike choice might allow me to get close enough to use my skystone blade."

"Mum, don't take any unnecessary risks."

"The way I see it, Dannor, he'll make the first move. A sling might stop him or at least give me a chance to get away from him to find safety if I have to."

"Good thinking, Mum. And Da'll have your back too. I'm going to the stable now."

"And I'm going up to the cliff to call Danuka. I have questions for her." She went back in for her weapons.

On her walk up to the cliff, Nagora stopped to reorganize her scrip. The sheathed golden-handled dagger would fit in the false bottom of her scrip if she placed the blade end alongside the small leather-wrapped box that contained the vial of the healer's secret. All she had to do was lay the scrip on its side, pull the tab that revealed the false bottom, and place the dagger there. *It'll be safe there until I need it.*

At the cliff, Nagora called to her dragon. *Okâwîmâw, if you can, please come to me. I have questions for you. The answers you give will help me plan my next moves when I go to the king's oak forest.*

Nagora looked out to sea as she waited. *Do I count the times I admire the waves until I no longer can? Would that do any good? No. I'll enjoy it while I can. When the time comes, it will be just another step I take on my journey as a Dragon Talker.*

Danuka glided into view, set down before Nagora, and spoke to her mind-to-mind.

You have questions. I will answer if I can.

Thank you for coming, Mother. Dannor told me you had the Mêmêkwêsiw measure him and the assistants of the Dark Twins to make armor for a journey he will take. From the plans I shared with you, can you say now that trip will happen?

Almost with certainty.

Can you tell me about Dannor's journey? Why is he going to Kemet? Will he return? How will he return? Does this have to do with the name they call him "Golden Boy"?

*He is the Golden Boy in the dreams of the Dark Twins. Should love blossom while he is with them in Kemet, he will become their husband. He will also be their Dragon Talker guide, helping them with hatching the eggs the dragons will lay and the shedding of their skins and those of their young as they grow. When conditions in the Land of the Danu are in harmony, he will return by boat to deliver a major portion of the dragon gold his grandfather tracked. After that, whether he returns to stay or only to visit will depend on his choices.

Nagora spoke the thought that had come to her mind: May my son find happiness on his path as a Dragon Talker.

Okâwîmâw, do you want me to tell him about his journey, or will you?

I will tell him he is going to Kemet to be a Dragon Talker guide. Time will provide him with answers to the questions he will have.

In that case, when you bring me to the oak forest of the king, could you leave earlier and bring Dannor also, so he may visit his father before leaving? If his armor is ready, we would be invisible when we land on the cliff above Lars's encampment. Dannor would not be in danger. At the same time, I will warn Lars of the mission your dragons will undertake so he can prepare the strike force for the consequences.

Then Dannor could come with me to watch the Gold Planter unwittingly reveal her own Leafer hoax. Again, since we will be invisible, no harm will come to him. Since it will be dark, I will try to unclasp the chain holding the golden oak-leaf medallion around the neck of King Raynhard, hoping he will regain his senses. I'll try to do the same for the other Head Leafers.

And one more thing, *Okâwîmâw*, if the *Mêmêkwêsiw* can confirm that Heqet lives with Worsham in the Oracle Inn, could you fly us to a place near there so Dannor and I can see for ourselves how she takes on the body of a woman at night to go about her business as the Gold Planter? If we are there invisible before she returns, we will have the answer. We will only observe and not disturb anyone. Will you allow Dannor to come with me?

Danuka brought her snout to Nagora's forehead, touching it to her Tiwaz brand. She stood still as her dragon looked inside her to read her deepest thoughts. When the dragon pulled away, she spoke. *Ka Peyakot Mahihkan*, you rightly fear for your daughter. You do well to keep the dagger from her. I trust you will not allow harm to come to Dannor and that, if you find what you seek, chances are you will be able to protect Sarah. I will ask the *Mêmêkwêsiw* to have his armor and that of the women from Kemet ready for a flight lesson tomorrow, so he will have it when I bring him with you to warn Lars.

Then in two days, Dannor will join the women from Kemet to practice the formation we will use to fly there. After that practice flight, I will tell him he will go with you for the mission you described to me. And I will warn him to keep safe.

Thank you, *Okâwîmâw*. Trust me. I will care for my Golden Boy.

The next morning, not wanting the dragons to show themselves over the maze and around Maze Point, Danuka had the flight lessons start in the cave. First she spoke to Dannor and the women from Kemet, mind-to-mind. The princesses translated for their servants.

Nagora guessed her dragon had just instructed them on the use of the invisibility armor and perhaps had given them a tip about wearing it as the servants of the princesses helped with their braids. With one hand they held on to the golden arrow band of the long braid behind their mistresses' heads while their other hand wrapped it into a tight bun, tucking its tip under a pleat on the tops of their heads.

Dannor's hair was not long enough to braid. He pulled it back and tied it.

Danuka must have been clear and strict with her instructions because the five weren't smiling as they climbed onto her wing to retrieve their scrips from her saddlebag. They seemed worried as they returned to stand before Nagora, peeking into their dragonskin scrips labeled with their names.

Her dragon's words came into her mind: *Ka Peyakot Mahihkan,* show them how to put on the dragonskin armor.

Nagora undressed. "Do as I do."

She pulled her armor from her own scrip. "With your fingers, find the belly hole. It is a small fold of skin that stretches beyond belief."

The five showed they had found it.

"Good! First, put one leg in and then the other. Pull until the hole is above your hips. Yes! Like that.

"Next, reach back in with your arms to find the sleeves. Pull way up. Reach to the back of your shoulders. Grab the hole. Pull it up over your head and then keep pulling it down over your belly and the hole shrinks. See! Your head slipped right into its place without you having to try."

She watched them spread and clench their fingers and bend their elbows and knees. She wondered if they were hearing their hearts beat and feeling the muscles of their bodies pulse with extra strength like she did.

"Now watch me. To make this work, you must believe it has the power to make you invisible. Will the dragonskin to make you invisible!" She disappeared before their eyes. The Kemet women held onto each other. Dannor chuckled. She reappeared. "And will it to make you visible again!" Nagora waited for the princesses to convey her instructions to their servants. "What are you waiting for? Try it!"

Kalhata and Khensa disappeared first, then Tabiry, Nefruke and Dannor. When they reappeared, they were giddy, and Nagora was curious. "Will yourselves invisible again, but this time wait for my signal to will yourselves visible." They did, and it confirmed what she had seen the first time. Through her dragonskin, she saw the outline of their bodies as an iridescent shimmer. That makes sense. Dragons need to see each other when flying invisible in formation. It'll be helpful for the twins and Dannor if they have to stay invisible wherever they land until they know it's safe to show themselves. "Make yourselves visible." They did. "What did you notice?"

Dannor said, "We see our bodies with many colored flickering lights around them."

"With changing colors," said Kalhata.

"We are beautiful ghosts," said Tabiry with a laugh.

Danuka's next words into their minds caught their attention. Nagora and Dannor will take turns with each of you on short flights with me out to sea and back to destinations on the coast where we will safely become visible and practice landing. You, Kalhata and Tabiry, will control me with your thoughts. Tell Khensa and Nefruke they will not have control, but to give their complete trust in the dragons they will fly to Kemet.

Then when we return here, Kalhata, Tabiry, and Dannor will ride with me. Khensa and Nefruke will each fly on the dragon they will ride to Kemet. Nagora will ride a dragon of her own. Once you are in the saddle and holding on tight, will your armor invisible. We will fly invisible at high speed so you will experience the distance we can cover in a brief time.

Nagora climbed onto Danuka's wing to take the first flight with Kalhata. She spoke to her dragon. *Okâwîmâw*, you have a new, bigger saddle. The three you will carry to Kemet will be comfortable.

Ka Peyakot Mahihkan, the *Mêmêkwêsiw* made this saddle to measure for that purpose.

Past noonday mealtime, Dannor returned from going to fetch the light meals Sarah had prepared for the riders. He was just in time to see his mother and Nefruke land with Danuka at the mouth of the cave.

The women from Kemet hugged Nefruke and danced together, obviously sharing the excitement of their flights on Danuka. After thanking the dragon and hugging Nagora and Dannor, they settled down to eat, and the mother dragon flew from the cave.

"No one will believe their eyes when we return to Kemet on the backs of dragons!" said Tabiry.

"Such power! We are bigger and stronger than the biggest of birds!" said Kalhata.

Dannor smiled as he nudged his mother. "The joy of their first flight. Do you think they'll sleep tonight?"

"Probably not, though if they do, they'll have dreams of wonder."

Much later, Danuka returned to the cave with three dragons. All were wearing dragonskin saddles. She spoke to the riders' minds, reminding them of the flight of speed they were about to take.

Do not guide us on this flight. When we return, we will fly slower so you can see the terrain. For Dannor and his mother, this flight will be over familiar territory.

Dragon Talkers, know that with our new knowledge, we dragons now have a new skill that will help you. If, while riding her dragon, Nagora wishes to speak to you, Kalhata and Tabiry, she can do so through her dragon to me and to you, from her mind through ours to yours. In the same way, you can answer Nagora. If Nagora thinks of a memory from her past, she can share it with you through us. Images of the memory she shares will appear in your minds. In the same manner, you can share yours with Nagora. For this flight and the flight to Kemet, Khensa and Nefruke will only be able to speak to their mistresses since they are not Dragon Talkers.

After a slow exit from the cave, the four invisible dragons, with their invisible riders, skimmed over the waves, following the coastline. Nagora began counting; at ten, they raced past the entrance to Skull Bay. At thirty, they flew over Sandy Hook Bay, in the Land of the Danu, and turned inland. By thirty-six they were over Yhorgal, and at forty, they climbed high in the sky above the mountain where Nagora had spent almost a year in the secret cave, protecting Danuka's eggs.

Then the dragons slowed their ascent and began a slow downward glide in ever-widening circles. Nagora recalled shoveling snow at the mouth of the cave to share with the Dark Twins and Dannor. She then remembered giving birth to Sarah with Paruline's help.

Over the abandoned fortress at Yhorgal Cliffs, Nagora shared her memory of rescuing the girls from the dungeon. As Danuka glided along the beach at Sandy Hook Bay, Nagora thought of making curraghs at the beach hut with Uncle Dangor, and lying on hot sand after a cold swim in the bay.

The dragon circled back inland over Cairnmase, causing Nagora to remember learning to loose arrows from horseback with Paruline and Geirador.

From there, they flew onward, following what now was becoming the trade route. After crossing the Blood River into the Land of Skulls, they flew over Godomor's hunting lodge, where frightened signers from Gabe's border patrol had greeted her.

Closing in on Skull Bay, she brought back her memory of riding ahead to meet her mother and sister face-to-face for the first time.

Gliding over the gates of Skull Bay, the image of King Godomor saluting her with his great sword as she left with his Hundred Best for the Land of the Danu came to mind. Over Godomor's Grand Hall, she recalled her branding.

When the maze came into view, she recalled the mound of stones it was before the rebuilding started. The last memory she shared with the Dragon Talkers was Dannor's birth.

Back in the cave beneath the maze, the riders thanked Danuka and the other dragons for the flight. The twins took Dannor's hands and brought him to his mother. "Hold your mother's hands. Tell her how much you love her. She is a remarkable warrior with an enormous heart."

"Mum, I love you." Dannor took her in his arms. "I cried when you showed the branding."

Nagora reached for her son's cheek. "I know. I felt your tears." She stepped away from him, blinking back her own. "Best we take off our armor."

As Nagora removed her armor and dressed, the others followed her example. Kalhata held the dragonskin in her hands, stroking it as she folded it. "Now we understand why we must respect the rules for using this remarkable skin. It gives us great powers."

Tabiry nodded. "Powers to do good or evil. We will use it to do good. It will be our secret." She kissed the skin she had folded and placed it inside its scrip before storing it in her bigger one.

"Mum, did you wear your armor at the castle in Windhaven?"

Nagora held a finger to her lips, winked at him, and whispered, "Don't tell. Three years ago, I walked circles around you in the courtyard as you waited for Danuka to return."

He smiled and shook his head.

On returning to the lodge, Nagora let Dannor go in with the Kemet women while she stayed to speak to a guard on watch at the door. "Where can I find Prince Gabyndor?"

"He's at the barn now. Shall I fetch him for you?"

"No thanks, I'll go to him." She adjusted the strap of her scrip on her shoulder as she walked down the slope. The added weight of the two Stone Stander war stones was making a noticeable difference since she had added them to her bag that morning.

Nagora found Gabe and Raean tending to the horses. "You two are keeping busy."

Gabe smiled and winked at her as he glanced at his son, who was brushing a mare. "It comes with the job. Between watches, time can feel long. Better we keep busy instead of

becoming lazy. It helps us be more alert on watch, right Raean?"

"Right." The boy paused long enough to smile at his aunt
and give her a quick wave. "I have another one to brush before I can take a break." His eyes flitted to his father. "Orders
are orders."

She looked to Gabe. "Can I talk to you outside?"

"Sure. Raean, finish that one. Then take a break until I return."

"Aye, sir!" His brush strokes became more vigorous.

At the side of the barn facing the maze, Gabe said, "In my
daily report to my father, I mentioned the news I learned at
the evening meal yesterday. He'll be glad to learn how the
Leafers' promise will be exposed as a hoax."

"Well, I hope that goes as planned. I imagine the Gold
Planter will try in desperation to explain to the Head Leafers
that what they're seeing makes sense. I doubt they'll accept
whatever she comes up with unless she has extraordinary control over them. Coins are not nuggets, and then if the dragons
drop all those oaks where I've asked them to, that will help."

Gabe nodded. "And not surrendering the dragons will
change the giant's expectations. He'll be mad at you, but also
wary of you. I wonder if he has ever had to deal with dragons
that had Dragon Talkers caring for them. With the audience in
attendance at his circus, he'll try to attack you. Lars's support
will be even more important. Be careful."

"I will. It's not the first time I kick a hornet's nest. This
time I'll have surprises of my own to use against him. Anyway, that's a matter for me to deal with. I want to talk to you

about something else. Something I didn't mention, and no one asked about."

"I'm guessing it concerns the dagger."

"Aye, you're right, Gabe. What I'm about to tell you, I want you to tell no one else except your father. The others will find out soon enough."

"You have my word."

"When I spoke to Godomor about choosing to become blind to see the curse of the dagger, he told me I was to go to him before I did. I assumed he knows of a way for me to become blind, one I would not choose. If he does, he had a reason for telling me. I want you to tell him it is my choice, and if I survive my encounter with the giant, he is to expect me soon thereafter."

Gabe reached out to Nagora and pulled her into his arms. "I will tell him. He will say: 'My heart adopted a daughter who is braver and stronger than I imagined.' He will prepare for your visit. As you say, he has a reason."

"Thank you, Gabe." She stepped back from him and held his gaze for a moment before leaving.

The next morning, Nagora brought blankets so she could sit with her daughter, sister, and mother at a spot on the cliff overlooking the sea. From there, they could watch the Kemet women and Dannor ride low over the waves out to sea, visible on their three dragons.

"Will Danuka stop along the way to Kemet?" asked Tagnyoriva.

"For sure. Even with their new strength, the dragons still need to eat and drink, as do the riders. They'll need to stretch their legs and sleep. Danuka will find safe places to stop on the way. And the weather might influence where and when she stops." Nagora wanted to talk about the benefit of the invisibility armor to keep a rider warm, but she chose instead to respect her dragon's wishes. The more she thought about it, the more she realized those not having experienced wearing the armor would, if they knew about it, suggest being invisible as a solution to many of the issues they might face. Your turns will come in time, Sarah and Sagora.

Nagora was conscious of how she had moved her scrip to keep it between her and her mother, away from her daughter. Rather than think about discovering the dagger's curse, she focused instead on taking in the features of Sarah's face and comparing them to Tagnyoriva's. Even with the crease lines on her mother's face, their smiles were identical, as were the profiles of their noses. Also, the set of their eyes was the same. There was no mistaking whose granddaughter Sarah was.

Sagora pointed seaward. "I see them! Danuka's in the middle, with Dannor's sitting behind the princesses! Khensa and Nefruke are riding low on their dragons, each to a side and slightly behind Danuka! They're hugging their dragon's necks! They must be so excited. I wonder if they're scared."

Sarah laughed. "Right now they probably are, but they have no choice but to trust the dragons."

When the dragons and their riders became specks on the horizon, they disappeared as they rose skyward on the practice flight that would prepare them for the long trip back home.

"Out of sight," said Sarah.

Nagora leaned toward Tagnyoriva. "Mum, tell us about Da. What does he look like now?"

"Aye! Tell us!" said Sarah and Sagora in unison.

"Well, like me, he's gotten older. He's three years older than I am. At sixty-four, the hair on his head is almost all white. His beard still has streaks of black. He's strong. His muscles are like ropes. He's not as heavy as when he was younger, but I'd say he's just as agile. He's regained his smile. For a few years after you freed him from the cave, he wasn't easy to live with. I'm not blaming him. It was all those years with Danuka. Another man would have lost his mind. It scarred his. Yogari needed this hunt for the king's gold. It gave him a new purpose in life.

"And to be on the sea again! For him, it was like finding his old self. His crew! By the stars! They would follow him anywhere. He made sure the Sea Wolf was always in its best sailing condition. Safety of ship and crew always came first. I'm glad I went with him. I hesitated, but I made the right choice. When Yogari comes back, you'll see he's a cheerful man once again. You know, Nagora, like Geirador and your uncle, Dangor, always were."

With the mention of Geirador's name, the conversation turned to the life he and Paruline were living and the great connection they had with their new in-laws. Nagora brought her mother up to date on that front.

When the day drew to a close, Nagora wondered how it would have gone had her family known of the choice she had made. Would it have encroached on all they had talked about? Better they learn it after the fact.

After their evening meal, Dannor took Nagora outside for a walk. This time his aunt and Sarah had teased him, accusing him of using his mother to get out of the after-meal chores. Even Kalhata and Tabiry chimed in.

As they walked up the trail to the cliff, Dannor said, "Tomorrow they'll be on my case big time. Danuka told me where you're taking me. She warned me about staying safe. She said you'd give me the details about what we'll be doing."

"Before I do, I want to know if Danuka told you about the trip you'll take with her."

His laugh was a nervous one. "Aye, well, she told me I'm to be their Dragon Talker guide, to share what I know about dragon eggs, hatchlings, and the sheddings as the dragons grow. That means I'll be there for a while. We'll have to find a safe place for the dragons to hatch their eggs. Who knows what that means? Apparently, there'll also be Little People there to help us."

"How do you feel about that?"

"I'm going there blind, not knowing what I'll find. It feels like it's going to be an enormous responsibility. I don't know if I'll be able to handle it."

Nagora took Dannor's arm and turned him so he faced in the direction of the maze. She pointed to it in the distance. "How do you think I felt when I learned that's what I had to rebuild? Like you feel right now. How did I do it? One stone at a time, with help from Lars and the Little People. We got it done. Whatever it is you must do over there, I'm sure you'll get it done, and done well. You're a smart young man and a Dragon Talker. Take it one day at a time." She put her arms around him and hugged him. "We'll talk more at the top."

Deception
Wayesihiwewin

Nagora brought Dannor to the same spot where she had sat with her mother and Sarah. She filled him in on the details of what they would do at the three places Danuka would take them. Dannor was glad that he would see the battlefield. Nagora was pleased that he would have time with his father who would describe the layout on the plain, their tactical plans, and how they might change given the recent information she was bringing. It would be Dannor's opportunity to let his father know about his coming trip; for that, she would give them time to be alone.

After describing the circle of oaks to which they would go, Nagora shared an added aspect of her plan with Dannor. "It'll be dark. We'll be invisible. The Leafers will be engrossed with the uprooting of the oaks. The conditions will be right to act. What I hope to do is remove the gold-leaf medallions from around the necks of as many of the Leafers as I can, but first from King Raynhard's neck. Most of these old Leafers wear their heavy medallions with the stem of the leaf resting in a pocket on the front of their robes. The clasp is a simple S hook on one end of the chain that slides into an O loop on the other end of the chain. If the clasps are visible at the back of their necks, I'll pull the S hook from the O loop, reach the ends of the chain over their shoulders, pull up to release the stem, and then let the medallion fall down in front of them to the leaf-covered ground. I'm hoping that in their excitement they won't feel it missing or hear it drop. I'll have a bag I can will invisible as long as it touches my armor. I'll place the medallions in it."

Dannor touched her arm. "Danuka said I'd have such a bag too. I can guess what you're doing. You hope to remove the control Heqet has over them through those medallions, like you did with the rings at the castle three years ago."

"Exactly! And I'll have them to show on the battlefield the next day when I confront the Head Leafers."

"If the Little People are there, do you think they'll have the gold nuggets they switched? If you had those too, they would help show what Heqet did," said Dannor.

"Aye, I'll ask them when we get there. Now, about the Oracle Inn: We'll have seen the Gold Planter disguised in the body she has gone into. We'll be watching for her return. I haven't been inside that inn, so I can't say how crowded it might be. We may get a glimpse inside to give us that information. When she shows up, we'll follow her in. What we want to find out is how Heqet becomes the Gold Planter, how she goes from a frog's body by day to a woman's body by night.

"Dannor, if for whatever reason there is a confrontation, keep out of harm's way. If action has to be taken, I'll do it.

And if ever something happens to me, you're to go to Danuka without me."

"I know, Mum. She warned me."

The next morning, Nagora walked with her mother along the well-tended garden rows, admiring the growing plants. "You know, Yogari has talked about having a garden when he returns," said Tagnyoriva. "He doesn't know where yet. His only condition is that it will have a view to sea."

"Does that mean he'll no longer be a Dragon Talker?"

"I don't know. He never talks about that as it relates to him. He will still be one, but not only that."

"And you? Will you still be a healer who collects medicinal plants? You and Da will have to agree where to settle so you're both happy."

"That's true. I think he wants me to be happy too. We'll work it out."

What'll I be when I no longer can see? How will I adapt? Are my days as a Dragon Talker ending? I'll find out soon enough.

"Come. We'll go talk to Jari and Jenni if they're not busy."

For Nagora, the day seemed to drag on. Dannor had spent most of it with the women from Kemet as they trained for their flight home. She wondered if they would leave the day after the battle, ahead of the time Danuka had scheduled. It would make sense if they did. The sooner Danuka left, the sooner she could return and prepare to deal with Golgotha.

In the cave below the maze, Nagora and her son donned their armor and prepared their bags. Danuka was ready. As soon as they climbed onto her saddle and willed their armor invisible, the dragon did the same and leapt from the cave entrance to take flight over the sea. She followed the coastline all the way past the remains of the Isle of Smoke. From there the dragon glided in a circle above the sentinels from The Guard and the Stone Standers. As Lars had said, they stood watch on the forest perimeter along the high ground above the trainee encampment.

Danuka landed on a bare patch of land near the edge of the cliff. It gave Nagora and Dannor time to dress and put on their weapons before heading to the nearest sentinels to announce their presence. Nagora whistled to get the attention of a young Stone Stander paired with an archer from The Guard. After their initial surprise, they welcomed Nagora with dragon-chord salutes. "Our commander didn't warn us you were coming, Edana."

"We come with urgent news for him. Where is he? And where is Trowan?"

They both pointed in the same direction. "You'll find Trowan that way. I'll take you to her. Commander Lars is in the camp below," said the Stone Stander.

Trowan greeted them with the warrior-style embrace and a smile. "You bring important news?"

"Aye, urgent news for Lars."

Trowan strung her bow and reached for an arrow in her quiver. "He will come." After taking a dozen paces to the edge of the forest, she loosed her arrow at a target near the line of tents. No sooner had it struck, than a trainee on watch went to retrieve it and disappeared behind the tents. Moments later, Lars was on his way up the slope, twirling the arrow on his uphill trek.

While they waited, Trowan pointed to the enemy encampment in the far distance. "They are ready for an attack." She crossed the fingers of her hands, creating X's. "Sharpened pickets planted all around. Eight wagons in the middle, two to a side. Wooden panels on outer sides to protect archers who will shoot from the wagon beds. They are higher off the field, advantage to them. Inside wagon area, one ballista. Wagons have space to move so it can fire bolts. Troop tents all around wagon space."

"Why would they set up their camp like that? Are they expecting to be attacked? Is it out of precaution? Or is that their usual practice?" asked Dannor.

"Good questions," said his mother.

"We not trust them. They not trust us because we hold the high ground here. Maybe they know others come to help us, making our force bigger than them. If we attack, fire arrows will take care of wagons and ballista," said Trowan.

Nagora scanned the circus battlefield scene before her. Now tents occupied all the empty spaces. The evening cooking fires were still burning. Golgotha's tent was lit up. Is he there? Fires dotted the edge of the forest all along the other side of the plain. Early onlookers who've set up camp? I wonder how many are reinforcements.

When Lars joined them, he handed Trowan her arrow before taking his wife and son in his arms. "We weren't expecting you. What brings the two of you here?"

While Nagora ran through the change in plans the dragons would bring, Lars and Trowan listened. When she finished, Lars took a deep breath. "Well, that will change the battlefield and Golgotha's mood. This afternoon on the battlefield, he was a jolly jouster on his horse with his big lance, as the drummers and trumpeters accompanied his prancing and charging at invisible foes. If the dragons deliver those oaks, he will not have room to maneuver his horse.

"And with the rain storm starting tonight, it will dump a lot of water on the field. It'll be a muddy mess down there. No one in their right mind will ride a horse. I can't imagine Golgotha even trying to walk onto the field in his armor. He'll sink to his knees. He might be a no-show two days from now. Thanks for warning us. I'll have something worthwhile to report when I meet with the strike force commanders later. We'll have interesting scenarios to consider on our extra day of waiting in the rain. When you come to confront Golgotha, don't count on there being sunshine for our shields to help you."

"I won't. Dannor wants to talk to you. It'll be dark soon; in two counts we must leave."

Lars led Dannor away further along the tree line.

While Nagora waited, Trowan showed her the cache of quivers the archer sentinels kept in their tents, and the stone caches the Stone Standers had built up by using ropes to climb down to the beach below the cliff to gather stones. Most of their stones came from the beach. In an unlikely attack from the plain, they would defend with the bigger beach stones instead of their smaller war stones.

...

When Lars returned with Dannor, he smiled at Nagora. "I'm proud of our son. He's about to embark on the adventure of a lifetime. Thank you for bringing him to visit me before he leaves. I'm sure he'll send us news from over there. Both of you be careful tonight."

"We will."

He hugged them both and kept hold of Nagora's hand. "I suggest you come back here for a view of the dragons' work before confronting Golgotha. We'll update you on what we've observed and how we'll have your back."

"Good. I'll do that."

Back at the cliff, before packing her clothes and weapons in her bag, Nagora put the gold-handled dragon dagger in its special pouch and fastened its belt at her waist. Invisible, she and Dannor climbed into the saddle. When Nagora signaled they were ready, Danuka took to the air.

The dragon glided over the king's forest. Nagora spotted lit lanterns within the stone circle where the twelve oaks stood and at two places outside the circle. She had Danuka circle over it one more time. This time, she spotted men harnessing horses to the ropes that led from the pulleys to the chain-lever hoists.

She saw no signs of the Leafers, but further along near the parked wagons, lit lanterns hung from the trees along the trail. Danuka alighted a hundred paces from where the forest trail opened onto the field.

As soon as their feet were on the ground, a voice spoke in Nagora's ear. "Dragon Talker. We have two pouches of gold nuggets for you. You will find them at the base of that tree. See the tiny light blink?"

"I do."

"Put them in Danuka's bag now, in case you have to leave in a hurry. You saw the lighted trail. Follow it to the wagons. From there, you know the way to the big circle of oaks. Wait there for the Leafers. Soon they will arrive."

"Thank you, *Mêmêkwêsiw*."

Nagora turned to her son. "Did you hear that, Dannor?"

"Barely."

She pointed to the tiny blinking light. "There are two pouches of gold nuggets by that tree. Follow me. We're going to put them in Danuka's bag now and then go to the circle of oaks."

After Nagora had showed Dannor the system to uproot the oaks, they climbed over the stone fence using the fence ladder for the Leafers; then they walked to a long rectangular table in the middle of the circle.

On it sat a balance scale with a set of weights, a candle lantern next to them, a wooden tray, two buckets of water, and a stack of clean, folded linen cloths. Beneath the table were eight more pails of water, and one that appeared to be empty. Nagora bent down and reached into it. "It feels like empty leather pouches," she whispered. "Come. We'll wait by that tree. It's halfway between the two prepared for uprooting."

They were in the dark, except for the half dozen pole-planted hanging lanterns which lit the scene of each hoax tree. Dannor pointed to the one to his left with ropes wrapped around its trunk and whispered, "Is that the tree that wasn't treated with dragon blood?"

"Aye, so said the Little People."

He touched Nagora's arm. "We must be careful when we stand behind them. They might back away quickly when that oak topples."

"True. We'll choose Leafers whose chains are visible at their necks, and we'll not make our move until their attention is on the oak uprooting. Keep in mind, we're invisible to them. Our game will be to avoid touching them at all times."

Nagora heard voices in the distance. "Here they come. They must have tied their horses near the wagons." As the voices got closer, she heard a woman's voice explaining how the workers would uproot the trees.

The king and Kiviran were the first to climb the fence ladder. They helped the older Leafers come down it. Several had walking sticks with them. The last one in the circle was the Gold Planter. She had stood by the ladder offering the Leafers encouragement as they helped each other up. The Gold Planter led the group to the table, stopping long enough to point to it and say: "To clean, dry, and weigh the nuggets we will harvest tonight." She led them closer to the lesser yield tree. In the light of the lanterns, Nagora saw an ordinary-looking woman, not one of wealth or, judging by her simple attire, one with a taste for finer garments.

"This first tree is ready for uprooting, as is the other I showed you. I did not treat the surrounding soil with dragon blood, like I did the other. This one will give you an idea of the average yield of gold nuggets. You saw the table behind you. I invite you to pick the nuggets from among the roots and bring them over to rinse them off and place them on the tray. Once you've picked them all, we'll weigh them. Then we'll uproot the other tree so you can gather the nuggets it harvested. That one will show you a hundredfold yield. Are you ready to witness my promise of gold nuggets gathered by the oaks?"

"Get on with it," said an old Leafer, whose voice cracked and wheezed as he shook his walking stick.

As soon as the men, working the horses harnessed to the uprooting rig, yelled orders, the branches of the tree jerked. Mother and son approached the group from behind. Nagora stood behind Raynhard. His chain wasn't in sight. It's beneath the hooded cloak he wears. At least the hood is not on his head. With care, she pulled the collar of the cloak back. Now I see it.

"Back away! Dirt might fly up as it gets pulled from the ground," said the Gold Planter, as the tree's shaking became stronger as it leaned more and more with each pull of the chain-lever hoist.

Nagora danced back away from the king, keeping her eye on the clasp. When he stood still, she made her move to unfasten the S hook, reach the chain ends forward, and let them drop, hoping the S hook didn't catch on his clothes.

She stepped back enough to spot the medallion lying on the leaf-covered ground at his feet. Bending to one knee, she made a quick grab for it and pulled it behind him. She opened the mouth of her bag and dropped the medallion inside, closing it as fast as she could.

"Look! Look at the ground! It's lifting!" The Gold Planter was pointing to the growing arc of fresh soil being exposed. Some Leafers took a step back. Nagora chose one whose chain was visible. He was one of the older men, leaning forward on his walking stick. She guessed he might be squinting to spot a gold nugget. He took no notice of his medallion dropping to the ground. Nagora added a second one to her bag.

"Here it comes! Watch out!" There was a ripping sound of roots being torn from the ground and gasps from the Leafers as many of them stepped forward, pointing at the gold coins. The rootlets had trapped some, while others fell into the earthen hole left by the uprooted oak. The Gold Planter had her eyes on the Leafers, relishing in what she thought was their excitement, but it wasn't. It was bafflement. She only turned to look when one of the Leafers exclaimed, "Those aren't gold nuggets! They're gold dragons!"

Raynhard didn't move as several of the Leafers rushed forward past the Gold Planter. They were pulling coins from the earth-laden roots and bending to poke, dig, and comb the soil in the hole with their fingers to bring up more coins. One of them, with both hands loaded with coins, held his haul up to the Gold Planter's face. "What kind of fools do you take us for? Next you'll tell us the oaks harvest gold nuggets and mint them into coins for us?"

The Gold Planter stared at the coins in the Leafer's hands, her mouth agape in disbelief.

He turned to those near him. "All these years! All these bloody years, we believed in her promise! Look at these coins! New minted gold dragons on one side! What's on the other side? See that symbol? You know what it is, don't you? Aye! It's Edana's Tiwaz! She's sending us a message with these coins. She's telling us the Gold Planter has duped us! There's no way she's going to surrender the dragons to slaughter! I'm willing to bet all these," he paused, holding up the coins cradled in his hands, "that we'll find more like them in the roots of that other oak. A hundred times more!

"If that doesn't make her message clear to you right here tonight, then go to the battlefield tomorrow and witness what Edana will tell Golgotha! She'll kick his ass! There's no bloody way I'll say that I'm sure beyond any doubt about the Gold Planter's promise. If any of you do, you'll be fooling yourselves. Double duped, you'll be! I'm a Leafer no more!"

The man looked at each person in the group of Leafers who listened and then lowered his coin-filled hands to his medallion. He glanced to where it should have been and then back at the group. "Those who side with me, stand with me!"

The king and four others joined him. Kiviran remained with the others.

The man continued to speak, stepping closer to those who had not moved. "Look at us, and then look at yourselves. What are you wearing around your necks? Look at my chest! Is that what controls your belief in her promise? A gold-leaf yoke? I dare you to remove them as you watch the other tree get uprooted. Then tell me you still believe her promise. Aye! You will lose face! Better you admit it now rather than wait for others to tell you to your faces that she fooled you twice. That'll make you three times the fools!"

The man strode to the table and dropped his coins in the bucket on the table before going to stand near the lanterns that lit the other tree.

Those who had sided with him followed, doing likewise with the coins they had gathered.

The Gold Planter appeared stunned, almost disoriented, as she stepped into the hole and approached the mass of soil-covered roots. She dug furiously until she found a coin, then another, and another. As she returned to one of the hanging lanterns to examine them, she rubbed dirt from them and turned them over in her hands, while nervously looking up at the Leafers, who stood nearby.

She rushed over to the table, threw the coins into the same bucket as the former Leafers had, and swirled the water around before reaching in to bring all the coins out, dropping them onto the wooden tray.

Next, placing a single coin in one bowl on the scale and a small counterweight in the other, the Gold Planter adjusted the weight marker. When the scale balanced, she ran her finger under the marked weight, as if to note it. Then she scooped up the rest of the coins, dropped them into the bowl, and repeated the weighing procedure with heavier counterweights. When the scale balanced, she appeared to calculate the weight of the coins as the fingers of her left hand clenched into a fist. She bent to retrieve a leather pouch into which she poured the coins from the scale.

Clutching the pouch to her breast, the Gold Planter looked around as she backed away from the table. The grin on her face was a snarl, revealing the chattering teeth in her mouth. "Damn you, Edana! May the dagger be the end of you!" She rushed to the fence ladder, clambered up it, and disappeared down the other side.

Raynhard had been watching her all the while. Now he looked around at the others. Among the group who still wore their medallions, two held the gold oak leaves in their hands, staring at them. When they looked up at Raynhard, he made a sign for them to cast off the medallions. They threw them to the ground and joined the king's group.

A man's voice called from the top of the fence ladder. "Do we pull it down or not?"

"Pull it down!" To Nagora's ear, the king's voice sounded like he was back in command.

Dannor whispered in his mother's ear, "Do we wait around and try to remove more medallions, or head for the inn?"

"We don't have to watch this. The farther away she gets, the more they will come to their senses, especially when they see the mound of coins buried under that other tree. Let's go."

Mother and son, each carrying their bag of medallions, left the edge of the forest to the waiting dragon. Now Danuka's bag would be heavier with the six gold medallions added to the two heavy pouches of gold nuggets. As they refastened the bag to the back of Danuka's saddle, Nagora spoke to her dragon, mind-to-mind.

Okâwîmâw, did a woman rider leave the forest alone on horseback?

One did.

The two climbed onto her saddle. Mother, we're ready. Take us to Walker Way.

Witch Sanctuary
Kîskwehkan Iskwew Katanohk

Locals knew Walker Way as Lonesome Lane because the only buildings along a short section of it were mostly smaller inns with dubious reputations. These inns, however, still required delivery of ale, spirits, and foodstuffs to satisfy their clients and residents; as such, wagons entering the narrow way had to travel beyond the inhabited section to the turnaround at the edge of the forest. It allowed wagons to do that and exit the lane. Only those on horse or on foot could continue further on Walker Way, which became a trail.

The dragon floated down and settled inside the darkness of the turnaround.

Okâwîmâw, leave if you must. I will call for you if you are not here when we return.

Nagora and Dannor walked toward the lighted section of the lane to search for the Oracle Inn. It was the first building on their left on the high side of the way. Two lanterns hung from hooks, illuminating the carved wooden sign above the doorway. A big O was at its center. Beneath it were the letters "r a c l e" and below those the letters "I N N." Around the perimeter of the O were the twenty-four rune symbols. Within the circle of symbols, two forearms crossed at their middles, the left over the right, with palms facing up and fingers slightly bent. Black paint illustrated the major lines in the hand, the rune symbols, and the letters of the inn's name.

Nagora pulled her son aside before getting closer. "Inside, we'll most likely find tellers of good fortune, who, for a coin, will tell you what the future holds by casting rune bones. Others will read your right palm to tell you what your past did for you and your left palm for what the future might do for you."

"Is there truth to what they tell?"

"Like storytellers, some are adept at telling stories that hold you, others are not so good. The word to remember is 'stories.' As for truth in them, that's for listeners to decide."

"Have you ever had your fortune told?"

"Aye, once on the bridge at Twin Rivers, the witch, Hag, had me choose eleven tiles from her rune bag. I was disguised as Tars then. It was my first encounter with her."

"What did she tell you?"

"'Child, a dragon awaits you,' were her words. They bore truth, though at the time, I didn't realize it. My amulet was just starting to reveal its powers."

"Will there be witches inside?"

"Perhaps one. That's what we want to find out. Let's not wait out here until she returns. If we go in the next time the door opens, we stand a chance of finding Worsham. If we find him, we might find the frog. My guess is, if Heqet only comes out in someone's body at night, wherever she hides in the day must be somewhere dark. If there's a cellar in this place, I want to look there."

"That makes sense to me. When we're inside, we'll look for doors on this floor that might lead to the cellar."

Across the way, two women came out of the Two Hounds Ale House. They were in a tipsy mood, laughing as they held onto each other. "Pig's knees, it is! I'm starving!" said one, as she pulled the other along with her.

"They're headed our way," said Dannor. "Get ready."

"Pig's knees, and another mug of ale!" said the second one. "And then we'll cast the tiles."

One pulled the door to the Oracle Inn wide open to let the other in. Nagora made it inside before the second woman, and Dannor followed before the door closed. Nagora watched his outline move past the dining tables toward the back, beyond the kitchen's service window in the wall. On the shelf of that opening sat several wooden platters, holding small iron skillets of pork-knee bones, stripped of their meat.

Not seeing any other doors near the front, Nagora headed toward the back. She stopped at the other end of the long bar where mugs of ale were being filled by the bearded man who tended it. She moved to peek behind the bar where she spied a trap door on the floor not two paces from where she stood. *How long will I have to wait for a chance to go down there?*

She moved on to join Dannor. He pointed to the two doors on the wall at least a dozen paces away, clearly marked "Latrines," and then to the one near the corner, and close to the privies. He whispered, "It leads outside." He showed the one on her right, near where they stood. "To the kitchen," and then to the one opposite it with the wooden bar across it, "Look above the door."

Nagora squeezed his arm. Scratched onto the top door-frame piece was an outline of an oak leaf.

"What's our next move?" asked Dannor.

"Other than the bar, the door has no locks unless it's locked from the other side. If it's not, we hold hands and stand close to it. You watch the barkeep and the activity at that end. Let go of my hand if it's clear for me to slide the bar to its rests on the wall and go in. Follow me when you can."

Nagora's followed the opening door into the darkness past the doorframe. To her surprise, her foot landed lower on a step, causing her to lurch just as she found the handrail, her other hand keeping hold of the door handle. She went down two more steps to wait for her son. While her eyes adjusted to the dark, she listened. Is that snoring I hear? Could this lead to Heqet's lair?

The momentary light from the door opening warned Nagora to hold up a hand to prevent Dannor from taking a spill. Once he was in and the door was closed, she whispered, "No lock on this side of the door. Listen. Someone is sound asleep down there. Whoever it is would have to either stoop or slide the door bar out of the way when leaving the cellar." She found his hand on the rail. "Follow me. I'm guessing that's Worsham snoring."

At the bottom of the staircase, they stood on an earthen floor. The dank smell of the cellar was more apparent. To their left, a dozen paces away, a dim light shone behind what appeared to be a black curtain of thin cloth that covered a doorway three quarters down. In the dim light cast ahead of her, Nagora counted six sets of wooden kegs, stacked three high, lined up against a wall near a wooden door. She guessed the door led to the kitchen side of the cellar.

With care, she walked toward the light. The irregular snoring was louder. At the doorway, she pulled aside the curtain to look. The bed on the wall opposite the doorway was empty. Two lanterns hung from a ceiling beam. One lit the area near the doorway; the other lit a long table near the wall at the other end of the room.

A third lantern sat in the middle of the table on which Worsham's upper body rested. His head lay on his left arm, which extended toward a pitcher, while his right hand lay flat on the table next to a mug. His lower body occupied a wooden chair with armrests, like the one at the other end of the table on which his open basket of bulrushes sat. A set of heavy black curtains, as wide as the table was long, hung on a section of the stone wall, covering it from the ceiling to the floor.

Dannor followed his mother into the room. Nagora stopped to point to her nose and then her son's. "What's that smell?"

"It smells like a swamp," answered Dannor.

They walked around the table to the curtains on the wall. Nagora touched the edge of the first one before grasping it in her hand. The weight of the material reminded her of that used in Raganora's Temple of Fire. She remembered when Moreena had first told her about it.

†

"Inside the Temple over the dragon window hangs a black curtain on which young virgins are now embroidering flames with copper, silver, and gold threads. Queen Raganora says she'll destroy the last stained glass window the day after she executes the last dragon."

†

That memory made Nagora's skin crawl. Who controlled Raganora back then? Hag or Heqet? That window is still there. Perhaps it has been in Heqet's sights all along.

Standing in the middle of the curtains, Nagora looked at Worsham. He appeared to be sleeping. She motioned to Dannor to move the lantern to the edge of the table, showing she wanted to light what was behind the curtain. Together, they each pulled back a curtain.

What Nagora saw shocked not only her. Her son's mouth hung open in disbelief. She forced her eyes to take in the scene. It wasn't a picture in a frame, though, from a distance, it could be mistaken as a grotesque image painted with ghastly realism.

Imbedded in the stone wall was a basin of water. Gold dragon coins lay strewn on its bottom, making a bed upon which lay the naked body of a woman, submerged except for her face. In her wide-open mouth a green frog sat, its bulging eyes closed. The edge of a gold coin separated the frog's lips.

Dannor must have overcome his initial shock, for now he took hold of the lantern on the table and moved it along the length of the basin.

The withered, emaciated skin on the legs, hips, and ribs of the woman had a pale green tint to it, except in its folds and creases where the green was dark, almost black. The skin on the part of her face out of the water was as white as boiled bones, and as smooth. Her bulging eyes were open wide, lending her an air of terrible fright. Her long hair, white in the portion above water and green below, had settled over her shoulders and onto her upper arms and elbows. A gold bracelet fashioned to resemble a snake with amber stone eyes circled her bony left wrist.

"Who is she?" whispered Dannor.

"I don't recognize her." Nagora replied in a hushed tone.

Dannor raised the lantern to light the timber frame that supported the imbedded stone basin. Carved into the wood of the top piece was an oak leaf. Beneath it were the words, "My Dear Raganora," and beneath them, "faithful in life and in death."

Nagora reached out and touched the frog between its eyes. It did not move. As they let the curtains fall back, Dannor set the lantern on the table. *Raganora's crypt is the frog's refuge when Heqet's spirit takes possession of a woman's body at night. Heqet is not here now; she's in the Gold Planter's body. She can't have returned to the inn before we did on Danuka's back. If she was here, could I kill her? Worsham, her daytime caretaker, would protect her. Even so, there are conditions to the dagger's curse I don't know. They might prevent me from killing her.*

This much of the curse I know: A dagger cursed to a line of queens. They shall in turn, knowingly or unknowingly, carry with it life and death, mother to daughter, and daughter to mother, until dragons fly no more, and Heqet rules as queen forevermore.

Ha, and she'll cover herself in gold in her royal bed if the curse plays out. And tonight Heqet damned me, wishing the dagger to be the end of me. What is the remedy? If I am cursed to die by the dagger, who will wield it? Sarah? Is that why I fear for her? If I, as queen, gave Sarah life, can she give me death? She is not a queen.

Those thoughts gave birth to one that Nagora had never imagined. *Am I cursed to turn the dagger on myself with my own hand? Is that what blindness will do to me? Now I have* another reason to understand the curse. Until I do, how do I prevent Heqet from ruling as queen forevermore? I'm doing my best to protect the dragons. How will I protect them when I'm blind? How will I protect myself? Who will protect me?

Nagora reached for her son and pulled him to her. "We have nothing more to do here. We need not see how the witch moves out of the woman's body she conscripted and back into her frog body. Now that we've found where she lives, in Raganora's body, let's go."

At the top of the stairs, Dannor opened the door just enough to judge whether to step into the passageway. Once he did, he stood next to the door, waiting for the next opportunity. When it was right, he opened the door and slipped through, his mother joining him.

Past the kitchen, Nagora took in the dining area. To her right was a section that was a step up from the main floor. She counted five tables at which sat women plying their trade as tellers of good fortune and adventure. Three used rune tiles, one used tea leaves, and the third read palms. Nagora wondered if those who paid for a glimpse into their futures took what they were told as entertainment or as potential events to look forward to.

To Nagora's left, the two women who dined on roasted pork knees were the only diners still attacking the meat on the big bones. Patrons at other tables were into their drinks. Two musicians, a young man with a flute and a young woman with a flat table harp, sat at a table near the bar. They had their eyes on the entrance, probably waiting for another player to arrive. That guess made Nagora pick up her step to make it to the door.

...

Before long, a young man with a bodhran pulled open the door. Nagora squeezed out. Dannor was late and had to stop it from closing, which brought calls of "Willy, close the damn door!" from the young man's fellow music makers. Dannor made it out just in time.

When mother and son reached the turnaround, drops of rain began to fall. Nagora saw the outline of Danuka's saddle and the bags tied to the back of it. As they climbed onto the saddle, the dragon warned them to hold tight, as she would have to jump to clear the trees before using her wings.

From Windhaven, Nagora's dragon flew in a straight line through the falling rain, using the cross wind to her advantage like a sailing ship. She required less effort to maintain speed. By the time Danuka sailed over the high stone plain that made up most of the Stone Stander territory, the rain had slackened to a fine drizzle that died out for the rest of the flight to Maze Point.

As Danuka flew closer to the cave entrance below the maze, Nagora saw two dim lights shining on its side walls. She realized they were lanterns, hooked in place, that would allow her and Dannor to see, but they weren't necessary for the dragon possessing inner eyelids that permitted her to see in the dark.

They untied the bag at the back of Danuka's saddle, re-moved their bags and the sacks of gold nuggets, and set them on the cave floor. They gathered the medallions together on one of the empty dragonskin bags. As they dressed, Dannor asked, "What will we do with the gold nuggets and medallions?"

"Those bags of nuggets are heavy. I don't see myself carrying them onto the battlefield, but I will bring the six medallions. They will be the proof that the Leafers, who witnessed the Gold Planter's proof, were not convinced of her promise. That being so, I won't surrender the dragons because they haven't respected my first term of surrender. We'll leave the nuggets in the forge room. The Little People will take care of them."

Dannor watched his mother remove the dagger from its dragonskin pouch. "May I see the dagger?"

Nagora hesitated for a moment before handing it to him. "Be careful. The blade is sharp."

Dannor stepped closer to the wall to examine the dagger in the lantern light. "I've only seen it sheathed like this once, when you used it to gain an audience with King Raynhard.

"You talked about it with Pare and Geirador when we stopped to visit them at Yhorgal Fortress, explaining you would have to convince Sarah to help you use it to kill Alizarine.

"I've asked Sarah about it a few times. She only told me she hoped never to see it again. She refused to talk further about it."

He pulled the dagger from its sheath. "It's so beautiful. What are you doing with it now that King Raynhard sent it to you?"

"That's what I'm trying to figure out. I don't think I'll have an answer for you before you leave. Eventually, when I find an answer, you'll learn about it. Until then, I can't tell you more."

He returned it to its sheath and handed it back to Nagora. She hid it beneath the false bottom of her scrip. "Thanks for the sling and war stones. I don't want to forget them." She dropped the medallions in next to them. "Put our dragonskin bags in the bag on Mother's saddle and make sure it's tied."

While he did, she spoke to Danuka mind-to-mind.

Thank you for bringing us back. Rest tomorrow. Have you decided when you will leave for Kemet?

The day after the battle.

I hope I will be here to see you leave and wish my son and the women from Kemet a safe journey with you. Tomorrow, I will write a letter to my father. Dannor will deliver it to him.

Rest, *Ka Peyakot Mahihkan*.

I will.

When Dannor joined her, Nagora reached for one of the leather bags of gold nuggets. "Grab the lantern and the other bag. We'll bring them to the forge room and then head home. Please keep what we saw at the Oracle Inn to yourself."

"I will."

"Can I ask you a question about me?"

"Sure, Mum!"

"Have you ever heard me talk in my sleep? Or has your da ever told you I do?"

Dannor laughed. "No, to both questions. Why do you ask?"

"Something someone said to me once. It's not worth talking about. I was curious to know if I did or not. If I did, you two would most likely know, right?"

"I guess so. Do I talk in my sleep?"

"All the time! About a maid who works at the inn."

"Mum! Come on! I don't."

Nagora grabbed his arm and gave it a squeeze. "I'm just teasing. Thanks for coming with me today. I bet your da was happy to have time with you."

"Aye. He says if ever he becomes a Dragon Talker, he'll come visit me."

"You know, Dannor, I hope that happens."

On their return to the lodge, a guard on watch informed Nagora that Gabe had a message for her and offered to go fetch him. She declined, took the lantern from Dannor, and headed for the barn herself.

Again, they went outside to speak. The wind had freshened with the possibility of rain. "It was raining when we left Windhaven," said Nagora. "The Little People predict it will rain there day and night tomorrow, a heavy rainstorm. Lars says the battlefield will become a field of mud and Golgotha's horse will sink to its knees in it."

Gabe shook his head. "I wouldn't want to be in Lars's camp. They'll get soaked to the bone."

"Well, at least I warned him it will rain, along with a storm of falling oak trees."

Gabe grinned. "A definite game changer for their strategy on the field. I'm sure he'll make adjustments."

He raised a finger. "On that topic, my father has made adjustments. He met with the domain counselors and has asked them to advise his vassals to place their warriors on a war footing, ready to be called to Skull Bay on a day's notice, which could be as soon as you report to him on the outcome of your battle with the giant."

Gabe reached for Nagora's hand. "If Golgotha comes our way by sea, my father and I will meet with the domain commanders to prepare a defensive strategy that will contain the giant's force. My father wants a force of five hundred, two hundred of which will join the Skull Bay forces, while the other three hundred will hide in strategic locations."

Nagora felt reassured by Gabe's words. "Your father truly wants to protect my dragons. I wasn't expecting that many warriors, only a contingent from Skull Bay. Let me tell you what I saw on the battlefield." Nagora described the giant's fortified troop encampment.

Gabe rubbed his chin. "It sounds like he's prepared for an attack. Not intending to respect the terms of surrender, Golgotha is wary of Lars. He wants the spectacle of the kill all for himself. It's his circus."

He pointed to Nagora. "From what you've told us, there's nothing he likes better than to spill the blood of the dragons he kills. I bet he suspects that when Lars sees he won't be getting blood for his oak seedlings, he'll want revenge. He must know by now that half of Lars's trainees have secured a patch of high ground. And if he's aware of the reinforcements in the forest hills, he won't risk troops outside of their compound other than those backing him up on the field so he can fall back with them if he's attacked."

Gabe paused, as he appeared to be thinking on the information Nagora had provided.

He continued. "Once your dragons do the damage with the oaks, Lars will have interesting options to consider. If they have fire arrows like Trowan says, they could set the compound on fire. Troops slinging mud to douse the flaming arrows will become easy targets if there's not much smoke."

Nagora grinned. "If the battle ends up taking that turn, Golgotha just might want to go home with his tail between his legs, and I'll have little to report to Godomor."

Gabe shrugged. "That remains to be seen." He raised a hand. "If he does, he'll return another time to finish what he came to do. He wants to add your dragons to his kill list. That would be fifteen more flags."

"Not if I can stop him," said Nagora through clenched teeth.

Gabe placed a hand on her shoulder. "My father thinks you can, and so do I. He wants you to know he has prepared what you will need when you go to him."

"Thank you, Gabe, and please, thank him for me."

Back in the lodge, Nagora found Dannor speaking to an attentive audience about his meeting with his father and what he had seen of the battlefield. He paused when he saw his mother, but she made a sign for him to continue.

As Sarah stood and pointed to the empty chair next to hers, she also pointed to the top of the table. Dannor, using cloths, spoons, knives, and overturned bowls, had built a makeshift model of the circus battlefield layout and positions of the opposing forces on the plain. Nagora sat, noticing the Kemet women's interest in understanding potential battle scenarios.

They had many questions about the ballistae, wondering if they would be worth using against a dispersed mobile strike force, or even against the dragons who knew of the danger they posed.

What they liked was the Stone Stander force with their slings. The four of them claimed to be adept with that weapon, though the war stones fascinated them. They surmised that for slingers to take such care in carving them, it probably made them more careful when they used them. They'd not waste their shots and would recuperate as many stones as possible after a battle. Kalhata asked if she could keep the one she held in her hand to bring back to Kemet, to ask their potters to make molds from it and to come up with a way to make war stones out of baked clay.

"Dannor, give her at least six with no blemishes," said Nagora. "Their potters will make more molds to experiment with faster. And show her how the grooves in the stone fit to the sling's woven pocket. I think the Stone Standers would be proud to see the idea of their war stones exported to the warriors of Kemet for adaptation and adoption."

Dannor nodded. He then continued his explanations of where the dragons would drop trees during the rainstorm, and how that would change conditions on the battlefield.

Kalhata and Tabiry wanted to know what outcome Nagora expected.

"Given the conditions Golgotha and his troops will be in and the fact I'll not surrender the dragons, if he cares about the lives of his men, he'll order his circus to pack up and leave the plain. If he gets news of the conditions in Windhaven and the condition of the Gethsemane, his pride might take a beating. His anger could make him look for a way to strike at me. I don't intend to get close to his lance, and I don't expect he'll fight fair. I might be walking into a trap when I go before him, but I'll do my best to turn it against him. He must know Lars will have my back. He's going to learn what it's like to fight a Dragon Talker. If I can strike a fatal blow, I will. If not, it'll be a blow to make him think twice. Though, it may anger him more."

"By making him angry, you control him. His anger gives you that power. Use it well. He will regret it," said Tabiry.

The next morning, Nagora awoke before the others and snuck out of her lodge in the cold, grey, pre-dawn drizzle. The two guards outside her door paced back and forth, shivering under their waxed woolen rain capes. She gave them a quick smile and took the trail up to her spot on the cliff to practice her ritual exercises.

It was the first time she had ever used a sling loaded with a war stone to go through the hundred slow repetitions of her twelve movements from ward off to center balance. With each movement, she focused with eyes closed on how she held the sling, registering the weight of the stone in each position until she felt the sling was a natural extension of her arm. All the while, her left hand held the other war stone, which she touched to the sling at the end of each movement as if to re-load.

When Nagora finished, the light rain had drenched her, but she was not cold as she looked out on the whitecaps of the waves of the agitated sea. *What are the conditions on the plain right now? Is Golgotha taking stock of the work of the dragons? Or did the noise of falling oaks keep him awake and worried most of the night? How will he busy himself today? Will he venture outside without his armor? Dare he?*

While returning to her lodge, Nagora thought of the missive she would write to her father. *I want to be the one to tell him about my decision. Will he return before I am blind? I fear I won't have the choice to wait until he does. Shall I wait until the last moment?*

I need to know what threat the dagger's curse poses. Being blind to it could be the end of me as Heqet wished last night. I don't think she's expecting me to blind myself to learn the curse. She doesn't know what I will do for the dragons. The sooner I confront the curse, the better my chances will be to overcome it, and defeat Heqet. Ha! Here I am planning for a future event that will not happen if I die on the battlefield tomorrow. The letter can wait. Today I'll rest, like Danuka.

Muddy Battlefield
Pasakoskowakâw Nôtinikewin

In the quiet of the next morning, after her exercises, Nagora laid out her weapons on the bed and emptied her scrip to re-pack it before leaving for the maze. Her skystone blade and throwing knives were sharp and in their sheaths, ready to wear. In her scrip, she placed only what she felt was essential: the smaller scrip containing her dragonskin armor, her sling, the two war stones, and the six gold oak-leaf medallions. Something was missing: her small pouch of fire starter with the flint stone. As Nagora reached for it, she thought of her uncle, Dangor, who had trained her to be a warrior. He had reminded her only once. "You never know when you'll need to start a fire. If you carry these, it'll be easy." Experience had reinforced his words. Since she had other plans for the gold-handled dagger and the healer's secret, they were the last items she put in.

The night before she had made it clear to her children and the Kemet women she did not want any long goodbyes as she left to join Danuka at the maze. She wanted her mind to be clear and focused. Her words to them were: "I want no hugs or kisses tomorrow. Not a word from any of you. Give me dragon-chord salutes to send me on my way." She felt they might have considered her request harsh, but that was the way she wanted to leave them.

Without a word that morning, Nagora returned their salute once before stepping out of her lodge.

Right after climbing down into the well, Nagora lit a lantern and went to the wagon room. She removed the dagger and the healer's secret from her scrip and placed them on the topmost shelf behind one of the polished stone boats.

A voice spoke in her ear. "Dragon Talker, you must have an excellent reason to place such a precious instrument there alongside such a dangerous poison."

Since she wasn't expecting to meet the Little People today, Nagora shared her honest reason. "To tell the truth, I am worried that, in some strange way, the curse of the dagger destines the giant, Golgotha, to kill me with it. For all I know, he could be a woman and a princess if Heqet were a queen and Golgotha, her daughter."

The voice completed her thought. "And thus complete what you know of the curse of the dagger."

"Yes! I do not want to take a chance that it, or the poison, falls into his hands today. Leaving them here is my way of planning for the unknown. If I survive today, they will be here when I come back."

"They will. We will guard them for you.

"We have just received news for you from Windhaven. On the night the Gold Planter unwittingly exposed her promise as untrue, the Head Leafers returned to the castle to collect their belongings. Each carried with him a gold dragon coin with the Tiwaz and the weight of an undeniable truth. As the truth of the revelation set in, we wondered if we should describe their reaction as one of great deception or of great remorse. Their assistants accompanied them home.

"Today they will have much explaining to do in their hometowns because of what the dragons did to their oaks. They will have no choice because news of the oak piles on the battlefield, in Windhaven, and on the giant's ship will spread. The claw and tooth marks on the trunks and branches of those trees will be proof it was the work of dragons. Edana promised the dragons would return. They did with a vengeance, a warning to those who would harm them.

"As for King Raynhard, his trusted Captain of The Guard, Ardal, has returned to his side. He had never left, but on the order of the king, he did not become an active Leafer. Instead, Ardal was to be a discrete observer when the king took the Leafer medallion. Now, as the king regains his senses, they plan how they will deal with Golgotha. Today, you go to the plain as a warrior with a plan to confront the giant.

"If you win your battle with the giant, as Queen Edana, you could become advisor to the king. You, Dragon Talker, are in the best position to advise King Raynhard. You might ask why. The answer lies in the actions you have taken to protect the dragons; your observations of the giant since his arrival; witnessing the king under the control of Heqet; and your continuing quest to undo a threat you fear hides within the curse of the dagger. Though you have accomplished much, you still have work to do. Stay the course."

"Thank you, *Mêmêkwêsiw*. This news is most helpful."

...

At the mouth of the cave, as Nagora changed into her armor, she advised Danuka of her intention to return to the seaside cliff above Lars's encampment.

Ka Peyakot Mahihkan, did the Little People give you the news?

Yes, *Okâwîmâw*. You and your dragons worked hard. From what they say, your mission was a success.

Many of the Leafer stone rings are now without oaks. We used the wind from the rainstorm to help us fly the trees to the plain.

I cannot wait to witness the oak piles with my own eyes.

We will fly over it, invisible, for you to see before we land.

That is an excellent idea. After Lars reports to me, I will have you bring me to a safe spot on the plain beyond the range of any arrows.

Nagora tied her bag to the saddle. Once seated, she willed her armor invisible. Ready, Mother.

The dragon circled downward in a slow glide from high above the plain, giving Nagora ample time to take in the whole area. The closer her view, the more she appreciated the great number of trees the dragons had flown to the battlefield. A pile of oaks rested in a tangle on top of the butchering tripods they had obliterated. Streams of rich black earth from the roots now puddled on the ground around the pile.

On the long sides of the field, the uprooted ends of the oaks created a haphazard and wet dirt wall, three to four felled trees high. Their leaf-covered top branches seemed to point at each other from across their sides of the field. So many of them touched and tangled in great snags that Nagora wondered if she'd be able to walk through them.

One big oak had landed on the viewing stand and broken it in two, instead of landing in front of it. Where the two ballistae had stood was a mound of broken oaks, hurled on top of each other. The wagons and the lone ballista inside the troop compound had suffered the same treatment. An enormous broom appeared to have swept aside the defensive cross pickets surrounding the troop compound.

No one from the giant's circus was in sight, not a single soldier, no Leafers, and no one from any of the support tents or the musician tents. Not a tent flap was open, not even Golgotha's. Two saddled horses, tied to the guylines of the entrance, waited.

Only the shelters of the onlookers along the forest's edge showed signs of life.

The Little People were right. Maybe I won't be a warrior today.

Okâwîmâw, take me to the cliff.

Once Danuka had landed, Nagora willed her armor to make her visible. She dressed and put on her weapons and scrip. She walked to Trowan's station. Before she arrived, she understood why she had seen less than half of the trainee tents in Lars's camp. Most were here on the high ground. Those who saw her saluted her. They seemed to expect her arrival. They were still busy taking care of their wet clothes from the soaking of the previous day.

When Nagora found Lars and Trowan, they didn't seem unhappy. "Still drying out from the deluge?"

Lars chuckled. "We took our chances and brought every-one up here except those who volunteered to take care of our horses. It's damper up here under the trees, but we'll dry out. Did much rain fall in Maze Point?"

"Some rain, mostly drizzle. We caught the edge of the blow. Looks like you people had a direct hit. What's happen-ing on the field?"

"Come see," said Trowan. She led them to the spot where she had loosed the arrow to call Lars on Nagora's previous visit. "So many trees dropped in the wind and rain. It was like thunder come from the ground when they struck. A sound to scare anyone."

"Where is everyone down there?"

"Reports from those on watch say the troops have split up and moved," said Lars, as he pointed, "to the Leafers' tent, Golgotha's tent, his stable tent, and into that line of service tents."

"What are they doing?"

Lars took a deep breath and crossed his arms before speak-ing. "My guess is they're waiting for Golgotha and his commanders to decide on their next move. The night before last, lookouts reported that a single rider had arrived as the rain started and left after only a brief stay, probably after re-porting how the Gold Planter's hoax was exposed, since King Raynhard and the Head Leafers haven't showed up.

"Today, nine counts after sunrise, two riders arrived and haven't left yet. We're guessing they are messengers bringing unpleasant news. These two are probably reporting on the damage done to the Gethsemane. That news, and knowing a strong opposing force has them in their sights, must cause them to weigh their options."

Lars pointed at Nagora. "Put yourself in the giant's place. What do you want? You want to kill dragons. They are your trophies. The delivery of fifteen dragons won't happen. That means you have to go hunt them where they are. How will you get there? By land?" He shook his head. "Not with a force like the one that surrounds you now and will be on you as soon as you announce your intentions."

Pointing seaward, Lars asked, "By sea?" Nodding, he answered his own question. "Yes, if you announce your intentions are to leave the way you came. After seeing the damage done by the trees, would you risk moving your troops by sea to Skull Bay, knowing death from above awaits them?"

He pointed skyward. "If dragons can drop trees, they can drop boulders. Is it worth it? Should I just go home without trophies because Dragon Talkers protect these dragons, and they fight back in ways other dragons never have?"

Lars crossed his arms again. "Anyone leading a force they care for would clearly see that they would fight a losing battle if they attempted to hunt the dragons at the maze. Is that the case with Golgotha? Perhaps. Unless another reason motivates him."

Nagora kicked at a twig on the ground. "Such as to fulfill the curse of a dagger that states in part ' … until dragons fly no more, and Heqet rules as queen forevermore.' If Heqet is his mother, and he lives his life by the motto on his kill flags, '*nam mater mea*,' then yes, that might be the motivation, but how does he convince his commanders?"

She pointed at Golgotha's tent. "How were they motivated? With a promise of payment in gold? Has the Gold Planter, Heqet, accumulated any gold so far with her long-standing promise to the Leafers, or was it to come from the sale of dragon blood?"

Again, Nagora pointed at the giant's tent. "And what about the profits Golgotha expected to make from his circus show? No dragons, no show; no show, no profits; only losses so far. How will he pay his people? He has debts to merchants in Windhaven. How will he pay back the king who paid off the traders so his ships could dock?"

"Nagora, are you thinking what I'm thinking?"

She stared at Lars with worry on her face. "That Golgotha will turn pirate and plunder Windhaven, or hold it hostage by threatening to burn it to the ground unless the king pays the ransom he'll demand?"

Lars nodded. "Aye, either way, he'll want payment of some kind. The king and Windhaven's citizens are in danger. My guess is that, come noon today, Golgotha will want to negotiate terms of surrender so he can leave with his troops and his circus."

Nagora's mind lit with a sense of urgency to protect the people of Windhaven—not from Golgotha, but from Heqet. Was she the one in the past who, through Hag, had poisoned the well water of the towns and villages of the Land of the Danu during Raganora's reign? If she was, she could do it again! She's the one who has to be stopped! To stop Heqet, I must know the dagger's curse!

Nagora grabbed Lars's arm. "We have a problem. More than one. If our guesses are right, who will Golgotha want to negotiate with? Do we force his hand and make it us? Let's not give him that choice, because every moment counts. I have six gold oak-leaf medallions proving Heqet's plan has failed. Will Raynhard come forward to negotiate with Golgotha? Or should we go in his stead? Has the damage done by my dragons given me that power? I would think so because of my direct involvement in this conflict as the giant's opponent."

She explained her fear of Heqet poisoning Windhaven's water supply. "That brings us to the dilemma of one of the terms of surrender we must weigh. Do we allow Golgotha into Windhaven? Or do we have him camp outside its walls? Either way, they will be weaponless. If they are within the walls, there'll be less likelihood of Heqet poisoning the water supply. I say we have them surrender their weapons, camp outside Windhaven walls, and only allow safe passage to the harbor to embark on their ships to leave, one crew at a time, to limit the number of feet on the ground in Windhaven."

Lars held up a finger. "And we could force them to use drinking water from Windhaven's wells. One cistern wagon a day should take care of their needs."

Nagora smiled. "Aye! I like that. And Golgotha will be the last to embark. That will make him our hostage, our guarantee."

The clouds jostled with each other in a battle to decide whether the sun should shine through. The greys were winning as noon approached. Nagora told Lars and Trowan of her earlier conversation with the Little People, when they gave all the reasons she was the most suited to advise the king. "They speak truth. It must be you!" said Trowan.

"I agree, Nagora. The sooner the better," said Lars.

Nagora pointed in the direction of the giant's tent. "Should I go down there now?"

"Not yet! With the dragons' help and the Little People, you made your moves. Now it's Golgotha's turn. He knows it."

Lars looked to the sky. "It shouldn't be long now. He'll give you a sign."

In less than a count, soldiers lifted and secured the entrance flaps of the giant's tent. As they did so, other soldiers carried out a panel made of planks tied to cross pieces. It was about three paces long and an arm's span wide. They laid it on the muddy ground just outside the tent.

Then two men stepped from the tent. One carried a pole with a white flag on it, the other had saddlebags slung over a shoulder. The men untied their horses and walked them toward the broken viewing stands. When they slogged past the stands up to their ankles in mud, Golgotha, in full armor, walked out onto the wooden panel and appeared to watch the two.

Lars touched Trowan's arm. The archer left. When she returned, she held a white flag wrapped around a stick, sharpened to a point at one end. "We thought this might come in handy." He handed it to Nagora. "Walk down the slope past the squared-off logs, stand in front of them, plant the flag there, and wait. Our archers and slingers will line up here along the forest edge well in view, no arrows on their bows, no stones in their slings. Those two will come to you. Do you want me to be your second?"

"Aye, come with me."

The one with the saddlebags on his shoulder had pointed to Nagora and Lars as they descended the slope. He then fastened his bags to the saddle and led his horse past the support tents. The one with the flag followed. As Golgotha watched, the red-and-black plumes on his helm bent in the wind.

...

By the time they reached the bottom of the slope, Nagora recognized the one who was removing his saddlebags. He was the harbormaster who had supervised the docking of the giant's ship. A trainee from the horse line approached the unarmed men to hold the reins of their mounts. The one who carried the white flag seemed ill at ease as they approached. The harbormaster seemed minded on doing his duty as he led the other. He pointed to where the man should plant the flag.

As soon as he did, the harbormaster took a step forward. "Greetings, Edana, from His Majesty, King Raynhard. My name is Mikkola Marko, Harbormaster of the Port of Windhaven, sent here along with," he pointed, "Captain Hugo Rech, Fleet Commander and Skipper of the Gethsemane, Golgotha's ship.

"King Raynhard sent the captain here to inform Golgotha of the state of his vessel in the bay; the state of his accounts owing to local merchants; the reimbursements due His Majesty; the current situation with the members of the Community of the Leaf who invited him here; and that he is to give serious and immediate consideration to the conditions of his surrender before undertaking any further movement in the Land of the Danu."

Marko reached into one of his bags and pulled out a letter. "Which brings me to the delivery of this royal missive to you." He took two steps forward and handed it to Nagora. "I invite you to read it now, and if you are agreeable to the king's request, I will then inform you of my further duties."

Before she did, Nagora pointed to Lars. "Meet my second, Lars Marraden."

Marko bowed to Lars. "Forgive me for being so hasty as to not allow for proper introductions. I had little sleep, and the ride here was long. That's not an adequate excuse. Never in my life have I dreamt of being put in this extraordinary position."

Lars smiled. "Neither have we."

Nagora slipped a finger under the folded vellum page to release the king's seal, the same that had sealed his letter to Sagora, which she read a month ago.

✝

✝

In my 44th year at Windhaven Castle, Land of the Danu

Dearest Nagora,

Once again, I am in your debt. Urgency this day dictates I offer you my thanks only when next we meet. Until then I have dispatched Mikkola Marko, Windhaven's harbormaster, having authority over all vessels in our port, to deliver my request to you.

Will you, with his aid, negotiate with Golgotha the terms of his surrender favorable to protecting the people of Windhaven and the Land of the Danu?

Marko speaks the Franca language of Golgotha and his Captain Rech who, as Fleet Commander, I have ordered to render an account of the condition of his commander's vessel, the Gethsemane.

If you agree to my request, Marko will, among the other duties I have conferred upon him, record the terms of surrender as you best see fit to negotiate, and ask for the signatures and seals of the parties and witnesses to the terms upon their agreement.

As Edana, Queen of the Land of the Danu, you have the power and authority to speak and act in this matter in my stead. As Dragon Talker, you have faithfully cared for our dragons and prepared some to return to our land. Thus, it is with a humble heart and on behalf of the people of the Land of the Danu that I confer my complete trust in you.

King Raynhard

†

†

This doesn't sound like the same king I spoke to in his bedroom. Nagora handed the missive to Lars. "I agree with the king's request."

Marko nodded and gave Nagora a quick smile. "Excellent! You make my task easier. Because you agree, I will act as broker in this negotiation. Since Golgotha refuses to meet with you face-to-face, Captain Rech accompanies me as his representative. With the captain's help, and in Golgotha's presence, I have put in writing the conditions Golgotha looks upon as favorable to his surrender.

"To hasten the negotiation, I suggest first you indicate the terms you wish to see respected. Once I record them, we will then compare them with Golgotha's, establishing common points of agreement. On the points where clear agreement is not present, I will record your counteroffers and whether you judge them as negotiable or non-negotiable.

"As broker, I will then return to Golgotha to express the points where you agree and the counteroffers you make on those you disagree with. If he accepts your proposals, I will draft the final document of surrender for you to sign and appose your seals. If not, and he has counteroffers, I will bring them to you for consideration, and so forth, until we reach a compromise. Should you agree to proceed in this manner, I will explain to the captain before we get to it."

"I agree," said Nagora.

Marko pointed to the squared-off log. "It'll be easier if I sit. Have you given thought to your terms?"

"I have."

Again he smiled at her and then, as he spoke to the captain, he pulled a rectangular box from his saddlebag. It contained writing implements: a bottle of ink, a brush pen, a candle, a royal seal, and a stick of red sealing wax, which he set on the log. The vellum sheets remained in the box. He removed the lid from the bottle and dipped his brush.

With the box on his knee and a wet brush in hand, Marko looked to Nagora.

She gave him the terms she and Lars had discussed earlier, adding more details on how and when his troops were to surrender their weapons and the forfeiture of a ship or ships, should he default on paying his debts. She also included a warning.

Then, after comparing her terms with Golgotha's, the major disagreements concerned the enemy, keeping their weapons, and living inside Windhaven's walls. "They are non-negotiable," said Nagora, "as is the forfeiture condition he does not mention in his terms."

While Marko packed away his writing kit, he explained Nagora's position to the captain. Rech shrugged, shook his head, and made a motion with one hand, as if turning something over as he spoke. "What did the captain just say?" asked Nagora.

"He said, 'What did Golgotha expect? He has no choice. The giant won't be drinking dragon blood in celebration today. It is just as well he leaves his goblet overturned.'"

"He's got that right."

Nagora watched Marko and Rech return to Golgotha's tent. "I came here expecting to fight the giant. Instead, I'm negotiating his surrender. I have the feeling this won't be the last I'll see of him."

Lars crossed his arms over his chest. "With no casualties so far, only his self-esteem has taken a beating. What he will do remains to be seen. I doubt he'll make any counteroffers. He'll want to get busy packing up to leave so he can start repairs on his ship. Your warning that the dragons could sink his ships should he or his people not abide by the agreement will keep Golgotha in line, especially when he sees the damage done to his ship."

"What I wonder is, will he pay his debts?" said Nagora.

"Perhaps he will, if the Leafers paid him up front to come here. Then again, depending on the agreement he struck with them, he might owe them."

When Marko returned, he had a surrender agreement ready for her and Lars to sign. Into the red molten wax, Nagora pressed the side of the handle of one of her throwing knives upon which she had carved the Tiwaz and Dagaz symbols inside a circle. Dagaz resembled a dragon's wings in shape.

One of its many meanings was "disappearance." It's even more appropriate now that the dragons have the power to become invisible whenever and for however long they choose. Then she signed "Edana" with the brush pen.

Nagora watched Lars press his seal into the wax. He had carved it on the handle of the small dagger he wore on the belt at his back. The Tiwaz and Algiz symbols inside a circle were his seal. Algiz, the one that most resembled his sword, meant "protection." He is my protector. He signed his name.

Golgotha's seal was a helm with two curved plumes. His signature was illegible.

Marko also signed the document before folding it. As he was about to place it in his scrip, Nagora said, "I'll take it to King Raynhard myself."

The harbormaster smiled at Nagora. "Thank you for making this happen. I will ride easier knowing you will deliver it." He bowed, as did Captain Rech. This time, they cut across the plain to the road leading back to Windhaven.

Nagora was staring at Golgotha standing outside his tent. Lars turned to her and asked, "Do you think he's looking at you?"

"It's hard to tell from this distance. Does he feel defeated, or let down like I do? I thought I'd be fighting for my life today. Striking the face of his helm with a war stone in the hopes I'd at least knock him out was all I hoped to do. I feel no satisfaction in what I've done today."

Lars put an arm around her. "Well, take satisfaction in knowing that no one has lost their life. The giant didn't kill a single dragon. The Little People helped you expose the Gold

Planter's false promise. And your dragons helped you wound Golgotha's pride. May he leave here and never return.

"And the strength you did not spend today will serve you well in your battle with Heqet."

"Aye. First, I'll go to the king to give him the news of Golgotha's surrender, and that your strike force will keep an eye on him until the royal forces arrive to take over from you. I'll warn him of what I fear Heqet will do.

"Then I'll return to the maze for the dagger. In five days at most, Danuka leaves for Kemet. I may need her help before she leaves. I must act as soon as I can to uncover the dagger's curse."

Warnings
Neyak Wihtamâkewin

When Nagora returned to the dragon, she asked Danuka if they could fly invisible to the castle and land on its roof.

Lone Wolf, I have grown since the last time I landed on the roof near the skylight. The castle trembled then. I can instead alight on the stone wall of one of the corner guard stations and set a wing talon on the roof for you to climb down.

Okâwîmâw, that will do.

After I meet with King Raynhard, we will return to the maze, and possibly from there to Skull Bay to meet with King Godomor. Mother, I feel an urgency to act, to learn the curse of the dagger. I believe Heqet is a threat to the people of Windhaven.

Two guards manned the castle roof at the far end. They appeared to be watching the work in the courtyard. Danuka alighted as quietly as possible at the corner behind the skylight, allowing invisible Nagora to climb down to the roof and rush into the empty guard station, where she changed before running to the doorway opposite the skylight.

Down the narrow wooden stairs from the roof to the stones of the third floor, Nagora hurried along the hall that would take her to the top of the main staircase.

She surprised the on-duty guard standing there. "Sorry about that. You weren't expecting someone to come from behind. Where can I find the king?"

He pointed downward. "In the maps room."

That's a good sign. Already it has reverted to its original name.

Nagora skipped down the three staircases and walked past the throne to the maps room. The door was open. Raynhard, Ardal, and an officer of the king's forces were leaning over sheets of vellum spread on the big round table. She stood in the doorway. "I bring news of Golgotha's surrender."

The three looked up. Raynhard stepped around the table in her direction. "Nagora! He has truly surrendered?"

"Aye. Your man Marko is on his way back here, but I carry the signed and sealed agreement we reached." She removed the document from her scrip and handed it to Raynhard. As he looked it over, for the benefit of the other two in the room, she gave a rundown of the terms and of how the negotiations had gone.

Raynhard looked at the two who had been listening. "We couldn't have asked for better terms. Thank you, Nagora." He pointed to the two men. "I believe you've met Ardal."

Nagora gave him a warm smile. "Aye, his daughter and I share a name. How is Edana?"

"Thanks to you, she is well-married with two children, a boy and girl."

"You must be a happy grandda."

"That I am."

Raynhard pointed to the other man. "Meet Fredriksen, Commander of the Windhaven Force."

The man bowed. Nagora returned his gesture and then looked at the three men. "Lars Marraden and the reinforcement forces of The Guard and the Stone Standers are watching over Golgotha's people and collecting their weapons. If the force you send needs their help, the reinforcement forces are to advise them. Lars suggests men from The Guard join your force to escort Golgotha's return. The Stone Standers plan to leave when your force arrives at the plain. And Lars wants to leave with the trainees as soon as possible to return to Maze Point."

"Excellent! We can make that happen," said Fredriksen. He turned to Ardal. "Having The Guard with us will make our work easier."

"Your Majesty, I want to warn you of the threat I fear the witch, Heqet, poses to the people of Windhaven," said Nagora.

"The witch? Heqet? What is this about?" asked the commander.

In her mind, Nagora questioned what they knew about the Gold Planter. "I won't give you a lengthy explanation of who the Gold Planter is. But believe me, she is a powerful witch named Heqet who has been with us since the witch, Hag, arrived. She controlled Hag for a reason other than to kill the dragons, a reason yet unknown."

"What threat is that?" The king's face showed his concern.

She pointed to Raynhard. "Poison in Windhaven's water supply. Remember when my mother and sister came to test the wells of Windhaven and teach people how to remove the poison from them?"

"Of course."

"That was most probably Heqet's doing, not Hag's as we first thought. I fear she'll do it again. Right now you must issue an order that people not drink water from Windhaven's water system until someone tests it. That will create problems. Those with their own wells should be safe from poison. Perhaps, until it's safe for all, they can share rationed amounts with those who rely on the water supply. Do you recall the names of the people my mother trained years ago?"

Raynhard shook his head. "I must inquire. Tagnyoriva had created tools to test the water and instructions on how to clean the wells of the poison. Someone here must remember."

"My mother has always kept written records of her treatments. Would one of her records be here?"

Raynhard shrugged. "Perhaps, but I don't know where."

Nagora felt her irritation build, but she didn't want it to control her. "Search for it and for the people she trained. Tomorrow, I'll have Danuka bring her and Sagora here. I'm sure Mum has that information. If not written in her notes, in her memory."

"Tagnyoriva has returned? With Yogari?"

Nagora waved her hand. "I'll let Mum tell you about it."

Ardal spoke. "This information might delay Golgotha's arrival. We don't want his people competing for drinking water if we limit the supply for our citizens. The sooner we can test the water, the better."

"I'll post guards at our cisterns," said Fredriksen.

"Excellent!" said Nagora. "If I can learn more about Heqet, we might stop her threat. Leave that to me. As soon as I figure it out, I'll inform you. I have nothing else to report. If you have no questions for me, I'll leave now."

"Thank you, Nagora," said the king. Ardal and Fredriksen nodded.

Raynhard reached for her arm. "Nagora, I'm ashamed for not seeing what was happening in my kingdom. I didn't realize how vast the Community of the Leaf had become and its growing influence as the number of its members grew.

"It was Ardal who suggested I fight fire with fire by joining them, letting them control me, and having him watch for a way to stop them. He said he was losing hope because he felt he was fighting an invisible force of evil he didn't comprehend. For him, there was no path to a solution until the night the Gold Planter came with Worsham and asked for the golden-handled dragon dagger."

Nagora looked to Ardal. "Why didn't you send a warning to me about the Gold Planter?"

Ardal turned to Raynhard, who answered her question. "That was my doing. I had told him I would send word with Geirador to warn you. I didn't think Worsham would arrive ahead of Geirador.

"When Ardal heard that the Gold Planter wanted Worsham to deliver the dagger to you, to call you to your destined duty and persuade you to join the Community of the Leaf, he knew there was hope because you, Edana, have always battled evil forces. Nagora, you do that now with Heqet. That's something I could never do. For that, I am in debt to you. Words of thanks are but a pittance in the balance of what I owe you. Riches hold no attraction for you, nor does the royal title I conferred on you. I'm at a loss at how to express my deepest gratitude to you."

"Your Majesty, allow me to be blunt. You crowned me queen because I asked you for a reason. That was to crown our daughter a princess so she and I could rid you of the hold Hag had on you, and to protect the future of the dragons. To-day, you don't yet realize that it was the witch, Heqet, who, through Alizarine back then and the Gold Planter recently, had control of you. And she still might control you. Raynhard, all I want from you as thanks is to act if I ask you to. Do not hesitate. Don't doubt my words. Your life could depend on them. Be the king I know you can be."

Before Raynhard could speak another word, Nagora turned away and walked out of the maps room.

Raynhard followed her as far as the throne.

Nagora was already running to the staircase. Only glancing back once, she bounded up to the second floor. From there, she slowed her pace until she reached the rooftop.

Before climbing up the dragon's wing, she removed her clothes and weapons and packed them into her bag. After tying her bag in place, Nagora climbed onto Danuka's saddle.

Seated, she willed her armor invisible. Ready, *Okâwîmâw*, take me to the cave under the maze. On the way, I will tell you my plans.

If Tagnyoriva and Sagora agree to go to Windhaven to test the water supply, could you bring them there tomorrow morning at first light?

I will if they agree.

And on your return, could you bring me to Skull Bay? I must seek to learn the secret of the dagger. I have no choice.

Ka Peyakot Mahihkan, you must bring Sarah with you.

But Mother! I fear the curse of the dagger is destined for her. I want to protect her. You even told me I did well to keep it from her.

I did, Lone Wolf, but destiny has arrived at your door. To thwart it, you must face your fears. Involve Sarah in uncovering the curse. Have her go with you. Like the last time with the dagger, she will choose. Is it not true that if one knows the danger, one can best prepare to combat it?

The dragon's question made Nagora feel she was in a quandary.

Look how you dealt with the giant. Would the outcome today be the same if it had been the first time you heard of him?

The answer was obvious, but Nagora felt there was another way.

Could I bring Dannor instead?

You surprise me, *Ka Peyakot Mahihkan*. He is about to embark on a journey of unknowns, yet you do not fear for him. Is it because the curse of the dagger calls into play a line of queens, mother to daughter, daughter to mother, that you fear for Sarah? You seek to understand the curse. When you do, who will be better equipped to deal with it, you or Sarah? Or will both of you need to act together again, as when you killed Alizarine?

Okâwîmâw, I do not want to bring harm to the ones I love.

But you choose to bring harm upon yourself to learn the curse. Do you not think the ones you love would not want to help you? As concerns the curse of this dagger, I see none better than Sarah to be at your side.

Nagora leaned forward in her saddle to reach for Danuka's neck, resting her cheek against it. *Okâwîmâw*, your wise words give me guidance. I will heed them. Mother, I worry that these extra trips will tire you before your journey to Kemet.

Fear not that these flights will sap my strength. I am so much stronger since the transfer of knowledge; and my upcoming flight to Kemet will be in formation with my daughters, lessening the strain upon any one of us.

Tomorrow, I will bring you and Sarah to King Godomor. And if they agree, I will fly Tagnyoriva and Sagora to Windhaven in darkness this night to land unseen in the castle courtyard. The guards will have cleared away the debris by sunset. Bring your mother and sister to the cliff above your lodge. The *Mêmêkwêsiw* will wake you when it is time. Warn Sagora she must hide her brand and wear a disguise when traveling in the Land of the Danu. The Dark Twins and their attendants are to camp with Dannor in the maze until I leave with them for Kemet. You and Sarah will join them when you return from Skull Bay.

Are the Dark Twins in danger?

I wait for the Little People to confirm Windhaven is secure and free of Leafers, who would be a threat. The prince and his troops guard your lodge and the entrance to the maze, and the Little People guard the maze, its paths aboveground and the caves beneath. I am cautious with those I will bring to Kemet. Like you, I still fear Heqet and Golgotha. So must you.

Mother, I will be careful.

Back at the cave below the maze, out of her armor and dressed again, Nagora put on her weapons before tying the bag once more to the saddle. Thank you for your help, *Okâwîmâw*. You continue to make what I try to do easier. As a Dragon Talker, I am privileged to be in your service.

Ka Peyakot Mahihkan, we help each other.

Danuka turned from Nagora and pushed off from the cave's mouth to glide out to sea. Nagora watched the dragon disappear in the distance. *She is not letting her guard down, and she reminds me to do the same. Does she see a threat I cannot? Focus on my task. Be aware of my surroundings.* A chill took hold of her. *Without sight, I'll be in the dark. My other senses will work overtime and may not suffice. It will be my weakness.* She reached for the lantern hanging on the wall, lit it, and headed for the far end of the cave with it.

In the wagon room, Nagora retrieved the dagger from the top shelf and placed it under the false bottom of her scrip. She was not sure if she should leave the healer's secret there. *I know a better place to hide it.*

Nagora brought the poison to the forge room to hide it in the secret coal room concealed behind the pivoting shelf unit. As she approached the laddered shelves, a voice spoke. "Dragon Talker, do you remember the shelf on the other side where we had placed your dragonskin armor?"

"I do."

"Place it there."

"*Mêmêkwêsiw*, my mother gave me the poison on one condition: If I do not use it, I am to burn it in a deep outdoor firepit. If I die before I can do that, will you destroy the poison for me?"

"We will. Consider it safe until then."

"Thank you." Nagora placed the lantern and the healer's secret in the shelf cubicle next to the one that would allow her to unlock the pivoting door. She reached into the smallest square cubicle for the handle hidden at the back of the compact space. She pulled on the T-shaped handle and heard a thunk sound. It made her remember to push the handle back in and pulled it outward again, before turning it. When she did, metal slapped against metal. The door unlocked.

Nagora stepped to the right side of the shelving unit and pushed on the outer frame. The entire unit pivoted inward at the middle. The smell of coal filled her nose. She returned for the small leather-wrapped box that contained the poison vial. Then she walked to the other side of the unit and found the shelf space for the poison, thanks to the Little People who lit the way.

After pushing the shelf unit closed, Nagora locked the secret door by reversing the steps taken to unlock it. She then reached into her scrip and took out the gold, oak-leaf medallions and placed them inside one of the square shelf spaces.

Between the forge and wagon rooms, Nagora stopped at the image of the dragon on the stone wall. *This is most likely the last time I'll admire its lifelike details. Few eyes have gazed upon it. I'll keep it in my memory.*

After climbing out of the well into daylight, Nagora looked up at the lintels of the inner and outer hatching circles. *If I'm blind, will I still be able to tend the dragon hatchlings? It'll be the task of the other Dragon Talkers, Sarah and Sagora, and perhaps Yogari. I'll be better off not trying to imagine my* future as a sightless one. Take it one day at a time. Now it's time to go home and answer questions.

Nagora surprised the two guards who stood outside the maze entrance. "I hope I didn't give you a fright. Is Commander Gabyndor on watch?"

They both pointed in the barn's direction. "You'll find him and his son tending the horses. The lad has taken a liking to the work."

"Thank you. That's where I'll go."

The main door was open, so Nagora went in. Raean was spreading fresh straw along the row of stalls. The sound of someone working a pitchfork in the loft above had her guess it might be Gabe. "More coming down!"

Raean turned to look up, and he saw his auntie. "Hold the straw! Auntie Nagora is here!"

Gabe peered over the edge of the hayloft. "Let me throw this pile down before I join you."

When he reached the bottom of the loft ladder, Nagora nudged Raean and winked. "I see the commander has been promoted to stable hand."

Gabe laughed. "Aye, the commander leads by example. It encourages young recruits such as the one standing at your side. For someone who went to battle today, you show no wear and tear."

Nagora smiled. "Well, some battles are not fought with the usual weapons, and so have unusual outcomes." She laid an arm across Raean's shoulders. "If you two will escort me to my lodge, I'll tell you and the others about the battle that wasn't."

...

As Nagora spoke in the Language of the Dragons, Tabiry translated for the attendants, while Sagora translated for her mother, husband, and son.

"That's how it ended? Not an arrow loosed? Not a war stone slung? Words on vellum, a negotiated surrender! Just like that!" said Dannor. "It's hard to believe."

Nagora shrugged as she looked at the faces around the table. "Not an exciting tale, but true. That's what happened."

Gabe leaned closer to the table. "Golgotha didn't have a choice. Even if the dragons hadn't dropped oaks on the battlefield, the giant wouldn't have fought in those muddy conditions. He didn't have the field advantage, and he was outnumbered. King Raynhard will have his hands full with him still around. He'll breathe easy once Golgotha's fleet has left Windhaven Bay."

"Mum, I'm just glad you weren't hurt," said Sarah. "Will Lars return with the trainees soon? It seems to me they still have lots to learn before riding the dragons. Two dragons less will make a difference."

"Most likely, once the king has Golgotha and his people in a guarded camp outside the walls of Windhaven, Lars will set out on the return trip. I don't see that happening for another five or six days. Add to that the time to travel back here. If all goes well and they travel fast, perhaps in twenty to twenty-five days from now, they'll be back here. The trainees will need to rest by then."

Kalhata wanted to know if Nagora had confirmed the Gold Planter was the witch, Heqet.

Nagora glanced at Dannor, who sat between the princess twins. His eyes told her he understood he wasn't to speak on the topic. "The Little People have yet to confirm it. They think, and I believe they may be right, that somehow Heqet can take control of a woman's body and inhabit it at night, while in the daytime, Heqet lives in the body of a frog in hiding somewhere."

Nagora looked at her mother and Sagora. "This brings me to why I fear Heqet might poison the water supply of Windhaven."

When Sagora translated, Tagnyoriva's jaw dropped and her hand covered her mouth before she spoke. "Like Hag had done years ago?"

"Aye. I warned the king to issue an order to the residents to not drink the water until someone tested it. I told him I'd ask you and Sagora to go to Windhaven to help, like you did in the past. Do you still have notes of the test and treatment you devised to eliminate the poison?"

While Sarah translated for the Kemet women, Tagnyoriva and Sagora looked at each other. They were obviously searching their memories. "Mum, you made notes of everything we did, not just in Windhaven, but in all the towns and villages we visited. Where did you put them?" asked Sagora.

Her mother was nodding as she closed her eyes in thought. "I know where they are! They're at the castle. Before we left for Kemet, Yogari had prepared maps of our planned route and destination to leave with Raynhard. When we delivered them, we met with the king in the maps room. A servant called him away just as we entered. Sarah was with us. Since she and I wanted to visit Sagora and her babies, Yogari suggested I put my notes in one of the empty drawers of the two map chests that stood in the room."

"You put them in the bottom drawer of the chest on the right!" said Sarah. "I remember because I closed the drawer for you. Then we took the staircase up to Auntie Sagora's room."

"Yogari must have forgotten to tell Raynhard I had put my notes there. That's possible since they spent a good while discussing the maps," said Tagnyoriva. She turned to Sagora. "I'm willing to go to Windhaven if it means saving lives. I'd appreciate your help."

Raean took hold of his mother's arm. "Mum! You're a warrior healer, just like I told you! Go with Grandma Tagnya! I'll take care of Da while you're away."

Sagora placed a hand on Raean's as she looked at Gabe. He smiled at her. She looked at her mother. "I'll go with you. Mum, it'll be your first flight on a dragon."

"You are both sure about this?" asked Nagora.

The two women nodded.

"Say hello to King Raynhard for me," said Raean.

"Now I must tell you Danuka has conditions for flying you there and precautions she wants you to take." Nagora looked to the others at the table. "And she has instructions for Sarah, Dannor, the women from Kemet, and me. She wants us to understand she is doing this for our safety and hers," said Nagora.

After Nagora finished conveying the dragon's instructions about setting up camp in the maze, Sarah asked, "What will I be doing with you in Skull Bay tomorrow?"

"Helping me solve a problem, one that I can tell you about only when we get there."

Dannor stood. "That means the meal this evening will be our last one together." He pointed to the women from Kemet. "Do we set up camp in the maze today?"

"Tomorrow, so it will be ready for Sarah and I when we return," said Nagora.

The table became a mix of excited voices, speaking of what they would pack for their journeys and how they would camp in the maze. Nagora found herself a lone observer until Gabe approached. "I'm going to leave now to write a quick report for my father. A messenger will take it to him as soon as I finish. I should be back here in time for the meal. I'll leave Raean with his grandmother."

After Gabe left, Sarah came to stand beside Nagora and placed a hand on her shoulder. "Do I have to bring anything else besides my weapons?"

"Not that I can think of. We'll be meeting with Godomor."

"Should I bring vellum and ink to take notes?"

Nagora looked up at her daughter. "Come to think of it, Sarah, that's an excellent idea. Notes of what we discuss and how we plan to deal with the problem are always worth having."

Nagora glanced at her mother. "Like your grandma Tagnya's notes will help her deal with a potential poison problem in the water supply. They'll be a point of reference to guide her. She'll be able to act faster. Sarah, we're lucky to have you as our record keeper. Tomorrow, you'll be my personal record keeper." She leaned her cheek on her daughter's hand. "I'm fortunate to have you."

"Mum, come with me upstairs. I need to talk to you."

Sarah pulled back Nagora's chair and headed for the stairs.

· · ·

Sarah sat on the wide window seat in Nagora's room, which sat over the notch of the huge stone outcrop against which Lars had built their lodge. The room's only window gave them a narrow view to sea. Nagora detected worry on her daughter's face as she sat next to her. "What's on your mind?"

"This morning, after you left for the maze, I followed. Not to follow you—I knew you would be gone by then. I wanted to see if any dragons were in the caves below. When I reached the bottom of the well hole, the Little People had me follow them to the dragon painting. They asked me to remove my clothes and lie on the floor. They measured me and told me not to tell anyone else except you, and that you would explain why."

Nagora put an arm around Sarah and pulled her close. "You have nothing to worry about. You will receive a gift of dragonskin armor. When you wear it, you can will it to make you invisible."

Sarah looked at her mother in obvious disbelief. Nagora explained how she had received hers, how Dannor and the four women from Kemet got theirs, the conditions for using it, the advantages of wearing it when flying on a dragon, and with whom she could discuss it, but only after she received the armor. "I'll show you how to put it on and make it work. It's hard to believe, but once you've tried it on and experienced how it feels, you'll realize how powerful it is."

"Auntie Sagora doesn't have one?"

"Not yet. Danuka said all the Dragon Talkers will get a suit. The Little People are most likely making them in order of priority."

"Does that mean I'll need to wear it soon?"

Nagora shrugged. "Could be. Do you feel better now?"

"Aye. That explains why the Little People take the dragonskins after the sheddings. They make valuable things with them. And it explains how you come and go so fast when you're with Danuka. The dragonskin armor is a true advantage for us Dragon Talkers."

Khensa and Nefruke insisted on serving the meal as they did back home in Napata. They honored Tagnyoriva by serving her first, followed by her daughters, her grandchildren, Gabe, and the princesses. They served themselves last. Whenever someone asked for another serving or more bread or tea, the royal attendants circled the table, dancing and singing a song as they delivered the requested items.

To the amusement of Gabe and the other women, Dannor and Raean took turns asking for more of just about everything to see the women dance and hear them sing again and again. The cousins didn't yet know their repeated requests would earn them the after-meal chores, and that they would have to sing while doing them, as was the tradition in Napata.

Nagora wished Lars and Yogari could have shared in the meal and the laughter with them. Still, she savored the radiant smiles of these people who, like her, enjoyed the moment without worries of what was to come.

Blind Revelations
Pâskâpiwin Kîkway Ka Wihtamihk

That night, when all were in bed, Nagora sat to write her letter to her father. She realized it was most likely the last missive she would ever write. Her hand trembled as she held the brush pen to form the letters of the words on the page. She had to stop and breathe to steady her hand. My eyes won't be able to connect to my hand to control it.

She exhaled. Images of when she had crossed the chain bridge into the Stone Stander territory to flee the mercenaries flashed in the back of her mind.

†

As Nagora approached the bridge path, the noise from the roiling river in the gorge below rose out of the mist and fog generated by the warm rain. She saw the chains. These are the bridge? I don't believe it. But sure enough, the closer she got to the ledge at the edge of the chasm, only two chains stuck out from the huge boulder into the mist above it. There was plenty of space on the ledge near the boulder, allowing her to stand before she set foot onto the bottom chain.

✝

Nagora took a deep breath. This is a different bridge. No turning back now. You're on it. You're more than halfway across. Deal with the other side when you get there.

Before sealing the letter, Nagora reread it.

✝

✝

In my 37th year at Maze Point, Land of Skulls

My Dear Father,

What I write to you now, I do so because I still can and because it is possible that my son and the women from Kemet might not yet have this news, given the circumstances of the events I am involved in. Though, it is also possible that they will have this news to share with you. If they do, you will hear their version of it. My intention is to tell it to you as I feel at this moment.

In my battle with the witch, Heqet, and the giant, Golgotha, to protect my daughter and the dragons I serve, I will become blind to learn the curse a golden-handled dagger holds. It will be the key to allow me to win the fight. If I win, my eyesight will have been a minor price to pay to save the lives of the ones I love.

I look forward to your return home.

Your loving Dragon Talker daughter,

Nagora

✝

✝

It's brief. No use in repeating the other news Dannor and the Dark Twins will give him.

Tiny flickers of light blinked around the perimeter of Nagora's third-floor window, accompanied by persistent tapping on a glass pane. She had lain on her bed dressed after finishing her letter and hadn't been asleep for long when the noise woke her. She sat up to pull on her boots in the dim light of the candle lantern.

With lantern in hand, Nagora climbed down the loft ladder to the second floor and stopped to wake her sister and mother. "It's time to go. I'll meet you downstairs."

While putting on her weapons and sheepskin vest, Nagora kept her eyes on her son and daughter as they lay sleeping on their cots near the fireplace. It'll be our turn later, Sarah. Sleep for now. I'll try to when I get back.

Tagnyoriva and Sagora came down the stairs, wearing their skystone blades, scrips, and carrying their coats. Her sister showed how she had tied the long scarf she wore: a knot at her forehead, the two ends down over her ears, and crossed behind her neck, ending in a last knot at her throat.

Nagora pointed to the tam her mother wore and shook her head. Tagnyoriva took it off, and her daughter went to the closet beneath the stairs to bring back a sheepskin hat with earflaps that tied under the chin. "It'll be cold in the sky. This will keep you warm," whispered Nagora.

Tagnyoriva stuffed her tam in her scrip and put on her coat. She looked to Sagora. "Do we have everything?"

When her sister nodded, Nagora opened the door and led the way out with her lantern.

...

Gabe and Raean were on watch outside the door. "Go with your mum, then come back with Auntie Nagora." He hugged and kissed Sagora. "Be careful."

"I will." She took Raean's hand as Tagnyoriva hugged Gabe.

Danuka was waiting at the cliff with one of her wings extended and lowered. Nagora hugged her sister and mother. "I hope you'll have little work to do. Sagora, you know your way around the castle, perhaps more than Mum. Don't let her get lost."

Raean accepted the last hugs from his mother and grandmother. "Good luck!"

Nagora held the lantern high to light the wing as Sagora helped Tagnyoriva climb on and grip her way to the saddle. "Mum, you hold on tight to Sagora. Enjoy the ride. It'll give you a fresh way of seeing the land and sea. Good luck!"

"Someday I'll be a Dragon Talker like my mum," said Raean as he watched the dragon flap its wings and rise into the darkness to become a shadow crossing the starlit sky.

Nagora pointed to the stars overhead. "My uncle used to tell me star stories to put me to sleep when I was young. It was his way of telling me about the mother I believed had died giving birth to me. See that group of stars like the letter W? That's her, *The Woman Waiting*, lying on her side, one knee bent, resting on her elbow to see out her window, watching for her husband's return." Mum, once again, you're waiting for Da to return. He will soon.

Nagora pointed to another constellation. "That's *The Dragon Tamer*, my father, who I believed was away at sea and would return someday."

Raean pointed. "Aye! I see the dragon!"

Again, Nagora pointed. "The twin sister I didn't know I had, your mum. Those stars are *The Twins*."

"Which one is my mum?"

"The one closest to you, Raean."

The boy laughed.

"My uncle kept secret their true existence to protect me until the time was right to reveal the truth to me." The painful memory of the day she learned those truths brought tears to her eyes. She wiped them and looked at the sky again. "Can you find *The Hunter* with his bow?" Uncle, I know the stories you told about him weren't about you. However, if there is a place among his stars where you belong, it would be on his bow. Tomorrow, I need you to watch over me. I'll feel better if you do.

Raean took hold of Nagora's hand as he pointed with his other. "There he is! Who is he in the star stories?"

"My uncle never said that was him, but I like to think so. He was the greatest bowman in the Land of the Danu."

Nagora scanned the sky from one edge to the other, where the waning moon was sinking below the horizon. She blinked at the tears that blurred her vision. "Take me back to the lodge," she said to her nephew.

Sarah woke Nagora from a deep sleep. "It's time to get ready. The Little People warned me Danuka will arrive soon. You'll have time to eat something. I'll have tea on the table for you when you come down. Dannor and his women have already left for the maze."

Nagora rubbed her eyes. "His women?"

"Well, most of the time they're with him, almost stuck to him. If he had a bed of his own instead of a cot next to the fireplace, they'd crawl in with him."

"Are you jealous of the attention he's getting?"

"No! I'm happy for him. It'll make it easier for him when he leaves with them. I hope it lasts, and he doesn't get home-sick."

Nagora stretched. "Those are my thoughts too. I think we'll both miss him. Thanks for letting me sleep. I needed that. I'll dress and be right down."

Nagora patted her belly before putting on her weapons. "Where did that honeycomb come from? It doesn't taste like Jari's."

"Gabe brought it from their supplies. Could it be from Godomor's hives?"

"Aye! It could. Do you have your vellum?"

Sarah pointed to her scrip. "All in here."

On the way up the trail, Nagora stopped to look back at the garden plots and buildings below. How will I help with the harvest? I must wait and see. The irony of her last thought almost made her burst out laughing.

"Are you coming?"

Nagora turned to wave at Sarah. "I'm coming."

Mother and daughter set foot on the cliff just as Danuka was landing. They climbed onto the saddle. Nagora let Sarah sit in front so she could hold onto her for the flight and enjoy the view.

The dragon flew them along the coastline all the way to the entrance of Skull Bay, over Skull Rock, and, to Nagora's surprise, to the space at the bottom of the steps leading up to Godomor's Grand Hall. Had the Little People told Danuka that Godomor would be here and not at his lodge?

Ka Peyakot Mahihkan, call to me when you are ready to return.

I will. Thank you for bringing us, *Okâwîmâw*.

The last time Nagora had climbed the wide stone steps to the Grand Hall was three years ago when she branded Sagora with the Othala symbol. She paused before setting foot on the landing where Sagora had knelt. Two guards stood by the entrance doors of the hall. One stepped forward to ask them to wait a moment for the last counselor and the four throne guards to come out.

"This will be my first time inside the hall," said Sarah.

"Have you heard anything special about it?"

"Do you mean how it's made?"

"No. Something your grandmother placed in there. When you look up and see it, you won't have to guess who put it there. I'll let you ask her how she did it and why."

The door opened and out came the counselors, followed by four guards, two women and two men. They took positions on the landing near the door. One guard held the door open and motioned Nagora and her daughter inside.

...

It was the third time Nagora entered this hall. Her eyes took a moment to adjust to the dim light of the tallow lamps, affixed to the huge support timbers that rose from the stone floor to the ceiling on each side of the hall.

Her eyes followed one support timber up to its roof-framing rib. It and the other ribs curved upward and in, supporting the ceiling's wooden planks right to where they met at the main center beam. It ran the length of the hall, like the keel beam of a huge drakkar turned upside down.

At its far end, Nagora could just make out Vorpinger's axe. Her mother had thrown it to hit her chosen target on the beam. The story of how her mother had beaten Vorpinger at his own game made her smile with pride. Will Sarah spot it?

Now that her eyes had adjusted, Nagora walked down the terraced levels of the stone floor of the hall. Sarah followed.

Godomor was sitting on his simple wooden throne on a raised platform of carved stones. On the cliff wall behind him hung the curtain that covered the entrance to the cave where he had once lived. Now, the sixteen dragon eggs were there; two were hatchling eggs, one male and one female.

A table with two chairs sat on the level just below the throne. It was where Godomor would sit with his aide when meeting with his domain counselors. A single lit lantern sat in the middle of the table. To the right of that table was the counselors' wooden bench. It was long, with a carved backrest. Four skulls sat along its top, and it had a curved arm rest on each end.

On the same level, to the left of the king's table, was a backless bench where an old woman sat in a long forest green linen dress. A knitted red shawl covered her shoulders. She wore her long white hair in a braid that ran down the front of her left side and down to her knee. In her right hand, she held a single raven wing spread over her breast. Who is she?

Nagora had seen such a wing only once before, on the day she left with Godomor's Hundred Best. The king was standing at the wall above the gate in the fine drizzle. Occasional gusts of wind had bent the single raven's wing, attached to the crown, over his head.

Now here I am, ready to battle a witch's curse. Nagora and Sarah sat on the ledge of the bottom terrace and waited for Godomor to speak first. It was the way. It allowed her to gather her thoughts, and Godomor his. And it gave time to Sarah to spot the axe overhead.

Nagora studied the old woman's creased face. She appeared to be wise and at peace, like Godomor when she spoke to him in private. Is she related to him? Could she be a descendant of *The First People of The Land*? If so, why would he want her here? Will she be the one to blind me? Nagora felt her stomach knot.

"*Ka Peyakot Mahihkan* and *Piwi Mahihkan*, welcome to my Grand Hall." He had spoken his welcome in the Language of *The First People of The Land*, the language the dragons spoke. Then he reverted to Skullian. "Nagora, is it still your wish to learn the curse of the gold-handled dragon dagger?"

Sarah grabbed her mother's arm. "What is this about? Does it involve the same dagger we used to kill Alizarine? Are you going to convince me to kill again with it?" She stood, clenching her hand into a fist. "If you are, I'll not be a part of it! Not this time!"

Nagora reached for her daughter's hand. "No killing for you this time, I assure you. And perhaps none for me either.

But this concerns both of us." She eased her daughter's fingers from the grip of the fist. "Please, Sarah, sit and listen as I explain. Then you will understand how you can help me."

When Sarah sat, Nagora kept her daughter's hand in hers. She explained the details she had omitted when telling Sarah of her encounter with Worsham. Then she described how she had sought Moreena's help to reveal the dagger's secret, and then how Danuka brought them to the secret cave to examine the golden dragon harp.

"The same cave where you took me to prove I am your daughter, and explained how we would have to carry out Heqet's curse?"

"Aye, Sarah, the same cave." Nagora described the events in the cave and the riddle the dagger revealed to Moreena. "These are the words Moreena spoke when she held the dagger in her hands: 'A dagger cursed to a line of queens. They shall in turn, knowingly or unknowingly, carry with it life and death, mother to daughter, and daughter to mother, until dragons fly no more, and Heqet rules as queen forevermore.'"

Sarah was shaking her head as her mouth moved without speaking words.

"Sarah, don't waste time to understand the riddle. I've puzzled over it more times than I can count. I've lost sleep over it. The fact remains, I want to know the curse because I fear it's destined for you. I want to protect you from it. To know the curse, I have to be blind. Heqet believes I would never choose to do that, otherwise she wouldn't have instructed Worsham to tell me the about the curse and how to learn it. That's why I've never told you until now. That's why I need your help today. I've chosen to trade my eyesight to get rid of the threat Heqet poses to the dragons, and to protect you.

"It may look good that Golgotha surrendered, but the witch, Heqet, hasn't waited all this time to give up on becoming a queen forevermore. Just those words show Danuka and her dragons are still in Heqet's sights. Danuka fears her for good reason, and so do I. That witch has underestimated my loyalty to the dragons. If knowing the dagger's curse can remove Heqet as a threat to our dragons and to you, then I, as a Dragon Talker, will do all in my power to eliminate her. It's my choice, Sarah, not yours. All I ask is your help. Record what the dagger reveals to me when I am blind. I fear it could be another riddle. If it is, every word will count to decipher it."

Sarah let go of Nagora's hand and covered her own face with her hands for a moment before letting her fingers come to rest at the sides of her chin. Her eyes filled with tears as she looked at her mother. "What if the dagger reveals more nonsense?"

"Was Heqet's curse on Alizarine clear?"

"Aye, but you had to become queen and crown me princess to make it work."

"That's right! There were conditions. This dagger's curse must also have conditions to meet. Otherwise, if it didn't, its curse wouldn't make sense. You and I are part of that curse. We are in that line of queens. That's why we have to understand it, so we can protect ourselves. And get rid of Heqet."

Sarah wiped away her tears. "Mum, are you sure? You seem so determined."

Nagora took her daughter's hand. "I'm sure. Time is running out. My sister and mother are in Windhaven, doing their part. I know what the consequences are. I'll live with them.

You carry no blame in this, Sarah. I've decided. I want to continue doing my part."

Sarah hugged her mother. "I'll help you." Then she turned to face Godomor. "Your Majesty, today my mother wishes to know the curse of the dagger, and I wish to assist her."

The king pointed to the old woman and spoke in the Language of the Dragons. "Meet my grandmother. She is a healer who carries stories of *The First People of The Land* and much wisdom. As a free spirit, she comes and goes as she pleases. Where she goes to her secret places, neither I nor anyone else knows, but she turns up in times of greatest need. Though, when I was dying from the poison smoke of the candles of Vorpinger, I could not find her. Later, she told me she saw in a dream the daughter of Tagnuska bringing medicine, and so my need for her was not great. Today, she is here to help you become blind. You may call her Grandmother."

Grandmother spoke in that same language. "Know, daughter of Tagnuska, a medicine to bring back your sight exists, but it is not mine to offer to you. Know also you cannot ask for it. You may only accept it if it is offered."

Sarah squeezed her mother's hand.

Daughter, I too feel the hope offered.

Grandmother waved Nagora and Sarah to her with the raven wing. Her other hand patted the space next to her on the bench, showing Nagora where to sit. With a touch of the raven wing to the folded blanket on the bench, she motioned Sarah to sit next to it.

Her ancient eyes looked deep inside Nagora as she reached to take her hand. Warmth radiated from Grandmother's hand, bringing peace to Nagora's quaking insides and calming her worries. "*Ka Peyakot Mahihkan*, let *Ohkomimâw* help you."

"How, Grandmother?"

"I will need what you wear around your neck. If you give it to me, I can help you." She held open her hand.

Nagora reached for the pierced gold dragon coin hanging on the fine leather lace around her neck and placed it in the old woman's hand.

Grandmother set the raven wing on her lap and, with care, undid the knot that tied the lace ends together. She returned the lace to Nagora before setting the coin face down on the black wing so the Tiwaz symbol on the coin was visible.

Next, she reached into a pocket in her dress and pulled out a leather pouch. Inside it was another leather piece and a braided wick of dried sweetgrass. She placed the wick on the wing and unfolded the other leather packet. Inside was a finger-thick section of a plant's green stem. It was half the length of Nagora's little finger. That leather piece with the plant stem went onto the wing as well.

"*Piwi Mahihkan*, spread the blanket at my feet." Grandmother moved the wing from her lap to the space the blanket had occupied on the bench and then knelt on the blanket. She held the green stem piece with the square of leather, squeezing a drop of thick, white sap onto one side of the coin, on the Tiwaz arrow tip, and a drop on the other side. The tip of the Tiwaz symbol was between the two holes in the coin.

"*Ka Peyakot Mahihkan*, lie on the blanket. *Piwi Mahihkan*, you will hold her eyelid open as I let fall a drop of this poison onto her eye. It will burn for a few moments until her eye stops blinking. Then I will do the other."

When Nagora was on her back, Grandmother set the raven wing on her chest. She smiled at Nagora and made a sign to Sarah to hold open the right eyelid. With a steady hand, the old woman brought the coin over Nagora's eye and tilted it, causing the white drop to ooze out from one hole in the coin and fall onto Nagora's eye. "Tar piss!"

Sarah lifted her fingers away from the blinking eye. While Nagora's tears built, the burning sensation subsided.

"*Ka Peyakot Mahihkan* is brave." Sarah and Grandmother repeated the procedure to Nagora's left eye. The falling drop was the last thing Nagora saw. Nagora shouted her cuss once more. As the pain subsided, the pale grey shadow turned to pitch black.

Nagora sensed movement nearby, heard a snap of fingers, and then smelled burning sweetgrass.

Sarah spoke. "*Ohkomimâw* just lit the grass wick. She is burning the sap off the coin. I cannot explain how she lit the wick or how she can hold the coin. It must be hot. Now that side is turning black. The flame is out. She is rubbing the coin on the knee of her dress. It is free of soot now. Hold open your hand. She will give you back your coin."

Nagora did as Sarah said and threaded the leather lace through the holes. While tying the figure eight knot, she realized that visualizing it in her mind made that task easier. "*Ohkomimâw*, I do not know if I should thank you or not. Allow me to offer you this coin in payment." She held out the laced-coin where she hoped the old woman stood.

"Keep it, *Ka Peyakot Mahihkan*. It will be of greater use to you than to me."

Nagora felt a brief gust on her face and then something springy touch the top of her head, followed by a powerful hand on her shoulder. It was Godomor's.

"Daughter, we leave you now to the curse of the dagger. I will meet you outside."

Her ears caught the gentle sway of Grandmother's dress as it moved away from her, and then she heard the first footfalls as she climbed the terraced levels with her grandson, the king.

Nagora reached into her scrip, lifted the false bottom, and pulled out the sheathed dagger. "Sarah, shall we sit at the table to do this?"

"Aye. It'll be easier for me to write."

"Go there. I want to find my way on my own. I'll follow the sounds." Nagora listened for her daughter's soft steps and the sound of her scrip being put on the table. There it is. With tentative steps and holding her left hand in front of her, below hip level, she walked to where her ears guided her. The back of her hand bumped the corner of the table. Like her friend, Moreena, she let the backs of her fingers guide her around it until her leg bumped into a chair, making it scrape the stone floor.

"I'm in the other chair, Mum."

Nagora set the dagger on the table and then with both hands, she worked the chair into position to sit. She sat and realized it was close to the table. A quick adjustment made the space more comfortable.

"My writing hand is away from you. You're sitting on my left. Let me uncap the bottle and dip my brush."

She heard Sarah take a breath. "I'm ready."

Nagora pulled the dagger from its sheath with her right hand. Will I have to touch the blade's tip like Moreena did? She leaned forward so her elbow rested on the table. The fingers of her left hand contacted the crossguard. She let her finger and thumb glide along the flat sides of the blade. Almost there. She lifted her thumb from the top side and let her finger slide to the tip. Her right hand trembled, causing her to prick her finger. She felt the slight trickle of blood as she pulled her finger away. Her right hand shook, but she clenched tight on the handle to keep the dagger over the table and not flail toward Sarah.

Nagora felt a spasm move through her arm. The shaking subsided to a slight tremor. This must be it. She swallowed, and the words spilled out of her mouth.

> Dragons' future condemned by ancient witch
> in battle with one who uttered first curse,
> calling upon a mother, reluctant queen,
> destined to duty with golden dragon dagger
> hand-in-hand with princess daughter
> together to deliver fatal blow of death.

> Despite cruel words, prescribing death,
> vanity's lust inhabits Alizarine witch,
> betraying Heqet, who called her daughter,
> and so onto giant brother to be, as a dagger,
> she wills the seed of love a one-eyed curse
> to search for his mother turned frog queen.

> Not to be dissuaded, anger of Heqet queen
> conjures to renew on Hag the sentence, death,
> to be delivered in time to come by dagger.
> When failing her task in exile, Alizarine witch
> shall suffer in pain the unbeatable curse
> spoken by mother in dragon cave to daughter.

> Shall come a time when the hand of a daughter,
> crowned princess by hands of a mother queen,

shall together, hand-on-hand, carry out the curse
pronounced and labeled a sentence of death
by Heqet in last judgment of Alizarine witch.
Each with a hand on dragon's golden dagger,

without remorse, together plunge the dagger
in the heart of Alizarine, Heqet's daughter,
to end on that day her reign as witch.
But unbeknownst to the brave killing queen,
in handing Alizarine Heqet's gift of death,
with it comes Hag's last confounding curse.

Without necessary eyes to see the curse,
Regina knows it hides within her golden dagger.
Will she choose blindness to see the death
destiny reserves within, if her daughter
so grants mother and father Hag's last curse
to become the final resting place of Heqet, witch?

For in parents' death is royalty's gift to daughter,
fulfilling curse, unless hand of Rex on his dagger
kills who would be queen forevermore, Heqet witch.

"Mum, that's too many words! I can't remember them all.
Can you? Or can you speak them again?"

Nagora set the dagger on the table and then picked it up
again. The words came again. When they stopped, Nagora
again rested the dagger on the table. "Sarah, words repeat
throughout. I hear 'daughter,' 'queen,' 'witch,' 'death.'"

"And 'dagger' and 'curse,'" said Sarah. "Those six repeat,
but not in the same order. Try again. I'll list them in the dis-

tinct orders they repeat. Then it'll be easier for me to fill in what's missing."

As soon as Nagora held the dagger, out came the words. When she came to the end, she set the dagger down. "Do you have the list?" Sarah was counting.

"Aye. I have seven sets of repetitions. None of them repeat those words in the same order."

"Good, Sarah. In the last set of six, the words repeat in shorter phrases. That set and the one before it reveal the curse. Aim to get those two down. Are you ready?"

"Aye. Do it!"

Nagora felt her throat become raw as the words issued from her mouth, and with them came greater clarity of their meaning. She let the dagger fall onto the table and listened for Sarah's brush strokes. They were barely perceptible, as were her daughter's whispers of the words she wrote. In her mind, Nagora could see them form on the vellum.

"Mum, I have the last two sets and half of the one before them."

While Sarah read from "But unbeknownst" to the end, Nagora spoke the words along with her. Her body shivered as she realized what she now understood.

"Mum, when we killed Alizarine, we released Hag's last curse?"

"Aye, and now that I'm blind, I see Hag's last curse on you, Sarah."

"But Mum, I don't understand how I can grant Hag's last curse."

"If, with the dagger, you kill me, Queen Edana, and your father, King Raynhard, that will make you Queen of the Land of the Danu."

"But what's the connection with Heqet?"

"That, my daughter, is the part that makes me sick. To rule as queen forevermore, two conditions would have to be fulfilled. One, all the dragons killed. Two, you would have to kill us, your parents, with the dagger so Heqet could take over your body and live inside you to rule as queen forevermore." Nagora waited for Sarah's reaction, trying to imagine the look on her face. Or is she rereading what she wrote?

"Is that what Heqet does to become the Gold Planter, take over women's bodies at night? But this curse states she takes over mine, day and night, forever! Am I right?"

"Aye, Sarah. Such is the curse. In your body, she would rule as queen forevermore."

"But Mum, there's an 'unless,' right?"

"Correct! Tell me what it is." Again Nagora waited.

"It says 'hand of Rex,' meaning the king, has to kill Heqet with his dagger."

Nagora touched the handle of the one on the table. "Is it this one?"

"No! That would be the one marked 'REX' in the golden harp's secret compartment."

Nagora nodded. "Now you know what you have to do if you don't want Heqet to inhabit you."

"I must convince King Raynhard to kill her. That will involve so many steps. I'll need your help to plan them out. Before we do, speak the words one last time so I can note them all. Then I'll clean it all up to have it to show the king."

Nagora reached for the dagger. One more time, out came the words. She felt certain they would live in her mind for the rest of her life because of the sordid but true tale they told of her and Sarah's relationship with two witches.

Sarah put her brush down.

"Mum, if I understand this, it's all about a fight between Heqet and Alizarine.

"Heqet adopts Alizarine as her daughter.

"Alizarine gets caught lusting after Heqet's lover.

"So then Heqet curses Alizarine to live in exile in Hag's old body until she kills all the dragons. If she had been successful, Heqet would have rewarded her with eternal beauty in the body of Alizarine."

Sarah paused before continuing.

"However, Alizarine gets caught, and then she curses the seed of Heqet's lover, so that Heqet gives birth to a one-eyed giant.

"Heqet in turn curses Alizarine with a death sentence, to be carried out by a queen and her princess daughter together with their hands on a dragon's golden-handled dagger. Alizarine is cursed again because she failed to kill all the dragons and because she still has lustful intentions."

Again, Nagora's daughter paused.

"Finally, Hag curses Heqet to live in the body of a frog until a princess kills her own royal parents with the dagger to become queen.

"If that comes to pass and all the dragons are killed, then Heqet can live in the new queen's body forevermore unless the king, with his dagger, kills her first."

Nagora nodded. "That's the gist of it, a fight between two witches, involving the two of us, and two golden-handled dragon daggers."

"And Mum, let's not forget the dragons." She felt Sarah lean against her as she reached to take the dagger and its sheath. The sound of the blade sliding into its holster told Nagora she would never hold it again. Now it passes to Sarah.

"No, we won't forget the dragons. We've been destined to protect them. Let's go." After pushing back her chair, Nagora waited for Sarah to finish packing her scrip.

She heard her daughter buckle the flap of her scrip. "Mum, one thing bothers me. Why did Heqet curse this dagger in the first place? Because it would come into your possession? How would she know that? Or did she know that only after the king gave it to you? And what about the mention of the other dagger in the curse?"

"Sarah, answers to those questions might remain mysteries we'll never solve." They both stood to go.

Sarah guided her mother out the door, into the sunlight. Nagora closed her eyes and turned her head until she felt the warmth on her face.

A hand gripped her other arm. "Daughter, the sacrifice you have made in duty to your dragons impresses me. You have the heart of a brave warrior. What is your next move?" asked Godomor.

"Father, my daughter now carries the full weight of her duty to the dragons. She will bring the message of the curse to King Raynhard. It will be his obligation to act, for only he can kill the witch Heqet with his dagger."

"Prepare her well, *Ka Peyakot Mahihkan*. Tasks that appear simple often have hidden dangers. Your uncle, Dangor, trained you in the warrior skills you have, and you learned from your experiences. She will have only her courage, her own skills, and your words to guide her."

"And now, should the king fail to act, the knowledge of what the curse holds for her," said Nagora.

"This morning I met with the domain counselors. Despite the report Gabe sent me of the surrender agreement you negotiated with the giant, I have asked my vassals to keep their warriors on alert. I have ordered increased coastal and road lookouts for irregular movement coming our way."

"Thank you for your help and concern."

"Little Wolf, go about your task with care and heed the counsel your mother gives you."

"I will. Thank you for helping us."

Godomor took Nagora's hand and squeezed it. She imagined he did the same to Sarah. In her mind, she called to her dragon. *Okâwîmâw*, we will meet you at the bottom of the steps.

Halfway down the steps, Sarah squeezed her mother's hand. "Here comes Danuka." The dragon glided toward the Grand Hall, pivoted her wings, and alighted in the square. She spoke to Nagora in her mind. Recall all you saw and heard to learn the curse of the dagger. I want to know it all.

As Sarah guided her to the saddle, Nagora obeyed her dragon and continued for the duration of the return flight to the maze.

Danuka landed near the well in the center of the maze.

Thank you, *Ka Peyakot Mahihkan*, for the courage of your choice today. Prepare Sarah for her task. In nine counts, I will return for her. Before then, have her go to the wagon room below with Dannor, Kalhata, and Tabiry. They will show her how to put on her armor and instruct her in its use, along with the bag to carry her clothes and weapons. She will need to be at the castle in Windhaven before sunset.

Mother, *Piwi Mahihkan* will be ready when you return.

Thwart Destiny
Ka Pometisahoht Awîyak Ohcitaw

As soon as Sarah had guided Nagora down from the dragon's extended wing, Danuka leapt to the inner ring lintel to spread her wings wide and fly away. Dannor was the first to approach them. "Mum? What happened? What's wrong?"

Nagora didn't know if Sarah had signaled him to hold off on his questioning or not. The sudden silence seemed awkward to her when the twins from Kemet cut short their queries; so she spoke. "As Dragon Talkers, events often call upon us to make sacrifices in service to the dragons we love and care for. Today, I made such a sacrifice to learn the curse of a dagger, to understand its threat to the dragons." She lifted her daughter's hand. "Now Sarah knows what she must do to help prevent Heqet from killing all our dragons. Let us go sit at the encampment you have set up. Sarah will tell you how we did it. Then, with the help of my son, I will go through the steps I believe Sarah should take."

She felt a hand take her other arm. "It will be easier if only one of you guides me."

Sarah let go. "Guide her, Dannor."

Nagora could only imagine Sarah signalling her brother to hold off on expressing his feelings and asking further questions.

After Nagora and Sarah relayed what had happened in Godomor's Grand Hall, Nagora stressed the urgency to act.

Two points on what Sarah must do caused discussion. First, should she advise Moreena and Bardas that she was taking Raynhard to replace the queen's dagger for the king's in the golden dragon harp, or should she go only with Moreena? Sarah's words settled that issue. "I will tell Moreena and her father. She can come if she wants, but I will insist the king be there to see the two daggers with his own eyes. It will be further proof to the words of the curse I will show him."

Second, should Sarah go with the king to the Oracle Inn to witness him kill Heqet? If she does, will she be in danger of Heqet taking possession of her body? Certainly. But if she doesn't, will Raynhard be able to prove that he accomplished his task, given his past vulnerability to encounters with the witch, Hag? Who knows what Heqet is capable of? Again, Sarah provided the answer. "If I have my invisibility armor, I would feel safe observing the king's actions at the inn. Witnessing him kill Heqet would give me peace of mind, knowing that I'm no longer her target."

"Mum, I could go with Sarah to protect her," said Dannor.

"You know Danuka will not allow it because of the possible violent confrontation that will take place. She had allowed you to go there with me because we went as invisible scouts, simply to observe and gather information. And if you went with her, you might interfere with Raynhard's actions, depending on how many soldiers he brings with him. What I suggest is you draw a map of the inn to show the way to Heqet, and give Sarah a clear description of what the king will see when he goes there, but do not label the map. 'Oracle Inn' should not appear on it, just in case it falls into the wrong hands."

Then Nagora relayed the dragon's earlier instructions concerning her daughter's armor. "Sarah, as you can see, Danuka senses it is urgent to act, not only because of the threat she feels Heqet still poses, but because soon she must fly Dannor and the Kemet women back to their home. Be prudent.

"Inform the king of the steps he must take, but do so as if a spy were listening to your conversation. Have him read the curse without speaking it aloud. If he needs explanations, whisper them in his ear. Once he's understood the curse, destroy the written words. They're etched in my memory should we need them again."

Sarah nodded. "And in mine."

"Good." Nagora continued. "When you take the king to Bardas, tell Raynhard the destination only when you are on the way there. Before taking him to the cave, swear him to secrecy in front of Bardas and Moreena. Since Raynhard doesn't have invisibility armor, Danuka will only fly under cover of darkness.

"Before revealing where Heqet is, have Raynhard describe how he would secure a place the size of the Oracle Inn based on the plan of the inn Dannor will draw; and how many soldiers he would need to guard the exits, to control people inside, and to go with him to Heqet's hideout.

"Ideally, Raynhard should only go when he is certain Worsham is with her. He protects her and transports her. Only when Heqet is in another body is she away from him."

Nagora paused before continuing. "Sarah, when you go to the wagon room for your armor, call out to the Little People to ask if they will inform you if Worsham is with Heqet while you are with the king in Windhaven.

"Sarah, I'll say it one more time. Be prudent. Be on your guard. Warn King Raynhard to be careful. Remember when we killed Alizarine. She was in a child's body—it was difficult. Heqet must be in the frog's body when Raynhard kills her. Otherwise, how will he know whom to kill?"

Dannor asked, "What about Raganora's corpse? Somehow it's the frog's resting place when Heqet leaves it to go into a woman's body. What evil magic makes that possible?"

Nagora shook her head. "The line 'to search for his mother turned frog queen' could hold a deeper meaning. If Heqet were a queen cursed by her 'daughter,' Alizarine, she needed to inhabit the body of a queen to keep her royal status. That would be Raganora's. Sarah's body would allow her to rule forevermore."

"Is it possible," Nagora heard Kalhata's voice, "that when Heqet exiled Alizarine to the Land of the Danu to kill all the dragons, she also came here and took possession of the living body of Queen Raganora to spy on Hag as she tried to complete her task?" In answer to her own question, she said, "When Hag failed, Heqet cursed her with death, but she followed Alizarine as her pet frog until you two were ready to carry out the curse."

Next, Tabiry spoke. "When did Raganora die? How did she die? Who killed her? Could it have been Hag after Raganora sent her to her death in the cave in the volcano vent shaft? What keeps her body from decay? If Heqet prevents the decay, how does she do it? How did she recruit Worsham? Was she one of the women who nursed him back to health? The power of this witch frightens my sister and me."

Nagora realized the witches had preoccupied the princesses' thoughts. She replied, "I wish I knew the answers to your questions and mine. I doubt we will get an answer from Heqet. All we have left is speculation and uncertainty. I take those as warnings that my daughter must be careful."

When Sarah left with the others to fetch her dragonskin armor, Khensa and Nefruke made Nagora comfortable near the fire where they heated water to make tea. The attendants hummed songs Nagora found to be relaxing and contributed to reflecting on the day's events. How she wished she could go with Sarah. Did Uncle Dangor worry about me when I left on my mission? I was seventeen, a trained warrior, and I still made so many mistakes. She's nineteen. All I can hope for is that all the training I've given her will serve her well. If she follows the plan we worked out, she should be fine.

Upon the group's return from the wagon room, they joined Nagora and the attendants. Sarah sat next to her mother. "Mum, the dragonskin armor is incredible! I can't believe you have been able to keep its existence secret from me all this time!"

Nagora reached in Sarah's direction, searching for and finding her daughter's hand. Because they knew what they were touching, her fingers detected the dragonskin. "Consider it a most remarkable gift to use in exceptional circumstances.

Never discuss it with others who were not given the armor. Realize if you did, they would call upon you to use it for their whims and purposes. Respect its secrecy, and it will serve you well."

"I will, but what if someone should find the armor in my possession, or if they search me? What do I tell them?"

"If they know you are a Dragon Talker, tell them it's a dragonskin shawl or a scarf. There is no way they can figure out you can stretch it to fit on your body. Tell them it helps keep you warm when you ride a dragon. Otherwise, tell them you found it on your visit to Maze Point when exploring the maze, and that you've been told it's the shed skin of a young dragon.

"Did you speak to the Little People?"

"Aye. They said they track Worsham as he travels to and from the Oracle Inn; and that they will inform me of his whereabouts when I am in Windhaven."

"Good. That will help." Nagora heard eggs being cracked and then stirring in a bowl.

"Mum, Khensa and Nefruke are going to cook eggs in butter, mixed with goat's milk and spring onions from the garden. Will you eat with Sarah before she leaves?" asked Dannor.

"Aye. That'll be good."

"Nefruke will make pan bread to eat with the eggs," said Tabiry.

"Even better!" said Nagora.

While they ate, Sarah wondered aloud if she would be back in time to wish the women from Kemet and her brother a safe trip, as only three days remained before their departure.

The meal turned into a goodbye celebration with three Dragon Talker princesses, exchanging wishes of safe journeys and happy futures, and a brother and sister swearing to meet again someday. Khensa's and Nefruke's cheerful songs did not stop until Danuka arrived.

The maze camp occupants became silent after the dragon left with Sarah. Now all Nagora could do as a mother was wait and try not to worry. She would have to find something to do to occupy her mind. *I'll take a nap first and then go speak to Gabe and Jenni and Jari. That means I must ask Dannor to bring me.*

A tugging at the leather lace around her neck and whispering voice in her ear interrupted her thoughts. "Dragon Talker, wear your coin over your shirt. When you speak your destination, we will guide you wherever you want to go, here in the maze and outside of it to your buildings. Trust us."

"Thank you, *Mêmêkwêsiw.*"

At night, two days later, Danuka returned to the maze alone. She reported Raynhard had switched the queen's dagger for the king's dagger; the first of Golgotha's force had arrived and was setting up camp outside Windhaven's wall; Lars's contingent had turned over the surrendered weapons to The Guard and would start their return trip to Maze Point as soon as possible; and Sagora and Tagnyoriva had begun discrete testing of the water cisterns and planned to stay in Windhaven until poisoning was no longer a threat.

Danuka advised Nagora she would rest for a day and leave as planned the day after. The dragon's news gave Nagora an excuse to leave the maze the next morning to report the findings to Gabe. She kept secret how she could find her way around inside and outside of the maze, explaining she had committed to memory the number of steps from location to location before her blinding.

The next day, Nagora returned to the maze with Gabe and Raean so they could share a last meal with Dannor and the women from Kemet and say goodbye. Nagora regretted not seeing the reaction on her son's face when Raean said: "Dannor, when I become a Dragon Talker, I'll go visit you and Kalhata and Tabiry and Khensa and Nefruke." The happy sounds told her the women from Kemet were covering the boy with hugs and kisses as they sang their farewell song.

Kalhata translated the words to the song:

With joy, we carry your smile in our hearts
to sing it back to you when we meet again.
Sing-sing, sing this song from your heart
to our hearts until we meet again.

We too will sing-sing, sing this song from our hearts
to your hearts until we meet again.
And when we meet, our hearts will sing
your smile back to you.

Nagora wondered if she could hear someone smile by the sound of their voice. I think so. Now I'll listen for smiles.

In the pre-dawn darkness, after Danuka's day of rest, Nagora awoke to the sound of Dannor lighting the fire in the small camp stove. The other muted sounds told her the women were putting on their dragonskin armor.

Experience told her early morning departures to unknown destinations were always ones of personal introspection, at least for her. Was it her awakening mind that needed quiet time with its own thoughts to prepare to face the unknown? She had taken such journeys on foot and on horseback. These five will be on the backs of dragons, visible only to themselves as iridescent, shimmering outlines flying over land and sea, above and below the clouds for two days. I envy my son.

Nagora joined the group for their simple morning meal of porridge with honey, dried grapes, hazelnuts, and goat's milk. A piece of pan bread cleaned her bowl for forest tea.

"Will you stay here or return to the lodge?" asked Dannor.

"I will spend my nights here. Danuka wants the Little People to watch over me. I will venture out for food and firewood, and to check in with Gabe and Raean. I will visit Jenni and Jari and ask them to set stakes with twine fastened to them from the bridge to the lodge, to the barn, and to their home to make it easier for me to find my way. Don't worry about me. I'm learning to adapt."

"Do not worry about your son. Tabiry and I, and our servants, will take care of him and protect him," said Kalhata.

"Our parents, King Nimabaka and Queen Kamenirdis, will hold us to our duty to protect the Golden Boy. He brings much knowledge and more. We are most grateful and honored he has accepted to join us," said Tabiry.

"I know that whatever Dannor does, he will always make me proud. That you will care for and protect my precious son reassures me. Thank you for the knowledge you brought to our dragons. May your dragons grow and multiply with that knowledge to help them and you."

"Nagora, Tabiry and I leave to you and Sagora our clothes and weapons from our homeland. When you see Umma, thank her, and thank King Godomor for his welcome."

"Thank you. I will convey your messages. Have a safe journey. Until we meet again, I keep your smiles in my heart."

Nagora heard the gentle flap of Danuka's wings as she slowed her glide to land near the well. Khensa and Nefruke sang the farewell song as Dannor helped his mother stand to accept the warm embraces from the princesses and their servants.

"The other two dragons are landing on the outer circle lintels," said Dannor.

Danuka spoke to Nagora, mind-to-mind. *Ka Peyakot Mahihkan*, sleep in peace here in the maze. I will be away for six days before I return with Yogari. Though, a delay of a day or more is possible. Do not worry. You may call upon my son to help you. He is the eldest by hatchling age. When you speak to him, you will speak to all. The *Mêmêkwêsiw* will place the saddle with the bag and a bridle in your tent should you need them.

Okâwîmâw, may your trip to Kemet and your return with my father be safe.

Dannor took his mother in his arms. "I will miss you, Mum." He kissed her forehead.

Nagora reached into her scrip for the letter she had written to her father. "Give this to your grandda."

"I will, soon as I see him."

Nagora's hands sought Dannor's, and she pulled him to her in a silent embrace. She felt tears spill onto her cheeks. How I'm going to miss you, my young man! How long before I get to hold you again? After a final hug, she released Dannor with a smile.

Kalhata and Khensa hugged Nagora, followed by Tabiry and Nefruke. She listened for Dannor to tell Danuka they were ready. "Goodbye, Mum!" She waved as the displaced air brushed past her like a gust of wind when her dragon leaped to the top of the inner ring to flap her wings and take flight.

Then one of Danuka's daughters landed to take on her passenger and leave. No sooner had she left, the other daughter landed. "Nagora! Goodbye!" It was Nefruke's voice. Nagora waved and wished she had gotten to know the Kemet women better. They must be happy to return home. She wiped the tears from her cheek. Dannor will have his hands full training the princesses when Danuka's daughters lay their eggs.

In the middle of the night, tugging on the leather lace at Nagora's neck woke her. Once she sat up in her bedroll, a voice spoke. "Dragon Talker, we have urgent news. We cannot locate your daughter in Windhaven. The last time we saw her was on Harbor Way. She is not at the Oracle Inn, nor at the castle. We fear she was taken aboard a sailing vessel. Confirmation of that will follow soon."

Nagora's heart raced at the news. "What about the king? Where is he?"

"At the Oracle Inn. His men, dressed as civilians, surround it and occupy it to give it the appearance of business as usual."

"Is Worsham there?"

"He is not."

Nagora's hand clenched into a fist. "Is the witch, Heqet, there?"

"So far, we cannot confirm she is."

"Do you know the whereabouts of my sister and mother?"

"They are with your friend, Paruline."

That's good news.

"Soon as you know about Sarah, tell me." Tar piss! She shook her head. Always the unknown!

"I have another service to ask of you. I need to know the king's situation in the Oracle Inn in Windhaven. Is he in control? If he is, did he kill the witch, Heqet? If he hasn't killed her, why not? Is he aware that Sarah has been taken captive?"

"We will relay your questions."

"Thank you."

Nagora's mind raced with possibilities. Calm down. Wait for confirmation. Sarah might have an excellent reason to be on a sailboat. Nagora knew sleep wouldn't come again.

I'll make a fire in the stove to boil water for tea. Focus on that task for now. Take your time. Gather the twigs, kindling, and two small logs. Load the stove in that order. Stick the milkweed fire starter among the twigs. Take your flint from your scrip and a throwing knife from its holster. Strike the flint to make sparks to light the milkweed.

That was easy to say. Now, can I do it?

Three counts later, Nagora was sipping her tea next to the small ceramic stove that was radiating the last of its heat. She had no time reference other than her counting since getting the news. No night sky to inform her of the coming daylight. What does it matter? Anyway, what would I do? Plan. Plan for what?

She poured the last of the forest tea into her bowl.

Later, possibly near early morning judging by her hunger, the voice spoke again. "Dragon Talker, here is what we can confirm. Worsham led Sarah to the dock at Harbor Way. He was carrying a basket made of woven bulrushes."

Worsham! "Was it nighttime?"

"No, in the late afternoon. At the dock, a wagon from Golgotha's camp carrying lumber, ropes, and tools arrived to offload those materials onto a fishing boat tied to the wharf. Sarah followed Worsham onto the boat, and then the two men from the wagon and Golgotha got on. The giant wore leather except for a black metal helm, the armor on his right arm, and the gauntlet on his hand that held his lance. He had been hiding in the wagon."

"Where did they go?"

"To the battered ship of the giant. Days before, dock hands had tied skiffs to it to haul it away from its berth at the wharf and anchor it in the bay. Two men then offloaded material from the wagon onto the ship. Crew from the Gethsemane replaced the men from the fishing boat. They hoisted sail and tacked out of the bay to the sea."

"With my Sarah on board?"

"Yes, and Worsham and the giant."

"How many sailed away on that boat?"

"Seven in all. That fishing boat is smaller than any of the ships of the giant's fleet and faster under sail."

"How long would it take to reach Skull Bay with fair winds?"

"Four days, five at most if they sail night and day."

I'll ask Gabe to send this information to King Godomor.

"Where is King Raynhard?"

"He is with your mother and sister at the Oracle Inn. They are tending the wounds he sustained in the cellar there."

Nagora's jaw dropped as she tried to comprehend what had gone wrong. "Is the king in danger of dying?"

"It appears not. He suffered a minor puncture to a lung, causing it to collapse, a cut to his forearm, and a cut to his head from being knocked unconscious. As soon as his breathing returns to normal, they will move him to the castle."

"Do you know the details of what happened?"

"Not yet. As soon as we do, we will inform you."

"Thank you, *Mêmêkwêsiw*."

This must be Heqet's doing. The curse says Heqet needs Sarah's body. Could Heqet have taken over her body somehow? Why would Worsham be carrying that basket? Is Heqet in it? She can only die at the king's hand. Can she take Sarah's body if Raynhard and I are still alive? Why would Sarah be with Worsham? Wait! Heqet needs Raganora's body to go into another woman's body at night. Or does she? No! Can it be? Is Heqet truly in my Sarah's body at this moment? That can't be! She was wearing her armor! Or can it?

Golgotha's coming after me. He'll use Sarah as a hostage to come here and bargain her life for safe passage from Skull Bay to Maze Point. Once in here, will he threaten Sarah? Not if she's to be Heqet's vessel forevermore, and the witch is already inside her. Worsham, Heqet, and her son must think the king died of his wounds. Now they're coming for me.

I need to speak to Gabe. She placed the coin outside her shirt. "To the guards outside the maze."

...

The breeze from the wind that curled around the maze wall and into the entrance told Nagora she was near. She cleared her throat.

"Can we help you?"

"Is it daylight yet?"

"Aye, the sun has just risen. Do you wish to be taken to Commander Gabyndor?"

"Please, if one of you would be so kind."

When they approached the barn, the guard informed Nagora that Gabe and Raean were at a table near the cook's wagon, waiting for the morning meal. "Auntie Nagora, come sit with us." The lad took her hand and guided her to sit opposite them. "Will you eat with us?"

"Aye, please Raean, whatever you're having will be fine."

"I'll tell cook you're eating with us," said the boy.

"We thought we were up early. What brings you here, Nagora?" asked Gabe.

First, she relayed the situation with the king, followed by the other news the Little People had brought concerning Golgotha, Worsham, and her concerns for Sarah. "Can you convey this news to your father?"

"Of course. You are right to be concerned. Golgotha won't kill Sarah because, like the curse says, she is to become the host for his mother. It would be in his interest to keep her safe for that purpose," said Gabe.

"For Sarah's sake, I hope he will. Now my greatest fear is that Heqet is in Sarah's body. If she is, can Sarah still be alive?"

"Nagora, you don't know that for certain yet. What you know is that Golgotha is coming with only five in support plus Worsham. I doubt he's coming to kill dragons. He's coming for you. You put him to shame. Like you say, he'll use Sarah to gain safe passage to the maze. We can be thankful that Raynhard has two healers taking care of him.

"My guess is that the Little People will somehow inform Raynhard of what happened to Sarah. We don't know if he still has the dagger and if he'll be in any condition to carry out his duty. What if Sarah has it? Or should I say Heqet, if she's in Sarah's body?"

The thought of the dagger's whereabouts and how that affected Raynhard's ability to end the curse sent a chill down Nagora's back.

Gabe continued speaking his thoughts aloud. "What are Golgotha's intentions if we assume Maze Point is his destination? Will he try to force you to kill all the dragons? It wouldn't be his usual way of doing things. Perhaps he doesn't want to be humiliated again; perhaps he just wants to settle a score with you. Or do what he can to help his witch mother."

He touched Nagora's arm. "You won't know until he gets here. You need to come up with a plan so he won't harm Sarah. Something that will distract him from his goal, like you did to Vorpinger with the axe in the center beam of the sawyer's log-cutting frame. That put an end to his attack on Skull Bay."

Raean set bowls of porridge before his aunt and father. "Spoon's in the bowl, Auntie. It's hot. I'll be back with bread and honey."

"That something I came up with back then almost got me killed. What about Lars's plan to battle the giant in the maze?"

Nagora heard Gabe stir his porridge and then set his spoon on the table. "That was meant to fight the giant's full force coming into the maze. Lars wanted to block the four exit gates at the center and flood the middle of the maze up to the top of the well rim with seawater that the dragons would fly in with big makeshift waterskins made from tarps. Then he would release the water through the true exit gate once all Golgotha's troops were inside the maze walls. He figured the force of the water going down that slight slope might drown at least half of them and injure many of the others. Not to mention getting the giant's armor wet."

"I understand. I need a plan of my own." Already her mind raced with a plausible one. I'll beat him at his own game.

"Nagora, you won't be able to face him alone."

"Why not? Because I'm blind? That just might work to my advantage. If Golgotha lands in Skull Bay, I want Godomor to make it clear to him that I'm blind and I no longer have the golden-handled dragon dagger to kill the dragons.

"The only advantage I'll have is to be in the maze I built. If he wants to get to me, Sarah will be the only one able to lead him into the maze, unless Heqet is not in Sarah's body already. I'm expecting Sarah to lead him in. I can't imagine the giant following a frog into the maze.

"Once he sees that I'm alone, I'll test the loyalty of those who come with him by having the Little People seed the maze path with gold dragon coins. After all, if the giant can slay dragons, he can surely handle an unarmed, blind woman. I'm hoping greed will tempt them to gather up as many coins as they can carry. All they'll have to do is follow the coins on the maze path. In no time, they'll get lost in the maze."

"I hope your gamble pays off in that respect."

Nagora kept her smile to herself. *If it doesn't, we'll see how they fight an invisible foe supported by her invisible dragons.*

Raean joined them at the table with his bowl and a plate. "Cook boiled some eggs for us, Auntie. They're on the bread plate with honeycomb and goat cheese."

Her concern for Sarah had almost taken away her appetite. *I'll need my strength to plan and face the giant.* "Thank you, Raean. I should eat here every day. I feel spoiled!"

"I'd like that, Auntie!"

"Gabe, I have the seed of an idea that's germinating in my mind. If things work out like I hope they do, could I bring Raean into the maze with me to test something? No harm will come to him."

"Of course. He'll be glad to help you. A change in his routine will do him good."

"When do I start?" asked the boy.

"Tomorrow or the day after, at the latest. I'll come for you." Nagora's hand found the plate, took an egg, and cracked it on the tabletop. As she peeled the shell away, the long-ago memory of eating a hard-boiled egg surfaced. The day before, she had escaped the dungeon sea cave and would have drowned if someone hadn't saved her.

†

She stepped out of the streambed onto the shore. While waiting for the dripping to stop, she cracked the shell of the hard-boiled gull egg, salvaging the charcoal-drawn heart before biting into the white flesh.

How would she ever thank the one who had saved her? With the heart resting in the palm of her left hand, she gingerly ate away the white flesh of the egg until she held the solid orange sphere of yolk between the thumb and pointer finger of her right hand. She inhaled its distinctive odor and popped the sphere into her mouth to let her tongue play with it before crushing it to the roof of her mouth to savor its rich flavor.

†

That was a gull egg, and Raynhard was my savior. How many times have I repaid him? I had Sarah give him the dagger to save himself. Who has it now? If I can't save Sarah and myself, how will he save himself?

Nagora bit into the white flesh. "Are these from Jenni's hen house?"

"Cook brought his traveling coop. He has a dozen chickens in it, all good layers," said Raean.

The boy's words sparked another idea. "Gabe, when you send your messenger to your father, ask him to bring back two of the feeder eggs the dragons laid at his Grand Hall. I'll ask Danuka's son for permission to use them. And Raean, the princesses left two white robes in their sea chests. You'll find the chests in my room at the lodge. They are gifts for Sagora and me. Bring one robe here, please."

"I will, Auntie."

"Are you working on your plan already?" asked Gabe.

"Aye, it's coming together. Oh! Gabe! I would also need a goblet, a big one to fit the giant's hand. It could be made of anything, as long as it stands on its own when full."

Raean said, "Grandda Godomor has that big ram horn with the four brass legs. He says it looks like a strange animal howling at the moon. He told me he drank from it only once. Maybe he would lend it to Auntie Nagora?"

Gabe chuckled. "I won't be surprised if he gives it to her. He won that a long time ago in an axe throwing contest. I'll ask him."

"Thanks, Gabe." She popped the yellow sphere into her mouth.

When Nagora finished her bowl of tea, she stood. "Please, thank the cook for the meal. I couldn't have asked for better."

"Raean, take Auntie Nagora back to the maze. I think she will have a busy day ahead of her."

Back in the maze, Nagora walked to the rim of the well. Before calling to Danuka's son, she wondered about names. Da told me that female dragons choose their names when they mate, and that the name usually relates to the place where they reside. He didn't mention how the male dragons are named.

In her mind, she called to the young dragon. Son of Danuka, I need to talk to you. I am at the well in the maze. Please come to me as soon as you can.

While waiting, she let her plan play out in her mind as if the dragons and the Little People had agreed to help her. She had an alternative to one aspect of her plan should the dragons not want to play a part in it; but if they did, the trap for the giant would be set. The only question remaining is: Will Golgotha fall for it?

The sound of the slow sweep of dragon wings from above and behind her told her a dragon had just alighted on the inner ring. She stood to turn in his direction.

His voice was clear in her mind. *Ka Peyakot Mahihkan* calls to me. You have questions in need of answers. Ask them. If we dragons can help, we will.

Son of Danuka, thank you for coming. Is this how I should call you, or do you have a name?

Male dragons are called the sons of their mothers, as you have called me, in honor of my mother, Danuka.

Nagora smiled. I need your help if you and the other dragons can give it without coming to harm. Before I describe what I will ask of you, I must know if you are aware of the danger posed by the witch, Heqet, and her son, the giant, Golgotha.

Since after the Dark Twins brought us the gifts of knowledge of dragons present, dragons past, and dragons future, all of us are aware of all the details of that situation and all the conversations you have had about it with our mother. We also know of the messages the *Mêmêkwêsiw* bring to you and your talks with them.

Nagora felt awkward speaking to a dragon she could not see. She nodded. That is good to know. She spoke the details of her plan, stressing the safety of the dragons was foremost in her mind, and that the choice to take part was theirs, right until the last moment. She also asked permission to use two of the feeder eggs should the dragons choose not to take part. When she finished, he did not reply right away. She guessed he was discussing her plans with the other dragons.

Ka Peyakot Mahihkan, you have our permission to use two of the feeder eggs for your alternate plan. Our mother was one of the three dragons that practiced the illusion of a three-headed dragon in flight. A dragon has offered to replace her and learn to fly that formation with them. That will be the sole role of those three.

If the Little People can make the instrument you need and it will not cause me harm, I will play the submissive dragon lying before you near the well. For my protection, in an instant I can disappear and fly away. I believe the *Mêmêkwêsiw* can make the instrument and test it on me beforehand. Tell them what you need, then I will discuss with them to decide if they will proceed or not.

Of all the parts of my plan, this was the one I feared the dragon would not go along with. Yet he will test it. For that, I admire him. If it works, it will lure Golgotha. If not, I'll have the dragon eggs to fall back on.

As for your request to have invisible dragons be your eyes to send what they see to your mind, like when you transmitted your memories to the women from Kemet on that flight with the dragons, first, you must try that with me now.

Almost at once, the image of her standing before the well and looking up flashed in her mind. She moved her arm to wave her hand. The image in her mind moved also with a slight delay.

Turn to look at your camp.

She did and saw it as if from the height of the dragon's eyes.

This is amazing! I see it as you see it from the lintel. She turned in each direction he looked. The sky! Those clouds! You are looking at my back.

Face me now.

She turned in his direction. The feeling of seeing herself, watching the slight delay in time between when she moved to when she saw it, almost made her dizzy. This is better than I imagined.

I have called four dragons to come. We will test what it is like for you to see with their combined help. Move to the exit gate. They will land near the well and take up positions beneath the outer ring to place their heads at your eye level.

Then I will land near the well and lay down, as you suggested. I will call you to me when I am ready.

Nagora did as she was told. Feeling her heart beating with the excitement, she felt surprised her. Having vision again, even if only for a moment, made her happy and gave her hope that her plan might work.

Come to me now.

She counted her steps as she did.

Stop where you are. My four sisters will look at you. Describe the images.

The four images are fighting to take position one over the other. They fall in and out of focus. They disappeared.

Come to me. One will move your stove to where you last stood. You will face in that direction. When you do, the four will look at the stove. Tell us what happens.

Two images come together. Both show the front of the stove. One shows the left side, the other the right. The two come together and lock in place as one. Have one dragon glance away. That was the one to my right. The tents came into view and I lost sight of the right side of the stove.

We will try with only one looking over your right shoulder. Go to the stove and then walk to whatever comes into view.

Nagora laughed as she walked. The back of my head just came into view. Now down to the back of my knees. I see all of me. I bent to touch the stove and felt it before I saw my hand touch it. Ha! The delay is almost the time I take to speak the name of my son. I say "Dann" and just begin "or" and the image of what I do appears. It is amazing how clear the image is, like seeing with my own eyes.

She stopped at a tent. This is where I sleep. She pulled the flap aside and saw only a sliver of what was inside. She turned to face the dragon. You are lying on your side like I asked you, one wing stretched out on the floor stones. You are holding the other up and back, resting your wing talon against the lintel. This is what a different dragon sees. The first one stopped looking, and this one took over.

Correct. Let us try something else. Each dragon will watch the direction you walk in. The one who has the most favorable view to help you will send it. Each will decide when and for how long to transmit before another with a better view takes over. Walk wherever you will within the inner ring and as fast as you want. Make the movements you want. They will track you.

Nagora followed the dragon's suggestion. She walked slow, walked fast, sprinted, stopped to change direction, and then reverted to her original course. When she caught glimpses of the four dragons squatted on the maze floor, leaning forward on their wing talons, and holding their heads at the level of hers, it made her realize that not only their eyes followed her, but their necks too were in continual motion. She imagined the concentration it took. She stopped next to one of the stone pillars.

Tell us what you saw.

She turned toward his voice. The son of Danuka was sitting upright with his wings folded to his sides, their talons resting on the stone floor before him as he looked at her.

I am amazed at how well they tracked me. Though, the shift in view has the muscles in my legs reacting before my mind adjusts to each new view. If my movements were more predictable and slower, it would be easier for them. For my plan, I do not expect to hurry, as I want to appear blind to the giant while the dragons act as my eyes. If I have to move fast, seeing my opponent and where I will go would be useful.

Tomorrow, with your permission, I will fetch my nephew Raean and practice with him. The four dragons will be invisible. I will not tell him they are present and helping me. It will be a test to see if he detects the dragons.

That is possible. Call them before you bring the boy in. They will take and hold their positions while he is here.

Son of Danuka, I thank you and all the dragons for helping me. You give me great hope my plan will work. Please, before you go, look at the sky and show it to me. Nagora savored the dragon's slow scan of the blue sky with its tiny wisps of white clouds chasing the bigger ones. The lintel's edge came into view, and then her, standing with eyes closed and a smile on her face. Ha! You give me sight with my eyes shut. Thank you.

One after another the dragons left, leaving in their wake the soft turbulence of their wingbeats.

Nagora found her way to the well and sat on one of the rim stones. Did the Little People return to the caves below, or have they been watching and listening to the plans I shared with the son of Danuka?

A voice answered her thoughts. "Dragon Talker, you are planning to confront the giant here in the maze, and you need our help. More details on the instrument you want us to make are necessary. Speak them as clearly as you can so we can explain to the son of the mother dragon what we will make, and how it will function, to cause him as little discomfort as possible."

"I need a special dagger. Its handle, crossguard, and a short section of its blade, when pressed against the skin of the dragon, will give the appearance the rest of the blade has lodged in the flesh of the dragon.

"In reality, the dagger does not have a full-length blade, but what it will have is a needle with a hole inside its length, attached to the other side of the handle. It will pierce a vein and allow blood to be drawn. A simple mechanism attached to the needle would allow me to start or stop the flow of blood. To the giant, when I press the goblet to the skin of the dragon with one hand, I will also appear to twist the dagger to make the blood flow."

"When you remove your hand from the dagger, it must stay in place to give the appearance that you had stabbed the dragon. Is that correct?"

"Yes. I will need another piece affixed to the side of the dagger's handle not visible to the giant: A small bulb to containing a slight amount of water into which I can place three drops of poison. To release the poisoned liquid, I would only need to tilt the bulb to empty it into the goblet." Nagora explained.

"To repeat, your special dagger appears to be lodged in flesh, draws blood in controlled amounts, and dispenses a poison only once. Is the poison the one you hid on the shelf in our coal room?"

"It is."

"If we make this instrument, and for your safety, shall we fill the bulb for you?"

"Yes, please. Will you be able to make it?"

"We will discuss and study the possibility. It is a challenge, and the son of Danuka will decide if it is to be used. We will inform you."

"I have two more favors to ask of you. Can you make a sling for me made of dragonskin that I can will invisible when I touch it and that will hide the war stone I place in its pouch?"

"That will be easy to make."

"Finally, the well hole here gives access to the caves below. Can you disguise it so the giant will not recognize it?"

"We have thought of that. Those looking into the well hole will behold water, level with the stones they stand on. If they bend to touch it, water is what they will feel."

"Excellent! Thank you, *Mêmêkwêsiw*. Your help is invaluable to me."

Nagora walked the perimeter of the inner circle from pillar to pillar as she imagined Golgotha coming into the maze with Sarah. Will she be wearing her armor? If she is, my trap will be more convincing, but if Heqet is in her body, she won't be wearing her armor since it would prevent the witch from entering. Or would it? Sarah said she would wear it. If she wore it, why would she remove it?

Will Golgotha remove his helm? He must if he wants to drink the blood. How fast will the poison act on him? What if it doesn't?

I'll wear my armor and carry my skystone blade in the special bag from my saddle to render it invisible. Perhaps I could attach both the bag and the pouch I used for the dagger to my belt and wear them beneath the robe. If they are touching my armor, I could will them invisible. Are the belt and pouch in the bag in my tent with the saddle? I'll check.

"Is there anything else I need?" Nagora asked her question aloud and then laughed when the voice spoke to her: "If we can, we will get it for you."

She thought for a moment. "A leather ball like the one my son played with when he was young."

"The ball you speak of is in the barn. The lad, Raean, sometimes plays with it when not on duty."

"Perfect! I will have him bring it tomorrow when I go fetch him."

The next morning, Raean followed Nagora back into the maze. "How can you find your way?"

"I rebuilt the maze with the help of the Little People. Because I'm a Dragon Talker, I know my way in and out, but now that I'm blind, they help me get around in here."

"Da said you're not bringing me here to play games, but to test something. He thinks you want to prepare for when the giant comes to the maze with Sarah so you can protect her in the best way possible."

"He's right. You will play the giant. You'll help me test if I can spot him or not when he's in the center of the maze with me."

"Okay."

After passing the gate, Nagora stopped on the edge of the inner ring. "You have the ball. Stand right here. I'll walk to the well rim in the middle. When I get there, I'll turn to face you. First, you'll roll the ball in my direction. I'll listen for it and try to intercept it before it gets to me.

"Then you'll walk or run to any pillar of the inner ring. I'll try to follow where you go and roll the ball to you. We'll start with that."

When in position, thanks to a dragon, she could see Raean. "I'm ready." The smiling boy swung his arm to send the ball in Nagora's direction. The head-sized ball, made of wrapped layers of leather stitched together, having been kicked around by Dannor for many years, had lost its tightness, hardness, and roundness; and so it no longer rolled with the speed it once did. The stone floor slabs in the middle of the maze were flat, with plenty of rough spots that affected the path of the rolling ball. Still, Nagora intercepted it.

"Wow! How do you do that? Your ears must be sharp!"

"Pick a spot, Raean."

Trying as hard as he could not to make a sound, still Nagora followed him. When he stopped moving, she rolled the ball to him. He easily stopped it.

Nagora held her hands at chest level. "This time, run to a spot, stop, and throw the ball at me."

"I'll do my best to reach you."

Again, she watched his moves and the ball arcing toward her. To catch it, she had to move forward. The slight delay in what she saw was enough to make her miss catching it. It struck her knee and rolled away. "I'll get it. This time I'll throw it at you. You can catch it or dodge it, but I want you to be moving when I throw it."

"Okay!"

Throw ahead of where he'll be, not where I see him. She held the ball at shoulder level as she tracked him, taking a guess where he would be, and threw with all her might. She was on target, but he dodged it at the last moment.

"You almost got me!"

"Take ten strides closer to me. Try to hit me with the ball. I won't move, but I will try to protect myself. Throw with all your might."

"Okay!" Raean stepped forward, his lips moving as he counted to himself.

Nagora held her hands shoulder high and at the ready to protect her face. The ball came at her fast. She lowered her hands, expecting to catch it at waist level. Instead, she knocked it down. The time delay was making it difficult to judge how to match her actions with the outcome she expected. Will practice help me improve? Yes, but how much time just to master this? Maybe I won't be able to use the sling. It could end up being a guessing game for Golgotha and me. "Let's try it again."

Raean was on the move and again her throw came close. She almost caught the return throw. "Ten more times, Raean!"

By the fourth throw, the boy was more accurately guessing when Nagora would hurl the ball and he would change directions as fast as possible, causing her to miss by a greater margin. How can I adapt to that? If I use the sling against the giant, I must think in terms of having a single shot. That'll mean picking the right moment of distraction to strike.

She caught Raean's last pitch. "That'll do, Raean. Now I know what I must do. It won't be playing catch with the giant. Thanks for your help. I'll keep the ball for two days to try something on my own."

"For someone who is blind, you're amazing! I can't believe how good you are."

"Well, neither can I." Nagora rolled the ball into her tent.

"Wow! How did you know where to send it?"

"A good guess. Before I take you back, I need your help to take down these two tents. First, we'll move a cot and the blankets from this one into mine."

"The one the princesses slept in?"

"That's right. They found our nights cool and damp compared to where they come from. Go to Dannor's tent to check if he left anything behind."

Nagora found six blankets folded in two neat piles on one cot. As she stepped from the tent with three of them, she almost ran into Raean.

"Auntie, I found these two bundles of kindling. Other than a cot, there's nothing else in his tent. Shall we move his tarp and the stove over to yours?"

"Excellent idea. We'll keep a cot to place under the tarp, fold the other cots, and lean them on the wall behind my tent. Then we'll take the tents down."

Nagora sat on the cot between the two tents they had folded as compact as possible. "Good! I have enough clearance above my head when I lean forward to stand. I like the way we've set up the tarp. If the wind veers to bring rain, this lean-to gives me a windbreak to cook under."

"Your firewood and kindling are all within easy reach of the stove. The cooking pot, bowl, and spoon are on the other side in that wooden tray," said Raean.

"Thank you, young man, for helping me set up my camp so well. Now I have only one set of guy-lines to trip over." She held out her hand. "Help me up. We're ready to go."

"Da's messenger should be back from Skull Bay. If he is, the feeder eggs and the robe you asked for will be waiting for you. Have you planned how you'll use those eggs?"

"I have, Raean. They will be my backup plan in case my first plan doesn't work. The eggs will help me distract the giant just enough to strike a fatal blow. It might not go the way I want. He will be on his guard, even if he knows I'm blind. I stand a better chance with my first plan."

"Da thinks you are brave beyond belief. He hopes that whatever your plan is, you'll succeed."

"So do I, Raean."

Nagora returned to the maze, carrying a large leather scrip. In it were the dragon eggs, packed in the folds of the robe. Tied to the scrip's leather strap was the big ram horn goblet. In a linen bag slung over her other shoulder, she had a loaf of Jenni's freshly baked bread, a half dozen eggs, a handful of tiny washed carrots, and a packet of smoke-cured pork belly already sliced into strips. That the hardworking woman had thought to send her these provisions made her feel good.

Also, Nagora had filled her own scrip with stones from the stream. They were about the same weight as the war stones, not ideally shaped, but they would do for target practice. I'll tie a rope to the leather ball, throw it over a lintel to let it hang at the height of the giant's head, and call for a dragon to be my eyes as I set it in motion and try to hit it with my sling.

Now in her tent, Nagora emptied her bags, put away their contents, and readied the ball as best she could before calling to the dragons. Dragons, you who are my eyes, I need one of you to help me. Please come when you can.

The ball hung above her head, out of her reach. She used a vertical support pole from a tent to strike it to set it in motion. She dropped the pole and stepped back thirty paces. I'll start from here. Just as she was about to return to the pole, she heard a dragon land behind her.

Nagora turned to face it, speaking to it mind-to-mind. Thank you for coming. Which daughter of Danuka are you in the hatching order?

Nagora, I am last in that order. You need my eyes to help you?

She pointed. Yes, I will sling stones to try to strike the leather ball.

When you face it, I will look at it from over your shoulder. The dragonskin sling the *Mêmêkwêsiw* made for you is on your cot. It will be best if you practice with it.

On returning with her new sling, Nagora loaded it with a stone. From the feel, its pouch was slightly larger than the Stone Stander sling and more intricately woven. She held it up so it dangled before her, and then she turned away from the dragon. Danuka's youngest daughter allowed her to see the sling. It's beautiful. She willed it invisible. It works! I can't see the stone in the pocket either. Now to try it.

The ball swung in a slow, short arc. It would soon stop. She spun the sling three times and released the stone. It sailed past the ball. The second stone caught the edge of the ball, causing it to spin on the rope and lengthen the swing of its arc. The third stone missed, but the fourth was a direct hit, sending the ball up in the air. Now it swung in her direction. Can I hit it when the rope hangs vertical? Her next stone made the ball jump.

I better make it move sideways. As she approached the stick, Nagora watched herself walk toward it. Reaching for the ball with the pole as it appeared to her gave her a strange sensation. Her swing missed, as if the ball were not there. She had to concentrate as she watched herself line up the pole to make contact. This time, her swing set the ball in motion like she wanted.

To see herself walk back toward the dragon caused her to feel unbalanced on her feet, almost dizzy.

Once Nagora faced the ball again, it took a moment for her to feel in control. *What I see has already moved on in reality. I must think ahead to where it will be. Focus. Aim ahead of its destination.* The stone caught the back edge of the ball. Almost smack on. *Aim.* "Aye! A direct hit!" Voicing her excitement gave her encouragement as she went to adjust the swing of the ball.

I've got this. I just have to imagine it ahead of where I see it, two ball diameters in distance ahead. The next dozen stones proved her right.

I will take the ball down and gather the stones. Then you will be free to go. Thank you for being my eyes today.

I will show you the sky.

Not a patch of blue was visible. Instead, black clouds were stacking up. *It will rain by nightfall.*

Correct, and for two more days. Conditions at sea will not be easy. Though, if the crew of the giant is competent, they will use the wind to their advantage to ride the waves on a beam reach.

As long as my daughter is safe.

We keep watch on the vessel.

Thank you for doing so.

...

When the dragon left, Nagora heated water to boil four of the eggs and then make forest tea. She wondered if the weather would delay information from Windhaven. First, my questions have to reach the Little People. They'll investigate and then send the replies here. Will I have answers before Golgotha arrives? Will Danuka return with Yogari before the giant's arrival? Is work on the instrument progressing? Have the Little People discussed it with the son of Danuka? Will they test it on him soon? I have all these questions. Only time will answer them.

What can I do besides worry and wait? How will I conceal my weapons? I must remove the holsters of the throwing knives from the straps of the sheath of my skystone blade. If it weren't necessary to hide it, I could strap the skystone blade to my thigh. That won't be possible with it inside the invisibility bag. I'll let the bag hang from the belt. To pull the sheath out could be awkward. Though there might be a way. Tomorrow, I'll do my exercises in the rain with it. A solution will come.

Even if I can will it invisible, I'll hold the sling pocket armed with a war stone in my armpit. Its two strings will hang inside the sleeve of the robe. I'll reach for them with my other hand, pull them, catch the loaded pocket end, and then attack. I'll hide the second war stone behind the nearest pillar for a chance to reload for a last strike. I'll try that later.

The next day, Nagora awoke in her damp tent from a dream of the Dark Twins. As wind-driven rain pelted her shelter, the image that stuck in her mind was one of the princesses reuniting with their parents, who were in awe of the dragons in their courtyard. Is this a message Danuka is sending to me?

Perhaps with her new powers, it is possible. Does she know what I'm preparing for?

The warmth of her bedroll was inviting, given she had little to do. I'll try to sleep some more. When I wake again, I'll wear my dragonskin armor. It'll keep me warm. With thoughts of Sarah at sea in these miserable conditions, Nagora closed her eyes. If she's wearing her armor, at least she won't be cold.

Tugging on the leather lace at her neck awoke Nagora. She did not know how long she had slept, only that it was a deep sleep. "Dragon Talker, let us be clear with you. If we are to make the instrument you request, we are the only ones who will pierce the vein of the dragon with it. The special dagger will hold in place with invisible dragonskin strings tied to its crossguard. It will be in place before the giant arrives. You cannot pretend to stab the dragon.

"However, you can pull the dagger from the wound. Knots in the strings will permit that if you pull in one swift motion. When you do, two things will happen: First, the needle will stay in place in the closed position to stop blood flow. Some blood will appear around the wound. We will remove the needle when the dragon returns to the cave. No harm will come to the son of Danuka. Second, from within the handle of the dagger, a complete blade will emerge. The small bulb on the back side will stay and not be visible if you hold the dagger.

"These are the conditions the son of Danuka agrees to. If you do too, we will build it."

"I agree. I am amazed! Does that mean I could use that dagger as a weapon?"

"You could. Once the blade emerges, only we can return it to the handle."

"Thank you! Of course I agree! I am most pleased no harm will come to the son of Danuka."

"Tomorrow we will bring news of the test."

"I look forward to your news."

"Dragon Talker, you asked for details of the events in the cellar of the Oracle Inn."

"You have that information now?"

"Yes, as retold by the king. Somehow, against his wishes, Sarah had followed the king, Ardal, and two guards into the cellar. Worsham was there and Heqet too in the body of the frog resting on the mouth of Raganora.

"Worsham appeared to be in a drunken sleep at his table next to an empty mug and a pitcher of stale ale. The king woke him. Ardal and the guards disarmed him. When the king demanded he wake Heqet, Worsham refused, saying that he could not, even if he wanted to, because too many were present. He could only wake Heqet on two conditions: if he were alone, or with a woman in whose body she would live.

"A moment later your daughter entered the room of Worsham, saying: 'Perhaps my presence will help. If this man values his life, he'll do his best to wake the witch.'

"Worsham said: 'Still, there are too many present.' He pointed to Ardal and the guards. 'They must go back upstairs. If the king stays and hides wrapped in the curtain, I can try to wake her as I usually do in the presence of a woman.' The king ordered the three men to leave.

"After they left, Worsham moved his mug and the pitcher to where his head had rested on the table before sliding the lantern to the side farthest from the curtain. He said Sarah had to lie on the table to be visible to Heqet. She did. He had the king stand in the place where the curtain would create a shadow as he pulled it aside.

"The king waited with the dagger in his hand as Worsham drew the curtains back. Before reaching for the sleeping frog, he motioned for the two to keep quiet. He took the frog from the open mouth of Raganora, held it over Sarah, and pointed to the edge of the gold coin that rested between the frog's lips. He whispered to your daughter, 'Touch the coin with your nose. It will fall into the stomach of the frog and Heqet will awaken.'

"In his telling, the king regrets having misjudged Worsham, in that moment, to be a slow-talking drunkard and allowing his daughter to lie on the table and do as the man told her. She did as instructed. The coin disappeared, and in the next instant, the frog clung to her face and breathed into her mouth, croaking what sounded like words the king could not comprehend.

"Before the king could react, Worsham struck him with the pitcher. The next thing he remembers is Ardal on his knees leaning over him, telling him help was on the way.

"Then the king recounted what Ardal had told him. Your Sarah and Worsham came up from the cellar with an order from the king to fetch a body basket of specific dimensions. Ardal said he would go, but let Sarah and Worsham leave before going to hear the order from the king himself. That is when he found the wounded king and sent for your mother and sister.

"Dragon Talker, we can only hope that your daughter will have some recall of the events that followed."

"*Mêmêkwêsiw*, these details do not portend well for my daughter. I asked for them. Thank you for delivering them to me."

Despite the news she had just received, Nagora felt encouraged. *Chances of my plan succeeding are weighing in my favor. If my appeal to Golgotha works, I stand to defeat him and perhaps save Sarah at the same time.*

Confrontation
Nôtinikewin

Two days later, news from Windhaven arrived first. According to the Little People, the king was back at the castle resting, and his wounds were on the mend.

Next came news from Skull Bay. The sailboat Golgotha had commandeered docked in the dark of night. Before daylight, a wagon with a team of six horses carrying the giant and six others left for Maze Point. As Nagora had predicted, Golgotha had used Sarah to gain safe passage.

Sarah must have given them the information they needed to navigate past Skull Rock. He's determined to reach the maze by afternoon. I wouldn't want to ride in that wagon. It'll be worse than being at sea and more jolting.

The dragons that would be Nagora's eyes, for the time being, perched invisible on the outer ring lintels, ready to give Nagora their unique view of the giant's arrival.

...

Sarah walked through the gate first. She had a rope noose around her neck. Golgotha had the other end tied around his waist. His black helm had two slits, one for his eye and the other for his mouth. He wore a long, sleeveless, black leather vest, pants, boots, and, as the Little People had reported, the metal armor on his right arm and the gauntlet on his right hand that held his dragon-killing lance.

Nagora did her best to appear to focus on the sounds she heard coming from the entrance without looking directly at them. Something about Sarah's demeanor did not seem right. *Is she wearing her armor? If so, can Heqet be inside her?*

Three armed men followed the giant. Behind them came Worsham, holding a basket of woven bulrushes with both hands.

While still appearing to focus on the movement of the giant and his men, her dragon eyes allowed her to see Worsham go to stand with his back against the maze wall. *Is he carrying Heqet?*

The armed man who had followed Worsham now stood on guard with a sword at his belt and a spear in hand, so he had a clear view of the maze path they had just travelled.

Golgotha spoke something Nagora guessed to be an order. He waved his lance at the same time. One spear carrier moved to his side while the two others, with swords drawn, followed the circular wall of the maze center, looking for a hidden defender. Nagora ignored the beating her tent took. Instead, she focused on the giant. *He's staring at me and the dragon, waiting for his men to report. Will they dare to peer into the well behind the supine dragon with a dagger lodged above its belly?*

After they reported, the men took up positions behind the giant.

"Mother, I'm sorry! I had no choice but to lead these people in!"

That's Sarah's voice, but not the words I'd expect her to speak. She hasn't expressed concern for the dragons. Do I detect a warning, or is Heqet speaking those words through Sarah?

With the dragons now at ground level, Nagora adjusted where she looked to focus on her daughter. "Sarah, don't blame yourself. Destiny guided Mighty Golgotha here to learn our Dragon Talker secrets. Once he does, I am sure he will no longer want to harm our dragons, but want to join us and gain the powers our dragons give us as Dragon Talkers."

Nagora raised a hand, showing five fingers. "My ears told me Golgotha has come with an escort of five men. Unfortunately, you and I, Sarah, cannot reveal our secrets with them present."

She waved her hand. "If they look to their feet, the gold coins on the ground will lead them out of the maze. Each will have more than they can carry for not staying, and then you, Golgotha, will be witness to the power we Dragon Talkers have. Your men can wait for you outside the maze."

The giant's armed men had their eyes on the coins. Nagora did not understand the pleas they made to Golgotha in the Franca language. Whatever they said or promised moved him to wave them away. Or was it his impatience to finish his task?

Worsham did not move. Nagora avoided looking directly in his direction. Soon the sounds of gold dragon coins being dropped into improvised, folded shirt-front pockets faded as the men scrambled along the maze path, gathering their treasure.

"Golgotha, I take it you hold the life of my daughter in your hands, and I imagine you hold a weapon to kill her should you judge that necessary. You have the advantage."

She pointed to the dragon behind her. "As you can see, I stabbed this dragon with my only weapon. I could kill it if that was my desire; but if I did, I would waste the benefit its blood procures me.

"Let me show you just how submissive a dragon is to a Dragon Talker. A power that could be yours should you become a Dragon Talker instead of a dragon slayer."

Nagora let the robe she wore fall from her body while keeping the invisible armed sling tucked in her armpit as she turned to face the dragon.

She bent, reaching with a tentative hand to find the ram horn goblet. With her left hand, she felt along the dragon's chest to grasp the handle of the dagger just within her reach before pressing the goblet in place. She moved the blood-flow control and imagined Golgotha watching the blood trickle from the crossguard into the horn.

Stopping the flow, Nagora faced the giant with the goblet, raising it high, as she took several steps in his direction. "Now I call on you to witness the true power of dragon blood freely given to a Dragon Talker." She brought it to her lips, drank, and disappeared. Thank the stars he doesn't know I'm wearing dragonskin armor. Only the horn was visible.

Golgotha's helmed head turned to Sarah and then back to the horn, as he pointed to it with his lance.

When she reappeared, she held the goblet in Golgotha's direction. "Such is the power you could have! The same power my daughter and I have! Sarah! Shall I draw blood from this dragon for you to show Golgotha the power he too could have?"

"Mother, I think what Golgotha has witnessed is more than enough to convince him."

What, or should I ask who, stops you from drinking the blood, Sarah? "As you wish, my daughter. Then perhaps you will bring Golgotha a goblet of dragon blood to drink." Will she bring it to him, or offer an excuse not to? If she's Heqet, she might not want to make me suspicious.

With deliberate care, as a blind person would, Nagora returned to the dragon. This time as she prepared to draw blood, she held the strings of the sling as she reached up to grasp the handle of the blade to fill the goblet a second time, adding the poison to the seeping blood.

Nagora held the goblet before her and walked in Sarah's direction.

Golgotha let the young woman walk to her mother and take the goblet.

That's when Nagora saw the gold bracelet on her daughter's wrist. The same snake with amber eyes as was on Raganora's arm! Heqet, you are not a queen yet! Your greed for gold has betrayed you. Does my daughter still live in her body?

Sarah turned and walked toward the giant, holding up the horn for him to take.

What will he decide? If he removes his helm, I'll attack in that moment his eye won't see. She waited. What's he thinking?

"I not believe you. You try trick me." The giant's voice echoed from inside his helm.

"Trick you? Not at all! I offer you proof! All you have to do is drink the blood and watch your hands disappear. They will stay, but not be visible. Of course, with another secret ingredient added to the blood, we Dragon Talkers can stay invisible for days at a time."

He pointed to Nagora with his lance, shaking it from side to side. "I not trust you."

Nagora pointed to herself. "You do not trust me?" She pointed in Sarah's direction. "You know we are the two who killed the witch who cursed the seed of the one who fathered you to be born with one eye. We are on your side. This would be your opportunity to live your life for you, not to fulfill your mother's desires."

Golgotha shook his lance and spoke something that sounded more like a growl.

"Have you found her yet? We know the curse. We know she lives in a frog's body. A witch cursed you to search for her and cursed you to kill dragons for her. Let's say you do that for her. She'll live as queen forevermore. What will she do for you? Reject you like everyone else has, except for those who fear you? Will she fear her son? What thanks will she give you? Will she, as queen, give you a prince's share of her gold?" Sarah set the ram horn on the floor and then reached out with both hands, taking a step in Golgotha's direction, seeming to plead without speaking.

Nagora continued. "I've just shown you a glimpse of the power you can have over dragons if you don't kill them. What has your mother offered you? Nothing, if you think about it. The curse has ruled your life. If she becomes queen, what will you have left to do? Mission accomplished. Yes, you enjoyed the kill when you had an audience. Yes, you drank the blood of the dragons you slayed, but what's next if there are no more dragons to slay? What do you become? What do you have to show for it? Flags that depict your kills? What will become of your circus if it has no main attraction?"

Again the Giant growled, but louder this time.

Sarah's hands were at her face as she shook her head.

Nagora cocked her head to the side. "I know what you're thinking. Look at her. It cost Nagora her eyesight to learn the curse of some dagger just to protect her dragons. True enough! Nevertheless, look at what they give me in return! Have you ever had a dragon obey you and submit to you like this one? One that would allow you to spill its blood for your benefit?"

Nagora detected Worsham's agitation as he stood by, clutching the bulrush basket. His eyes darted repeatedly from the giant to Sarah and to Nagora.

"What you are witnessing today," Nagora raised her voice, "is what Dragon Talkers can do with their dragons when alone with them! We would never do this in a circus. If we did such a thing, they would never give us the power to become invisible! There are so many more powers they give us!

"Think about it. Destiny has brought you to the maze, like it brought me here to rebuild it. It didn't bring you here to kill the dragons. It didn't bring you here to kill me!"

Nagora pointed to Sarah, who was pacing back and forth, hands on her ears, as she glanced from the giant to Worsham and back to her. "A curse says my daughter will kill me and her father so she can become a queen. Right now she is a princess, and King Raynhard crowned me Queen Edana of the Land of the Danu. I crowned my daughter princess so she and I could kill the witch, Alizarine, who cursed your parents!"

Golgotha growled something and slammed the heel of his lance against the stone slab at his feet.

"Think about that! Think about the task that lies ahead of you!" Nagora pointed to the sky. "Are you prepared to fight this dragon?" Many years ago, having seen Danuka do what these three were about to do, she was eager to watch the spectacle.

The three-headed dragon appeared above the maze, swept down, and each head blasting a stream of fire from its mouth, hovering for a moment above Golgotha before flying off out of sight. The giant had raised his arms and crouched in fear. Then, as he stood tall, he searched the surrounding sky.

"Did you feel the heat? That dragon could have cooked you right where you stand! If it had, right now you would be a mound of charred, burnt flesh, no longer alive so as not to bear the pain. No one, except for my daughter and I, would have witnessed it. And that dragon! No circus audience. If your men inquired about you, we would say you disappeared before our eyes. We would fly no flags nor tell tales of your defeat. What need would there be?"

Nagora pointed to her daughter again. Sarah was glaring at her. "There's no way Sarah will kill me. Dragon Talkers don't turn on Dragon Talkers. Golgotha, you have no control over her to force her to do that, and there is no way you can kill our dragons. However, there is one thing you can do to free yourself of that curse. I am certain my daughter has explained the curse to you. If she has, then I want you to tell me what it is you have to do."

Golgotha rested his lance in the crook of his arm as he reached to untie the rope at his waist to release Sarah. "You right on both counts. I know what I do."

He's making his move. Nagora turned to the dragon. "Go! Leave now!"

Sarah turned to face Nagora, kicked the ram horn away, and slipped the noose from around her neck. "Queen Edana, I will kill you like I killed your king, and then live as queen forevermore in this beautiful body." She drew from inside the vest she wore the gold-handled dragon dagger.

"Nooooo! You promised me revenge! She's mine to torture for what she did to me!" Worsham hobbled his body along as fast as he could, waving his staff. "Let me at her! Let me at her now!" He hurled the bulrush basket, almost stumbling to the ground as he did. It landed past Golgotha, halfway between him and Sarah, spilling the frog onto one of the floor stones at the center of the maze.

Taking advantage of the distraction Worsham caused, Nagora swung the sling three times and released. The stone hit the side of the giant's helm, knocking it askew on his head as he looked at Worsham. In that position, the helm blocked the giant's vision. Now his free hand struggled to remove it.

Nagora removed the sheath containing her big blade from the invisible bag tied at her waist and put it on as she strode toward Worsham, who was coming at her with his walking stick. His face was red with his anger. Spittle streamed from his crooked, gaping mouth as he yelled what Nagora could only guess were obscenities, so hoarse was his voice.

Nagora caught a quick glance in Sarah's direction, showing the girl on hands and knees chasing the frog.

Just in time, Nagora sidestepped Worsham's lunge, swinging her skystone blade to cut his staff in two as she spun on one foot, slicing through his robe and cutting into the back of his trailing leg just above the knee.

Nagora didn't stop moving toward Golgotha as Worsham screamed and fell face first to the ground. The giant still fought to remove his helm, while jabbing and swinging his lance to defend himself. Would she trust what she saw, thanks to the dragons, to attempt an attack on the disadvantaged giant? Nagora kept her distance, intent on watching him to find a pattern in his dangerous flailing.

Stepping back, Nagora turned to find a dragons' view of Sarah. She was on her feet, dagger in one hand and frog in the other.

"Golgotha!" What Heqet yelled next, Nagora did not understand, but she guessed the witch had just told the giant where his opponent stood.

Nagora turned to bring him into view. Golgotha had paused long enough to adjust his stance and was now taking a step forward, brandishing his lance with one hand as his other worked the helm up from his face.

"The kill will be mine, Golgotha!" Heqet screamed in Sarah's voice.

Not if I can stop you. "Dragons! Show yourselves!" A quick glance around the lintels of the inner circles told her most of the dragons were present and a peek over her shoulder confirmed the four who were her eyes were still in place. "Today, I, Nagora, your Dragon Talker, release you from your oath to not harm our kind. If you must kill every human standing here in the maze to prevent Heqet from ruling as queen forevermore and being a threat to you and to dragons in the future, do so, knowing that I offer my life to protect you. As for my daughter, Sarah, who loved you all, I fear she is no longer in this world. It is the witch Heqet who inhabits her body now. Son of Danuka, Heqet tried to kill you with the acorn poison. Now you are free to seek your revenge!"

Just as the giant had lifted the helm above his single eye, the three-headed dragon swooped down on him. He raised his hands to fend off the flames as they breathed his way. The dragon hovered in place as the heads blasted the blade of his lance with flames until it became molten red, bent, and wrapped itself to his helm. His motion to jab with his lance pulled his helm back down on his head, muffling his screams. He released the lance to reach for his helm with both hands.

Sarah-as-Heqet stood frozen in shock as she looked from her son to the dragons on the lintels peering down at her. The terror she must have felt invaded her face, making her whole body tremble. She dropped the dagger to clutch the frog with both hands.

Nagora made her move, running to the giant with her sky-stone blade. Standing behind him, she swung her blade twice. The cuts brought him to his knees, one after the other, as they severed the muscles and tendons just below his calves. He might have fallen forward had it not been for the shaft of his lance and the sword in his belt that kept him propped up. Nagora sheathed her blade and yanked Golgotha's sword from its scabbard.

Golgotha toppled onto his side, the fall dislodging his helm. In doing so, it tore away a wide ribbon of skin and scalp in the pattern left by the blade of his lance where it had melted onto his helm. His lone, swollen eye squinted up at Nagora and then up to the dragons around the lintels.

Nagora lifted the heavy sword to rest its blade on her shoulder. "I'll get back to you in a moment. First, I have a promise to keep with your mother's protector."

Sarah-as-Heqet was on her knees, holding the frog to her lips and mumbling words Nagora did not comprehend.

Worsham moaned as he lay on his side and held the knee of his wounded leg bent to his belly. Nagora stood at his back. She let the flat of the big sword's blade drop onto Worsham's hip. He screamed and then reached back with a hand, the one with the scar. "No! Please! Have mercy. I beg you!"

"I've a mind to give you as much mercy as you did to those girls in the dungeon." Nagora dragged the blade back over his hip, letting the tip scrape over it and then lodge between his buttocks. "Well, well, Golgotha's sword has just found a new scabbard. What do you say, Worsham? Should I slide it in slow so you can tell me it has gone far enough or do I thrust it in fast all the way to the crossguard to make you scream?"

Thanks to the full view of the scene the dragons' eyes provided, Nagora's eye caught the frog hopping away. Sarah's body now appeared to lie lifeless on the maze floor. Nagora rested the hilt of the sword on the ground, leaving its tip lodged where she had placed it.

Then she rushed to Sarah, taking hold of her shoulders and turning her onto her back. Her daughter's face did not move, but when Nagora placed a hand on her cheek, she felt the dragonskin armor pulse. *That's what I feel when I wear mine!* "Sarah! You're alive! That's your heartbeat! I know you're in there! Come back to me." She bent and kissed her daughter's forehead. "Sarah, my Sarah! Don't leave! You're safe now."

The girl's eyes opened, and she gasped, taking in a long breath. Her lips moved, but no sound came until she coughed and caught her breath again. "Mum, where am I?"

Nagora hugged her. "In the maze with me and your dragons! Look around on the lintels. They must be happy to see you're alive."

Sarah lifted a hand, waved, and then pointed.

Nagora looked. "Don't you dare touch that sword, Worsham! I'll be the one to place it in its new scabbard."

Worsham's moan was one of desperation.

Nagora helped her daughter sit up and pointed to the giant. "Have no fear, Sarah. He's in no condition to harm us."

"Where is the witch?" asked Sarah, as she looked around.

"Back in the frog's body, probably hoping a dragon won't roast her alive."

Sarah reached for her mother and pressed her face to her bosom. "I think I killed my father. I stabbed him with the dagger. If only I had listened to him, but I wanted to witness him kill Heqet like I witnessed you get blinded."

"Sarah, listen to me! You didn't kill him. He's alive and on the mend. Ardal found him. Grandma Tagnya and Sagora have taken care of him."

"But I caught sight of Worsham strike my father with the pitcher. The dagger fell to the table near my head. The next thing I remember is a voice that sounded like mine saying over and over: 'I'm killing the king!' It wasn't me saying those words. I'm sure I was wielding the dagger! Worsham held Father up from behind and yelled: 'Be quick! Do it!' I stabbed him twice. He let Father fall to the floor.

"Then Worsham leaned on the table. He appeared to catch his breath before saying: 'I'll hide him over there. He'll bleed to death before they find him.' I was kneeling on the table. I felt so tired that I curled up on the table with the dagger still in my hand. I heard a dragging sound and my father groan. After that, I can't recall a thing. Now I'm here with you."

Nagora took Sarah's face in her hands. "It wasn't you. It was Heqet who was in you that made you do it. She used your body to do the deed." Nagora reached for Sarah's wrist and, as she pulled the golden snake bracelet off her arm, said, "See! This is Heqet's. She must have put it on after taking your body."

Sarah rubbed her wrist as if trying to remove a stain.

Nagora's vision changed. Now she saw three perched dragons staring down at the bulrush basket.

"I'll be right back." Nagora stood and walked over to it. "Where are you hiding, frog queen? In your basket? My! How convenient. Do you think your keeper will protect you? I think not, given the predicament he's in. I'll take care of you." Nagora bent and set the basket upright, dropped the bracelet into it, and closed the lid, buckling it shut.

Then she brought the basket near Worsham, but well out of his reach. "Say goodbye to the Gold Planter." As she walked around to the ex-jailor's backside, she motioned to her daughter to cover her ears and look away. "This won't take long."

Worsham's screams lasted only the time it took Nagora to position the sword's tip and align the blade with his spine. She shoved the sword with all her might. When done its journey through the man's body, the tip had sliced through his nose bridge and split his two eye sockets wide, freezing his mouth wide open in a silent scream. An arm's length away from the former jailer's forehead, two eyeballs dangled by their nerves from the sword's tip. The crossguard stuck firmly in the fold of his robe between his ass cheeks.

Images of the cruel treatment the young women suffered at the hands of the jailor and Prince Acindor in the dungeon fortress at Yhorgal Cliffs flashed in Nagora's mind. *It has taken a long time, but today I have kept the oath I swore to you: I will be your justice. I will be your vengeance.*

Nagora walked around the body and nudged the basket with her foot. "I have a feeling you'll get your turn soon enough."

Nagora helped Sarah to her feet. "Don't bother looking at him. He got what he deserved."

She felt her daughter touch her face. "Mum, you can see again? How?"

"With the help of dragons. I'll explain later."

The two Dragon Talkers stood before the giant, who was in obvious pain and losing blood. As they looked down at his bloody, swollen face, he spoke. "I not come to kill your dragons. My fight is with you." His eye looked from Sarah to Nagora. "You killed my sister. She the only one who love me. Alizarine made me a giant, a slayer of dragons. I want to give her gift she desire most—eternal beauty. I not want my mother know I was on Alizarine's side. My flags lie. My hope was kill you two so she not rule queen forevermore. Promise me she will not, and then end my pain. Cut my head from my body. Put my dead frog mother in it. Burn it."

Nagora looked at Sarah and made a sign they should speak at the same time. "We promise Heqet will not rule as queen forevermore."

Nagora pointed Sarah toward her tent. "You'll find a waterskin and a bucket in there." She turned to have the dragons' view of the well. *It's back to its original state. The Little*

People didn't waste any time. "Bring them to the well and fill them with water. While you're gone, I'll end his pain. I'll meet you in the tent."

She waited for her daughter to disappear down the well before turning to Golgotha. "Can you sit up?"

"I will try." He rolled to put some of his weight onto his arm. The metal plates of his armored arm scraped on the stone as he positioned his gauntlet-covered hand to help push himself up.

Nagora moved to stand behind him and out of reach, waiting for him to be upright before she would swing her blade. *Better I do it without warning him. It'll be swift. He won't have time to think about it.*

As soon as he sat straight, she stepped close and swung. The skystone blade cut clean all the way through his neck. Blood squirted onto Nagora's right forearm, side, and leg. His head fell forward, landing between his outstretched legs. His upper body slumped over.

Nagora walked to her tent, skystone blade in hand, covered in the blood that dripped down from her arm.

"The center of the maze is a mess. I don't look forward to cleaning it up," said Sarah. "I didn't mind helping you clean yourself and your blade, but those two bodies are … "

Nagora didn't let her finish as she dressed. "Killing is messy. Don't worry. You won't have to deal with the mess. When we're ready, I'll have the Little People bring the giant's four escorts back here to do it. If they refuse, they'll suffer the same fate. Thanks for your help. I'll truly feel clean once I've bathed in the stream. For now, this will do." She put on her sheathed set of blades. "Do you have the sheath for the dag-ger?"

"Aye, it's in my vest pocket, but I don't recall putting it there."

Nagora held out her hand. "Don't worry about it. Give it to me. I'll pick up the dagger and take care of it for now. While I put Golgotha's head in the bucket, can you go get the robe over there and put it with my other garments?"

"That, I don't mind doing."

Having set the bucket and the basket next to a nearby lintel support pillar and placed the golden-handled dagger in the pocket of her vest, Nagora waited for Sarah to come out of the tent.

Sarah's pale features worried her. *The kills have surely af-fected her. She looks tired. Then again, I might look that way too had I spent almost six days with a witch living inside my body. What harm has come to her? She'll never be the same, especially if she carries guilt about what she did to her father.*

Nagora's view changed, breaking her away from her thoughts. The dragons' eyes showed her the other dragons perched on the lintels. As she counted them, including the four at floor level, she realized the perched dragons were all looking in the same direction, and that two were missing.

Then her view changed to one of the sky beyond the maze and above the buildings on her land. "Sarah, come here."

"What is it, Mum?"

Nagora pointed. "Watch the sky. You'll soon see two dragons. One carries two riders, the other a single rider."

The voice of the male dragon spoke to Nagora, mind-to-mind. *Ka Peyakot Mahihkan*, they bring good news from Windhaven. Sarah will be relieved.

Nagora reached for and found her daughter's hand. "I'll let you tell me who the riders are." The closer the dragons came, the stronger was Sarah's grip.

"Mum! It's my father! Grandma Tagnya's riding with him. Auntie Sagora rides the other dragon." The dragons flew by and glided in a circle above the maze, finally landing on the other side of the well. Sarah let go of her mother's hand and ran to her father.

Son of Danuka, how long have you known?

Since the king has been out of danger, three days ago. He insisted to the *Mêmêkwêsiw* that dragons come for him. He wanted to see the situation here, to learn if he could complete his task. When Tagnuska and Sagnuska said he would be ready to travel today, yesterday I sent two of my sisters with the special saddles the Little People have been making.

What if he were coming upon a scene where I had died at Golgotha's hand?

Then it would have become his fight. But it was yours, *Ka Peyakot Mahihkan*. Our mother told us that any evil-intentioned foe seeking to harm us would have to first defeat you, our lone-wolf-warrior Dragon Talker, for with your self-less courage, strength, and devotion, you protect us.

Son of Danuka, I take those words as a compliment. Know that I do my duty as Dragon Talker to the best of my ability—no more, no less. King Raynhard could not have come at a better time for Sarah, and to carry out his destined duty. Nagora patted her vest and made her way to the group on the other side of the well.

...

Sarah had hugged the three arrivals and now had an arm around her father's waist. From the motions of her hand as she spoke to him, Nagora guessed she was recounting the events in the maze. She stopped when Nagora approached. "Mum! He's alive, like you said. Grandma and Auntie took good care of him."

Raynhard patted the right side of his chest. "The dagger made a small puncture wound to my lung, and," pointing to his left forearm, "I'll have a nice scar here to remind me of the event, and," touching the side of his head, "another scar here when I lose my hair someday. Ardal found me and sent men to find Sagora.

"Luckily, she and Tagnya were nearby at Paruline's place. They stopped the bleeding and moved me upstairs at the inn where they treated my wounds to prevent infection. They didn't move me to the castle until two days later when my collapsed lung truly showed signs of healing."

Tagnyoriva placed a hand on his shoulder. "He's lucky the wound was small and that he's strong."

"And he took our advice," said Sagora, waving a finger as if they had to scold him to follow their instructions. "Otherwise, we wouldn't be here right now."

"Speaking of you people being here, what's the situation with Golgotha's force and the Leafers?" asked Nagora.

Raynhard looked at Nagora's mother. "Do you want to speak first?"

"Aye, I will. No signs of poison in any of the wells. I posted guards for the next thirty days, day and night, until the king's investigators report on all former Leafers living in Windhaven. They'll question them about any feelings of retaliation they might have about the events they perceive as having reversed their future fortunes. To those who helped us, we left instructions on how to test the water of the wells randomly. If they find anything, they'll sound the alarm." Tagnyoriva waved to Raynhard to take his turn.

"All of Golgotha's vessels have sailed away, except for the one with his fleet commander, Captain Rech, on board. He awaits news of Golgotha and his escorts before he will set out to sea. As for the Gethsemane, it awaits Queen Raganora's corpse, and any others you want to join it at sea, where we'll set it on fire."

"I have a question," said Sarah. "Since I don't recall most of the events after Heqet took control of me, I want to know how Worsham and I got past Ardal and the guards when we left the cellar."

Raynhard smiled. "You came up first and told the guards I was ordering them to go buy a body basket of specific dimensions to put Raganora in. It had to be that size, and they were to insist the basket maker build one on the spot if he didn't have one that size. Ardal said he would go.

"Then, right after, you led Worsham out of the inn, telling the guards inside and outside that you were on an errand for me and that you would return within a count.

"As soon as you were out of sight, Ardal went to the cellar to confirm my orders. That's when he found me and your weapons." Her father reached into his scrip and handed her the wrapped set of blades.

"Thank you. I had taken them off before joining you in Worsham's room, thinking I would appear as less of a threat to Heqet since you were armed and ready to kill her." Sarah gazed at the ground and shook her head. "I should have gone in with my skystone blade in hand."

She sighed and looked at her mother. "Now we know."

"Aye." Nagora looked from Sarah to Raynhard, and back to the girl. "Did you tell him what Golgotha asked us to promise?"

"I did."

Nagora removed the sheathed dragon dagger from her vest pocket. "In that case, Raynhard, this belongs to you. Now would be a good time to do your duty. There'll be no interference from Heqet's protector, or her son. Sarah and I will witness your actions. The frog queen waits in her basket. Golgotha's head is in a bucket. The frog should fit in his mouth. I can knock his jaw shut if you won't."

Nagora turned to her sister and mother and pointed to the area on the other side of the well. "The scene over there is not pretty. I spilled a lot of blood. You would probably find it offensive and sickening. I suggest you wait here."

The king fastened the sheath to his belt and placed his hand on the dagger's handle. "Let's get this over with."

Nagora had Raynhard and Sarah stand next to the pillar on the other side of the inner circle of lintels and opposite from where her tent was. "I'll fetch the basket and the bucket."

Her view changed to that of the dragons perched on the lintels. They watched her walk past the slain bodies.

After slipping the strap of a waterskin over her shoulder and picking up the basket and the bucket, her view changed again. She saw herself walking toward the king and her daughter. She wondered if they were aware of the invisible dragon crouched behind them.

Nagora set the containers on the ground before Raynhard, shaking the bucket until the giant's open mouth faced upward, while imagining the invisible dragon craning its neck over her from the lintel above to allow her to view inside the bucket. Then she unbuckled the cover on the basket, leaving it closed. As she stood next to Raynhard, Nagora said, "There are no instructions on how to do this other than what is said in the curse. Take your time. We are your witnesses, as are the dragons."

With decisive movements, the king drew the dagger from its sheath, knelt on one knee before the basket, and flipped the lid open, reaching one hand in to pin the frog to the basket's bottom. He then stabbed Heqet more times than Nagora cared to count.

Then Raynhard set the bloodied dagger down before pulling the bucket closer. His other hand came out of the basket covered in blood, clutching the limp, punctured body of the frog. He squeezed it while working his thumb against his fingers until a gold dragon coin fell next to his knee.

He stuffed the frog into Golgotha's mouth, taking his time to squeeze in every piece of flesh and the stubborn toe digits. With one hand over the giant's mouth, his other tilted the giant's head to stand it upside-down in the bucket. Resting the heel of his hand on the chin, the king leaned the weight of his upper body onto his arm until the mouth shut, sealing the body of the frog witch inside.

Raynhard took the gold bracelet from the basket, picked up the coin and the dagger, and stood before the witnesses, holding the objects before him. Without a word, Nagora poured water for him to rinse the blood from them and his hands.

Sarah broke their silence. "Is it over? Is that the end of the curse?"

"Now you can thank your father. He has met the conditions of the curse. Heqet is no more. Let there be no more curses in our lives."

Sarah put her arms around the king. "Thank you."

He kissed the top of her head. "I did my duty. It doesn't make up for all my missteps." He held up the coin and bracelet. "I'll put these with the coins from Raganora's bed. Sagora told me the Little People will disinfect them all and melt them down to mint new coins. Sarah, the witch is no longer a threat to you. It's over. You are safe."

Sarah reached for her mother and pulled her close. "Mum, I have to thank you too. Words will never be enough."

Nagora's view switched to the dragons that were gliding to the outer ring of lintels and looking skyward. What are the dragons seeing that I don't? "Sarah, what's in the sky?"

"Nothing but blue. Not a cloud. Why?"

"The dragons who allow me to see are looking there."

"Mum, could it be Danuka is returning?"

"That must be it."

"There she is! To seaward! Just above the lintel ring," said Raynhard.

"Now I see her!" said Nagora. She couldn't hold back her tears. Danuka is bringing Da home.

Sarah took her mother's hand. "Grandma and Auntie have moved to give Danuka room to land."

Nagora took Sarah's hand. "Let's go join them." Raynhard followed, holding his daughter's hand.

...

With the others near a pillar of the inner ring, they watched the mother dragon glide in a slow circle above the maze before making her approach.

As Danuka controlled her landing next to the well, she spoke to Nagora's mind. *Ka Peyakot Mahihkan*, I want to hear the news from you.

Okâwîmâw, it is over! Look there! The frog witch is dead! King Raynhard killed her with his dagger, as the curse demanded. He buried her in the mouth of Golgotha. Such was the wish of her son before I beheaded him. His head will join the corpse of Raganora on the carcass of the Gethsemane to be hauled out to sea and set on fire. I served just vengeance on Worsham, as I had long ago promised the victims of his cruelty. Worsham, Heqet, and Golgotha are no longer a threat to you.

Thank you, Lone Wolf.

Yogari climbed down from the saddle and jumped off the outstretched wing. Nagora ran to him. The others followed. Her father took her in his arms. "My child! My daughter! I have come home to you!"

Nagora shook as she choked back her tears and clung to him. "You don't know how happy I am to see you." She laughed as she spoke the words, realizing the irony of them. "How is Dannor?"

She felt his hand caress her cheek. "He told me to tell you he misses you already, but he wants you to know he is happy with the challenges he faces. And he has ordered me to build you a new door for your lodge, just like the one of his new home. I promised him I would since he will pay for it."

Nagora laughed and reached for Sarah. "Did you hear that? That's your brother being funny! I will get a new door! Give your grandda a hug."

"My! You have grown! I wasn't expecting to see your father here."

"How are you, Yogari?" asked Raynhard.

"I'm happy to be home, King Raynhard. Give me a moment." With Nagora's hand in his, he beckoned his wife and Sagora to come closer. He joined their hands in his. "This has been a long time coming. I promise you that from now on, we'll be together as a family. Let all the adversities we've faced in our separate lives strengthen our bond." He hugged them to him.

Wiping away his tears, Yogari faced the king. "I take it Tagnya spoke to you of our adventure."

"That she did. You have my complete admiration for what you accomplished."

Yogari looked past Raynhard beyond the well. "Is that your handiwork Danuka is examining?"

"Mostly Nagora's, though Sarah and I helped." He gave Yogari a quick description of his execution of the frog witch, Heqet, and how he would dispose of her and her son, along with Raganora's corpse. "As for all the details leading up to this, there'll be a time and place for the telling of them, most likely when Lars returns and all involved assemble."

Nagora cleared her throat and touched Raynhard's elbow. "Earlier you said Golgotha's fleet commander, Captain Rech, was waiting for news of the giant and his escort. How do you plan to deliver that?"

"Are the men who accompanied Golgotha still alive?"

"Aye, they're lost in the maze on a greedy treasure hunt, separated from each other because they've followed the gold coins the Little People laid out for them. I can ask the Little People to show them back here, unarmed and coinless." I know they're watching and listening and will act when the time is right.

"Good. I want his men to witness the giant's corpse. Then they'll use his sword to cut the hands and feet from his body. When they sail from Skull Bay, they'll have those body parts, along with the giant's helm and sleeve of armor, to show to Captain Rech in Windhaven."

Nagora shook her head. "I don't want the bodies of Golgotha and Worsham rotting in the dragons' maze. I'll have the Little People lead a contingent of Gabe's men here to help you. While you're at it, have them remove the corpses and throw them off the seaside cliff. When they're done, the Little People will lead you out.

"Then you can have troops from Gabe's contingent return the giant's men to Skull Bay under armed escort. You might give them some incentive to return to Windhaven with proof of Golgotha's demise. Once you've sent them off, Gabe's men will escort you to my lodge."

Raynhard nodded in agreement.

"One more thing. I want the giant's sword. Have it washed well in the stream before bringing it to me." Turning away, Nagora said, "Excuse me now. I must speak to the dragons."

Before thanking the dragons who had helped her, Nagora joined Danuka near the giant's corpse and spoke to her mind-to-mind.

Okâwîmâw, do you agree with my instructions to King Raynhard?

Ka Peyakot Mahihkan, you spoke them like the queen you are. My daughters who flew here from Windhaven today told me they, and two more dragons who have mated with my son, are ready to return to Windhaven with Sarah as long as they can return here with their hatchling eggs.

The *Mêmêkwêsiw* have found a cave on a seaside cliff close to the inlet to Windhaven Bay. It will be an ideal place to hide their eggs until hatching time nears. Only Sarah, the dragons, and the Little People will know its whereabouts. With our new power to fly invisible as long as we desire, keeping it secret will be easy.

Mother, this is good news! Sarah will be most pleased to hear it when you inform her. It is a challenge she has been looking forward to, and it will help her overcome the ordeal she has been through with Heqet.

Your Sarah will call to me when she is ready to return to Windhaven with her father and the dragons. That day will be memorable. Your daughter will fulfill the promise Edana made.

True, Mother, Sarah will make me proud, and the people of Windhaven will be happy.

Okâwîmâw, I wish to thank your son, the dragons who were my eyes, and the three who created the illusion. All of you helped me survive this battle. Thanks to you all, my beloved daughter still lives. For that, I hold you dear in my heart.

Nagora turned to face the dragons perched on the lintels. Son and daughters of Danuka, I thank you for trusting me and helping me. Thank you, *Okâwîmâw*, for bringing my father home to me.

Ka Peyakot Mahihkan, we thank you for what you have done for us.

She felt Danuka's snout touch her forehead.

Ka Peyakot Mahihkan, in your life as my Dragon Talker protector, you have witnessed firsthand that to know the future is a curse. It is a gift we dragons can live with. You humans cannot; though you are gifted with hope. Its seeds are sown in the reality of your present, allowing you to aspire to a better future. Permit me, with the knowledge I now possess of dragons past, present, and future, and the knowledge I learned while in Kemet, to show you whence the witches came and why. This will confirm what you have learned, what you know, and perhaps what you have suspected all along.

First, Lone Wolf, know that there are good and evil witches. The good are selfless, living in the moment in harmony with themselves and nature. They have the gift to heal. The evil are selfish, living in greed and chaos. They lie, deceive, and curse to do harm.

Days ago, you met Grandmother, the good witch who blinded you to allow you to see as only the blind can see; and years ago, Yogari told you of Old Mother he had sought on the Ice Islands when no one else could cure his illness. She gifted him with the amulet he gave to your mother, who gave it to you at your birth. It guided him to the Land of the Danu and eventually you to me.

Evil Heqet, whom you battled, was an ancient witch from the Black Lands, cursed to live in cycles of one hundred years in the body of a young, beautiful woman, followed by a century in an ancient body. When young, her greed made her a seductress who mingled with those of royal blood to grow her fortune of gold coins.

In the final year of her cycle of living in a youthful body, she adopted a young beauty, Alizarine, whom she did not know was a witch. She was an orphan maiden, like all the girls who worked at the dye pools of the scarf maker, dyeing silk scarves bearing the color of her name. The intention of Heqet was to break the upcoming cycle of living in an old body by taking possession of the body of Alizarine. She had found a forbidden spell with instructions that would allow her to use the young beauty as her vessel and live forevermore in that youthful body.

The spell required three essential ingredients: a virgin maiden, a bed of a thousand gold coins bathed in the light of the full moon to lay her upon, and the words of the incantation to work the magical outcome. With Alizarine, Heqet would have all three, or so she believed.

As in all such spells, conditions and limitations bind those involved. If not met, they change the desired outcome in ways the participants can never suspect.

The scarf maker certified the virginity of Alizarine as he had found her abandoned on his doorstep only days after her birth, with two golden-handled dragon daggers wrapped to her sides. He and his wife took the baby in, raising her until she was of age to join the other orphan girls in their dormitory to learn the craft of dyeing and the art of dancing with silk scarves.

The girl's attachment to her daggers was such that she would only dance with them in her hands. Sultans travelled from afar to the scarf maker to seek virgins for their harems. They paid in gold coins, but shunned beautiful Alizarine out of fear of her daggers. The scarf maker knew Alizarine would eventually fetch a high price. Heqet had him name the amount and doubled it in payment, so long as Alizarine brought along her golden daggers.

At her home, and to show Alizarine how much she loved her, Heqet gave the girl a room of her own, with a bed of gold coins to sleep upon.

In the evenings before retiring to bed, Alizarine, in a wanton dance, would remove her silk scarves one at a time with the blades of her daggers until she was naked. The dancing brought great pleasure to Heqet as she admired the young body and golden daggers she would soon possess as her own.

On the day before the full moon of the magic ritual, Heqet invited her lover, a rich seafaring trader back in port, to witness the dagger dance of the one he would make love to the following night; but he could not wait, such was his infatuation with Alizarine. After satisfying the needs of Heqet and ensuring she was asleep, he crept into Alizarine's bed.

The following night, Heqet prepared for the magic ritual and waited with her lover for Alizarine to fall asleep. When she appeared to be sleeping, Heqet pulled aside the curtains of the window to let in the moonlight. Then, standing at the foot of the bed, Heqet chanted the magic words. When nothing happened and her lover suppressed a laugh, she reached for one of the golden-handled dragon daggers and threatened him.

Alizarine, who had been pretending to sleep, sat up, grabbed the other dagger, and spoke: "I gave myself to your lover last night! Mother, you do not recognize me, do you? I am the daughter you cast aside centuries ago because I was more beautiful than you. Now it is my turn to cast you aside."

That night, daughter and mother cursed each other with improbable deaths. Because the forbidden spell had failed, it bound them together in exile in a mutual competition to witness who would survive the curses they had uttered upon each other.

Prior to coming to our land, Heqet gave birth to her cursed son, Golgotha. Alizarine, in the body of Hag, cast her mother aside into the body of a frog while she herself nursed Golgotha and raised him. Eventually, Alizarine hoped to convince him to help her kill all the dragons in the land where the daggers had originated, thus gaining the eternal beauty Heqet promised her if she succeeded. To that end, Alizarine encouraged Golgotha to seek warrior training and become a slayer of dragons.

When Golgotha was old enough to leave home, the two witches exiled themselves to the Land of the Danu on the boat of the former lover of Heqet. They began attacking us dragons, but the Dragon Talker of that time did his best to defend us before his death. With the help of the Little People, he got his hands on the golden-handled daggers.

Before my mother dragon succumbed to her fate, she used her knowledge of the future to infuse one dagger with a warning of the curse and the other with its consequences; then, she instructed her Dragon Talker to give one to King Bernhard and the other to the Little People to hide, never to reveal its location. Nagora felt Danuka lift her snout from her forehead and guessed she might stare into her eyes.

Okâwîmâw, the leftover puzzle pieces in the back of my mind have fallen into place. Now I see how destiny helped forge the path of my life and my submission to you.

Ka Peyakot Mahihkan, you submitted to my will to save me and my kind, and in doing so, you suffered. You were banished, branded, betrayed, bred, blamed, and blinded. At all those turns on the life path set for you, you never gave up. You always fought for the truth, and to protect us. You helped us survive to this day.

Mother, you know I have no regrets. I did it all in service to you. Nagora reached up to find the dragon's snout. *Okâwîmâw*, can you tell me one thing about the future you see?

Ka Peyakot Mahihkan, we dragons will live on forever, invisible to the eyes of humans.

A shiver ran down Nagora's arm. Without Dragon Talkers?

It must be so, as human will use one of our greatest gifts of communication for much good and for much evil. However, if tended properly, it will be a seed of hope for their future.

Nagora returned to the group. Now the view she had was of them watching her approach. She guessed the smiles they wore were of admiration for her, but believed they were looking at her with love. She felt her face blush.

Nagora reached for her sister's hand, and placed it into her father's hand, while she herself reached for his other. "Sarah, take your grandma's hand and lead us home, but first stop at my tent. I have to collect some things." In her heart, she hoped her father had spoken true about them being a family, and that he would find a plot of land nearby to build a lodge. If he and her mother lived with them, she would be happy. If I can keep them with me until Lars gets home and for a time afterward, I hope they'll want to call it home.

Sagora helped her sister by carrying the big leather scrip containing her clothes. Nagora found the linen-cloth bag with the remains of her food. She felt the bag to make sure the two feeder eggs were still intact. "Dannor's leather ball should be in here somewhere. I'll give it to Raean. We can leave the saddle and the bag tied to it. The dragons will find them."

"When can I expect Golgotha's men to arrive?" asked Raynhard.

Nagora turned to face him. "We have finished our work here. We'll be on our way. As soon as we exit the maze, if Gabe agrees, the Little People will lead his men here. The giant's men will arrive before them. No need to fear Golgotha's men. The Little People will have disarmed them, and the dragons will watch them do the butchering you assign them. We'll see you later."

Raynhard took hold of Nagora's wrist. "Before you go, I have something to give you."

Nagora held her hand open and felt the king place something in it. It wasn't until he folded her fingers over that she recognized the wedding rings Lars had woven from willow branches. She swallowed and blinked back a tear. "Thank you, my king." Her other hand dug into her scrip to find the inside pocket where she would place them.

Holding the hands of his daughters as they walked the maze path, Yogari spoke words of admiration for the work Nagora had done. "Dannor and the princesses described the maze to me and I saw it from the sky on Danuka's back, but seeing these stone walls up close is amazing. Even if the Little People helped you and Lars build it, it's beyond belief!"

Nagora squeezed his hand. "Da, wait until you visit the caves beneath. We didn't build those, but they are worth seeing. You'll newly appreciate what it means to be a Dragon Talker in a place like this."

As soon as Nagora stepped out of the maze, a dragon's view of the whole scene came into her mind. Gabe and Raean, along with an armed contingent, met them. The boy released Sarah from the hug he was giving her to run to his mother. "Mum! We saw you fly over with King Raynhard and Grandma Tagnya! Is your work done in Windhaven?"

Sagora hugged her son. "It is, and more. King Raynhard made me promise to let him tell you about it." She stepped to her husband to hug him. "Raean, I see you've taken good care of your da while I was away. I want you two to meet my own da, Yogari."

He extended a hand to the boy. "The last time I saw you, you were a baby."

"And I had a twin brother then. So you're my grandda, Yogari." He shook the man's hand.

"That I am, and happy to meet you. I remember your brother. I'm sorry for your loss. The things witches have put us through have marked all our lives." Yogari turned his gaze to Gabe. "The likeness in this man's face tells me he must be your father, and these lined up on each side of the gate must be the men he leads."

"He is my da, Prince Gabyndor of the Land of Skulls, and these are only twelve of the men he leads."

"Yogari, we finally meet," said Gabe, taking Yogari's proffered hand.

"It's about time, son-in-law! Dannor holds you in high esteem. I hope to be around here to get to know you well."

"So do I."

"And so do I!" said Raean. "And you too, Mum, aye?"

"Oh! Aye! Me too and your Auntie Nagora too."

"Well, if I can convince Tagnya," Yogari squeezed Nagora's hand, "we'll make that happen."

"You'll have no argument from me," said Tagnyoriva.

"That's good to hear," said Gabe.

I hope it will be so. I want you and Mum near me, near all of us.

The lad pulled on Nagora's sleeve. "Auntie Nagora, did you slay the giant? Did you?"

Nagora handed the boy the leather ball. "I did, Raean. And King Raynhard killed the witch, Heqet."

"He did? How did he do it?"

"Well Raean, would you rather hear him tell you or me?"

The boy twisted his jaw in thought. "I think the king because he did it. Can I see the giant's body?"

"That will be a decision for your father to make. For some warriors, it's never a pleasant experience to look upon a dead foe, even if they weren't the ones to strike the fatal blow."

"Auntie Nagora, what's the king doing in the maze?"

"Well, Raean," she saw Sagora whisper to Gabe, "there are some duties a king must attend to that are not pleasant to discuss, even with adults. I'll just say that he's having Golgotha's men take care of two bodies."

"The giant and that man, Worsham?"

"That's right, Raean." With a tentative hand, Nagora reached to touch the leather ball. "No playing with this while on duty, archer Raean." She embraced the boy.

"Gabe, I want to warn you. In a while the king will come out with a burial detail. They'll take the bodies to the seaside cliff. Before they do, if you permit it, the Little People will guide six of your men in to help King Raynhard. Have your men follow the gold coins. About ten coins apiece should take them to the king. They can keep the coins as payment."

"My men will be at his disposal for any duties he assigns them."

"Thank you, Gabe."

When the group crossed the bridge over the stream, Yogari spoke. "Nagora, your lodge looks great!"

"From here it does. Wait until you see the door up close."

On the path, nearing their lodge, her father exclaimed, "Wow! That has to be the garden Dannor told me about."

"Isn't it grand?" said Tagnyoriva. "You've been dreaming about one like it."

"I have!"

"Thanks to Jenni and Jari who work for us, we benefit from it," said Nagora.

"Dannor told me he often helped them. Do you think they will let me help? I want to learn to grow things!"

"They won't say no!" said Sarah.

Nagora sensed they were now standing in front of her lodge.

"I see what you mean. That door needs to be replaced," said Yogari.

"With Dannor being away, there'll be no more war stones slung this way," said Nagora.

"Especially with a new door," said Sarah.

"Before we go in, I want to take Da to see the view from the cliff." Nagora pulled the linen bag from her shoulder. "Let's leave our bags here while we walk up."

"Wait until you see it, Yogari! You're going to love it," said Tagnyoriva.

"Sarah, when we get up there, you show him where we sat with your grandma Tagnya to watch Dannor take the women from Kemet on their preparation flight for their journey home."

At the spot on the cliff, Sarah said, "Mum had brought blankets for us to sit on. Dannor and the women flew out to sea from the cave beneath the maze."

Yogari stared out to sea in silence. When he spoke, Nagora guessed his words were for her mother. "We spent a lot of time on the water. Now we're home. It's good to have this view to remind us there's no comparable feeling to that of a heart that knows it's coming home."

Yogari put an arm around Nagora's waist. "You don't see her, but I do. Danuka's flying toward us. I think she caught something for me. Oh! That looks like a big salmon! I told her I missed the taste of that pink meat. She must've gone to feed herself and caught one for me. There'll be enough for all of us. She's coming to land."

Nagora felt a brush of air being displaced by the slow flap of her dragon's wings.

"Don't move, Nagora. I'll go get the fish."

Lone Wolf, come to me.

Nagora stepped forward, waiting for the dragon's next command.

Her father patted her shoulder as he walked past her. "It's a big one."

Stand still now.

She felt Danuka's snout touch her forehead.

Ka Peyakot Mahihkan, with one of the hatchling eggs King Godomor holds in his Grand Hall, his grandmother can make a medicine to give you back your eyesight.

Nagora's eyes watered and she swallowed hard before answering. No, *Okâwîmâw*. The life of that dragon to be is too precious to sacrifice. I will not accept your offer. Please, Mother, bring the hatchling eggs back to the maze so I can protect them. That will make me happy.

Ka Peyakot Mahihkan, you honor me and my dragons. Danuka lifted her snout from Nagora's brand.

For a higher cause, *Okâwîmâw*.

A gust blew over Nagora as Danuka leaped into the air to take flight.

Her father took hold of one hand and Sarah the other.

"Take me home," said Nagora. "We have a meal to cook."

THE END

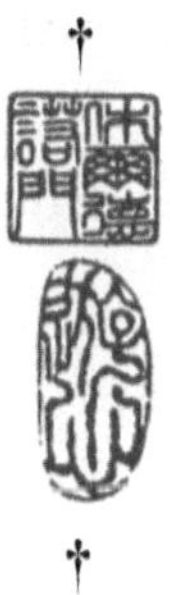

Dear Reader,

Thank you for reading *BLINDED*, the final book in The Dragon's Game series. For the benefit of future readers and to help me as an author, you would truly warm my heart by leaving an honest review at:

www.hnhenry.com/#testimonials

OR wherever you purchased this copy of *BLINDED*.

Sincerely,

H. N. Henry

P.S.: If you haven't read the other books in The Dragon's Game series, you can find out more about them here: www.hnhenry.com.

ABOUT THE AUTHOR

Other than writing, his passions include kayaking, baking bread, and trying to learn how to play guitar. He shares the profits of his work with a local community cause, *Point de Rue.* They help homeless people on the streets find meaning and passion in their lives. Learn more about it here: https://pointderue.com/

To learn more about the author and the other books in the series, please visit: www.hnhenry.com

Titles in **THE DRAGON'S GAME** series:

†

BANISHED BOOK I

BRANDED BOOK II

BETRAYED BOOK III

BRED BOOK IV

BLAMED BOOK V

BLINDED BOOK VI

ACKNOWLEDGMENTS

The Dragon's Game books wouldn't have come about without the generous and invaluable support of these people throughout the creative process.

From the beginning, Staecy-Lee, my editor, gave my manuscripts tough, honest critiques. Her hard questions made me see my stories with fresh eyes for the benefit of my readers.

Randi, my proofreader, closely read the final formatted-for-publication texts, finding inconsistencies in details, descriptions needing clarification, and grammatical errors my own eyes could no longer see.

Staecy and Randi, avid readers of this genre, also offered truly valuable and insightful comments that have made me a better writer. Learning from them has been a pleasure and a privilege.

My passionate beta readers of the first original brick, in first name a-b-c order, Ann, Daniela, Danielle, Maria, Marie-Josée, Randi, and Staecy-Lee generously delivered invaluable feedback and constructive criticism that helped spawn *BANISHED*, Book I, and from the volume they read, give birth to Books II and III of the series. I am forever in their debt for their support and encouragement.

I am grateful to the stained glass window artist, Guido Nincheri (1885-1973), who over ten years (1924-1934) created the beautiful windows in the Cathedral of the Assumption in Trois-Rivières, QC, Canada. From the photographs of those windows that I took on February 27, 2006, I was able to digitally manipulate images from two of the panels to create the unique dragons that appear on the covers of the first edition of my books, a humble homage to Nincheri's masterful work.

Though not referenced as Cree in the context of my stories, I have used Cree, in Roman orthography form, for the chapter titles and chapter numbers throughout the books in the series. More importantly, it is the " … strange yet familiar language … " Nagora, the main character, a.k.a. *Ka Peyakot Mahihkan*—Cree for *Lone Wolf*—hears in her mind and eventually uses to communicate with her dragon and other characters. At those times, when used, Cree is referred to as the *Language of the People*, in reference to the *First People* of *The Land* where my story is set.

The *Language of the People*, or "dragonspeak" as some readers of The Dragon's Game books call it, in a way reflects the status of the Cree language in our land today. Though Cree is the most widely spoken Native language still spoken in Canada, it has yet to be recognized as one of this country's official languages. Similarly, in the fictional setting of *The Dragon's Game* books, the *Language of the People* is now only spoken by a few in a divided and renamed land where two different languages (those of the invading Outlanders) have become dominant in use.

To the Online Cree Dictionary Team: *Kinanâskomitin*. Thank you, I am grateful to you for making this resource available to all. It has been indispensible in helping me lend realism to that second language in my stories. I hope my readers will have as much pleasure as I do in discovering the living Cree language.

In the end, what appears on the pages of my books is mine, and I take full responsibility for any errors that show up in the final versions.